BURN LIKE AN ANGEL

HARROWDEAN MANOR #2

J ROSE

WILTED ROSE PUBLISHING LTD

Published by Wilted Rose Publishing Limited
Edited and Proofread by Kim BookJunkie
Model & Discreet Cover Design by The Pretty Little Design Co
Photographer: Wander Aguiar
Model: Stephen Dehler

ISBN (eBook): 978-1-915987-30-3
ISBN (Model Paperback): 978-1-915987-31-0
ISBN: (Discreet Paperback): 978-1-915987-32-7

www.jroseauthor.com

For those who've spent their lives silent. Small. Unseen. You squeezed yourself into the tight confines of survival mode, where no one can get close, and no one can ever hurt you again.

But your voice is your power.
Don't let anyone take it from you.

TRIGGER WARNING

Burn Like An Angel (Harrowdean Manor #2) is a why choose, reverse harem romance, so the main character will have multiple love interests that she will not have to choose between.

This book is very dark and contains scenes that may be triggering for some readers. These include strong mental health themes, drug addiction, graphic violence, psychological and physical torture, mentions of self-harm, allusions to childhood sexual abuse and suicide.

There is explicit language throughout and sexual scenes involving blood play, breath play, knife play, and orgasm denial.

If you are easily offended or triggered by any of this content, please do not read this book. This is dark romance and, therefore, not for the faint of heart.

Additionally, this book is written for entertainment and is not intended to accurately represent the treatment of mental health issues.

J ROSE SHARED UNIVERSE

All of J Rose's contemporary, dark romance books are set in the same shared universe. From the walls of Blackwood Institute and Harrowdean Manor to Sabre Security's HQ and the small town of Briar Valley, all of the characters inhabit the same world and feature in Easter egg cameos in each other's books.

You can read these books in any order, dipping in and out of different series and stories, but here is the recommended order for the full effect of the shared universe and the ties between the books.

More Information:
www.jroseauthor.com/readingorder

"Speak the truth, even if your voice shakes."

- Maggie Kuhn

Established in 1984, a world-first experimental program pioneered by global investment group, Incendia Corporation, founded six private psychiatric institutes across the United Kingdom.

Blackwood Institute
Harrowdean Manor
Priory Lane
Compton Hall
Hazelthorn House
Kirkwood Lodge

Hidden behind multi-million pound, state-of-the-art facilities and slick marketing campaigns, these institutes hide a far more harrowing reality. To find the truth, you must enter the gates of hell with the other patients assigned to Incendia's care.

These are their stories.

PROLOGUE

TWIN SIZE MATTRESS – THE FRONT BOTTOMS

XANDER

Present Day

Have you heard about those people who poke around abandoned buildings, waving around their bullshit ghost detectors and speculating as to the horrors the decrepit ruins they're violating may hold?

They pay off some cash-strapped security guard to sneak into the site without being arrested, usually by scaling chain-link fences or burrowing through boarded over entrances, carrying backpacks full of flashlights, energy bars and fancy cameras to document their exploration.

And that's where the show begins, right? We're sucked into the fascination from behind our phone screens, hearts pounding and palms sticky, awaiting the next dark twist in the story as they inch forward.

Hook, line and sinker.

I know we all watch those videos.

Not many of us can say that we were once the ghosts to

haunt the halls now immortalised on the internet. The flip side of the coin. Part of the fabric of the abandoned husk, and by extension, its story.

Our lives are a mystery that society then monetises and sells off to the highest bidder for entertainment. The human stories interwoven with the tragedy are erased. Written over. Forgotten. That's what happened to us.

Crouched low with the collar of my thick coat turned up to hide my face, I find myself in the paradoxical position of breaking into the institute I was once incarcerated in.

Now I'm the violator. Not the violated. I haven't returned to Harrowdean Manor in the last decade. Tonight is different. I'm saying goodbye for the final time.

Everyone thinks this tale has already been told. The book closed long ago for the short-term memory spans of the disinterested public. Once the uproar died down, the world continued to turn, and Incendia was forgotten.

We were forgotten.

One by one, each of the six private institutes that once fed the wealth and depravity of the corporation have been demolished. It's taken ten years to see the process through, and now Harrowdean is the final institute to fall. It's set for demolition at daybreak.

Most don't know this place still exists. It's kept off the books and quiet for this exact reason—the government and those in charge of the cleanup don't want curious bloggers poking around with their cameras. Instead, the place has been left to quietly rot.

In the pocket of my thick coat, I feel my mobile phone buzzing. I know who it will be without needing to check. Sighing through my nostrils, I answer the incoming call.

"I told you to leave me alone."

"You can't just storm off like that, Xan!" Lennox huffs in his gravelly, sonorous timbre. "We need to talk about this."

"I've made my position perfectly clear."

"Where are you?" he demands. "We're going to sit down and discuss this together. As a fucking family."

"Do what you want. I have nothing else to say."

"Ripley had every right to sit down with that journalist—"

"No," I interrupt him. "She didn't."

Hanging up, I pocket my phone. I may not be the stone cold, level-headed analytic I once was, but I'm not going to sit here and write some shitty pros and cons list to make this decision. I said no.

We've never entertained any interview requests before. I certainly won't be doing it now.

Creeping through long grass that's almost as tall as I am, the loading bay comes into view. Weeds have long overtaken the concrete foundation and brick pillars, cloaking the institute's rear entrance in a coffin-like, green shroud.

I hop up onto the platform, heading for the bolted door where deliveries once took place. My backpack slides off my shoulder and into my hands. After unzipping it, I sift around for the compact pair of bolt cutters I stashed inside amongst my other supplies.

The irony isn't lost on me.

Everyone wanted to escape this hell hole.

Here I am now, breaking back in.

Latching the curved blades around the padlock that secures the bay doors, I position myself then begin to cinch the cutters closed. It takes some manoeuvring, the rusted metal screaming in protest, loud enough to make me flinch.

Eventually, the padlock splits and falls. It thuds against the ancient concrete so loud, it feels like the metallic clank of a guillotine making impact with an exposed neck.

Lip curled, I shake off the thought. No one comes here. The security measures are fucking pathetic. I'm perfectly safe. As I ease the door open, the smell hits me.

There aren't adequate words to describe it... A pungent, stomach-turning concoction of animal waste, mould, burnt-out fires and something inexplicable. Something sinister. Perhaps the stench of long-removed corpses or faded bloodstains.

Stashing the bolt cutters, I swap them for an industrial flashlight then step back into purgatory. My flashlight providing the only guiding light, smashed glass crunches beneath my thick-soled boots, a breadcrumb trail leading me deeper into the suffocating darkness.

All of the evidence of the atrocities committed here was removed when CSI's swarmed, and the infamous Sabre Security picked over the remains. In fact, there's evidence of that—discarded plastic bags, crime scene tape and even the faint sprinkles of fingerprint dust.

The broken pieces of countless shattered lives were left behind, though. A random shoe. Used needles. Broken furniture. Torn books. Graffiti litters every wall with various tags and nihilistic messages left behind by forgotten patients.

One inked tag catches my eye.

WE SCREAM IN SILENCE.

Running a gloved hand over the letters, anger comes rushing to the surface. Strange to think I once felt nothing… until she came along. Now I'm not just angry. No. I'm indescribably, uncontrollably, ire-fucking-futably furious.

We did scream.

Yet all they heard was silence.

Hand falling, I swallow the thick lump that's now clogging my throat and push onwards to the south wing. The damage is worse here. Patients sought safety and refuge wherever they could when the institute fell. Some obviously hid here.

I'm not sure what possesses me to return to the art room at the end of the sagging corridor, now peppered with all manner of animal waste. The door is hanging off its hinges, the room brightly illuminated by moonlight spilling through smashed bay windows.

Gooseflesh rises on my skin, even beneath my heavy

clothing. I can feel it prickling and spreading. I numbly realise that I'm staring at a torn canvas, tossed on the floor and covered in stains.

Dirt. Blood.

Who can tell?

I recognise the brush strokes beneath, though. I've spent enough hours silently watching her paint. The way the lurid shades are liberally applied for maximum emotional impact... It's Ripley's signature style.

She doesn't just create art; she creates living, breathing replicas of her motherfucking soul. Each canvas holds a piece, torn directly from her chest then splattered against the material like a bloodied Rorschach inkblot. She paints with her own mortality.

Crouching down, I ignore the coverage of filth to lift the canvas. I don't recognise this one. My leather-encased fingertips skate over the intricate swirls of black, dark-green and crimson, painting a violent maelstrom with three lone figures at the heart of the storm.

It's signed and dated. She painted this not long after we arrived at Harrowdean Manor. I trace the first shadowy figure. She's flanked by two darker shadows, creeping up behind her like prowling wolves.

A low chuckle tumbles from my mouth. I suppose that's exactly what we were back then. Wolves. Predators. Enemies. Which is precisely how we survived. We had to become evil too.

Placing the canvas back down, I forcibly tear my eyes away from the twisted reminder of the past. The rest of the room is a disaster. Work benches are smashed and collapsed, stools upturned, electrical cables hanging from the ceiling. It's a war zone.

The other rooms are no better. My flashlight swings from side to side, illuminating each iteration of the institute's own apocalypse. Weirdly, it's silent. Deathly so. My footsteps are the only sound, not even the clamour of stray animals keeps me company.

The world abandoned Harrowdean Manor.

Much like it abandoned us.

My feet carry me without direction. I don't know what I came here to achieve. Not really. I just knew that I needed to see it one last time—to verify those dark times really happened and weren't some elaborate, fucked up dream.

On the fifth floor, it's a treacherous journey to room seventeen. The door hangs open, partially collapsed. Hoisting my backpack higher, I step into Ripley's old bedroom, the floorboards creaking beneath my boots.

As more moonlight spills through the window, a wave of déjà vu hits me amongst the thick plumes of dust. Like the rest of the institute, the bedroom is trashed. I move slowly and carefully, fearful the floor is going to give way at any moment.

My gaze is locked on the rusted bed springs, littered with scraps of decaying fabric that have peeled off the frame over the years. This is the bed where I held a knife to Ripley's throat, intent on ending the never-ending game for both of us before something stopped me.

She stopped me.

No—It was the way she made me feel.

That cruel vixen brought me to my knees without even trying. I couldn't have stopped her even if I'd wanted to. Deep down, I was always hers to claim. Even in the months I refused to acknowledge that.

Ripley Bennet stole me.

Broke me.

Fixed me.

Fucking *loved* me.

I knew what I was missing out on by refusing to feel or be vulnerable ever again—that's the thing the doctors and psychiatrists could never quite fathom. It wasn't that I didn't feel. Far from it. Rather, I used to feel so much, I instead simply chose never to feel again.

A silent scream.

And an unheard one at that.

But now our screams aren't just being heard. They're being documented. Edited. Cut into palatable soundbites to capture the public's eye. Our stories are being commercialised, swallowed and fucking regurgitated to secure some ambitious asshole's moment in the limelight.

She's enabling it.

Once again, Ripley's signing our death warrants.

I can't allow this documentary to happen. No matter what people's motivations are for getting involved, nothing good can come of dredging up the past. As much as I may hate the way this tragedy has been erased, I won't watch my family suffer the repercussions again.

If the world knows the true story, every last gory detail of what went on in this very manor, we can kiss the last decade of painful peace goodbye. No matter how horrific the long-lasting trauma has made these years. At least we're free.

Ripley's voice may change that.

I have to stop the documentary from airing.

CHAPTER 1
RIPLEY
HELP. – YOUNG LIONS

TEN YEARS EARLIER

I'VE RECENTLY BECOME acquainted with pure agony.

It's not the kind of pain you'd experience from a scraped knee or a sore cartilage piercing. That pain can be buried. Avoided. Numbed. Tucked away into a darkened corner until it grows tired of hanging around and fades.

The pain that's wracking my body now is a whole other level of intensity. Beyond exhaustion or emotional anguish. Survival isn't free—for any of us. It always extracts a toll, one way or another.

Escaping sometimes means leaving pieces of ourselves behind.

I imagine it's the same pain that semi-conscious Lennox is feeling. His injured hand hangs at his side as he's pulled along between Xander and Raine. I watch his bare feet drag against the ground, limp and useless.

"Where now?" Raine asks.

"Straight ahead," I croak.

With a trembling hand, I hold onto his hospital gown,

attempting to steer him in a straight line. It's a challenge as we trip and stumble towards the manor, dodging the mayhem unfolding all around us. It's spilling in from all directions.

"Careful," Xander calls out. "Body up ahead."

"Body?" Raine exclaims.

"A guard, I think. Dead or unconscious. I don't know which."

"What the fuck?"

"Be glad you can't see what's going on around us," Xander mutters.

Tightening my grip on his gown, I peer through the haze. "Keep going, Raine. I'll steer you."

Floodlights illuminate the nighttime air, and honestly, I wish they'd just plunge us into full darkness at this point. Then I wouldn't have to see the anarchy we've escaped into. We swapped one hell for another.

After months of malpractice and blatant abuse, the patient population of Harrowdean Manor has declared war. We escaped Professor Craven's sadistic Z wing, fleeing torture and imprisonment only to stumble out into a full-blown riot.

All around us, the madness is spreading like an airborne infection. Patients have turned into wild, almost rabid animals, attacking at will and destroying anything they can lay their hands on.

"Round them all up!" Rick's voice echoes in the distance. "I want every guard cuffed and gagged."

There's a chorus of agreements and various sounds of enthusiasm from the patients choosing to follow him. Most have descended into violence. Some fight, exchanging blows, while others begin smashing whatever they lay eyes on.

Those who've flocked to Rick's call are banding together to capture the remaining guards. Contrastingly, the rest of the patients are cowering or running. Sides have already formed amongst the anarchy.

The organised few—Rick, Rae, Patient Three and her

fellow escapee—are doling out instructions as they assume control. They seem to be operating under the delusion that we can pull this pseudo-heist off. Really, it's only a matter of time before the authorities march in here.

Then all our heads will be on the chopping block. I may have decided not to run, but we at least need to give ourselves a fighting chance of staying alive. That starts with getting Lennox help before he deteriorates.

"Ripley?" Lennox moans in pain.

He's unable to lift his head, the way my name slips off his tongue like a sorrowful prayer sending shivers down my spine.

"She's here, man," Raine mumbles back.

"Can't... go... farther."

"Like hell you can't," Xander spits.

"Xan," Lennox gasps. "Stop."

"We're getting you somewhere safe." Xander's usually curt voice carries a disturbing, almost high-pitched edge of apprehension.

Xander is... scared?

No. That can't be right.

"Just leave me," Lennox tries to plead.

"Not this crap again," I cut in. "We're not leaving you, Nox."

I don't miss the curious side eye Xander gives me, a single, midnight-blue orb slicing deep into my skin. It wasn't so long ago when I would've happily left Lennox to be trampled to death in a riot given half a chance.

Now the world has been swept away by a violent tsunami, and we're left to pick over the destruction to find our lives once more. Everything I thought I knew about Lennox, Harrowdean, even myself—it's all gone.

"What?" I snap at Xander.

"Nothing."

"Then stop staring, and get us out of here!"

The corner of his mouth quirks. "Whatever you say."

Dodging the dead or unconscious guard who's sprawled out near the steps leading inside, we head for the rear entrance to Harrowdean's reception. My cooked-spaghetti legs are barely carrying my weight.

We've both been wilfully battered in our time beneath ground, and though Lennox looks in far worse shape, I can feel the steady throbbing of my wrist along with countless bruises and other injuries from the beatings.

My wounds are bleeding, each droplet dripping in time to the rhythmic pounding of my skull. Between the water torture, subsequent beatings and lack of food or sleep beyond passing out, the trauma of our trip to the Z wing is quickly making itself known.

"Inside," Xander orders. "We're too exposed out here."

"How are we supposed to do this?" I ask weakly.

"Take Raine—don't let him fall." He shifts Lennox's weight onto himself. "I've got the big guy."

"I can climb a staircase," Raine grumbles.

Grasping his hand, I hold on tight despite the way it makes my wrists twinge. "We know. Just let me help."

"You're hurt, guava girl. I should be the one helping you."

"You are just by being here."

"I wasn't there to protect you!" His sunglass-covered eyes tilt upwards, like he's praying to the heavens for patience. "I failed you. Again!"

"Cry me a goddamn river," Xander drones with marked exasperation. "Get inside before having a breakdown please."

He tilts his head in the direction of Xander's once again lifeless voice. "Fuck you, Xan."

"He's right," I placate. "We need to hide."

"From who?" Raine shivers in my arms. "The guards? Or the patients?"

Xander releases a dry laugh. "How about both?"

I'm about to drag Raine up the damn stairs whether he

likes it or not when a cacophony of screams reaches us through the night, silencing us all.

"Burn, Harrowdean! Burn it all!"

"No more!"

"Burn! Burn! Burn!"

A gaggle of patients are high on whatever riot fever is spreading from one soul to another—eyes wild, fists bloodied, uncaring of who they hurt or why we're pushing back against the oppression at all. When violence takes root, reason soon evaporates.

Their chanting is growing ever closer. We're vulnerable out in the open, our only source of light the now-flickering floodlights that seem to be signalling impending disaster.

"Go!" Xander barks.

Semi-carrying Lennox up the first few steps, we're right behind the struggling pair when the patients catch up to us. It doesn't seem to matter that we're not dressed like guards or even a threat.

"Ripley Bennet!"

Fuck!

Lewis, an idiot from the sixth floor, recognises me. "Hey! Harrowdean's whore!"

Without hesitating, I shove Raine forward, wincing as he trips and falls. But I won't watch him get hurt because of me for a second time.

"Go. Get out of here!"

"Rip!" he yells.

"Move! Run!"

The only way to stop them from pouncing on Raine, sprawled out and disorientated, is to attack first. I fling myself down the steps to Lewis, determined to throw the first punch.

He takes the brunt of the fall. We hurtle towards the hard ground, landing in a tangle and both yelping at the pain of impact. His friends hang back, content to watch us brawl.

"Stay down," I warn. "We're not the enemy here."

"I've heard the whispers," he snarls in my face. "I know you're management's bitch. If we're taking them down... you're going down with them, Ripley."

"Look around you! This chaos only ends one way!"

Lewis grabs a handful of my filthy, bloodstained shirt to wrench me closer. "Yes. We're getting out of here. Not you, though. You're going to die here."

I ignore the sound of Raine's protests on the steps behind us, focused on my attacker. "Back off, man. Final warning."

"Or what?" he challenges.

With a quick glance at the group of onlooking patients, I realise how much of a target I've painted on my own back. They don't see a fellow patient. A victim. A survivor. Whatever bullshit fits the bill.

No.

To them, I'm the enemy.

Harrowdean's whore, right?

I didn't survive this long by making friends or exercising a moral conscience. And I'm sure as hell not going to start now.

"Your mates are leaving you." Lewis nods his head towards the institute where Xander's still struggling to shift Lennox. "I didn't think you had any of those."

Despite the voice telling me that Xander is right to leave me here to die, pain still cuts across my chest. He's here for Lennox. Raine. Not me.

"I don't have friends, and I don't need them."

Drawing back my fist, I deck the stupid son of a bitch. Agony explodes across my knuckles on impact with his square jaw, the vibrations ricocheting up my forearm to my elbow.

"Bitch!" Lewis screams.

His blow comes hard and fast, striking me in the cheek. My head snaps to the side, wrenching painfully. It's a mere drop in the ocean compared to the state of my body, though, and it doesn't distract me.

I use my position above him to my advantage and rain

down punch after punch. Not even the wailing of my protesting muscles slows me down. My mind narrows on one thought. Self-preservation.

I've always preferred to rule with words and threats. Most would fear the loss of their precious contraband far more than any physical damage I could inflict. But in a fistfight, I'm still deadly in my own right.

Lewis bucks and writhes, trying to throw me off. Clinging on, I slam my forehead into his as a last resort, a wail threatening to escape from my gritted teeth. Hitting the ground, his skull impacts with a rock, making him go limp.

"Move!" Xander yells distantly. "Now!"

At the sound of shouting, I flick my eyes up to the institute. Raine is still helplessly sprawled out, while Xander's almost inside, but his voice has taken on that disturbingly urgent edge again.

"Move, Nox!" he demands.

"No! Raine! Ripley!" Lennox replies in a weak bellow.

"I can't help them until you're inside, dickhead!"

Distracted by the sight of Xander shoving Lennox inside then rushing to help Raine up, I miss the attack heading my way. The long-limbed patient stinks of cigarette smoke, her face obscured by snarled hair and malevolence.

Air bursts from my lungs as I'm body-slammed, thrown sideways off Lewis's unconscious form. Hands wrap around my throat, finding a tight cinch that cuts off my oxygen supply. I writhe and scratch, frantic to find an escape.

"You used us all," she accuses.

My lungs are burning—filled with white-hot, molten lava that's permeating deeper into my chest. I can feel her blood on my fingertips, her hands seeming to squeeze ever tighter.

"You deserve to be cuffed and paraded around like the rest of them."

Warmth coats my skin from where her nails are slicing my

throat. My vision is beginning to haze, awash with bright, white spots.

CLICK.

"Let her go. I'll only ask once."

My attacker freezes, her head raising towards the new voice. The floodlights illuminate her blurry face. Tania. Seems her gratitude for the pink dildo I previously sold her was short-lived.

"You," she hisses at the voice.

"Step aside, inmate."

"You're outnumbered, asshole!"

Peeking over her, I spot the barrel of a black handgun. It's pointed directly at Tania's back. Looking higher, the person clutching the weapon causes shock and relief to blast through me.

"Do I look like I care?" Langley cocks the gun, ribbons of blood spilling down his face from a cut at his hairline. "Move. Now."

I've never heard such raw aggression from him before. The person looming over us both isn't the soft-eyed guard I know. Then again, I had no idea he was secretly working for Sabre Security until he tried to poach me as an informant.

Tania hesitates, her fingertips bruising my oesophagus. "You wouldn't dare use that."

His finger rests on the trigger, twitching in challenge. "Try me."

"It's your job to protect us!"

"Stand up, turn around and walk away."

"There are witnesses!" she screeches.

With a short laugh, Langley casts one of his baby blues around the state of disarray. "Where, exactly? I could unload this entire clip into your skull without anyone saying a word. Now *get up.*"

Her eyes now wide with genuine fear, Tania releases her grip on my throat. I splutter violently, sucking in frantic breaths, the rush of oxygen causing my insides to sear. Each inhale feels like drinking fire.

"That's it," Langley says in a flat tone. "Walk away now, and I'll let you live."

"What the fuck is wrong with you?" Tania exclaims.

"I have a job to do. So I'd suggest you get out of my sight, and take your little friends with you."

Langley boots Lewis in the ribs. He's beginning to stir, a semi-conscious groan escaping his mouth. With tears now streaming down her cheeks, Tania gestures for the others to approach and heave him up.

Once they've scuttled away, casting worried looks over their shoulders at the gun Langley holds poised, my surroundings filter back in. I can hear racing footsteps, speeding towards us from the institute.

"You." Xander's cool, clipped voice is unmistakable.

Langley swings the gun around, now aiming it at him. "I don't want any trouble."

"Then step away from her."

"Me?" Langley's dark brows knit into a frown. "Pretty sure she's the one who needs protection from you, last time I checked."

"And why exactly is her welfare your business in the first place?"

Groaning as I sit upright, I massage my aching throat. "Stop. Both of you."

Two pairs of eyes swing to me. Langley's track over me— cataloguing the various injuries, bruises and bloodstains like he's seeing them for the first time. Last time we spoke was before Noah's attack and our trip to the Z wing.

"I heard you were taken," he grinds out. "What the hell did they do to you?"

"No time." I look over to Xander's impassive expression. "Where are Lennox and Raine?"

"Safely inside."

"Then… why did you come back?"

His almost-black eyes make my skin tighten and prickle with awareness. The sheer intensity steals my breath far more effectively than Tania's attempt to choke me.

He's staring at me like it's obvious, but nothing about this complicated creature is ever fucking obvious. We've been playing an elaborate game of cat and mouse for years now, and I still can't fathom the broken mind that lies within his skull.

"You," he deadpans.

My windpipe closes altogether.

"I came back for you, Ripley."

Tucking the gun into his waistband, Langley flashes Xander an odd look. He stoops low to grasp my body. I let him tug me up, too exhausted to do much more than slump into him.

"They did this to you?" Langley grinds out.

"Professor Craven." I gasp in pain. "And… others."

"Jesus, Rip. How did you get out?"

"With a little help." Looking up, I find his concerned eyes scrutinising me. "What are you still doing here? Shouldn't you be running for the hills with the rest of your team?"

"The rest…" He grips his forehead. "How did you… Shit, not now. Can you move?"

Teeth clenched, I nod once.

"Good."

Xander takes one look at me then moves to my other side, a slim, scarred arm wrapping around my waist. "Let her go."

Langley snorts. "You first."

"Not happening."

With them both holding me, neither willing to let go, we awkwardly stumble into the reception. It's dark inside, still littered with debris and water damage from the storm.

That night feels like a million years ago, but from the failing power to the boarded windows and dirt-streaked flooring, the scattered remnants still paint a chaotic scene. The opulence has been destroyed by Mother Nature in all her almighty wrath.

Perhaps the most telling indication of that night's fateful importance has his arm around me. The cold-hearted man with empty midnight eyes who almost left me to drown in a pool.

Xander is my nemesis. The man who vowed to break me and keep the scattered pieces for his collection. Only now he's helping me, limping and half-dead, to safety. I must be delirious.

"I left them down here," Xander mutters in the gloom. "Lennox is in bad shape."

"He... We... They tortured him for hours." I struggle to get the words out. "Water. Beatings. His h-hand..."

"I saw. How did he make it out?"

"I, ah... helped him."

Pausing dramatically, Xander eyes me. "You... helped him?"

"Yes." I hold his stare, defiant.

"You." The word is half-question, half-statement.

"You really want to discuss this right now?"

"Later. But we are discussing it."

Xander leads us into an adjacent corridor leading towards the west wing. It's low-lit from the odd emergency light still working. My eyes adjust, and I spot two outlines slumped against a wall.

"Xan?" Raine's voice calls out.

"It's us."

"All I can smell is blood. Have you got her?"

"I'm here." I wince in pain as we trudge towards them.

Langley takes one look at Lennox, his partially mangled hand still limp at his side, then curses.

"What the hell?"

"You can thank your pink-haired friend for that one."

His blue gaze swings around to me. "What?"

"Alyssa, right?"

The silent bobbing of his throat is all the confirmation I need.

"You have some serious explaining to do," I demand. "Starting with who you really are and what you're doing inside Harrowdean."

Mouth flopping open, Langley's shocked to silence. Clearly, he never expected his cover to be blown so spectacularly. That only makes his betrayal all the more bitter.

"Yeah," he mutters numbly. "I guess I do."

"Shouldn't you be running off into the sunset with your team?"

He draws in a deep breath to gather himself. "It's complicated."

"Then uncomplicate it."

Interrupting our exchange, Lennox groans in pain. How he's still conscious and hasn't passed back out from exertion or blood loss remains a mystery.

"Medical wing," Langley announces.

"Explain yourself first. How can we trust you?"

"There's no time, Rip. I'll explain everything, but not here. We can temporarily secure the medical wing, and Lennox needs looking at."

"We were already headed there anyway," Xander snarkily retorts. "Feel free to fuck off, *Langley*."

"Need I remind you that I'm the one with the gun?"

"You think I need a gun to snap your neck?" Xander counters.

"Good luck getting close."

"I won't need it."

"Yeah? Well, putting a bullet between your eyes will turn around this shitty day. So, make your move."

"Enough!" I chastise them both. "Seriously."

Lennox grunts again before he suddenly collapses. Raine's

holding his arm, so he's pulled off balance by the weight dragging him down.

"Shit!" Raine yelps.

Xander releases me to catch his best friend before he hits the floor. He takes Lennox from Raine, throws his arm around his shoulder, then jerks his head to indicate we should all follow.

I steady Raine, taking his hand to steer him along with us. "This way."

"Aren't the guards supposed to be the enemy right now?" Raine whispers worriedly. "We shouldn't trust him."

I spare Langley a glance—stony-faced, his blue eyes darting from side to side, surveying for any threats. His posture betrays a persona I never spotted before. Shoulders square. Feet spread. Always alert and prepared to act.

He's the perfect mole.

Affable. Unsuspicious.

Unseen.

"Langley isn't a guard, Raine."

"What?" His head jerks in my direction.

I tear my eyes from the blue-eyed stranger. "He never was."

We struggle onwards. With the unlit medical wing in sight, I feel my last vestiges of energy dissipate. Xander shoves the door open, manhandling a now-unconscious Lennox inside.

"Anyone here?" he yells. "We need help."

Silence.

"I guess not," Raine murmurs. "Is it still dark? Morning staff probably got stuck outside when everything kicked off."

Jaw clenching, Xander continues to heft Lennox, his alabaster skin now dotted with sweat from the exertion. We limp behind them, slipping inside the deserted wing.

Langley glances at the door standing between us and the war zone. "Patients will come looting soon enough."

"Looting?" Raine repeats.

"Drugs. Weapons. Food. Riots can last days, sometimes even weeks. Survival instincts will kick in."

The reality of the situation hammers home with each word he utters. Hands raised, Raine follows Xander's huffing to help manoeuvre Lennox's now-unconscious body onto a bed.

"If there's no doctor, what do we do?" The concern in Raine's tone is audible.

Langley releases a long sigh. "I was a field medic… Well, in a past life. I'm not an expert, but I can take a look at his injuries."

"What do you need?" Xander straightens, his attention fixed on Lennox.

"A damn sight more than what we have available, I'd imagine." He looks around the deserted wing. "We're going to need some pain relief to start."

Watching them disperse to search, I suddenly teeter on my own two feet. Langley's mumbling is overcome by a loud buzzing in my head. Physical exhaustion coupled with the breakdown I've been holding back at all costs overwhelms me.

Lennox is badly hurt. There's no medical help. We're caught in a riot, surrounded by patients who hate my fucking guts, and have no idea when backup will arrive. Raine's barely recovered and shouldn't even be out of bed, let alone running around fending off attacks.

The odds are stacked against us.

Was this a huge mistake?

Staying here may have been the brave choice, but the violence will only escalate. People will die. Maybe we will too. And all the pain, the suffering, the sacrifice… it will all have been for nothing.

The magnitude of the past few days sucker punches me in the face. The Z wing. Lennox being tortured. Beatings. Sabre Security. Our pink-haired saviour. The bloodied corridor. Professor Craven's broken skull.

We survived.

We escaped.

But the real battle begins now.

"No," I choke out.

"Rip?" Raine cocks his head in my direction.

"W-We... should've... run."

The sight of Raine standing nearby while the other two get to work abruptly blurs. Now he's a pixelated jigsaw of fuzzy limbs and wobbly lines as my energy fizzles out.

"Ripley?" His voice sounds far-off, disjointed. "Ripley!"

Everything turns white. Spinning. Blurring. A hot flush of fever and dizziness sweeps me off my feet and sends me hurtling into the approaching blackness.

CHAPTER 2
LENNOX
MONSTERS – FOREIGN AIR

"I'VE DONE the best I can. I'm not a doctor."

A tired voice filters into my awakening consciousness. It sounds resigned. Perhaps a little defensive.

"Then what do we do?"

This one is flat, cold. Familiar. An iceberg carried to shore by my mind's rolling waves.

"Hope this riot ends fast. He's out of the woods for now."

Their two voices overlap, a confusing tangle of sounds and worried tones that permeate my thick brain fog. I can't drag my eyes open. Everything feels like it's wrapped in fluffy cotton wool.

The drug-induced fog offers me a brief escape from recent horrors. But as I come around, the peace dissipates. Pain comes rushing back in to greet me like an unwelcome house guest.

"Have you seen outside?" The tired voice speaks again. "People are going wild. This isn't ending any time soon."

"Then I guess we're all stuck here."

"We don't even have food!" This time, the second, colder voice sounds different—it's suddenly infected with something. Roughening into a low growl, I can almost taste the underlying fear and anxiety that's thawing the towering iceberg.

"Those patients outside will come looking soon enough."

"Agreed."

"Don't agree with me, Langley."

"I don't exactly like it either."

As the syrupy fog lifts further, I realise they aren't whispering at all. The two opposing voices are deep in a heated argument, their bickering overlapping a cacophony of other sounds that are slowly filtering in.

Screaming. Shouting.

Breaking glass. Loud whoops.

"Guys," a raspier voice interrupts them. "Quiet, both of you. They're right outside."

Banging. Smashing.

Excited hollers. More screams.

Trepidation slithers down my spine. I have no choice but to peel my heavy lids open. The light I anticipated to greet me never comes. Shadows and darkness douse my vision, broken by weak moonlight and blurry outlines.

"Xan," I moan weakly.

There's a shuffle, then a figure looms.

"Here, man. Don't move."

My tongue is glued to the roof of my mouth, a length of scratchy sandpaper that refuses to obey. I will my throat muscles to respond, swallowing repeatedly until I can form words.

"W-Where?"

"Medical wing," Xander answers, holding a bottle to my lips. "You've been out of it for a while. Are you in pain?"

I greedily gulp down lukewarm water, my throat screaming too much to respond.

"He's had the maximum dose," someone else interjects.

"Do you even know what those drugs do?" Xander hisses back.

"I wouldn't have injected him with them if I didn't."

A hand swipes down my arm, tracing a map on my skin. I recognise the rough pads of Raine's violin-worn fingertips.

"Ignore them, Nox." The shape of him sitting next to me becomes clearer as my vision settles. "How do you feel?"

Staring at their faces—Xander, Raine and for some reason, that piece of shit guard who's way too friendly with Ripley—it takes a moment for my brain to catch up. I must've blacked out as we ran.

"Peachy," I rasp. "How long was I out?"

"About… ten, eleven hours." Xander stares at the clock locked behind a metal cage on the wall. "You were sedated while he treated your injuries."

The *he* in question lingers behind Xander, arms folded across his built chest. Langley treated me? I hate that weird guy. He trails around after Ripley like a lost puppy begging for scraps of affection.

"Where is she?"

Xander narrows his dark-blue eyes on me. "What happened in that basement?"

Struggling weakly, I try to sit up in the hospital bed and fail. "Where. Is. She?"

"Lay still, for fuck's sake."

"Xan!"

The corner of his mouth twitches. "You should calm down."

"I will when you tell me where Ripley is!"

"She's in the bed next to yours," Raine supplies wearily. "Don't be a dick, Xan. Show him."

Relinquishing, Xander shifts to show me the view. The other hospital bed is lit by some kind of emergency flashlight resting on its side on the trolley between us.

Deathly pale and hooked up to an IV, Ripley is huddled on her side, unconscious. Her hands are curled up to her chest. In her sleep, she looks like a vulnerable waif, not the ballbuster I've always loathed.

The panic barrelling through my nervous system eases the slightest amount. Thank fuck I don't have the mental capacity to analyse that feeling too deeply right now. Or contemplate why I'm feeling it for her.

"Something to share?" Xander asks slyly.

With a huff, I sink deeper into the pillows. "Fuck off."

"You seem awfully concerned."

Ignoring him, I take stock of my body. Everything feels disjointed, like my limbs have been severed and reattached with makeshift stitches. The pain is a fierce, constant burn, despite whatever drugs I've been shot full of.

"Let me past, Xander. I need to check on him."

Langley is in rough shape. His dark hair stands up in all directions, face streaked with blood and dirt, like he got rugby tackled and punched to shit. It's a pleasing mental image.

I eye him warily. "Don't touch me."

"Easy," he placates with a frown.

Raine lightly squeezes my arm. "Don't be an ass, Nox."

"He's a goddamn guard!"

"Not strictly true." Langley fiddles with the IV line trickling into my body. "And in lieu of an actual doctor, I'm your best shot right now. I've had medical training."

"What training?" I stare at him.

Slender arms folded, Xander flicks his gaze back to the dickhead, a grimace twisting his thin lips. His platinum blonde hair is also a mess—shoved back, peppered with blood. In fact, he's covered head to toe.

"Care to elaborate?" Xander asks icily. "We've been patient."

Satisfied by his inspection of the IV, Langley turns his attention to me. "Just trust that I know what I'm doing right now."

I bite back a sarcastic response, letting the man go to work checking me over. As my limbs wake up, there's far too much pain wracking my body to protest any further.

"You're lucky that was a flesh wound." Langley nods towards the bandaged club resting across my chest where my left hand should be. "I can't be certain without an x-ray, though."

Looking down at the thick swathes of cotton, I internally wince at the memory of the drill digging into my hand, parting my flesh like butter. The entire limb feels completely numb, causing worry to flare up.

"Anaesthetic." Langley seems to read my concern. "I flushed the wound with saline and stitched you up. It'll hurt like a motherfucker soon enough."

"Can't wait," I drawl.

"Someone beat the shit out of you," he observes. "I can't rule out internal bleeding, but that's above my pay grade. You want to fill us in on what made that mess?"

He gestures to my bandaged club.

"Drill," I supply.

"A… drill? Like a fucking power tool?"

"The electrocutions didn't work." I hiss at the pain that attempting to shrug causes. "I'm stubborn."

"Fuck me." He scowls.

Xander remains silent, observing our exchange. I can see the memories dancing in his twilight-hued eyes. This isn't our first bout of torture. That's probably why my sanity is still semi-intact.

"You'll have a pretty scar on your face." Langley cracks his neck, trying to regain his composure. "Just pray the wounds don't get infected."

Suppressing a shudder, I force back the memory of the steel-tipped whip slashing into my face, parting skin and flesh. The bitch pretending to be a guard didn't have to go so hard, did she? The facial bandage feels huge and uncomfortable.

My gaze wanders back to the adjacent bed. "What about her?"

Ripley's face is swollen and misshapen. Slithers of her badly bruised body are visible around the sheet she's tangled up in. Her pale complexion makes the inked foliage on her arms stand out like dark thunderclouds.

With black-lined eye sockets, mottled purple bruises circling her throat and countless cuts and abrasions, she bears the evidence of all we endured beneath ground.

Bile burns the back of my throat as indignant rage threatens to take over. Those evil motherfuckers almost broke us. The pain-warped memories were real. It's a small miracle that we survived at all, let alone escaped.

The memory of fleeing Craven's house of horrors are blurred. Pain-laced fragments that no longer fit together in a neat patchwork.

"Similar story." Langley's forehead wrinkles with concern. "She's resting now, but her wrists are infected. You guys were chained up?"

"Shackled in a concrete cell."

"You were together?" Xander asks sharply.

Not trusting myself to speak, I merely nod. His pale-blonde eyebrows are furrowed, likely attempting to piece events together. I'm sure no one expected to see Ripley dragging me of all people out of the basement.

Langley visibly swallows. "I've cleaned her wounds and hooked her up to IV antibiotics. She'll recover. Now we wait."

Raine hisses through clenched teeth, appearing angrier than I've ever seen him. "What happened, Nox?"

A bubble grows and lodges itself in my throat. We've dealt with this kind of evil before. In Priory Lane, I saw the devil's face and lived to tell the tale. That gave me the strength to survive again.

But seeing Ripley, bare and battered as she fought to stay alive? Hearing her soft cries and whimpers while we clung to life? That did something to me. Something irreversible. Something far more crippling than their torture sessions. And I don't know if I can fucking fix it.

"Trust me." My voice is an aching rasp from all the screaming. "You don't want to know."

"Pretty sure we have a right to, though," Raine argues, his slender shoulders fraught with tension. "You both disappeared!"

"How long were we gone?"

"A couple days," Xander supplies.

Raine's grip on my arm tightens once more. "We were worried sick."

The panicked feeling is back. Breeding. Metastasising. In my head, I can hear Ripley's cries ricocheting, ping-ponging around the internal cavities of my skull. My own pain doesn't feature in the flashbacks—just hers.

Her body scrunched up, protecting itself from the battering water. Freezing-cold skin, snuggled into my chest, covered in gooseflesh. Her feeble whispers as she wrapped her fingers around the fleshy strings of my heart and ripped it clean out to keep it for herself.

If this is it... I just want you to know that I forgive you.

I didn't deserve those words. Hell, I didn't even know I wanted them. But now that she's given me her forgiveness... Lord, fucking help me. It's like an invisible dam has burst, and a torrent of guilt and self-loathing is spilling out.

Hatred has kept me safe. Protected. Immune. With that stripped away, I'm at risk of feeling things I've spent years trying not to feel. At least not for anyone but the family I chose in Priory Lane.

"Why didn't Ripley just leave you down there?" Xander stares at me like he's trying to figure something out.

"What?" I snap out of my musings.

"You tried to drown her alive, Nox."

The guilt building inside me explodes, spewing in all directions like an erupting volcano. "I'm aware."

"Then she used Noah to try to frame you." He shakes his head. "But what I can't figure out is why you're both lying here, and she didn't just leave you to rot or vice versa."

Now leaning against the wall, Langley is tuned in to Xander's interrogation. Raine's golden-haired head is cocked, demonstrating his attention, latching onto every hitched breath and note of hesitation.

My scalp prickles, a hot flush of awkwardness washing over me. I'm not telling them shit. Not about this.

"That was… before."

"Before what exactly?" Raine questions.

"Before everything."

"Everything?" Xander repeats drily.

The truth swirls through my mind. I can't explain. Not when I've barely wrapped my head around the whispered apologies we shared, the feel of her skin on mine, her soft lips and velvet tongue or bare breasts pressing into my chest…

"Nox!" Raine grips my arm, demanding an answer I can't give. "Well?"

"Raine," Xander cautions, reading something on my face.

"I have a right to know, Xan. She's my… She's… We… Fuck!" He pauses to blow out a frustrated breath. "Look, how can I help her if I don't know what happened?"

"You can't help," I snap back. "Not with this."

"I care about her. Far more than you do!"

Self-loathing quickly morphs into molten anger—the noxious fumes poisoning my thoughts. How dare he presume to know what I'm thinking or feeling? He doesn't know shit about what we just survived.

"And?" I scoff.

"And whatever game you're playing, stop. You can't keep me from being with Ripley."

"That's not what I'm doing," I quickly deny. "Well… anymore."

"Then what is this?" he challenges fiercely. "You despise her. What's changed?"

The pressure inside me boils over, a foaming, caged beast snapping through my veins as it breaks free.

"Everything!"

My voice carries, seeming to ricochet in the medical wing's gloom. Glaring at Raine like he can see the warning on my face, I breathe heavily, a tight ball of tension burgeoning in my chest.

"Take your hand off me."

Raine gapes at me, the borrowed aviators sliding down his nose. I watch his shock filter into defiance—mouth creasing, fists balling, his shoulders squared like I'm challenging his claim or some dumb shit.

"This conversation isn't over," he warns in a low tone. "Hurt her again and I'll kick your ass, blind or not."

Adjusting his sunglasses, Raine moves over to Ripley's bed. I watch him run his hands over the thin mattress, feeling for a spot to perch next to her. His hand moves to rest on top of her lifeless one.

My stomach clenches.

Get your fucking hands off her.

I swallow the words begging to spill out, imprisoning them instead in an imaginary steel box. Of course, he gets the right to touch her. I sure as hell don't. Not after all I've done.

The awkward silence is broken by the sound of more glass smashing outside the medical wing. Hoots and screams float through the windows, permeating the heavy air.

I glance at Xander, his attention now focused outside. "What's going on out there?"

He shrugs. "They've been securing the institute for a few hours. Barricading, bolting doors. The front gate's been chained shut to hold the authorities back."

Langley sighs, his attention focused on the bag of fluids hanging above me. "That isn't gonna keep management from sending a tactical unit in to retake control. There will be casualties."

"Are we safe in here?" I wince at another wave of pain.

"As safe as anywhere. You're both hooked up to IV antibiotics and need to rest. We can't risk moving yet."

"I'm perfectly fine."

With an eye roll, Langley finishes fussing over me. "You look it."

"Once the fatigue and hunger set in, the novelty of rebellion will wear off," Xander inserts. "Sides will form. They'll soon forget the enemy and turn on each other."

"Well… shit," I deadpan.

If Incendia were planning on sending in the cavalry to stamp out any resistance and retake control of Harrowdean, they would've done so by now. We must have enough hostages to stop them from storming the place.

We're on our own.

And I can't lift a damn finger.

"We should all get cleaned up," Langley suggests. "Then we'll make a plan."

"Help me up."

He shoots me a scathing look. "Fuck off, Lennox."

"What's your problem?"

"My goodwill only extends so far when it comes to assholes."

"Mind telling me what exactly I've done?" I ask caustically.

"Where should I begin?"

Temper flaring, I glower at the prickly son of a bitch. "By all means, from the top."

"Believe me, there aren't enough hours in the day to cover all the reasons why you deserved to be dragged into that basement. Ripley should've left you there to rot."

"Then why help me?" I fire back.

His gaze briefly strays to Ripley before he looks away. "I'm not here for you."

Turning away, he moves to pick through a cupboard of medical supplies on the opposite side of the room. Xander turns away from the window, frowning at Langley before he looks around the empty wing.

"They must keep spare clothes here for discharged patients."

"You could use some yourself." I jerk my chin, indicating his bloodied state.

Xander plucks the hem of his soiled shirt with a look of distaste. "He did bleed rather a lot."

"Who, exactly?"

"Davis," he answers casually.

I stare at my best friend, mouth hanging wide open. "Davis?"

"Yes. He's dead."

Xander drops the shirt hem then resumes scanning the medical wing. He doesn't spare my stunned expression a second glance.

"Did he say Davis?" Raine whispers from the other bed. "Like… Warden Davis?"

"You know any other Davis in here?"

"Fucking hell. He has to be kidding."

Watching Xander pick around the room, searching for clothing, the punch line never comes. He doesn't crack a smile or yell *gotcha!* For each second that trickles past, the dread blooming in my chest grows wings and takes flight.

"I don't think he is," I grumble.

"The warden, Nox?" Raine hisses in disbelief. "Xander… he… he wouldn't do that, would he?"

Honestly, there's no limit to the fucked up shit that Xander would do. He's just a hell of a lot quieter about it than the rest of us. That's how his evil so often goes undetected.

Ducking his head inside a tall cabinet, he pulls out a handful of second-hand clothes from a labelled laundry sack. Xander begins searching for the right sizes.

"I'm not kidding," he clips out.

A conflicting maelstrom rushes through my mind— disbelief, shock, fear. But for the life of me, I can't summon the humanity to pity the dead warden. As long as Xander isn't at risk, I'm glad he's dead.

"Was it an accident?" Raine inquires hesitantly.

Xander laughs under his breath. "Most certainly not."

Watching the colour drain from Raine's face, I refocus on Xander. "What happened?"

He yanks out a bundle of tangled clothing. "We had words."

"And?"

"And none of his were what I wanted to hear."

Dipping back into the bag to search for more suitable clothing, he halts as his eyes stray to Ripley. The man who doesn't bat an eye while telling us he killed the fucking warden now appears… uncertain.

What in the ever-loving fuck?

"He wouldn't tell me where you were." Xander's throat undulates as he quickly looks away. "Where either of you were."

"Were you seen?" I grit out.

"Of course not. The riot took care of that."

"Where…?" Raine pauses, swallowing audibly. "Where is he?"

Attention focused on sorting the clothing, Xander holds up an oversized t-shirt, seeming to consider the size. I watch his eyes flit back to Ripley's unconscious form, comparing her size to the shirt he holds.

"Office," he replies.

Nodding robotically, Raine now looks a little green. "So… he won't be found for a while."

"I suppose not."

Raine's been with us for long enough to know how Xander's bizarre mind operates. The boundaries of human emotion that fail to apply to him. Yet he's never quite accepted or even understood it.

Xander doesn't care. Not in the way normal humans do. He's destroyed his own ability to do exactly that. I've often wondered what he feels for us—his surrogate family. It can't be love. He isn't capable of that.

I didn't think I was either, but I'm fooling myself if I think I shared my body heat to stop Ripley from dying of hypothermia just for the company in hell. And I've deluded myself enough in the past.

That's how I lost everything.

I won't lose it all again.

We broke each other, and for good reason. But those reasons feel irrelevant now in the cold light of day. If it wasn't for her, I'd still be rotting in that basement, shackled and bleeding out in a padded cell.

Sinking into the hospital pillows, fatigue and weakness crash over me. I have enough energy left to turn my head to the side, giving me a direct view of the adjacent bed.

Raine's hand is still clasped over Ripley's limp one, his head tilted back as he contemplates. I can't help but stare at them. The familiarity. The intimacy. His palpable fear and clear devotion to her.

What I'm not prepared for is the piping-hot burst of emotion that stabs into me, over and over in a relentless assault on my damaged sanity. It isn't anger. That I can recognise, utilise, *control.*

It's… jealousy.

Well, fuck.

I'm jealous of Raine, sitting there like a goddamn guardian angel, holding the hand of the bitch who saved my life. He's earned her trust. Her love. Her vulnerability. That's why he gets to touch her and I don't.

That realisation only magnifies the feeling tenfold until I'm choking on the barbed wire lodged in my throat, taking the razor-sharp edges deep into my oesophagus and letting them shred apart my insides.

I want to shove him aside and take his place at her side. Ripley would certainly reject me. Deathbed forgiveness doesn't mean she's ready for all the thoughts running through my mind. I need to play this safe.

She's given me a second chance.

Now I have to earn her forgiveness.

UP IN FLAMES – RUELLE

HANDS BRACED on the edge of the bathroom sink, I stare into my hollow hazel eyes. Bloodshot. Lids drooping. Wrinkles pronounced. The brown and green swirls are overshadowed by black bruises and swelling.

I study my reflection, seeing a scared girl raising her hand, fingertips lightly dancing over each purple cloud and crusted laceration. Her eyes swim. The tears brim over, spilling down her cheeks in glistening ribbons.

"Rip?" There's a gentle tap on the door. "Everything okay in there?"

Sucking in a breath, I quickly scrub the tears aside, ignoring the way it makes my skin ache.

"I'm f-fine, Raine."

The door between us feels like an endless ocean, the raging torrent stopping us from clinging to each other to stay afloat until rescue comes.

"Can I come in?" he asks softly.

"I... I don't know."

There's a thud, like his forehead connected with the door. After straightening my septum piercing, I fill my hands with water, sloshing it over my face in an attempt to clean the blood. Dark, russet streaks cling to my skin.

"You don't have to do this alone," Raine coaxes. "But if you really want to be alone, then I'll go."

I stare at my reflection again. The water hasn't helped. I'm a fucking mess. Being confined to a hospital bed may have replenished my energy levels, but my entire body is now technicoloured with bruises.

I woke up to darkness after passing out then remained silently curled up for several more hours while the others bickered about what to do. It wasn't until the shouts and cries from a nearby fight roused me that I resolved to move.

"Rip? Are you listening?"

My mouth opens.

Shuts.

Nothing comes out.

I hear Raine sigh. "Alright, loud and clear. I'll go."

Chest spasming, an invisible fist tightens around my bloodstained clothing and seems to drag me towards the mirror. Closer. Closer. I'm spiralling back into the numbness, the detachment. Staring at a girl I don't even recognise.

No. I can't let myself fall into that dark, downward spiral. There will be no way back up. My mind is too fractured and exhausted to protect itself right now—I have to hold it together.

"Wait," I force out.

"Yeah?"

"P-Please..." My voice catches.

"Tell me what you need, Rip."

Head lowering, I squeeze my eyes shut.

"Please don't leave me."

The door clicks open and shut. I hate being vulnerable. Weak. Dependent on others. It goes against everything I've worked so hard to build here.

Hurried footsteps approach, then hands find my shoulders.

Raine searches me with his hands, banding his arms around my torso from behind in a tight embrace. A sudden, unwelcome sob tears at my chest.

"Never, guava girl," he murmurs. "Let yourself fall apart for once. You're safe with me."

Behind my closed lids, all I can see is blood. Slicked across the corridor in the Z wing, evidence from a dragged body. The gore spilling from Craven's broken skull. More blood spraying from the drill tearing into Lennox's hand. My own blood seeping from my wrists.

"Raine," I whimper.

"Shh, babe. I'm here."

"N-No… We're not safe! None of us!"

"Breathe, Rip. Come on."

One hand splayed over my belly, he raises the other to rub my arm in slow, comforting circles. His face is buried in the nape of my neck. Each time he exhales, I feel his breath tickle my skin. It feels warm and comforting.

Heart pumping.

Lungs expanding.

Tense muscles loosening.

Each small detail offers me something to focus on. It's a trick an old therapist suggested years back when I was first diagnosed. I haven't struggled to scrape myself together like this for a long time.

"That's it. Focus on me."

"You nearly d-died from the overdose." The air escapes my lungs like a popped balloon. "And for what? We're going to die here anyway."

"I just fancied a little getaway to the medical wing," he jokes quietly. "You get to stay in bed all day, you know? They even bring you food. It's like an all-inclusive resort."

Another choked sob breaks out of me. "Seriously?"

"Bad joke?" Raine chuckles into my hair. "Come on. The OD is old news now. I'm getting clean."

"It's not old news to me."

"You're deflecting, Rip."

My shivering body melts into his, seeking the reassurance of his sea salt and freshly squeezed orange scent. Raine smells like beachside breakfasts and sunshine, the perfect accompaniment to his golden boy persona.

Not many people get to see what lies beneath that deliberate façade. He's been blind since he turned eighteen. The honeyed jewels he keeps hidden behind specialist lenses, and now my borrowed sunglasses, brim with his secrets.

Raine plays the confident jokester, but deep down, he's broken like the rest of us. Uniquely traumatised. Lost. Clinging to vices to make him feel alive. That used to be drugs until he overdosed.

"Right now, I'm stable," he asserts calmly. "The meds are working. So let's focus on you and get cleaned up before Langley blows a gasket."

"Did he send you in here?"

Raine's head lifts from mine. "No, he's changing Lennox's dressings. And Xander's looking for food."

I wish the mention of their names didn't cause my heart to sputter like a faltering engine. Raine knows what complications are facing us. Xander's obsession almost killed me not so long ago, even if he did save my life before he held a knife to my throat.

What we shared that night has thrown everything into doubt. Our feud. The hatred between us. Years of resentment and violence. But now, after the Z wing and shivering in Lennox's arms, not knowing if we'd live to see morning... well, complicated no longer cuts it.

"I can't get the blood off," I admit.

Slowly turning me around, his fingers trace a path upwards, finding my wet face. "You're using cold water, babe. This crap is too dried on for that to work."

"Am I?"

Raine's full, thick lips quirk in a smile. "Yes."

"Oh. I… uh, didn't notice."

"Here, I can help."

Resting my tailbone against the sink, I let him take over. Raine has excellent spatial awareness, using touch and context to decipher his surroundings. I wait for him to locate the tap then test the water until it turns warm.

"Is there soap?"

Shaking my head, I realise my mistake and clear my throat. "No."

"Hang on." Raine inches backwards to fumble the door open. "Xander? Can you find soap? Or medical wash of some kind?"

A clipped voice responds, the seconds trickling past until footsteps near. Raine mutters a thanks, closes the door then returns to me. He's moving carefully without his guide stick in the small space.

"Let's hope this goes better than the time I shampooed your face instead of your hair." He cracks another blinding smile. "You should've just told me."

"I wanted to let you figure it out."

"Enough to let me shampoo your mouth?"

Sniffling, I bite back a grin. "I guess so."

"That's some serious love right there, guava girl. I'm swooning."

"Pack it in."

"Or what?" he challenges.

"Or you won't live to ever swoon again."

Locating a stack of paper towels, he begins to systematically wet each folded square. His smile widens until he's flashing pearly-white teeth.

"Ouch. I'm terrified."

"You're such a dumbass." A chuckle bubbles out of me.

"There's the laugh I was hoping to hear."

Dumping most of the medical wash everywhere but his

intended target, he lifts a wet paper towel to my face. I direct him to the bloodiest areas. Raine begins to wipe, the scent of antiseptic permeating the bathroom.

Gasping, I blink aside tears when he hits a sore cut above my eyebrow.

"Sorry, sorry." He momentarily pulls his hand away, chewing on his cheek. "This would be easier if I could see your face."

"Not your fault."

"Isn't it?" His easy smirk falls away. "I should've been there to stop this from happening in the first place."

"Raine—"

"Instead, I was laid up in a hospital bed for making a stupid choice. You had no one there to protect you."

The memory of Lennox's body fitted to mine flashes back through my mind. His warmth seeping into me, holding hypothermia at bay long enough for the torture to end. The asshole kept me alive.

"I wasn't alone," I blurt.

As soon as the words have escaped, I wish I could take them back. Raine's hand freezes, his head cocking ever so slightly, like he's attempting to read the clues my body is giving him.

"You hate Lennox."

My heart rate thunders. "Yes."

Raine rolls his lips together as he thinks. "You tried to frame him for beating Noah up."

"Yes."

"The Z wing is exactly where you wanted him to wind up."

"Yes." My voice catches on the word this time, forcing me to gulp hard. "But I didn't plan to end up in there with him."

"Yet… You weren't alone." He resumes cleaning, swapping out for a new paper towel. "So what? You're glad he was there?"

"I… I'm not… I don't know." I watch him toss a used, crimson-stained towel aside. "I don't know what I feel."

"Well, by the sounds of things, neither does he." His voice is painfully neutral.

"This isn't what you think it is."

"What do I think it is, Rip?"

The bruises ringing my throat throb, feeling a pair of hands squeezing the life from my lungs. Only this time, there's nothing choking me. Nothing but emotion—confusion, exhaustion, fear. This isn't the time to be figuring our situation out.

"We had to look out for each other." I try to focus my exhausted mind to explain coherently. "They tried to break us. If Lennox wasn't there, I wouldn't have survived."

He tosses another used paper towel. "Does that mean all is forgiven?"

"I didn't say that."

"Sure sounds like what you're *not* saying, though."

Eyes burning, the brewing tears return. I've never been much of a crier, but the barbed wire I've wrapped myself in for all this time isn't keeping me safe from feeling anymore.

Now the razor-sharp barbs have turned inward, and they're cutting deep into my soul. Tearing. Shredding. Scarring. My hatred and determination enabled me to survive Harrowdean… until now.

At the sound of my wet sniffling, Raine sighs. He ditches the last paper towel then tugs me back into his arms. I let him cradle me to his chest and stroke my back.

"I'm sorry," he whispers, pecking my temple.

"Don't be. This is all my fault."

"No, it's not."

"Noah… Nox… The Z wing… I made this mess!"

"Stop, Rip." He plants soothing kisses against my hair. "Have we all made mistakes? Sure. Plenty. I'm not blaming you for anything. I just don't want you to get hurt again."

My face hidden in his hospital gown, I let the relentless tears pour free. It's a battering waterfall, wave after wave of uncontrollable hysteria, obliterating my defences.

Years of pent-up emotion seems to be taking advantage and escaping before I can close myself off again. Raine doesn't say another word, holding me against his undulating chest as I fall apart.

It feels like we've been standing here for an eternity, wrapped up in each other's arms, when there's a hesitant tap on the bathroom door.

"Everything okay?" Langley's voice carries through.

"Fine. We're coming," Raine replies croakily.

"Xander's sorted clothes for everyone. I'll leave yours out here."

Pulling myself together, I breathe deeply as I raise my head from Raine's chest. There's a huge, wet patch on his hospital gown where I've sobbed my eyes out. I swipe a hand over it, biting my lip.

"I'm a bit damp." He smiles lopsidedly.

"Sorry."

"It's okay. So, ah… are we good?"

Raising my hands to grasp the aviators I lent him, I slide the frames off. Raine's molten caramel eyes are unveiled, darting side to side in the unfocused way that betrays the fact that he can't see at all.

"Was it ever in doubt?"

His cheeks flush adorably. "Maybe."

"Why?"

"I guess it feels like I've got some competition now… Maybe you want to upgrade to someone with two working eyes."

An amused smile tugs at my lips. "I'll pass."

"Sure?" He summons a tiny grin. "I wouldn't be offended."

"Positive. Your eyes work just fine for me."

Leaning in, I move my mouth against his in a hesitant brush then retreat. Raine's hand skates back up my shoulder, following his mental map until he cups the back of my head. "You call that a kiss?" he teases.

I'm quickly pulled back to him, our lips crashing together. Raine's mouth is hot on mine, his lips moving to a fast beat as his tongue pushes its way inside. He's lit with a visceral passion that takes my breath away.

Burying a hand in his golden locks, I kiss him back just as furiously. Teeth clicking. Lips massaging. Our tongues touch and tangle in a feverish waltz. In each touch, I taste his fear, desperation, and need to fix what's been broken.

He can't, though.

No one can.

A hot flush of toe-curling need sweeps over me. With the pain I'm in, I didn't think it would be possible. Yet the feel of Raine pleading with his mouth is enough to set my core alight.

Gripping his hair, I take control of the kiss. Raine backs up into the bathroom wall, trapped by my dominance. Fuck casual. Fuck whatever the hell we've spent months doing. I want him. I need him. I fucking *missed* him.

The low moan from his throat tells me just how much power I hold over him. All this time, I thought giving in to my feelings for Raine would make me weak. That allowing him to matter would expose a vulnerability.

I didn't stop to consider the possibility that having people who care about you does entirely the opposite. It isn't a weakness to love or be loved. Those connections are actually what make us strong.

Breaking the kiss, I press our foreheads together. Raine catches his breath, nose nudging mine as he chuckles lightly.

"Now that was a kiss."

I huff out a breath. "Smug, much?"

"Always, babe."

"Alright. Enough of that."

"Just reminding you that I was here first." He gently kisses me again, his citrus scent caressing me. "And I meant what I said before."

"Which part?"

"That I'm not going anywhere."

Leaving me reeling, Raine tentatively moves to the door to retrieve the clothes left for us. I suck in a breath at the thought of the two complications sitting in the medical wing. They may have something to say about Raine's promise.

I can't begin to fathom what either of them want from me. Xander hasn't exactly made his intentions clear since we slept together. Not to mention the clusterfuck that's me and Lennox.

"I can't tell what's yours and what's mine," he complains.

"Here. Let me look."

Taking the bundle from Raine, I search through the detergent-scented clothes. There's a pair of well-worn jeans and a t-shirt that looks around Raine's size, then some stretchy leggings for me with a man's shirt.

"Guessing you don't fancy second-hand yoga pants?"

He scoffs under his breath. "I reckon I could pull them off."

"No one needs to see that."

"Don't you think this ass would look good in Lycra?"

Biting my lip, I silently laugh as he strips off his medical gown, exposing slender limbs and tightly-packed abdominals that make my throat seize. He's slimmer than the others but no less attractive.

Raine clumsily steps into the jeans, refusing to ask for my assistance. They're much looser than his usual, tight style. Rips and scuffs mark the old denim.

"The leggings would look better," I comment.

"Stop being a shit stirrer and strip."

With a blonde brow cocked, he stretches out his hands in offering. I snort, stepping into his space so he can help me ease off the filthy shirt I'm still wearing. The way it clings to my skin makes me want to hurl.

Langley may have cleaned and bandaged my wrists before he hooked me up to the IV, but apparently, he didn't dare to strip me off. I'm thankful there's still some boundaries left between us.

"I'd kill for a shower right about now."

"You need another sponge bath?" Raine offers.

"I need a scourer and a bottle of bleach, I think." My gaze travels, cataloguing the bruises covering every inch of me. "At least the blood is off."

"The hot water seems to still be working. Maybe we can find somewhere to hole up that has a shower."

"Maybe."

Turning back to the mirror, I study the bird's nest on top of my head. My short, tawny ringlets are matted with sweat and blood. Cursing, I lean into the sink and transfer water from the tap onto my head.

It takes several minutes of scrubbing before the brownish stains stop swirling down the drain. Squeezing water from the semi-clean strands, I call it quits, picking up my share of the borrowed clothes.

"Be glad you can't see me right now."

Raine lounges against the wall, my aviators in place. "I still have my imagination. Though in that, you're lying naked on my bed."

"Behave."

"Why?" he drawls.

"This is kind of a life and death scenario right now."

Raine snickers to himself. "Is my dirty fantasy distracting you from our imminent doom?"

"Little bit, yeah."

Pulling on clothing, I grab the scuffed pair of Converse last and shove my feet into them. I feel infinitely better after getting dressed. The monumental problems facing us feel less intimidating with clothes on.

"Ready?" Raine checks.

"Yeah. As I'll ever be."

He clicks open the door, holding it ajar for me to step back into the now-lit medical wing. Combing my hair with my fingers, I move my throbbing limbs, keeping my gaze averted from Langley's stare.

While Lennox rests with his eyes closed, Xander has cleaned up too. His thin lips, exaggerated cheekbones and stony expression are now free from blood. He looks odd in old jeans and a too-big t-shirt.

"Feeling better?" Langley breaks the silence.

The cut on his forehead is now closed with Steri-Strips. His headful of thick, dark-brown hair is damp, hanging over his tanned face and fuzz-covered jawline.

Tucking wet curls behind my ears, I nod. "Yes. Thanks."

"Listen, Rip—"

"Who are you?"

His aquamarine eyes dart over my face, brimming with secrets. "You really want to do this now?"

"I think I'm owed some answers."

"Ripley, look—"

I can practically see the excuses he's preparing to roll out. My temper flares back to life. He has no idea what he's done.

"Are you familiar with Harrison?" I interrupt angrily. "Bald dickhead, works for Professor Craven in the Z wing?"

Langley hesitates before answering. "We've… met."

"Well, he found that business card you gave me. I had it stashed in my bra before they stripped us both to torture us with hoses. We were nearly frozen to death overnight… Then that damn card."

Xander halts searching through a box of snacks, hands freezing and head snapping in our direction. I ignore our audience as I stare into the face of a man I thought I knew. Perhaps even considered a friend.

"He dragged me into another cell and beat me with his fists until I blacked out. I refused to tell him where I'd gotten the business card from."

Head lowering, Langley stares at his laced boots. "I'm so sorry, Rip."

"I don't want your apologies. Why did you give me that card?"

"To help," he rushes to explain. "That's all."

"Is giving me cryptic half-truths helpful? I thought…"

Teeth clenched, I choke off my next words.

I thought we were friends.

Our roles didn't matter—patient and protector, faceless employee and stooge. He was still the only guard to treat me like a human being. And I came to see him as something akin to a friend.

"I gave you that business card because I work for Sabre Security."

"Wait." Xander straightens, hands flying to his tapered hips. "The people investigating the institutes?"

Scrubbing a hand over his face, Langley sighs wearily. "We're a private security firm specialising in criminal investigations."

Raine shuffles on his feet behind me. "Shit. You're really not a guard."

"I was given an assignment in Harrowdean last year to gather intelligence." Langley anxiously cracks his knuckles. "We've been investigating Incendia for a long time."

Vindicated, I glower at him. "I was right. You're one of them."

He nervously glances at me. "Yeah."

"Why are you here?"

"My job is to collect evidence. Flip key players. Line up

potential informants. Anything to pin down the truth behind these institutes."

A hot burst of sickness twists my gut. "So you've spent all this time pretending like you care? It was all an act?"

"No! I... I thought if you trusted me, I could turn you against management. Convince you to be our witness instead. But as time went on, I realised that you weren't the villain in this place."

An incredulous scoff emanates from Xander's side of the room. I deliberately ignore him.

"You played me." The sense of betrayal sinking into my pores practically coats my words. "I'm no saint, but you pretended to care so that I'd trust you."

Panic flashes through his azure eyes, darting from side to side as if searching for some excuse to offer. Sure, I've treated him like shit. I know that. I'm not excusing or even denying it. But I never once lied to him.

"It wasn't like that, Rip. You needed a friend."

"And you needed a lead for your investigation!"

"No," he balks, widening his eyes. "I wanted to help. I still do."

Angrily swiping at the moisture that's dared to grace my cheeks, I look away from his pleading expression. It's pulling at goddamn heartstrings I didn't realise I still have.

"I don't need your help."

"Our team can—"

"No!" Uncontrollable rage and hurt spike through my veins. "How can I ever trust a word you say?"

He steps closer, what appears to be genuine concern shadowing his eyes. "Because I care."

"You just admitted that you manipulated me to score yourself a star witness. Bet it came with a juicy bonus from the boss too, right?"

Focusing on anything but Langley, my gaze collides with two seafoam orbs daggering into me from across the room.

The pale, blueish-green hue is as captivating as the arrogant son of a bitch daring to look at me.

Lennox is awake.

He screams something unheard without ever opening his mouth. Any remaining air is sucked from my lungs as we communicate silently, the horrors we endured together snapping between us in lingering looks.

"We can still help each other," Langley attempts.

I forcibly tear my eyes from Lennox, pulling in a deep breath. "Forget it."

"Listen to me, Rip!"

"Never again."

Inching away from him, I'm suddenly itching for an escape. Somewhere to hide, far from these men. Their newfound kindness and concern expose the raw fault lines cracked across my fractured soul.

"The riot will end, and Incendia's days are numbered," Langley continues urgently. "You need to cut a deal while you still can."

"Numbered?" Xander repeats. "Do you know something that we don't?"

Langley seems to beg with his eyes. "Sabre will expose the corporation. You've heard what happened at Blackwood. Now this? It's only a matter of time."

"Good." I hold back a violent sob.

"Who exactly do you think they'll blame, huh?" Langley shakes his head. "I know the truth, but that won't stop Incendia from taking down everyone with them when they go. Stooges included."

"No one could ever blame Ripley," Raine protests.

"You think that'll matter to them?"

"It should!"

"We've all done things we're not proud of." Lennox speaks for the first time, his voice flaying my soul down to its bare bones. "Are you saying all our necks are on the line?"

"This will turn into a blame game very fast," Langley confirms in disgust. "My team is already working with a group of ex-patients from Blackwood. There are criminal charges on the table."

The white walls of the medical wing bend and contract, creeping ever closer like the bars of a prison cell slamming shut for an eternity. Terror curls in my lungs, filling them with acrid smoke.

"They're going to bury me," I whisper in horror.

"Not if you cooperate with us," Langley says emphatically. "We can offer you protection."

"She's not going anywhere without us," Xander announces.

His words have the impact of a killer blow to the solar plexus. I feel like I've been shoved into a freefall. The shock of his declaration only accelerates my rapid plummet into the bottomless pit I hoped to avoid.

I've gotten this far by compartmentalising the real Ripley into a deep, silent part of my mind. That mental prison is failing now. The unstable walls are collapsing with each realisation.

Worst of all? I hate how the sick tendrils of Xander's obsession wrap around me, forming a safe cocoon. I'm not alone in this. We're all implicated and caught in the firing line.

"Pretty sure that's her choice." Langley scowls at him. "Not yours."

Xander glares back, unfazed. "You think we're giving her a choice?"

"What the fuck is wrong with you?"

"Plenty." Xander shrugs. "Ripley stays with us. End of story."

"So you can have another shot at killing her?" Langley says incredulously. "I don't think so."

"Why don't you back off?" Lennox cuts in to defend his best friend.

Langley scoffs in disbelief. "I'll be doing her a favour by getting her away from you both."

"Because you're so perfect?"

"Oh, I'm sorry." Langley narrows his eyes on Lennox's prone form. "Says the guy incarcerated for burning his grandfather to death. I've seen your file."

Raine inhales sharply, whispering a curse.

Lennox's face is partially obscured by the thick dressing covering his cheek, but I can still see the angry red haze filtering over him. My attention catches the silver chain he never removes from his neck.

The military dog tags rest against the hospital gown he's been clothed in. After the raw emotions we shared in the Z wing, I finally understand why he's willing to wear that disgusting heirloom.

It's a reminder.

Lennox will do anything for those he cares about. Anything at all if it protects them from the same fate his baby sister suffered because of their grandfather's abuse.

Beneath the rage and hatred, his modus operandi is powerful, unconditional love. Lennox beats the world bloody so it doesn't have the opportunity to hurt his loved ones. That's how he shows that he cares.

"Congratulations," Lennox drawls sarcastically. "You can read words on a piece of paper."

"Just saying. You're in no position to talk to me about being perfect."

"Keep running your mouth," Lennox warns. "Go on. I dare you."

"What are you going to do from a hospital bed, huh?"

"Uh, guys?" Raine tries to interrupt.

Lennox acts like he didn't even hear him, too busy trying to escape the various lines tangled around him. Xander steps in to place a hand on his shoulder then shoves him back into the mattress and holds him there.

"Stay, Nox."

"No! I'm going to pummel his fucking face!"

"You think you're such a big man, don't you?" Langley goads. "And now you can't even get out of bed."

Still struggling, Lennox flushes red despite his sickly pallor. "I don't appreciate assholes sticking their noses where they don't belong."

"Guys—"

"I care about Ripley," Langley defends hotly. "Far more than you do. I'm trying to help her."

"By lying to her?" Lennox laughs.

"By doing my job!"

On a good day, even Langley's physique would be no match against Lennox's oversized bulk, packed with hardened muscle. His injuries are the only thing stopping him from beating Langley into a pulp.

Beyond the sheer size advantage he has in most fights, Lennox's deep-lidded eyes, round jaw smothered in unshaven stubble and slightly upturned nose give him a rugged, wild-like aura of threatening power.

"Guys!" Raine's worried voice cuts through their bickering. "Shut up for one moment and listen."

The room is quiet enough to hear the distant echo of voices humming through the early morning light outside. Langley moves to the window to assess the surrounding grounds.

"What can you see?" Xander questions.

"Well, everyone's awake," he replies. "Patients are gathering outside the institute."

"Why?" I frown at him.

"They're marching the guards out. Got them all tied up. Some look half-dead already."

Straining in his hospital bed, Lennox shoves Xander's hand away. "What are they doing with them?"

"Lining them up in front of the locked gates. I can't see

who's watching beyond the barricades, but it looks like a fucking parade." He blows out a leaden breath. "Fuck. Harrowdean is crumbling."

Trembling all over, I glance down at my borrowed Chucks, trying to get a handle on my emotions. The buzzing noise is back and louder than ever, a cacophony of shrill decibels cutting into my brain like miniature knives.

The guards were first to fall.

They'll come for me next.

The sound of the guys conversing is swallowed by my foggy brain, a spiralling cyclone dragging me into the depths of destruction with it. Fisting my wet curls, the sense of acute panic rises with Langley's words on repeat.

Harrowdean is crumbling.

I'll be crushed beneath the rubble.

He's right; the riot will end. When it does, everything will implode. The regime I've enabled was already hanging by a thread. If Sabre Security really is investigating, that means the institute will fall.

I may not be the monster behind this program, but I'm sure as fuck no angel either. I'll burn for their sins. There's guilt in culpability, and for every drop of suffering my fellow patients endured... I benefitted.

My gaze swings around, searching for an escape route. Reason dissipates as the instinct to run takes centre stage.

"Ripley."

His ice-cool voice laden with an odd softness, Xander abandons his best friend to follow my retreating steps. Each time I move, he closes the distance between us.

The look on his face could almost be described as concerned. But that can't possibly be right. I must be imagining the curve of his pale brows, the creases marring his marble forehead, all indicating fear.

"You need to stop and take a breath," he advises, studying me intently. "This isn't the time to make a rash decision."

"A rash decision?" I huff out.

Head tilted, his throat bobs. "I'm not letting you run away from us this time."

Features hard with determination, his thin lips press together. Each minuscule clue points to a far more petrifying reality beneath his stoic expression. It's pouring through the cracks in his mask.

"You want to talk to me about rash decisions, Xander Beck?"

He opens and closes his mouth, eyes swirling with a confusing maelstrom of ice-cold detachment and red-hot anger. For once, he has no smart retort or threat to levy. Not this time.

"I became Harrowdean's stooge to make myself untouchable. To protect myself. To honour the woman who became my family when my last relative abandoned me. I did this for her."

I can't tear my eyes from Xander, the slight twitches and near-invisible tells offering a glimpse of the man behind the machine. His human alter-ego, not the soulless psychopath who runs the show.

"Why did I have to do that?" Tears spill freely down my cheeks. "Because of your *rash decision*." I gesture to Lennox to include him. "Because of what you two did to survive. Because you killed her."

"Rip—" Lennox tries to intervene.

"Do you know what the worst part is?" I cut him off.

Both men stare at me, waiting for the guillotine to slam down on their necks. They're willingly giving me the fatal blow. Only this isn't a victory. Not for me. The time for revenge has passed.

This admission is a soul-destroying defeat.

My greatest failure.

"I can't even blame you." Acceptance dampens my words

into an almost-whisper. "Not anymore. Not after the things I've done with the exact same justification."

I turn away from them, my prickling skin pulling tight with the urge to run. The next words hurt to utter.

"I wish I hated you both, but I don't."

My fate seals, setting ablaze the last crumbs of my self-respect. I flee towards the exit, unable to look at any of them for a second longer. Overlapping voices chase after me.

"Ripley!"

"Wait!"

"Rip! Stop!"

Their concerned shouts fail to slow me down. All I can focus on is the foul taste of humiliation coating my tongue, reminding me of all I've sacrificed... for absolutely nothing.

They still won.

And I'm as broken as they intended.

CHAPTER 4
RIPLEY

YOU'VE CREATED A MONSTER –
BOHNES

HARROWDEAN MANOR is in pandemonium.

Hellish, uncontrolled, fatal fucking mayhem.

In my haste to get some space, I failed to consider what danger I'd be running headfirst into. After all, this place is my home. My kingdom. Nothing can surprise me, right?

Wrong.

All bets are off now.

Corridors littered with ripped antique paintings, scattered belongings and all manner of detritus stretch before me as I speed walk into the unknown.

I don't care where I'm headed. As long as it's away from them. My weakened body protests with each footstep, but I ignore it. The throbbing aches, mind-numbing pains and infection in my scaring wrists aren't going to slow me down.

Morning light illuminates the carnage that's unfolded. Clearly, we've been holed up for long enough to allow our familiar surroundings to transform. The opulent hallways no longer represent the extravagance and corruption I've come to hate.

My footsteps slow as I turn a corner, the sound of pleasured grunting quickly reaching my ears. I'm close to the reception where two patients are taking full advantage of the chance to indulge.

"You like that, baby?"

"Yes… Fuck… More!"

Her pasty ass on full display, a new girl I vaguely recognise from the sixth floor is bent over with her clothing wrapped around her ankles. Eyes screwed shut, she fails to notice me watching.

I'm shocked to recognise one of my regulars behind her—Luka. I've been selling him laxatives for months. He's ploughing into her like a man possessed. Damn. A twisted part of me wants to clap him on the back.

I race past them, keeping my eyes averted.

Light also reveals the dank mess and water damage. The flood that preceded the violence engulfing the institute trashed this area.

Adding to the destruction, patients have gone to town, smashing every available piece of furniture. I have to stop for a second to take in the sheer devastation. It gives me a sick thrill.

Windows shattered. Paperwork discarded. Computers broken. What looks like some kind of condiment from the cafeteria has been used to scrawl on the walls.

Chilled gooseflesh rises on my skin as my eyes follow the letters, spiky and rushed, seemingly written by any means necessary. An artefact left behind in the devastation for the world to read.

THE SYSTEM HAS FAILED US.

Staring at the words, the script screams the hard truth that nobody has ever dared to acknowledge. I want to trash anything left untouched in this false paradise. The emotion flooding my system isn't anger. It's pure rage, born of total powerlessness.

My attention strays to the entrance doors—somehow still

intact but swinging in the spring breeze that comes from outside. The sound of voices and activity are carried in.

I look back at the words. Feel the rage. The defencelessness. Every debilitating second caught in this state-funded trap, protected by an uncaring world's wealth and indifference. And I don't want to fucking hide.

They can hate me.

But we share a common enemy.

Fists clenched, I slip between the swinging doors into the new dawn. The entrance to Harrowdean Manor is usually heavily guarded by security, but it currently stands unprotected.

I can still remember being frogmarched past the gates and up the winding, cobbled driveway to the manor. The view looking out to the surrounding woodland has drastically changed since then.

On all sides, the same imposing cloak of juniper and birch trees remain as silent sentries. I can see the wrought-iron gates in the distance, embellished with the institute's crest.

"Get them in a line!"

Rick's voice booms over the hum of patients swarming all around me. A crowd has gathered to watch the unfolding circus.

"On your fucking knees!"

One by one, a group of eight or nine guards are being roughly shoved onto their naked knees. Daylight illuminates their exhausted faces, bruised and dirt-streaked, others bloodied.

They've all been stripped, mud covering their shivering bodies. I quickly catalogue their terrified expressions, making a mental list of who isn't here. Apparently, not all the guards were present when the institute fell.

Each one is chained to the next using interconnected handcuffs, forming one linked line of humiliation. Positioned execution-style.

Behind them, Rick prowls up and down, examining his handiwork. Beyond the barricaded entrance, cameras flash on repeat. Reporters are baying for blood behind the iron bars holding them back.

Harrowdean's gates are bolted shut from our side, keeping their desperation at bay. The chains may as well be flimsy cobwebs for all they matter, though. They won't keep us safe for long.

The hostages are lined up for their photoshoot, imprisoned like livestock and posed for the country's media to capture. Riots end fast without leverage, and Rick was quick to secure his. The guards.

"We have a message for the world." Rick's voice carries through the suddenly still air. "You don't know our faces. You don't know our names. That's because to you… we don't exist."

Microphones are thrust through the bars to capture his shouts. For every beady eye latched on to us, my stomach twists into a tighter knot. They aren't here out of concern. Our rebellion is nothing more than clickbait for them to utilise.

"And that's exactly how Incendia Corporation sees us!" Rick shouts angrily. "As commodities. Specimens. Fuel for their sick experiments."

Reaching out a hand to Patient Three who stands nearby, my heart convulses at the sight of the gun Rick took from Harrison in the Z wing. Raising the weapon, he aims it at the back of the first guard's head.

"What if we treat you like commodities too?" Rick screams. "What if you're the specimens this time? Will you remember our names then? Does that grant us the right to exist?"

I watch the guard's shoulders shake with petrified sobs. It's hard not to feel a shred of sympathy, but I quickly crush it. His sliced-up, bare chest is on display, a miasma of lurid bruises stark against his flesh.

Humiliated and hurt.

Just like us.

Scanning the crowd watching Rick's performance, I realise what's been gnawing at the back of my mind. What's missing from this picture is the reinforcements. Other guards. Elon. Bancroft. His goons.

The flashing blue lights accompany the sizeable police presence, but looking closely, they aren't even focused on us. The officers are supervising the crowd of reporters. Keeping *them* safe. They aren't here for us.

We've overtaken the property, seized their guards, publicly shamed management for all their misdeeds. And still, nobody cares. None of the missing guards or clinicians are here to plead with us. We're alone.

I heard Raine and Lennox's whispers as I came to earlier on. Warden Davis is dead. By all accounts, Xander was the one who took his life. Does Sir Bancroft know that? Has he declared Harrowdean a lost cause?

No.

I quickly discount the theory. That snake would never cut and run. He isn't the kind of man to walk away with his tail tucked between his legs. So this scene must be deliberate, luring us into a false sense of security.

He wants us to feel powerful. Vindicated. That'll make it all the more satisfying to storm in here and crush the riot with unfettered violence. Any bloodshed will simply be written off as a tragic accident.

"We will not surrender our hostages until Harrowdean's shut down and everyone is set free!" Rick proclaims, the gun still poised. "Those are our demands."

The surrounding patients shout and cheer, commending his words. When Rick turns to smile at them, his eyes sweeping over the substantial crowd, he catches sight of me lingering far behind.

We lock gazes.

Rick fucking *winks*.

He spins around to continue shouting. "If anyone attempts to penetrate the institute, we will begin killing hostages. Report that."

Pulling the gun back, Rick pauses to scan the baying crowd. I'm not the only one who gasps when he whips the weapon up so it collides with the side of the unsuspecting guard's head, eliciting a scream.

He slumps over, blood splattering his shoulders and back. Rick gestures for Patient Three and the other silent Z wing patient to step forward. They begin pounding on the fallen guard, kicking him until their target is a bleeding, unconscious lump on the ground.

"We will be heard!" Rick roars.

The panicked shouts of the other guards being tugged by their colleague's body makes my palms twitch. I want to march over there, take the gun then unload every last bullet in its clip into their heads.

Their little display over, Patient Three and her friend stumble back. They're both panting and sweaty from doling out the beating.

"Get them back inside," Rick orders curtly. "Show's over."

I look away from the guards being rounded up, their purpose now served, to find Rae's gaze on me. She looks unkempt, her voluminous, auburn curls frizzy and unbrushed.

My senses are on high alert as she approaches. I trust Rae, but there's still plenty of anger and tension floating in the air, and I'm not looking to get nearly strangled to death again.

"Rip!" She rushes at me. "Where have you been?"

I gingerly accept her hug, keeping a wary eye on the others. "Um, unconscious."

"Fuck, doll face. Are you okay?" Rae pulls back to skim

her eyes over me. "Stupid question. You look like you had angry sex with a woodchipper."

"Then I look better than I feel."

Her dark-brown, almost black eyes catch on my throat. It still feels enflamed and tender after Tania's attack.

"I guess I've made some enemies in here." I try to force a smile, but it feels alien. "You may not want to be seen with me."

Lips pursed, she looks around at the crowd dispersing to head back inside. "Rumours are swirling. Rick's been telling anyone who will listen the truth."

"Does that include you?" I ask tightly.

She hesitates, letting several people pass us. "I don't care where you got the contraband from. You didn't judge what I did to survive each day, so I'm not going to judge you for the same thing."

Heart sputtering, I can't swallow her forgiveness. She's a prime example of all I've done here. All the reasons I deserve to be punished for my role in the conspiracy. I enabled Rae, fed her addiction and reaped the rewards.

"How long do you think this can last?" I gesture towards the energised crowd.

"As long as it takes. We won't stop until we're treated like actual human beings. We're going to be set free, Rip!"

Her wide, excited eyes and the grin stretching her lips only intensifies the lead weight settling in my gut. She's as deluded as the rest of them, running around thinking this is some kind of pre-release party.

"Why do you think there aren't any reinforcements outside the gates?"

Rae sucks her bottom lip between her teeth, suddenly appearing nervous. "Because… they've given up, right? We won?"

Gripping her shoulders, I shake her roughly. "Wake up,

Rae! They will never give up! This is just the calm before the storm."

"But we have hostages!"

"You think management cares about a few worthless guards?" I scoff. "They'll cut their losses just to get their operation back up and running. Guards *and* patients alike."

Tears have filled her eyes, sparkling swells hanging on the tips of her eyelashes. She looks from side to side, cataloguing the roar of the nation's media trying to regain our attention as everyone disperses.

"I thought you wanted to take them down too."

"I want to walk out of here alive," I correct. "Do the smart thing, and keep your head down, Rae. Or you're at risk of losing it when this all ends."

Releasing her, she takes a big step back, rubbing her arms. We stare at each other as the shouts and hollers amplify, a group of hooligan patients running past with boxes of paperwork they're emptying out on the lawn.

Two others heave bundles of broken furniture between them, the polished mahogany now splintered into perfectly sized kindling. Adding them to a rapidly building pile, the addition of paperwork reveals their plan.

"Patient 2185," one reads from the thick file. "They didn't even give us names."

"Burn it! Burn it!"

In the distance, cameras are still rolling. I can imagine the madness sweeping over various newsrooms as they rush to report on the latest developments. Not even Incendia can suppress this story.

I recognise one of the instigators, yelling her head off with such gleeful rebellion, you'd think she was a kid on Christmas morning. Taylor hasn't even stopped to clean herself up, a curtain of dried blood still cascading from her sliced forehead.

Fingers pinched around a lit cigarette, she watches the pile of furniture and discarded paperwork grow. The hysterical crowd is emptying out the reception, adding anything flammable to the stash.

"Here!" someone shouts. "We raided the groundskeeper's storage."

I hear Rae curse next to me as a canister of fuel is paraded above their heads like the fucking holy grail. The kind of fuel you'd use to fill a lawnmower, I think.

With the canister emptied all over the broken wood, Taylor flicks her cigarette into the pile of kindling. The patient files scattered throughout quickly crisp and blacken, growing into a fireball.

"Yes!"

"More! More!"

The chorus of celebration fills the smoky air. Heat and acrid fumes pour from the bonfire, growing larger and more vicious by the second as it greedily consumes the destroyed furniture and files.

Smoke rises.

Patients cheer.

Harrowdean is burning.

CHAPTER 5
XANDER

SINCERELY, FUCK YOU –
PARDYALONE

FLASHLIGHT SWINGING from side to side, the beam illuminates my path through the pitch-black night. The emergency lighting that offered a little reprieve has now failed, plunging Harrowdean into total darkness.

Ripley didn't come back.

The fucking disobedience.

Trembling with a feeling I can't put a name to, I left the medical wing after growing tired of listening to the others' fretting. Even the meathead himself, Lennox, seems worried about his so-called least favourite person.

They both wanted to join the search party, but neither would've been able to navigate the war zone I've encountered while looking for Ripley. After only a handle of days, the institute is unrecognisable.

I didn't think I shocked easily. Watching patients physically fight over food, scratching eyes and pulling out clumps of hair is the least of what's unfolding. We knew it was coming. They're turning on each other.

Scanning my eyes over the crowded cafeteria, I peer through the gloom at various faces scattered all around.

Patients shout and threaten, arguing over whatever scraps of food from the kitchen are left.

Nothing.

She isn't here.

"Woo!" A dirt-streaked blur goes screaming past me. "We're free, bitches!"

Turning away from the cafeteria, I watch the girl stagger off, quickly deducing that she's wasted. Alcohol is a less popular form of contraband—too easily spotted by staff. Now, along with raided nurse's stations and riot fever, it's fuelling the carnage all around me.

I already had to punch some delirious guy a few hours ago when he came at me with a chair leg, screeching at invisible voices. I have no clue who he thought I was, but I wasn't hanging around to find out.

Sure, anarchy is fun. It's a romantic idea. Then reality sets in, and the delirium isn't so cute after all. The whole intoxicated, frat party atmosphere rife with explosive, unmedicated violence won't last much longer.

I'd usually enjoy the chaos. It provides ample opportunity to blend into the shadows and stalk my next plaything. Oh, the fun I could have right now while no one is watching.

It'd be easy to find something soft and vulnerable to slice. A pure, untouched specimen, ripe for the taking. Someone who would cry and beg. Vocalise their pain in a sweet symphony of desperation.

I haven't touched a soul since that night.

When *she* slept curled up in my arms.

Saucer-like, hazel eyes, brimming with tears. Tangled snarls of mousy-brown hair. Plump, perfectly proportioned lips, begging to be bitten. Her insults and protests turning into whimpers of submission.

My fantasies now have a face.

The woman I hate has become… What? Beyond fascination. Beyond obsession. Beyond everything I thought I knew and wanted from one of my targets. She's no longer just a toy.

Ripley Bennet has drilled her way into my bone marrow, infiltrated my blood cells and set up shop like a parasitic infection. My interest in her felt different than this before. Intense but under control. She was a collection of cells trapped beneath my microscope.

When she snuggled up to my bare chest, pressing the tip of her nose into my skin, tickling me with each relaxed exhale… my entire existence shifted. It happened so fast, I didn't see it coming.

I've never been touched like that—with gentle care and something akin to tenderness. In my experience, touch only brings pain. Humiliation. Degradation. I torture others to hold that agony at bay.

Without warning, my mind plummets into the black pit I never allow it to linger in for long. A place reserved for pathetic emotions. The weakness of a younger, smaller, more damaged version of the man I've become.

Walking faster, I head back in the direction of the medical wing, ignoring the way my lightly-trembling hand causes the flashlight's beam to shake. The institute's messy chaos is interwoven with lifelike memories exploding all around me like inkblots.

Mummy's asleep, Xander.

Don't wake her up. I'd hate to hurt her.

Revulsion writhes beneath my scar-striped skin at the voice accompanying my vivid flashbacks. I can still see the yellowing carpet adorned with a lumpy, striped mattress. The cracked, still functioning lamp lying on its side where I tried to fight back.

I always slept with that light on, terrified of what would happen in the darkness. It allowed me to stare at the newspaper cutouts of the latest 90s computer model tacked on my bedroom wall.

I loved computers even back then. I'd stare at those clippings through it all. Every second, minute and hour. Every night. Dreaming of the possibilities that my fingertips touching a keyboard would bring.

Technology intrigued me. I dreamed that if I could find a way to make money, I'd be able to run away. Or erase myself like the elusive secret agents I saw in crappy spy movies. I would never fucking return.

Shut up, brat.

I warned you what happens to boys who cry.

Over time, swallowing the sobs became a form of self-preservation. Clamping down on my wails. Extinguishing any protests. By the time my eighth birthday rolled around, I'd perfected the art of detachment.

Lost to the dark miasma clouding my thoughts, I trip over a length of bloodstained carpet that's been ripped up. I brace myself for a hard impact, dropping the flashlight and sending it spinning.

"Fuck!" I smack a hand against the floor. "Fuck, fuck, fuck!"

The whole world is tilting. Morphing. Crimson-dipped and filtered through a furious lens. I don't know how to hold this burden inside—the weight of thinking, feeling and caring about another human being. It hasn't happened since I switched all those vulnerabilities off.

Wait… Fucking caring?

Is that what this is?

Sprawled out, the most ridiculous details enter my awareness. The hunger pains in my stomach. How stray pieces of shattered glass have embedded in my palms. The coppery scent of a nearby blood spill.

My carefully constructed world is splintering apart. I've built it to the highest degree of perfection. Organised. Controlled. Emotionless. A shackled reality, the impenetrable bars of my indifference keeping me safely imprisoned from the entire world.

"We have their attention now. I want all the mattresses thrown outside next."

"From the windows?"

"Perfect. Wait for daylight so the cameras capture it."

Voices snap me back to the present moment as effectively as being dunked in ice water. I force a blank expression over the torment twisting my features.

Their footsteps crunch through the corridor's debris until they reach me. I peer up at the small group of patients holding flashlights. How fortunate. Perhaps I'll have an outlet for all this distracting emotion after all.

"You," I spit out.

Rick contemplates me through facial bruises and filth, his smile full of stupid confidence. "Xander, right?"

The son of a bitch beat the shit out of Raine not so long ago. If he hadn't been shipped off to the Z wing, I would've arranged a convenient little accident for him instead. He got off lightly.

"Correct. I was under the impression you were dead."

He shrugs casually. "Not quite."

"How unfortunate."

Sneering, he shares looks with his two friends. "Unfortunate?"

"For you, yes."

I don't recognise the patients with him, though the visible signs of torture and the dead look in their eyes are familiar. More of Incendia's little experiments. Ripley and Lennox clearly didn't escape the Z wing alone.

I know what this asshole did to her. So why didn't she leave him there to die? Yet another detail she's failed to share. Rage crystallises into an ice-cold shard that slices through my chest.

"Where is she?"

"Who?" Rick laughs.

Jump. Slice. Stab.

The temptation is strong.

"Ripley." I force a calm tone.

The amusement written across his face causes my teeth to grind in irritation. He can smirk all he likes. It won't change the satisfaction that slitting his throat will give me.

"Why do you assume I would know?" he retorts.

My blood boils. "Did you enjoy carving those marks into her?"

Rick's eyes flash with surprise. I knew Ripley wouldn't admit who hurt her; she has too much pride for that. The truth was easy to pry out of Raine's mouth, though.

"I'm far too busy cleaning up Ripley's mess to follow her around like the rest of you." His nose wrinkles in derision. "Look at you. Didn't take much for her to wrap you around her finger."

"What gave you that impression?"

He waves a hand over me, visibly dishevelled and sprawled out. "Not your best look."

Teeth gritted, I climb to my feet. "Perhaps go have a shower before commenting on my appearance."

I narrow my eyes at the male patient on Rick's right side who is eyeing me like a piece of meat he'd happily pummel.

"You want to call your attack dog off?" I gesture to him.

"Oh, don't mind him. He's just... focused." Rick casts his friend a smile. "We all want the same thing. You included."

"And what's that?"

"To see the institutes and Incendia burn," the female patient supplies. "Starting with Harrowdean."

Laughter rips out of me. "Why would I want that?"

All three of them gape, their silence punctuated by the loud chaos unfolding all around us. Anarchy has resumed, peppered with smashing glass and screeching.

"You think this means anything?" I gesture around at the people running wild. "This little rebellion of yours won't last."

"Is that what you want?" Rick's lip curls. "You think Ripley will return to her seat of power once we've all been eliminated? Maybe she'll toss you some scraps of attention, huh?"

"I have no interest in what Ripley does when this is all over."

Lies.

Swallowing my tongue to keep my composure, I stand firm as he runs his disgusting eyes all over me. The black shirt I located is short-sleeved, revealing layers of shiny scar tissue that he openly peruses.

"I suppose I did her a favour," he muses. "Her scars match yours now. You two freaks can compare notes."

"You touched something that doesn't belong to you," I spit venomously, my hands balled into fists by my sides.

"No, I simply made sure she'll never be able to forget what she did here."

My brain misfires with the surge of scorching-hot anger that barrels through me. I find myself leaping into his personal space before my common sense comes back online.

We're chest-to-chest with nothing but anger and violent threat trapped between us. All I see is red, causing my momentary calm to implode.

"For every mark you left on her skin, I'll break one bone. Would you care to choose which?"

Whatever Rick reads in my expression causes him to falter. He looks around for support, but his new friends don't jump to his rescue. Both look intrigued. Seems like loyalty only runs so deep.

"But… she—" he splutters.

"Never mind," I interrupt.

"Wait!"

"Too late. Dealer's choice."

My curled first snaps outward to connect with his face. I lavish the sight of his nose exploding into bloody fireworks upon impact. The lurid red splats coating his shocked face are mesmerising.

I wonder what the blood would look like spilling from his broken skull. Shards of bone and soft, squelchy tissue floating in the remains. He wouldn't lay another finger on Ripley then. Not without his head intact.

Bringing my knee up to smash into his stomach, I wait for his pained wheeze before punching him again. Over and over. The pain slicing across my knuckles is an exquisite shot of pure adrenaline. Heavenly.

His friends stand there, shuffling their feet like they're stuck watching an uninteresting theatre performance. Neither moves to intervene.

"Tell me, did you scream and beg for mercy when their experiments began?" I ask conversationally.

Punch. Crack. Ooze.

"Perhaps you prayed for someone to come to save you from the big, bad doctor."

Smack. Crunch. Splat.

"Truthfully? You should've stayed down there." I laugh loudly. "It would've been safer."

Thwack. Grind. Squirt.

His attempts to fight back are feeble at best. Inconsequential. I've switched gears and slotted into a less-visited corner of my mind. The primitive part that embraced violence and strength to endure the same torture he did.

The pain of each blow is insignificant. My tired muscles protesting. Stomach growling. Head pounding with exhaustion. Human weakness wasn't allowed in Priory Lane, so I quickly learned how to block it out.

Pausing, I hold him by the throat, watching the crimson rivulets spill over his cheeks. "At least down there, you were safe from me."

With a final, bone-grinding hit, I toss his unconscious carcass to the floor. Rick rolls through debris and sharp glass, a wet rattle pushing past his lips. Disappointing. I'd hoped he would beg before passing out.

As satisfying as it would be to bleed the bastard dry, a part of me is curious to see how many pieces Bancroft and his organisation will cut him into as punishment for leading the riot.

I look up at the two patients standing there watching the show, a single brow raised. Still neither moves to attack.

"This piece of shit is going to get himself killed when the authorities decide to intervene. Unless you'd like to join him, I suggest you consider your options."

"Options?" the female patient repeats. "We're here to fight."

"We know the truth about the real experimental program. Incendia will target us first when the riot ends."

"You weren't with us." She pulls her head back in confusion.

"Not in Harrowdean," I correct with a shrug. "But every institute in the country has a Z wing program."

Her eyes widen as she seems to view me in a new light. Even her close-mouthed friend seems thoughtful. Regardless of our choices, we're facing the same threat. Total fucking annihilation.

"This is bigger than all of us." I look between them. "Your pathetic riot means nothing to a multi-million pound corporation."

Colour drains from the female patient's face, making her bruises and visible injuries stand out. Her bravado is vanishing faster than our chances of survival.

"Do you really think we'll be rescued and released like this asshole is saying?"

"Well… The others… He…" she struggles. "We have hostages!"

The woman is as stupid as the rest of these morons, skipping around with their unearthed contraband and makeshift weapons, thinking this is some kind of game. It's laughable.

"The only reason management hasn't stormed Harrowdean and wiped us out is the media attention. When that dies down, they'll bring in the bulldozers."

Their posture changes—both seeming to shirk away from the writhing bag of organs at my feet.

"Or are you dumb enough to think Harrowdean will change?" I roll my eyes. "Perhaps they'll listen to your demands? Or let you skip off into the sunset and rebuild your lives?"

The more I speak, the further their unease seems to spread. Even Mr Silent is glancing at our surroundings and shifting on his feet. My words have made an impact. Good.

"Do what you want. It makes no difference to me." I draw my leg back to boot Rick in the ribs for good measure. "But think twice before throwing your weight behind this scum."

Dismissing them with a terse nod, I continue on to the medical wing to regroup. I've scooped up my dropped flashlight and taken a few steps from Rick when I set sights on her.

My lungs twist and knot. Oxygen collects in my oesophagus, burning hotter than trapped lava. Resting against the wall, Ripley is watching the interaction from afar, safe and fucking sound.

Relief swims through me.

Sweet, blissful relief.

My blood doesn't freeze solid in my veins like it used to at the sight of her. Those sad doe eyes and teeth-baring hisses used to be the equivalent of a cold plunge in liquid nitrogen. Enough to send my soul running for the hills to make way for my blood thirst.

Vulnerable. Lonely. Angry. Hate-filled. The most

perplexing combination of something so delicate and breakable yet reinforced with a pain-forged strength. I longed to break the last of her resolve.

Just like *he* once broke mine.

But not now.

Now… I want to bathe in her strength and formidability. To wipe the horrors from her gaze and soothe the pain that others have inflicted. She's mine to hurt. Mine to own. Mine to fucking cherish.

Standing on opposite ends of the corridor, we stare at each other. Two predators, sizing the other up, calculating the possibility of a quick kill. But… no, that isn't right at all. It isn't hatred I see burning in her eyes.

With long strides, I close the distance between us, halting with our noses mere inches apart. Her eyes are wide and glimmering through the dark bruises ringing them, fading from black to lightning-streaked purple.

"Where have you been?" My voice seeps with frustration.

"Why do you care, Xan?" she replies smoothly. "Worried I'll make a rash decision?"

Rather than strangle her black-and-blue throat like I'm longing to do, I brace a hand either side of her head. Seeing her whole and unharmed allows me to draw my first full breath since she disappeared.

I'm sucked into her orbit. Tumbling through a bottomless wormhole into the unknown emptiness beyond my line of sight. If I'm not careful, I'll lose myself along the way. Perhaps that would also be a relief.

"I didn't begrudge your rash decision the night we slept together."

"You restrained me and held a knife to my throat," Ripley snarks.

"Yet my little toy still shivered at my touch and begged for more."

I lean into her space, dragging the tip of my nose up her

throat and neck. She shivers against me, a whispered moan daring to break free when I trace the tip of my tongue behind her left earlobe.

"In fact, I think you begged me to fuck you." My lips follow her ear's curvature, leaving a featherlight trail. "Tell me, do I have to beg you in return now?"

Her body arches against the wall, pressing her round curves into me. "Hmm. The great Xander Beck begging?"

Sucked into the bottomless, hazel pits peering up at me, I don't bother to cushion the inevitable fall. I'll crash land in the innermost parts of her being and happily break every bone in the process. As long as I can stay there.

Seeing her disappear into thin air reacquainted me with an old nemesis. Fear. And fuck if the idea of losing whatever we are now feels far scarier than the emotions she's reigniting within me.

I lick my lips. "Yes. I'd beg for you."

"Me?" She drags in a shaky breath.

"Your acceptance." Blind hope forces me to keep going. "Maybe even your forgiveness."

Searching my face for any hint of deception, Ripley's brows crinkle. "You think I could ever forgive you?"

I raise a hand, vaguely noting the way she no longer flinches in my presence. Not a single hint of revulsion as I trace my pointer finger across her lips to map the kissable swell.

How would it feel to be touched by her?

Held by her?

Perhaps… even loved by her?

I don't know what that's like. My mother loved her bottles of cheap, supermarket liquor far more than she ever loved me. I doubt she even loved the monster she allowed into our home. And there was certainly no love in the string of foster homes that came after.

Before Ripley entered my life, I'd never been gently

touched. Held. Cherished. At least not without the expectation of pain. I have no clue how to earn her affections rather than plotting how to cause her pain.

"I doubt Lennox would be alive now if you hadn't forgiven him," I point out. "Why else did you save his life?"

"Because I'm not you."

A smile pulls at my mouth. "Perhaps we're not the people you think we are either."

Still pressing into me, whether consciously or not, she speaks a thousand words with her body language alone. Her grimace deepens as she wrestles with the words she doesn't want to say aloud.

"I want to believe that," Ripley finally admits. "I want to stop seeing the triumph on your face when they wheeled my best friend's body away. I want to forget."

"Can you forget?"

Her lips pucker and roll. "I don't know."

Flush with anticipation, I can't stop myself from acting on pure instinct. She's slipping through my fingertips. I can't have that. Whether she accepts it or not, Ripley Bennet belongs to me. She has for longer than either of us realised.

My mouth strikes hers without the pleasantries of a gentle reintroduction. I don't intend to entice her with some long, elaborate scheme—I want her to fucking submit. To accept the sick bond that's grown between us and join me in the torment.

I still want to own her. Break her. Shatter every last recognisable piece. But I also want to help her put those pieces together again. Her pain is no longer my obsession; instead, her will to survive against the odds is.

She hesitates for a moment before responding to my kiss. I wouldn't begrudge her punching me. Last time I touched her, we collided violently. Her response is no less rough as she bites my bottom lip.

I lift a hand to her short curls and seize a handful. Ripley moans into my mouth when I sharply tug, positioning her head to devour her at a deeper angle. Her lips take the brunt of my determination, smacking together with each kiss.

Her body writhes against mine, trapped between my onslaught and the hard wall with no room to escape. I grind into her soft curves, my cock hardening at the feel of each rounded angle.

Gripping her ass tight, she's pinned to my chest. I want her to feel the effect she has on me. A mere taste and I'm harder than steel. The sight of her crying out in ecstasy the night I saved her life has haunted me since.

I want that again.

I want her.

I'm ready to admit that.

Her desperate moans increase as I thrust my tongue past her lips, branding her mouth as mine. Our teeth clang. Lips wrestle. Breath intwines. The institute and all its madness fades into the background.

BANG.

Screams follow the loud crash. Ripley tears her mouth from mine, immediately on high alert. Two bickering patients race down the corridor, chasing each other to continue trading blows.

"Shit." She touches her swollen lips, stained an exquisite shade of cherry red. "We should move."

All I want is to bend her tight little ass over and roughly plough into her sweet cunt until she cries out my name in surrender. I swallow deeply and force myself to breathe instead.

"You're probably right."

"What about him?"

Ripley studies Rick's unconscious body in the distance. His companions have deserted him already. I wonder if her mind is chewing over whether she could forgive him... Whether she could forget.

Would his death appease her? If I find a sharp instrument to carve out his organs with, will I earn her forgiveness? Will she curl up in my arms again? All she has to do is say the word.

"Would you like me to go back and finish the job?" I ask plainly.

Her teeth seize her inflamed bottom lip. I'm calculating the best place to dissect the bastard, limb from limb, when she shakes her head.

"He'll get what he deserves. We have bigger concerns."

Stepping back from me, she crouches to pick up the bag at her side that I didn't notice. I move the flashlight to illuminate the backpack, noting that it's bulging as Ripley swings it over her shoulder.

"Some food I scavenged," she explains quickly. "And the last of my contraband stash."

"That's some survival kit."

Ripley jerks her head towards the medical wing. "We have mouths to feed."

"You're done running from us?"

"I'm done running. Period."

To my surprise, she stretches out a hand in offering. I stare at the tattoo-wrapped limb, uncertain how to respond. What is she offering me? Does she want me to… hold it? How do I even do that?

"Just take the hand, Xan."

Her palm is warm as it slots into mine.

"That wasn't so hard, was it?" she jibes.

Our fingers tightly intertwine, and she gives a barely-there squeeze. From the corner of my eye, I watch her frown at our connected grips.

Ripley tugs me onwards, leaving the bloody mess behind us. Illuminating our path to the medical wing, I let her guide the way as I keep a wary eye out for any more patients.

Creeping through the darkness, I'm so focused on our

surroundings, I almost smack into her back when she suddenly halts. The door leading into the medical wing is hanging off its hinges.

"Shit," she mutters softly.

I move fast, stepping in front of her. "Stay here."

"Forget it." Ripley quickly drops my hand. "Raine is in there!"

"Rip! Wait!"

Running after her, we race into the darkened wing, picking our way over smashed detritus. Gloom from outside and the swinging flashlight reveals a catastrophic mess.

Furniture overturned. Cabinets raided. Medical supplies scattered. Lennox's bed is empty, lying on its side with the sheets tangled on the floor. My gaze lands on a puddle of congealed blood smeared across the floor.

"Hello?" Ripley shouts frantically.

Her voice echoes—a panicked reverberation bouncing off the walls and vaulted ceiling. Its high-pitched tenor fades without a response.

The wing is abandoned.

They're gone.

CHAPTER 6
RIPLEY
FREEDOM – YOUNG LIONS

THE SHOWER SPRAY is freezing cold as it hits me square in the face. Whatever hot water remained when I woke up in the medical wing has petered out along with the electricity. We're truly cut off now.

Scrubbing myself with my papaya body wash, I continue to survey my mental map of Harrowdean, considering possible places where Lennox, Raine and Langley could be hiding.

Xander and I searched until the sun rose and our exhaustion refused to be ignored any longer. He was already dead on his feet when we started looking. We had to stop and find somewhere to get some rest.

I turn off the cold spray, teeth chattering as I step out into the chilly bathroom. My bedroom has been turned over, much like everyone else's on the fifth and sixth floors. The thieves didn't find anything, though. I'd already retrieved my stash.

As I set the makeshift shank made from a toothbrush and razor blade on the bathroom sink, a low-pitched whimpering echoes from the adjacent room. I left the door open a crack in case any wayward patients decided to surprise us with another sweep.

The noise stops before I can figure out what it is.

After hurriedly drying off, wincing at the pain of my aching body, I stand poised. It's silent. The floor is pretty much abandoned—during our searching, we found most still-lucid patients congregating in communal areas where light sources can be shared.

A smaller, almost incoherent group was attempting to break into the pharmacy to raid the medication stash when we passed. Unsuccessful, of course. The store is locked behind a reinforced steel cage that wouldn't budge.

Everyone's going cold turkey.

More fuel for the fire.

I pull clean leggings and my favourite oversized anime tee on, thankful to be back in my own clothes. The butter-soft, over washed fabric doesn't irritate my lingering injuries. It feels so good to be clean.

"No... S-Stop... Please."

My hands freeze while pulling the t-shirt down. The whispered pleading is barely audible. Confused, I glance around the bathroom, convinced my several missed doses of medication are taking effect.

It's definitely coming from the bedroom where I left Xander resting alone. I wasn't about to climb into the tiny, twin-sized bed with him, despite the kiss we shared. Surely, he isn't the one crying out?

"No! Leave m-me alone!"

Oh, shit.

It is Xander.

The sheer terror in his voice seizes hold of my heart and wrings the blood from it. I creep into the bedroom, now bathed in late afternoon sunlight leaking through the barred window.

My bed is occupied by a sprawled out Xander, his legs sticking out from the twisted sheets and arms flailing blindly to ward off something I can't see. In his fist, he holds a familiar pocketknife.

I should remain at a safe distance, but his mouth is frozen open in a silent scream for mercy. I can't just watch. He's keening like a frightened child, thrashing and kicking.

The powerful iceman is battling invisible demons and crying out to be saved from his own mind. Equal parts fascination and reluctant empathy carry me towards him.

Beneath his whimpering, I can almost hear the fissures in my heart cracking wide open. Hatred spills out in a violent geyser, leaving space for something else. Something unnerving. Something a lot like... understanding.

Xander Beck isn't only a monster.

He's a survivor too.

Just like me.

Resting on the edge of the bed, I tentatively place a hand on his cold, bare shoulder. He stripped out of his shirt and jeans to sleep, exposing the pale, defined ridges of his packed abdominals and pectorals.

While ganglier than Lennox, he's still wiry and muscular. His marble-like skin stretches tight across each chiselled tendon. The old, silvery scars that cover his arms and biceps also adorn his flat stomach and lower still.

"Xan," I murmur gently. "You're safe."

At the sound of my voice, the tension drains from his posture. Xander slumps on the thin mattress, a sigh whistling from his nostrils. I trace circles on his skin with my thumb, whispering under my breath.

"That's it, Xan." My throat thickens as my conflicting emotions battle it out. "You're safe."

The urge to climb into bed with him and hold this fragile version of the psychopath I thought I knew is overwhelming. In this moment, he looks so lost. So alone. So irreparably broken.

I know what that's like.

I've been so alone it physically aches.

Xander is evil, capable of inflicting incomprehensible cruelty. I know he craves pain and humiliation. To him, love is degradation. Power. Control. It's all he knows, and that's why he targeted me.

Being evil doesn't mean the person is all bad, though.

We contain multitudes.

There are a million reasons why he deserves to be left to battle his nightmares alone. Anyone saner would take one look at the terrifying brutality inside him and run away. But… fuck, there's something comforting about his capacity for violence.

How would it feel to have that power on my side? I've been alone for so long, I don't know what it's like to be defended by someone. To have the protection of another human being—even one who once hurt me.

When I try to put some space between us, a low moan rumbles from Xander's throat. His eyelids move, and before I can pull away, his weapon-free hand snaps out to capture my wrist in an iron-tight grip.

His long fingers tense, digging deep into the barely-healing wounds that ring my wrist. The hot throb of pain makes my breath catch, and at that tiny noise, his eyes suddenly fly open.

"No!" he shouts.

"Xan! It's me!"

Unseen ghosts haunt his shadowy cobalt orbs as the knife flicks out and swoops towards my face. I duck before he can stab me, trying to capture his attention so he can see it's me.

"Xander! Stop!"

Panting hard, he looks at me. The palpable fear warping his face into a child-like caricature morphs into surprise when he realises I'm the one touching him.

My chest expands with relief when he lowers the pocketknife. For the first time, he stares back at me with no defences intact.

Holy. Shit.

The truth is plain as day, written in blinding lights. He can't hide his secrets in this state. In his uncertain stare, I can see the tormented reality he hides behind cold smiles and indifference.

"Let go," I whisper in a small voice. "You're hurting me."

"Ripley?"

"It's me. You were crying out in your sleep. I thought…"

Not sure what to say, I purse my lips. He's still clasping my wrist, blinking hard to clear the sleepy fog from his mind.

Xander licks his lips. "You heard."

"Does this happen often?"

He looks away, blinking several times before answering. "Sometimes."

"What were you dreaming about?"

"Nothing," he replies flatly.

"That didn't look like nothing. You nearly stabbed me."

I wouldn't have put it past the old him to use physical violence, though that's more Lennox's style. Xander prefers mind games and careful manipulation.

The physical change is clear when he transforms back into the lifeless droid I'm used to. The fog clears from his gaze, and he wipes any trace of vulnerability away, smoothing a cool smile into place.

"Are you concerned?" Xander asks dryly. "I can assure you I don't need your pity."

"Fine, be like that," I snap in frustration. "I'm not the one who's scared to feel anything at all."

"Scared?" He laughs.

"Yes!"

"I don't get scared, Ripley. You should know that."

"Bullshit. I think you're fucking terrified."

His amusement makes my teeth grind. I finally see his cruelty for what it really is—a defence mechanism. The world shaped Xander into the psychopathic monster he proclaims to be. He wears it like a cloak.

"Fear is for children," he spits out.

"Is that who was crying out for help?" I lash back.

"I wasn't doing that."

"Bullshit! Tell me, who hurt little Xander?"

He physically recoils like I've slapped him. It brings me a shameful sense of satisfaction to see the hurt my words inflict. I'd rather he feel that pain than nothing at all. As long as he's feeling, there's hope.

When he releases my wrist and tries to wriggle away from me, I act quickly. Xander falls back on the bed with a huff as I pull myself on top of him, straddling his waist in a position of power.

I don't care that he still holds the pocketknife. He can lash out again if he so pleases. I'll take the blade and sink it into his chest to make him understand. This is our breaking point.

"Ripley," he warns.

"What? You're allowed to make demands and take my choice away from me, but I can't do the same?"

"Enough."

"No. It isn't enough, Xan."

Beneath me, his chest rises and falls in a fast rhythm. I trail my hand between his defined pectorals, over his breastbone and down his sloping abdominals. My fingertips catch on raised, puckered scar tissue.

His breath catches. "Stop."

"No. Not yet."

I watch indecision and torment flicker over him, breaking his act. My thumb strokes across a deep, jagged groove beneath his belly button, the shiny mark faded with time.

"I think the truth is… you feel too much."

Xander remains silent, so I plough on.

"It's why you bear these marks. It's why you hurt others to

feel in control. And it's why you won't open up to me. You're consumed by fear."

"That's... That's not true," he splutters.

"Then you won't mind if I walk away right now. I can't forgive or forget without first understanding the man demanding so much from me."

Climbing off him, I leave Xander looking startled. My gut burns with frustration and regret. For a brief, pathetic second, I dared to believe that he could be more. That *we* could be more.

I'm searching for my shoes to storm out when I hear movement behind me. Pale fingers wrap around my bicep.

"Stop."

I'm spun on the spot, forcing me to look up at Xander as the blade presses deep into my throat.

"Don't go," he croaks.

"You're threatening me to get me to stay?"

The pressure slicing into me is a silent bid for control. I don't think Xander knows how to communicate without threatening death in one way or another.

"I... I can't... I don't know how to do... this," he mutters awkwardly. "Talk."

When I try to pull away, his grip intensifies, holding me prone. He's clothed in nothing but form-fitting black boxers, his hair wild and eyes darting around like he's hoping to pluck the right words from thin air.

This Xander isn't in control.

"I was dreaming about your voice," he blurts abruptly. "Telling me I'm safe. No one told me that when I was a kid. No one... cared."

Holding still so he doesn't cut me, I carefully lay my hand over his. "Safe from what?"

Inhale. Frown. Exhale. Blink.

"Let me in, Xan."

"I... don't know when it started."

"Did someone hurt you?" I coax.

He licks his lips, avoiding my gaze. "You could call it that. I was too young to understand, I suppose. The memories are blurred, but the dreams about him are vivid."

Blood trickles down my neck, leaking from the shallow nick I can feel he's inflicted. If he needs to do this to feel in control, I'll take the punishment. A scar is a small price to pay for Xander's bared soul.

"So you were dreaming about... him?"

Watching his reaction, I'm unsurprised by his terse nod.

"Who was he?"

I've been able to deduce some of Xander's past from my conversation with Lennox. When he revealed the truth about his sister's suicide, he made it clear that he believes Xander was a victim of sexual abuse too.

"He was my stepfather," Xander grits out.

My stomach rolls. "Fuck."

"I never knew my real father. Mother spent my childhood at the bottom of a bottle. She almost died from liver failure when I was six. He was my only real parental figure."

My hand tightens on his, more blood sliding down my neck. Xander blows out a long breath and lifts his gaze to mine.

"He came most nights. I suppose Mother was too inebriated to hear or notice anything. We never spoke about the... the assaults. He just snuck in, left before dawn and always returned the next night. Every day for as long as I can remember."

His throat moves with a hard swallow.

"I was eight when the police came. I didn't say anything, the damage was done. He was actually arrested for assaulting a young boy in a park, nothing to do with me."

"That's so incredibly messed up."

"I guess he couldn't help himself." Xander eases the knife slightly, keeping it held at my throat. "The authorities took one look at Mother and sent her to rehab. I was taken into foster care. That's it."

Processing, I try to make sense of his words. "You never told anyone?"

Xander laughs humourlessly. "I didn't have to."

"Why?"

He drags his other hand over his weary face. "The bastard admitted it all. I wasn't the only person he hurt. He was charged with multiple counts of sexual assault and died in prison four years later."

Emotion boils behind my eyes, matching the white-hot sensation his blade is inflicting. I don't pity him. He doesn't need that. Yet the truth tears at my soul regardless.

"What happened after?" I ask in a guttural voice.

"I bounced between foster homes until I aged out of the system a decade later. No one wanted to adopt the antisocial kid who liked to cut himself. I scared off every potential adoption."

"Your mother never came back for you?"

Lowering the pocketknife fully, his shoulders slump. "No. I never saw her again. She could be dead for all I know and care."

Watching him breathe heavily, I can't comprehend how any mother could abandon her son like that. Sure, she was sick. But to never come back for him or make contact? After everything? It's plain cruel.

"When he…" His voice falters as he looks down. "When he used to hurt me, I'd cry and plead with him to stop. He warned me about what happens to little boys who cry."

"Xan. You don't have to keep going."

"I need to say it," he explains with a newfound fierceness.

I close my mouth, waiting for him to continue.

"After years of his nightly visits, it was easy to switch off to the pain, the fear, the confusion and disgust I felt… and feel nothing at all. He told me not to cry. So I stopped."

"He threatened you?"

My voice is barely a whisper, fraught with horror for that poor little boy, alone and scared, who found a sense of safety in not feeling at all.

"Me… Mother… His threats were indiscriminate. Crying wouldn't save me. If I laid there silently, the time passed quicker. The less I cared, the less it hurt each time he came back for more."

The broken person standing in front of me hardly resembles the white-haired demon I met in Priory Lane. The same man who tried to scare me into submission. Who kept me busy while his best friend ensured Holly's demise.

Xander scoffs, his gaze focused on the floor. "I never cared about anything ever again."

My attention latches on to his visible scars. I wondered about them for months in Priory Lane.

"These look old."

"It started in foster care."

"Can you tell me why?"

Xander pauses for a long moment, searching for the right words. He flips the pocketknife in his hands, uncaring of my sticky blood coating the surface.

"No matter how many times I sliced my skin until I ran out of space, I felt nothing. But I loved the act of doing it. The pain became a way to prove to myself that I'd never be vulnerable again. As long as I could confirm that the numbness was still there… keeping me safe."

I can't help but think of Rae. Her own addiction to pain. But for Xander, he wasn't cutting to feel something. He did it to check whether he still felt nothing at all.

His need for pain suddenly makes more sense. Not just his own, but the pain he inflicts on others. It's all a test of his control. A way to ensure his own survival. If everyone else is hurting, then they can't hurt him.

"That's why I didn't care about Holly." Xander finally

looks up at me. "I didn't care how much it would affect you either. I was willing to push her over the edge."

"Because it was necessary?"

He shakes his head. "I know how it sounds."

"The amount of times I've told myself the same thing." I laugh at the insanity of it all. "I guess nobody survives with their morals intact. Desperate people do desperate things."

Lips parted, Xander cocks his head. "Do desperate people forgive others' shitty choices?"

Even with a fresh wound, I'm twisted enough to actually consider it. Old Ripley would've left him, naked and humiliated. Lord, I'm fucking tempted. It would be no less than he deserves.

That was before I experienced for myself the true cost of survival. The evil that breeds when you're existing in a world forever weighted against you. We can all be a little monstrous when we're desperate.

"They try to." I touch the slick mess at my throat. "Even when it isn't easy or quick... they can try to make progress."

Stepping closer, I admit defeat and curl my arms around him. Xander shudders against me, his skin chilled and goose pimpled. He hides his face in my hair then grips my hips.

"For what it's worth," he says into my curls. "I'm sorry for the pain we caused you. For all that you suffered through because of our choices."

"I know, Xan."

"I mean it. We put you through hell."

"Well, yes." Pain prickles my throat at the admission. "But I suppose I did the same to you. You were tortured because of me."

Xander chuckles against my head. "It was no less than we deserved."

"As true as that may be, I don't want to hurt you anymore, Xan. I want us to be more than that."

A long pause is filled with the sound of his rapid breathing.

"I thought I knew what I wanted. What... I needed. Now I'm not so sure."

I tilt my head up to look at him. "What do you want right now?"

"Right now?" His tongue darts out to swipe across his bottom lip. "You."

CHAPTER 7

RIPLEY
FIXED BLADE – TRADE WIND

XANDER'S LIPS CAPTURE MINE. The anger that drove our kiss yesterday is absent. Instead, I'm overwhelmed by the urgent intensity his mouth embodies. He isn't punishing me; he's pleading with me. Begging for understanding.

Searching for a way to comprehend what he feels, Xander tattoos a frantic prayer against my lips. The voice that once screamed at me to never let this creature into my head has been beaten into submission.

He pulls my leg up so it hooks on his hip. I'm flush against him, the cold from his naked skin seeping through my t-shirt. His mouth massages mine before he sucks my bottom lip between his teeth to bite down.

I gasp as slick copper seeps between us. The piping hot flow seems to ignite something within Xander. When he squeezes my jaw tight enough to crack bone, the spark of danger makes my soaked core clench.

Stopping for a breath, Xander pushes his thumb through the blood dripping from my lip. He inspects the stained pad before taking his thumb into his mouth to suck it off.

"I want to earn it," he says emphatically.

"Earn what?"

His hand lowers, moving to clasp my injured throat. My mind can't keep up with the rapid fluctuations, a desperate man pleading for forgiveness as he squeezes the wound he inflicted.

This is how he surrenders. Xander could never tear down his defences without maintaining some control. The pressure at my windpipe demonstrates his internal struggle, fighting to shed his old self.

"You," he repeats. "Your trust."

Releasing my throat, he allows me to suck in a breath. Forcing me to trust him. To believe that even when he holds my life in his hands, he'll give it back to me in the end.

This isn't control.

This is trust.

When his grasp loosens completely, I grab his wrist, encouraging him to do it again. Xander's eyes blow wide. I finally get it. I know what he needs. And right now, I want him to hurt me. I want to give him the pain he needs to inflict.

"You want me like this?" he murmurs, eyelids falling to half-mast.

I nod, my chest searing.

"I'm not a good person, Ripley. I've hurt a lot of people. You included. Why are you still begging for more?"

Controlling my breath, he holds me in suspense until spots appear in my vision. I blink rapidly, unable to form words. The overwhelming pain of being choked feels good in the sickest way possible.

Xander releases me, allowing a short breath. "Well?"

"B-Because… I want y-you."

"How could you possibly want this?" he spits in disgust.

His choking hand caught between us, I lean in to press our foreheads together. "Because I'll always be safe with a villain on my side."

The molten determination that's replaced his icy stare steals my voice. I can handle cold Xander. Calculating

Xander. Obsessed Xander. But angry, emotional, fucking *possessive* Xander?

He's a different beast entirely.

A beast I'm longing to tame.

"I'll be your villain if that's what you want."

I nod in total compliance.

"No one is going to lay another finger on you," he promises menacingly. "Not if they want to keep that finger attached."

His expanding pupils are bleeding into his irises, spelling imminent attack. Xander's unfettered attention is an intense force, one that once terrified me. Now it feels fucking magnetic.

He's a powerful riptide holding me captive, repeatedly dunking me beneath the ocean waves, filling my lungs and nose until I'm reliant on his mercy to suck in a single breath.

Abruptly releasing my throat, Xander drops to his knees in front of me. He lifts my oversized tee to seize my waistband. I don't protest as he wriggles my leggings down over my hips and thighs.

Neither of us speaks. Not as he takes his pocketknife to my panties' elastic. Nor as the sliced cotton hits the bedroom floor. And not when his head lowers between my thighs.

His mouth travels from my hip to my public bone, planting wet kisses. I shove my fingers into his hair, fisting the strands tight. His teeth scrape against my sensitive inner thigh, teasing me.

"Xan… please."

"Hush."

My knees are practically knocking together with each second he fails to offer me relief. I'm lightheaded and trembling, the warring sensations inside me too much to hold.

"Be still," he demands.

His mouth descends exactly where I want it, his tongue licking the seam of my pussy. I hold back a shudder, terrified he'll stop if I move an inch. His tongue slides over me before he sucks my clit between his teeth.

"Oh God!" I moan.

Lavishing attention on my sensitive bud, he feasts on my core like a starving man shown a three-course buffet. I buck into his face, silently pleading for more as electric tension coils inside me.

Xander halts, glancing up at me. "I told you to stay still."

"You try to stay still."

Finding his feet, he eyes me with a knowing smirk. "Such a brat."

I yelp when he bends over to grab hold of my bare legs. I'm tossed over his shoulder, carried back to my own rumpled bed. Xander deposits me on the mattress with a huff.

Splayed out on my back, I'm exposed from the waist down. Xander drags his gaze over me, his boxers already straining from a large bulge. He discards the pocketknife on the bed.

The way he's looking at me while he strips is intoxicating. Every inch of Xander is on display for me to drink in. Whenever I see him naked, I learn something new. This time, I study his defined hips, guiding my eyes down to his cock.

He's many things, but shy isn't one of them. Nothing Xander does ever carries a hint of embarrassment. Particularly in the bedroom. He's made no secret of his proclivities, and a wanton part of me loves that.

"Open your legs for me," he commands. "Show me what you want, little toy."

That sick fuck with his stupid nickname.

Holding eye contact, I tug off my t-shirt to reveal my chest. I didn't bother to pull a bra on after my cold shower. My nipples are hardened spikes, tingling under his attention.

Squeezing my right breast, I feel my mouth quirking as I spread my legs wide open. The power I hold over him without a single touch is enough to get drunk on. Far more potent than any drink or illicit drug.

I was his obsession.

Now he watches me like I'm his god.

Playing with my nipple, I twist and tug, moaning with each painful jolt. I can feel the warmth pooling between my thighs, on full display for him to observe. Just his hungry gaze is enough to excite me.

Xander approaches, certain and purposeful. As he braces himself on the bed, moving to taste me again, I lift my leg high. My bare foot connects with his face, pushing him back so he can't lay a finger on me.

"I'll show you," I croon. "But right now... You have to stay still."

Keeping him a length from me, I dip my hand down to my dripping pussy. Xander curses under his breath as I circle my clit, coating my fingers in slick moisture. Holding him back is only making this power play hotter.

When I thrust a finger deep into my cunt, heat sizzles down my spine. I work myself over, stretching my pussy wide before pushing another finger inside. A moan spills from my mouth.

"Fucking hell," Xander rumbles quietly.

"Problem?"

He pushes his face against my foot, trying to get closer. I add more pressure, effectively shoving him backwards. I love humiliating him. Xander winces but doesn't try to move again.

"Stay." I grin broadly.

My hand moves faster. Pulsating back and forth, my walls clench tight around the wet fingers I'm taunting him with. I swipe my clit with each oscillation, using my spare hand to roll my nipple.

"You get to stand there and watch me climax. That's all you're allowed."

He breathes heavily. "Yes."

"Watch me fall apart, Xan."

"Yes." The word sounds like a plea.

"Stand there and watch, knowing how much I love seeing you get a taste of your own medicine."

"Fuck, Ripley… Yes."

I've always sought out a quick fuck during my sexual manic episodes, but I still know how to get myself off. My pussy clamps tight around my fingers as my orgasm explodes through me.

Spine curving, I let my release take over. I'm trembling too hard to stop Xander from wrapping a hand around my ankle.

He's focused on me—every shaky breath, the slippery warmth wetting my hand, my breasts shuddering as I pant for air, blood still leaking from my throat. I've become a filthy mess for him.

"My little toy likes to play games," he purrs, releasing my ankle. "I suppose turnabout is fair play."

Lowering my foot, I brace myself upright on my elbows to scrutinise him. His hand is wrapped firmly around his cock, pumping the veiny steel. It makes my mouth go dry.

"You're damn right it's fair." I trace my tongue over my lips. "Now, why don't you come here and fuck me?"

"I'm allowed to move now?" He quirks an eyebrow.

"Yes. But don't push your luck."

Xander prowls farther onto the bed. "Now, where's the fun in that?"

I shuffle backwards so my head rests on the pillows. He kneels between my legs, his thigh muscles bulging. But he doesn't move. The man hovers stiller than a statue and wears a goddamn smirk.

He scours every inch of me like he's seeing me for the first time. Or perhaps seeing me differently now that our rivalry has been thrown into question. The wait for him to finally snap and take charge is excruciating.

"Xan…"

"Something you want? You seemed quite content to deny me and satisfy yourself a moment ago."

Hissing, I stare up at the white ceiling. "You're a fucking asshole."

"As advertised."

The air displaces around me as I feel his hands seize my body. I'm quickly flipped, so fast I've barely sucked in a shocked breath before my face hits the pillow.

Xander lifts my hips to pull my ass up high before white-hot pain crackles across my left butt cheek. The smack is hard and fast. Fiery tingles spread, bringing a surge of pleasure with them. When he hits me again on the other cheek, I can't hold back a loud moan.

The constantly-shifting dynamic makes me feel raw and untethered. I know damn well that's his intention. He wants all the control for himself. Despite all my bravado, I'm far too ready to give in.

"I want to fuck your beautiful little cunt while I hold your life in my hands," he admits in a rough growl.

Twisted anticipation explodes through me.

"Yes," I mewl. "Do it."

Xander's heated skin brushes against my pebbled nipples as he reaches behind me. Cool metal kisses the side of my neck, behind my jaw. I don't need to see the knife to know that's what it is.

Xander strokes my skin with the razor-sharp edge. "So beautiful."

"I'm not afraid of you." I stifle a groan.

"Maybe you should be."

My body tightens as need pulses between my thighs.

"There are a great many arteries in the human neck," he says conversationally. "Internal and external carotid. Jugular. Vital muscles and branches. So many fragilities."

It shouldn't turn me on to hear his unhinged musings. The

man could end my life with a single slash. Once upon a time, I would've been sobbing in terror, convinced he'd do just that.

The pleasure spawns from knowing that he won't. Not now. This Xander wants to hold my still-beating heart in his palm, just so he can put it back behind my ribcage with the memory of his touch.

It aggravates my healing bruises and injuries to be bent over, but the moment his fingers press against my slit, pain is overtaken by near-animalistic need. His finger swirls over my pussy in a cruel taunt.

"So wet," Xander marvels before spanking me again, the jolt causing the knife to shift. "Is all that from putting on your clever little show?"

"Xan… Fuck."

"Or is it the threat of death that gets you so wet?"

"Please, just…"

"Just what?" His palm crashes into my ass so hard, it rattles my bones.

Hiding my face in the pillow, I cry out. Each hit blends agony and ecstasy in an excruciatingly perfect way. I could climax from his punishing spanks alone, I'm so wound up.

Xander slides two fingers into me, stoking the furnace with each deliberate pump. I rock into his hand, desperately trying to relieve myself.

"You asked me to fuck you." He tuts and withdraws them. "So behave."

Fucking behave?

"This is how it's going to work." Xander inserts his fingers into me again and resumes pumping. "I'll give you whatever broken excuse of a soul I have left. In exchange, I want you to make the pain inside me stop."

Fisting the anti-ligature bedsheets, I want to scream at the top of my lungs. Beg him. Plead with him. Use his fucking pocketknife to carve out my heart and offer it to him on a silver platter if it means he'll relent.

"How?" I gasp.

"By giving yourself to me. All of you."

"I… I don't know how."

"You do. It goes like this."

His fingers vanish, but before I can yell out in frustration, I feel his cock plunge into me. He doesn't inch in with any grace or patience. Xander buries himself to the hilt and waits for me to scream out.

The moment I do, he withdraws then slams back home with a loud grunt. He's blasting past my limits and fucking me as roughly as I'd hoped he would.

The room is filled with the sound of our bodies slapping together and my gasps each time his knife slices into me. Feeling every shallow nick is enough to keep the exhilarating danger ever-present. He knows exactly how to push my limits, and my body is addicted to the adrenaline rush.

Melting into a puddle of pure sensation, days of anxiety from watching our world erupt disappears. The fire he's injecting into my veins becomes my whole existence.

Now I'm the one burning.

Happily.

And he can keep the fucking ashes.

Xander keeps me suspended on the edge of the highest cliff as he holds me at knife point, moaning with each flex of his hips. He pulls out almost to the point of withdrawal before surging back in each time.

When he spanks me again, the blow makes his length spasm inside me. We both groan at the same time, overwhelmed by the deep, penetrating vibrations that ignite every last nerve ending.

"You did this to me," he accuses angrily. "You made me care, Ripley. You made me give a shit when no one else could. How?"

I'd laugh if I wasn't terrified of slitting my own throat.

Even like this, he's hung up on where the true power lies. He has to be the most obsessive creature I've ever met.

"I don't know," I whisper.

Xander's thrusts gain momentum, becoming deeper and rougher. "Neither do I. That's what terrifies me—not knowing how this stupid, goddamn useless organ in my chest works."

His heat pistoning into me abruptly disappears. I choke back a sob when the knife vanishes from my neck, totally overwhelmed by emotions. Relief. Frustration. The thrill is mind-boggling.

I'm on the verge of shouting at the sadistic son of a bitch when I'm flipped over. My back meets the bed, leaving me sprawled out in front of Xander.

Hovering over me, his sweat-dotted skin betrays how much his control has frayed. He can be passionate, but he was always clinical. There's no sign of that cold fascination right now, though. Obsession, sure.

But it feels personal this time.

Hunger has overtaken him.

Raw, famished, cannibalistic hunger for all the emotion he's never been allowed to feel. Every taut muscle shows how it's overwhelming him. I place a hand on his chest, easing him backwards.

He lets me guide him until he's on his back. Inelegantly manoeuvring myself on top, I ease the bloodied knife from his grip. He's had his fun. Now I want to have mine.

Bracing one hand on his shoulder, I lift the other to my neck. Xander's pupils blow wide as I collect the red spill, smearing it over my palm. His mouth falls open when I seize his cock, smothering it in my blood.

"I've given you all of me," I tell him. "My submission. My trust. My life. Isn't that proof enough that I want you?"

I guide his steel inside me. Xander's eyes roll back in his head when I sink down fully, allowing his bloodstained cock to stretch my internal walls. The crimson lubricant creates a silky mess.

"Goddammit," he hisses out. "Yes. It's enough."

"Then you will give yourself to me. Every day. I want this Xander by my side, not the detached man who felt no remorse for his actions."

Adjusting, he leans back on his hands. "I'm scared, Rip."

Part of me expected a fight, even wanted one. But I think I'm enjoying his vulnerability even more. The scales flipping back in my favour gives me an energy boost, numbing the pain from my aggravated injuries.

I begin to move, lifting my hips and pushing down on him in a steady beat. At this angle, he's breaching me deeply, his cock nudging the sweet spot inside me.

"You should be scared," I say between moans. "If I wanted to, I could take that stupid, goddamn useless organ and shred it to ribbons. But I won't, Xan. You need to trust me."

"I don't… trust anyone," he rasps.

"That's the problem." My nails dig into his shoulders, leaving crescent-shaped grooves. "Even if we can't forgive or forget immediately, we can learn to trust."

Riding him at an increasing pace, I batter my words into him with my body. We're a sweaty mess of limbs, both nearing the edge. The orgasm that's been slowly building is on the cusp of overwhelming me.

Xander drops a hand between us to find my clit. Extra sensitive, all it takes is one swipe through smeared blood to push me into the abyss. I throw my head back, calling his name.

His face buried in my neck, I can feel him finishing too. His body quakes beneath mine, and heat surges into me, creating an irreversible brand. Satisfying heat pulses through me as our essences mix.

The aftershocks continue, burst after burst, fireworks

pulling at my skin. My entire body is weak and spent. It's all I can do to collapse against Xander's chest.

My head slumps onto his shoulder, too heavy to hold up. Warmth seeps between us as he catches his breath. Completely drained, we don't move for a long time.

I can't summon a protest when Xander lifts me from his lap to separate us. He lays me down on the bed then curls up beside me. Any hatred I had left dissipates when he lays his head on my stomach.

"Trust is hard for me," he whispers faintly. "I've gotten this far alone."

Stroking through his unkempt hair, the usually silky-soft strands are coarse, in need of a wash. My heart is still hammering relentlessly behind my rib cage. It feels as badly bruised as the rest of me.

"You're not alone, Xan. You have Lennox and Raine."

His palm splays across my belly, leaking warmth. "What about you?"

"I guess I've got this far by myself too."

"You don't have to anymore."

"Don't I?"

"You're not alone now," he explains drily.

"I still feel it. Even when I'm surrounded by people."

"People like us?" Xander queries.

Uncertain, I lick my lips. "Sometimes."

"Well, people care about you. And Raine… I don't want to come between you two. He deserves happiness."

I don't dare speak, unnerved by this new, thoughtful Xander.

"And whether he's ready to admit it or not, Lennox wants something from you too," Xander muses tiredly. "You've managed to ensnare my entire family."

"Should I be apologising for that?" I ask honestly.

His spearmint-scented breath licks my skin. "No. I think it will take all of us to escape what Incendia has planned next."

"They won't go down without a fight." Trepidation crawls through me at the mere thought. "The gates will be blasted open soon enough."

"I agree. When that time comes, we'll need each other."

He falls silent, seemingly lost in thought. Harsh reality is crashing into our post-sex bubble. Violence and threats still surround us on all sides as an invisible clock ticks down to the unknown.

"Perhaps we're meant to be a fucked up family." Xander trails his hand up and down my back. "Maybe that's how we live."

"Together?"

"Exactly," he responds, tracing small circles with his fingertips. "Together."

My heart balloons to absolute breaking point. I want to tell it to brush his exhausted comment off, but that damned, sticky hope can never release its clutches on me. No matter how hard I try.

Family.

Could he possibly mean that?

I'm not sure I even deserve one.

CHAPTER 8
RAINE
SAID & DONE – BAD OMENS

MY ENTIRE BODY is wracked with violent shaking as damp claws sink into me. I'm overwhelmed with sounds, tastes and smells. None of them good. It's making it hard to focus on breathing through the nausea.

Mildew.

Old chlorine.

Floodwater.

Rotten wood.

Each individual scent helps me paint a picture of the place Ripley once brought me to. Only this time, the storm damage has worsened the swimming pool's state of disuse.

"Nox," I choke out.

"Coming. Shit, where are the pills?"

A scuffle betrays his frantic efforts to sort through our supplies. We weren't able to grab much when we fled the medical wing. A horde of patients came searching for food, drugs or weapons. They weren't exactly calm either.

Another burst of nausea causes pain to build behind my eyes. My stomach revolts, and it takes all my self-control to hold my meagre breakfast of stale cereal bars down. I can't afford to waste the food we scrounged up.

"For fuck's sake," Lennox hisses, clearly in pain.

"Be careful. You're still hurt. I can wait for Langley to get back."

"You need your damn pills, Raine. You look like shit."

I'd send him a glower if I knew where he was standing, searching through our two bags. I can hear his movements, but with all the dripping water and sporadic breezes, my spatial awareness is being thrown for a loop.

"Gee, thanks. You're always so complimentary."

"And you're a fucking idiot for waiting this long to take your dose," he hits back. "You know it takes the edge off the withdrawals."

"I'm trying to ration the pills. They're all I've got."

Another worry to add to the ever-expanding list. The longer the riot drags on, the more desperate our situation is becoming. I had one bottle of pills prescribed by Doctor Hall when it all went to hell.

No refills.

Without the methadone to manage my withdrawals, I don't want to consider what state I'll be in. Getting clean from several years of opioid use won't be an easy fix. I feel shitty enough even with the pills.

The sound of tablets clashing against plastic brings sharp relief. I hear Lennox's faint *aha* before his slow footsteps approach. He's up and moving but still in considerable pain, judging by his laboured breathing.

"Got them," he announces. "We'll find more."

"Where from, Nox?"

"I don't know, but we will," he insists. "I'm not watching you suffer. We both know that going cold turkey could kill you without help."

"But—"

"Take your fucking pills, Raine."

I suppose it's ironic, really.

I'm going through this self-inflicted torture to kick my

addiction for the last time. But to do that, I'm dependent on a handful of synthetic pills. I can't truly escape the power they still hold over me.

"Here, man." Rough fingertips touch my hand where I'm crouched against the wall. "How many do you need?"

"I'll do it. Pass them here."

"You need water?" Lennox asks.

Nodding, I close my fist around the pill bottle dropped into my palm. Lennox shuffles away, still trying to hide his pained grunting, and quickly returns with the sound of crackling plastic.

"Thanks."

"Yeah," he acknowledges. "Please just tell me next time? You look paler than a ghost. I could've found the pills hours ago."

Counting out my dose, I knock back the handful then let my head rest against the cold, cinder block wall. I doubt the pills will help my aggressive shivering. It's freezing cold in here.

Langley went searching for the other two and more food. Ripley and Xander have been missing since she stormed out. In this strange, lawless period, two days is a lifetime.

"That dickhead has been gone all night." Lennox loudly slumps back down. "You reckon some idiot's captured him for ransom?"

"Don't say that, Nox."

"I mean, it's possible. He is a guard."

"Apparently not. What's the deal with his... I dunno, colleague? The woman Ripley mentioned? Sounds like she works for these Sabre people."

His breathing catches. It always does anytime the topic of the Z wing or their escape is broached. Lennox plays a good game, but I've learned to read his unconscious tells. What he saw down there has left its mark.

"I don't know," he deflects.

"What happened?"

Lennox shuffles on the hard floor. "Some pink-haired bitch pretending to work for Incendia was torturing me. Maintaining cover, I guess. She admitted she was undercover and offered to get us out."

"Like… out of Harrowdean?" I enquire.

"Yeah. Ripley told her to leave us there."

"Why?" Confusion sits heavy in my voice.

"She refused to run without me." He clears his throat, sounding like he was barely able to utter the words.

I'd give anything to see his expression right now. To have even the smallest clue to the secret feelings he's harbouring. I've long suspected there's more to his hatred for Ripley, but recent events have made the situation ten times more complicated.

"That's why she helped you escape." I nod in understanding. "Ripley couldn't leave you there to die."

Lennox doesn't respond.

"Because… she cares about you."

Nothing but a sharp inhalation.

Come on, stubborn bastard.

"And you care about her," I add.

He still won't say it.

Not even to me.

Bizarrely, it frustrates me more than it angers me. I'm not even jealous. I just want him to admit it. Until then, we can't make any decisions on how to proceed.

"You can't avoid this conversation forever, Nox. Like it or not, the three of us are in neck-deep with this girl. I need to know where you stand."

"I…" He pauses. "Don't know."

"You don't know?"

"Ripley and I… It's complicated."

"You don't say," I mutter sarcastically.

"I know, alright?" he snaps in exasperation. "We've spent

months trying to kill each other, for fuck's sake. Then in the basement… Well, things changed. Now I'm fucking lost."

"What does that mean, exactly?"

"I don't know!" Lennox exclaims. "What's with the third degree?"

"Oh, I don't know. May have something to do with the fact you tried to kill the woman I'm in love with! Did that ever cross your mind?"

My words drop with the impact equivalent to a street-level explosion, holding the power to blow our entire lives apart. I can feel them reverberating in the chlorinated air as my confession lingers.

"You love her," he deadpans.

My throat aches with unspoken emotion. "I wouldn't get clean for just anyone, Nox. I want a future. One with Ripley in it."

The sound of his teeth grinding is a loud bullet in the silence. "Does she know?"

"It's complicated," I throw his words back at him. "She made it clear we were just casual for a long time. Then everything happened… Now I'm not so sure what we are."

"And the fact that Xander's got some fucked up claim on the woman you apparently love doesn't bother you?"

"Does it bother you?" I counter.

Teeth grinding. A sharp breath. More grinding.

"Who Ripley chooses to spread her legs for is none of my concern," Lennox replies flatly. "And frankly, she can do whatever the fuck she wants."

"Right. Because you don't care."

"Right," he repeats.

For all his fierce loyalty and commitment to his family, Lennox can be a thick-skulled bastard. This ridiculous denial phase is doing none of us any favours.

"I have no idea what your problem is, but you need to figure it out. Fast." I take another drink from the plastic water bottle. "I won't stand for you hurting Ripley ever again."

"If I wanted her dead, she would be," he says ominously. "We made it out of that wing together."

"Then fucking get over yourself!"

I want to get up and storm far away from him, but even if I could see to navigate the destruction we're hiding in, I doubt my shaking legs would hold me. The pills haven't kicked in yet.

Instead, I rest against the wall, focusing on anything but the pain fracturing my skull in two. I'd kill for a line right now. Even a single hit. Enough to take the edge off.

The awkward silence wraps around me like a blanket as Lennox stews. I have no concept of what time it is. The sharp hunger pains intermingling with my constant nausea are the only indications that several hours have passed.

Slipping into a trance-like state of deep concentration in an effort to manage my sickness, I startle back to reality when a loud bang permeates the building. Lennox curses, disturbing something as he moves.

"We've got company," he announces.

"Nobody knows about this place but us."

"Maybe that asshole Langley has given up searching?"

"Doesn't seem likely," I reply worriedly. "He was determined."

Bracing myself on the floor, I try to push myself up. I feel a little stronger though still shaky and weak. My spine doesn't leave the wall as I slide upright, trembling like a leaf.

Distinct footsteps are growing closer. Multiple pairs. Hope flares in my chest, but the very real possibility that more unruly patients looking to pick a fight have found us is acute.

"Just give them what they want," I whisper-shout. "You can't fight anyone off with one working hand, Nox."

"No one is stealing our shit. I'll crack their spines first."

"It doesn't matter!"

Between the two of us, one injured and one barely able to stand, we can't put up much of a fight if people are here searching for supplies. That's precisely why we abandoned the safety of the medical wing.

A resounding voice ends our bickering.

"You could've left a damn note!"

"A note? Seriously?"

"Well, I don't know! Anything but vanishing!"

The voices quickly burst the fearful balloon that's expanded inside me. Part of me was terrified I'd never hear her razor-sharp tongue chewing someone out ever again.

"It's them," I breathe out, letting myself slump in relief.

Lennox sighs, though I can't hear him moving to greet the others. The voices are nearing, exchanging heated whispers. Langley, Ripley and Xander. They're all safe. Thank fuck.

The door to the swimming pool slamming open announces their return. Taking a deep breath in, I feel myself smile. Papaya. The tropical fruitiness is like a homing beacon guiding me back to her.

"Raine!"

I could collapse from relief. "Guava girl."

"Did you show them my secret hiding place?"

Her rapid steps magnetise her to me. The familiar scent I've come to know and adore envelopes me as Ripley pulls me into her arms. I snuggle into her chest, getting a face full of fruity curls, but I couldn't be happier.

"Nah," I murmur.

"So how did you find your way back?"

"My idea," Lennox rumbles from far-off.

"I should've known," Ripley mutters acidly.

Squeezing me tight enough to ache, I feel Ripley running her hands all over me. Two small hands cup my cheeks, bringing warmth to my cold, clammy skin. She feels like a blissful furnace.

"You're pale and sweaty," she worries. "Withdrawals?"

"I'm fine, Rip."

"Nothing about you looks fine. Aren't you taking the pills Doctor Hall prescribed?"

"Under protest," Lennox supplies. "He looks better now than he did a few hours ago."

"Raine! You have to take them."

"I forced them down him," Lennox adds.

"Good." Ripley squeezes my hand.

I'm not sure how I feel about being the only thing these two agree on right now.

Using the memory of Ripley's body, I eventually find her jaw and begin searching it with my fingertips. Her face still feels swollen and a little hot to touch. My fingers coast over her neck, stopping when I feel several crusted cuts on her skin.

"What are these?" I ask, panic riding me hard. "Are you hurt?"

"It's nothing," she rushes to assure me. "I was coming back to find you guys when I found Xander. We holed up overnight to rest."

Oh.

Perhaps I shouldn't pull at that thread. I'm not about to judge how the pair sort their shit out as long as she… erm, consents. Then it's fair game, I suppose. Ripley is her own woman.

The sound of huffing follows something heavy hitting the floor.

"You lot were supposed to stay put."

I jolt at the sound of Xander's voice. "We had no choice."

"Let's agree not to split up again," Xander suggests.

A throat clears. Langley. "Well, about that."

Pulling away from me, I sense Ripley turn around to face the others. I snag hold of her t-shirt to keep her within touching distance.

"What does that mean?" she asks suspiciously.

"I need to re-establish communication with my team,"

Langley explains. "My mobile phone was in the staff lockers when the riot broke out. If it's still charged, I can use it to contact the others."

"Why didn't you check while you were out searching?" Xander asks.

"Because I was preoccupied by looking for you two," he claps back. "I do have priorities."

Xander has the good sense to stifle any response.

"Sabre can tell us what's unfolding outside," Langley continues. "We need to know when the authorities will move in. Perhaps we can still cut a deal."

"Perhaps?" Ripley barks. "You made that sound like my only option!"

"It is, Rip."

"Like hell it is."

"Look, I can't keep you safe if I'm hiding here, waiting for the fucking SWAT team to move in and start handcuffing everyone to be shipped off. It needs to be done now."

"You can't go out there." Ripley attempts to pull away from me.

Tugging her t-shirt again, I haul her back to my front. I can feel her trembling in the pointed nodes of her spine. Regardless of her anger, Ripley does care for Langley. And right now, guards are far more at risk than any of us.

"I have no choice," he justifies. "And I can take care of myself."

"What if you're taken hostage too? You didn't see Rick out there. He was waving around a stolen gun like a lunatic and threatening to shoot! This is serious!"

"Out where?" Lennox chimes in.

Ripley vibrates with a long sigh. "There were journalists outside the gate, filming us all. I watched Rick parade the guards out to make his demands to the world."

"Rick won't be making any demands for a while."

Xander's tone belies a hint of pride. "Though I wish it were permanent."

"Don't pretend you beat the shit out of him to stop the riot," Ripley challenges. "He was unconscious at your feet before you found me."

"You're right," he submits without hesitation. "That's not why I did it."

Xander's reply is silky smooth. Utterly shameless. Judging by Ripley's sharp breath in, a hell of a lot more happened while they were *resting*. I'm weirdly satisfied by Xander's clear possessiveness.

The more people looking out for Ripley, the better. Having Xander on her side is the equivalent of having a fanatical cult running headfirst into war for you. He'll do anything to defend those he deems worthy.

"The point is," Langley draws the conversation back to him. "If I can make arrangements with my team, we can find a way out of here."

Chuffing rudely, I can almost taste Lennox's mistrust. But Ripley doesn't give him a chance to speak for her.

She presses herself into me, seeking reassurance. "It can't go on for much longer. Something has to give."

"All the more reason for me to go now," Langley argues. "While we still have a chance."

"What would a deal entail?" Xander queries.

"Full cooperation in exchange for protection. You know we've done it with other inmates. If Incendia moves in first, I can guarantee that you will all disappear."

Wrapping my arms around Ripley's midsection, I hold her close. She's in their firing line, but Xander and Lennox aren't exactly innocent either. Hell, I'll be guilty by association. We'll all be erased.

"Go then," Ripley whispers.

"Rip—"

"No." She speaks over me, her voice gaining volume. "Go

make contact. We'll wait here. But I want protection for everyone—Xander, Lennox and Raine. I'm not doing this without them."

Not even Lennox has a comment to make as he processes her words. The magnitude of her request keeps them both trapped in silence.

"I never should've viewed you as a mark to be flipped," Langley says in a low voice, footsteps coming towards us. "I'm sorry for that. I'll make this right, Rip. I promise."

"You were doing your job," she eventually replies. "Just like I was doing mine."

"That doesn't make what I've done right."

"Well, me neither. But we all make mistakes." She pulls free from my arms. "Please be safe."

From the ruffling of fabric, I think they embrace. Ripley steps back into me shortly after as Langley clears his throat.

"There's something else," he begins with a hint of uncertainty. "I guess the time for disguises is over, right?"

"Langley? What is it?"

"That's not my name." His feet retreat, crunching over debris. "My name is Warner. You deserve to know that."

Bombshell dropped, he hastily leaves. The silence stretches on until the sound of the exit door slamming shut breaks it. Ripley is leaning so heavily into me, I wonder how she's upright at all.

"What now?" Ripley murmurs.

"Now we wait. And try not to die."

"Fuck," she whispers back.

Yep. Fuck indeed.

CHAPTER 9
RIPLEY

GOD NEEDS THE DEVIL – JONAH
KAGEN

ROLLING OVER on the folded cardboard box I'm using as a mattress, I tighten a stolen green parka around myself, ignoring the pain from my shoulder and hip digging into the hard floor.

Even if I were comfortable, I'm too agitated to sleep. The invisible fire ants are back. After a week since my last medication dose, it's inevitable. I'm surprised it took this long to set in.

I've managed to keep the signs to myself so far. Shaking hands. Agitation. Rising anxiety. I thought I'd adjust, but if this is an impending manic episode, I won't be able to keep it quiet.

The sounds of sleep around me offer a small sliver of comfort. Raine and Lennox are both napping while waiting for daylight. We've been taking refuge around the abandoned pool for the last two days, living off odd snacks shared between all four of us.

Warner hasn't returned.

Each passing hour is excruciating.

I can only assume that something went wrong, but when I suggested I go look, it was met with a resounding chorus of denials. Even from Raine. Xander stormed off to skulk around the abandoned building when I raised it again a while ago.

When did I sign up for three possessive men to tell me what I can and can't do? Even if I did barter for their lives, it doesn't give them the right to start this controlling shit. Our truce won't last long if this continues.

"I can practically hear the gears in your brain grinding," Raine whispers into the early dawn light. "Did you sleep at all?"

"How am I supposed to sleep?" I growl back.

"Typically, it involves closing your eyes, getting comfortable, dreaming about a stunningly attractive, blind violinist who can make your wildest dreams come true with his tongue…"

"Ha. Someone thinks highly of himself."

"That's not a disagreement. So you do love my tongue."

Huffing, I awkwardly turn over to face him. Raine is sleeping next to me, less than a metre between our cardboard boxes. Lennox opted to sleep beside him, still keeping a safe distance from me.

Raine is curled up on his side, the rich caramel of his unfocused eyes gleaming in the morning light. Beneath his golden locks sticking up in all directions, his gaze bounces around haphazardly.

"We can't just lay here and wait forever," I hiss under my breath. "What if he's been captured by Rick's merry band of idiots? Or he's injured? Or…"

"Rip," Raine interrupts. "Time out. Langley—or Warner —he's a big boy. He can look out for himself. You going out there is a shitty idea that we've already proven sucks."

"He needs our help!"

"We need to help ourselves," he disagrees. "That starts with laying low until we have a decent plan. The longer this goes on, the worse it's going to get."

Deep down, I know Raine's right. The nightly screams now bleed into daytime. From our hiding spot, I've heard bonfires crackling outside at all hours, the smoke leaking in through the broken roof and windows.

For the last two nights, we've been plunged into darkness to preserve our waning flashlight. The pitch-black cloak only intensifies the awful sounds all around us.

I've startled awake to wailing and sobbing several times. Sounds of people being assaulted. More brutal fights. Starving patients are turning to desperate measures to ride the riot out.

Something has to give. If Incendia's plan is to wait this out, it isn't working. Exhaustion and hunger aren't starving out the violence; it's just fuelling it. And Harrowdean's patient population has plenty to be angry about.

"How long was the longest prison riot? Like, ever?"

"In this country?" Raine questions. "I dunno. A couple weeks, maybe?"

"We've been trapped in limbo for almost a whole week now. It won't last much longer, surely?"

Skin prickling with trapped energy, I begin to scratch at my arms and neck, savouring the bite of pain. My injuries are healing well as the evidence of our torture slowly disappears. The memories remain just as raw, though.

I've seen the shadows in Lennox's eyes. He blinks them away when he catches me staring and always averts his gaze. We've woken up to the sound of him thrashing about in nightmare-filled sleep multiple times too.

The back and forth of my ping-ponging thoughts is only worsened by the physical symptoms I'm trying to ignore. I scratch my arms to the point of bleeding, watching the blood vessels burst in bright-purple streaks.

"Rip," Raine croons.

Ignoring him, I keep scratching. Harder. Rougher. My skin stains red from abrasions. The thick, gnarly scars beneath my touch are a harsh taunt. *Harrowdean's whore.* I've memorised each letter by touch alone.

Look at her now.

I'm a fucking coward.

With each second ticking away, I can feel the devil breathing down our necks. But in this case, the devil has a human face. One that now infiltrates every restful moment I manage to find.

Bancroft won't let me go unpunished. My uncle told me enough stories about his associate long before I experienced his cold calculation firsthand. He rules the corporation with an iron fist.

Now he's out there. Plotting and moving his chess pieces into place. I'll never take his silence for defeat. It's deliberate. The calm before a violent storm that destroys everything in its path.

Is my uncle helping him now?

Will he cheer Bancroft on when I'm sacrificed?

"Rip! Come here."

The sharp snap of Raine's command interrupts my downward spiral. I look over at him, sitting up and wearing a concerned frown that's directed in my vicinity.

"Now," he adds.

Blinking hard, I move robotically. My stiff body protests as I crawl over to him on quivering limbs. Raine grunts when I slam into him, climbing onto his lap and banding my legs around his waist.

"Shit, babe. You're shaking."

He strokes my back, letting me plaster against his chest like a fucking limpet. I want to crawl inside his skin and hide there until this is all over. I don't have to be brave around him.

"I'm scared," I admit shakily. "I can't hide it anymore."

I've spent years burying my fear, pretending to be some formidable badass, when deep down I'm just fucking terrified. I trust Raine to understand and protect that vulnerability.

"Breathe, Rip. I know how hard this is. We have to sit tight."

"Breathe?" I laugh. "We're going to die!"

"We're not going to die."

"Says who?"

"Says me," Raine insists fiercely. "You need to calm down."

Rocking back and forth, his attempts to soothe me fall on deaf ears. I may not be thinking logically, but my sudden urgency to be anywhere but here makes complete sense to my overwhelmed mind.

My head feels like it's on fire. The slow burn of rising hysteria only needed acknowledging for it to take full control. It's rushing in now, setting aflame anything in its path and gathering speed with each second.

We're running out of food. Freezing cold and constantly soaking wet. No medication. We have just a single flashlight with very limited life remaining. No plan for rescue or escape. Even Raine's withdrawal meds are running low.

My big, grand decision not to run is going to get us all quietly killed. That's how they'll keep our stories silent, and there's nothing I can do to stop it. We'll be forgotten. Erased. The slate wiped clean like it always is.

"Ripley," Raine urges. "Come back. I'm here. You're safe."

"We are not safe!"

"From the world? Fuck no." He chuckles bitterly. "But you'll always be safe with me."

I want that to be enough. It *is* enough. All I've ever wanted, beneath the role I've played, is for someone to make me feel safe in a world determined to prove otherwise. But I want Raine safe too, and that won't happen here.

"Come on, babe." Sliding a hand into my hair, he gently massages my head. "Focus on my voice. Can you feel my breathing?"

"Yes," I gasp.

"Good girl. Pay attention to it. I want you to block everything else out. It's just us."

Squeezing my eyes shut, I focus on the feel of his body pressing into mine. The lines I've memorised over the weeks and months. Soft angles. Muscled ridges. The smell of fresh oranges and tangy sea salt.

In a terrifying world, Raine is a solid constant. The confident, smirking jokester hiding a lifetime of trauma behind blacked-out lenses. Everything about him defies the odds. He's living proof of human resilience.

It's what first intrigued me, back when he was just another patient, sniffing around for contraband. The silver-tongued flirt with all the right words. Every syllable interwoven with deep, irrecoverable pain.

"Don't let the fear win, Rip. We're all afraid. Defeated. Exhausted. That just means we're winning the fight—because we're still alive to feel all those things."

"For how much longer?" I squirm on his lap.

"That I can't say. But I think every single one of us has proven that we're kinda difficult to kill. We've all survived shit beyond most people's worst nightmares. We can survive this too."

His fingers pressing into my skull causes me to flinch. My body is wound so tight, every small sensation is agonisingly intense. I don't know if I need to fight, fuck or flee. I'm longing for the oblivion of sedatives.

"Tell me what you need," Raine begs.

I can't possibly answer him, and the stirrings of another prevent me from having to confess.

"What's going on?" Lennox asks groggily.

With his long limbs stretched out, it takes him a moment to sit upright. He blinks rapidly to clear his seafoam eyes. Spotting me in Raine's lap, his spine stiffens.

"What is it?"

"She's okay," Raine replies in a gravelly rasp. "Just… struggling."

"Struggling?" I let out a strangled sound.

"You're supposed to be breathing, Rip. Not arguing."

"While we're sitting here waiting to be slaughtered? And Warner is out there risking his life! This is fucking stupid!"

When I try to climb off Raine's lap, determined to do what's necessary to abate the storm brewing beneath my skin, I find myself trapped.

"Stay." His arms imprison me in a steel cage, pinning me to his chest. "You're not going anywhere until you've calmed down."

"You can't fucking make me, Raine! I need… I can't… I…"

Running out of words, tears hit me hard and fast. The wave of mental torture rises from a deep well, a poisonous smog that gains speed until it's sweeping over me in a pyroclastic cloud.

"She's losing it." Lennox narrows his gaze on me.

"No shit, Sherlock. You want to try?"

"Isn't she your problem?"

The cruel bite of his words lashes into me, slashing skin and bone. Turning my tear-blurred gaze on Lennox, I want him to see just how much power the heartless bastard holds.

The power to heal.

The power to break.

The power to end it all.

"I c-could've run and left you to die," I snarl at him. "I could've been f-fucking free and safe right now."

"Maybe you should have gone," he replies softly.

"Is that what you want, Nox? To be rid of me?"

Sitting up straighter, he scrubs his hand down his face, careful to avoid the gauze on his cheek. Frustration quickens my pulse when I don't get the answer I want.

The old Lennox was as cruel as he was sadistic. That in

itself was safe. Predictable. Not this weird, introspective in between who runs so hot and cold.

"Answer me!" I thrash in Raine's arms.

"If it means you're safe, then yes!" Lennox suddenly yells back. "That's what I want! You... gone!"

The tears filling my eyes run over like burst riverbanks, the hot dribbles coating my cheeks and jaw. For once, Lennox stares back without flinching. A turbulent hurricane swirls in his conflicted gaze.

"Nox," Raine scolds. "Shut up."

"She asked for an answer."

"You didn't have to give that one! Fuck!"

Looking at Raine, the mental assault only intensifies. I'm surrounded by my failure on all sides. The man I saved who doesn't want me and the one who wants me so much I've ruined his life.

"I'm going to find Warner." I wipe my tears aside.

"No." Raine refuses to release his grip. "You're staying right here."

"Let me go! Now!"

"He doesn't speak for me, guava girl. I'm selfish enough to admit I want you here, even if it means you're in the firing line with us. At least we're together."

Raine's head lowers to my chest, the only place he can reach as I continue to fight his hold. I'd expect this from one of the others, but not my Raine. I hate how this horror show is changing us all.

He kisses my chest and clavicles exposed by the loose t-shirt's neckline. The small, simple touches are an attempt to distract me from spiralling.

"I know you're scared," he breathes into my skin. "But you didn't make a mistake by choosing to stay. You chose us."

Each kiss he lavishes me with drives his words home. I hate that Lennox is sitting right there, witnessing our intimacy, yet I'm also glad he's forced to see what he'll never have.

"Let us choose you back," Raine pleads. "Let us carry the burden with you. Let us help you get through this."

Lips coasting up my neck then skimming my jaw, I pour all my focus into the feel of his touch. Each gentle, delicate kiss. I home in on the way it contrasts the hatred I still feel pouring from Lennox's glower.

"Raine," I whine. "We have company."

"Ignore him, babe. Let the asshole see exactly what he's missing because he's being too stubborn to change."

Then his lips meet mine—plush and attentive. Raine pushes his mouth on mine to drive out every last horrid thought causing me to fracture. The kiss is passionate, demanding, full of desperation.

Pressure sears into the side of my head, intensifying Raine's firm kiss. I know Lennox is watching intently. What I don't know is how he's going to react. Not anymore.

Hysteria turns red-hot and liquifies as it fills my veins. Treacle-like heat pumps through me, warming my extremities even in the building's chill. I can feel every solid inch of Raine beneath me.

His tongue glides into my mouth, exploring every corner in his bid to pull me back from the brink. The fire ants morph into tiny, pleasurable explosions that cause my hips to shift.

I think I hear Lennox choke on a breath. Yet I couldn't care less. Not when Raine responds in kind and bucks up into me, the heat from his growing erection hitting my core.

"Rip," he breaks the kiss to rasp. "Let's… just take a minute. You're upset."

"Shut up, Raine."

Glancing to the side, I lock onto Lennox's hard stare. The column of heat stirring the still waters in his eyes encourages me to slam my lips back on Raine's mouth.

Fuck him.

He doesn't want me?

Fine. Raine does.

I don't care if it's the adrenaline talking. If a week of barely sleeping has frayed my sanity and I'm on the verge of an unmedicated breakdown. I need this release. Just the thought of it is already loosening my lungs.

Grinding on his hardening cock, I enjoy each toe-curling spike the friction brings. A groan builds in Raine's throat as he kisses me back, painting a bruise onto my lips.

His grip has slackened so he can clutch my hips, giving me room to touch him. I drag my hands down his chest, stopping at the waistband of the borrowed jeans he still wears.

I make short work of unclasping the button and pushing a hand inside. Lennox can continue watching if he likes. He can also fuck off to kingdom come for all I care.

Shifting backwards, I guide Raine's length free from his jeans. He groans when my hand clasps around his velvety cock, stroking the shaft in a slow tease.

"Watch your friend fuck my throat, Nox," I taunt brazenly. "Watch what I let him do to me. Watch what you could be doing… if only you cared."

Kneeling in front of Raine, I drag my tongue across his entire length, from tip to base. His cock jerks in my hands in time to his hissed breathing.

I don't spare Lennox a single glance as I suck Raine deep into my mouth. When his tip nudges the back of my throat, I lift my head, swirling my tongue back up to the end before taking him deep once more.

"Goddammit," Raine grinds out. "You're going to be the death of me."

Not him.

Just his asshole friend.

With each suck, I rotate my head to lick around his engorged cock. The light scrape of teeth causes Raine to curse again. Hearing him moaning in pleasure only spurs me on.

I'm going to make him fill my mouth with his seed just so

Lennox can see me swallow it. If he wants to play mind games, I can give just as good as I get.

Raine fists a hand in my short hair, using his grip to guide my movements. Each time he pushes me down, his hips lift to glide in deeper. I happily let him fuck my mouth.

Each thrust makes moisture gather in the corners of my eyes. I don't mind his roughness, though. I want Raine to feel good, to let go even if only for a second. For the burdens he's carried for me, he deserves no less.

"That's it," he encourages in a low rasp. "You take me so well, babe."

The burn of each pump is oh-so-satisfying. I love that he's completely disregarding Lennox and taking exactly what he wants. Something tells me Raine is just as mad as I am at the stubborn bastard.

Each tug on my short curls makes warmth pool at the apex of my thighs. I'm already clenched tight with need. At this rate, I'll let him strip me bare, bend me over and fuck me on full display.

In my periphery, I can see Lennox is unmoved. The man's frozen to the spot. He doesn't even have the shame to look away. I feel fucking powerful, yet I hate myself at the same time for even caring.

"Rip," Raine moans languidly.

His jean-clad thighs are tensing beneath my palms, telling me he's close. Increasing my speed, I'm determined to wring every drop of bliss from him. I want his complete and utter surrender.

"I'm going to pour myself down your throat, guava girl."

His cock jerks in my mouth, spasming with the force of his orgasm. My pussy quivers at the sensation of driving Raine to the brink. I don't stop sucking until he groans loudly, the hot spurts of his seed hitting my throat.

His painfully tight clasp on my hair loosens. Stilling, I slowly pull my mouth from Raine's cock, wiping at my bottom lip with a single finger. He's a panting mess beneath me, his liquid gold gaze burning bright.

I tilt my head to see Lennox. Eyes narrowed. Lips wet. Two wide pupils melt the skin from my bones with the violence of an acid attack. He doesn't blink as I make a show of swallowing Raine's come.

"Are you still here?" I ask bluntly.

Lips parted, Lennox sits stock-still. Stares. Falters.

"You may want me gone, but I'm right where I belong." I refuse to look away from him. "You're the one who should go if you don't want this."

His mouth opens and closes, like words are forming on the tip of his tongue. His facial expression twists and transforms, rapidly shifting between anger, lust and… Is that jealousy? Oh, fucking perfect. He's pathetic.

Squirming with need, I'm tempted to let Raine return the favour. Would that cause Lennox to relent? Seeing me ride his friend's face? I want to know just how far I can push him before he breaks.

"Rip." Lennox's lips form a narrow strip of anger. "I—"

The doors to the swimming pool being tossed open cuts him off. Xander runs in, his face flushed. He skids to a halt as Raine quickly rights himself, zipping up his jeans.

"Helicopters overhead," Xander rushes out.

"What?" Raine gasps.

"I was on the roof. I counted dozens of men, armed and wearing protective gear. The journalists have all been cleared out. Their weapons… I saw bullets."

"Bullets?" I repeat.

"This isn't a rescue mission. They're going to storm the institute and clear it out by force. No cameras, no witnesses."

"Shit." Lennox gapes at him. "What do we do?"

"We need to move. Now."

Focusing on me, Xander's face is grave.

"Incendia is coming."

CHAPTER 10
RIPLEY

OUT OF STYLE – KID BRUNSWICK
& BEAUTY SCHOOL DROPOUT

I'M ALWAYS PREPARED.

Harrowdean was my grand master plan.

Shoving dirty clothes, half-filled water bottles and the last of our scavenged supplies into my backpack, I realise how far I've fallen. My grand fucking plan lies in tatters. Along with my entire life.

I thought I had it all figured out. For a whole year, I made myself untouchable. Above reproach. An object of terror and fascination. That power was heady, but now I'm paying the ultimate price.

We're fleeing for our lives.

Lost, traumatised and alone.

"Pack faster!" Xander barks. "We need to move."

I accidentally drop the last remaining bag of sweets we have in our stash. The bag hits the floor, but before I can scoop it up, a bandaged hand grabs the bag for me.

"Here," Lennox mutters gruffly.

Snatching the sweets from his grasp, I shove them in the backpack. "Where the hell are we going to go?"

"I don't know."

"Then we shouldn't be running at all!"

"They're not coming in peacefully," he states plainly. "Weapons and riot gear hardly spell out a calm, orderly evacuation."

Avoiding looking at him, I continue shoving everything I can lay my hands on into the bag. Terror has condensed into laser-sharp focus. Adrenaline has a way of simplifying even the most complex emotions.

"Has anyone seen my guide stick and glasses?" Panic drips from Raine's words.

"Go help him." I gesture wildly.

Lennox straightens then moves to help Raine locate his belongings. After the show I just put on, being thrown into a life-and-death situation with him feels like a bad joke.

"Are we ready?" Xander questions.

"Warner's still out there." I zip the backpack and toss it over my shoulder. "We need to find him."

"There isn't time." He grimaces, shifting on his feet. "They'll breach the gates at any moment. We have to leave now before it's too late."

"And go where?" Raine asks timidly.

"I don't know… but if we stay, we'll be killed. Therefore, we run."

"This isn't a time for your stone-cold logic, Xan!" I snap at him. "Rick and the others swore to kill the hostages if anyone entered Harrowdean."

"I'm aware."

"If they've captured Warner… he's as good as dead."

"How is that our problem?" Xander throws his hands in the air.

"He's my friend!"

"Your friend didn't come back," Lennox interjects. "Perhaps his priorities lie elsewhere."

I flash him a furious look. "I'm not leaving without him."

"Would you prefer to stay here and be shot between the eyes when those men storm the institute?" Xander clips out.

"Obviously not!" I explode. "But... fuck! Where can we run? We have nothing. No money. Nowhere to go. We need Warner."

"Incendia's men are here to get the hostages out alive," Xander reasons. "If Warner has been captured, he'll be rescued. If he's in hiding, he'll be safe soon enough. Unlike us."

He's lying through his fucking teeth right now. There's no guarantee Warner will make it out alive, even if reinforcements have arrived. I don't even know if his cover is intact or if Incendia will kill him too.

"Xander's right." Lennox taps Raine's hand to pass his located items. "If we stay, we'll be dead by nightfall. Either way, we can't help him from here."

"So what? We make a run for it?" I laugh.

"I'll die running before I die on my knees." Xander picks up a bag and swings it over his shoulder. "They're storming the gates. No one is watching the perimeter."

Raine unfolds his guide stick as Lennox takes a final look around. We're running dangerously low on essentials. This plan sounds a lot like suicide. I don't know if we can even get beyond the perimeter fence.

"Let's move." Xander casts a final glance around. "No splitting up, no one gets left behind. Remove anyone who gets in the way."

"No!" I protest. "We said we'd stay and fight. I'm not running scared!"

Tapping his way over to me, Raine clasps my face. He softly strokes my cold skin, his sunglass-covered eyes reflecting my own terror back at me.

"We can't fight this if we're dead," he says quietly. "I want to see Incendia taken down too. Of course, I do. But this isn't the place to do it."

"But—"

"Please, Rip. We have to go. I need you to be safe, not

killed by Harrowdean's thugs or captured by the authorities investigating them. Then we can fight this war until the end."

Strangled by miniature knives cutting into my lungs, I can only nod. The words refuse to surface. Xander turns to leave as Lennox claps Raine on the shoulder.

"I'll take the rear," he announces. "Xan, help Raine."

Throwing me a loaded look, Lennox waits for me to step past him before slipping in behind. Xander leads the way out of the main swimming pool room with Raine, through the mould-ridden corridors and outside.

We step into the crisp dawn air as a group, all on high-alert. This part of the institute is always quiet, shrouded in mist and ominously swaying willow trees that obscure the outside world.

The abandoned swimming pool is surrounded by older, disused buildings separate from the main manor. I'm not surprised there aren't any other patients hanging around, though signs of destruction litter the grounds.

"Jesus," Lennox grunts behind me. "Did they leave any furniture inside?"

Eyeing a nearby smouldering bonfire with a blackened bed frame still intact, I choke on the cloying ash that hangs in the air. The destruction has gone beyond a defiant PR stunt now.

Loud humming rings above us through the interlocking birch trees. We're still tucked into the dense foliage that hides the abandoned building, giving us a precious few seconds to take in the scene.

"Our best bet is the rear fence on the south side of the property." Xander studies the landscape. "Farthest away from where all the attention is right now."

"What if they're patrolling the perimeter?" Raine whispers fearfully.

"We can handle it," Lennox answers.

I snort in amusement. "With your one working hand?"

Before Lennox can snark back, Xander intervenes. "Focus. We don't have much time."

We form a makeshift human chain, picking through the barbed shrubbery. Above us, spinning rotors seal our fate. We all knew the riot would end, but this doesn't sound like a resolution.

It's a massacre.

The last act of a crumbling regime.

The corporation has the power and reach to spin the narrative. It's the same game they've been playing for decades to cover up their brutality. All the world will hear is how they liberated Harrowdean and saved the innocent hostages.

Keeping close to Xander and Raine, my head is on a swivel as we creep forward. Far-off shouts pierce the sound of helicopters flying low overhead. It isn't long before we find our first group of patients.

Instantly, I spot Luka and his corridor hook-up among them. They seem to be searching for a hiding place, all wearing matching expressions of pure terror.

In the distance, the sound of metal screeching as entry is forced indicates the countdown to anarchy. Harrowdean's gates are being wrenched open. The cavalry has arrived.

"They're coming!" Kitty, one of the younger girls, wails in a panic. "We have to hide!"

Despite being adults—though some barely—they're too young to be caught in this situation. Doomed to endure violence and persecution simply because their brains work differently.

"Over there!" I yell at them, pointing to my left. "There's a building hidden by the trees! Hide inside!"

His gaze colliding with mine, Luka gulps hard. We're not supplier and customer anymore. Now we're just two petrified humans, tied to the same deadly train tracks. I nod at him, and he dips his chin in respect.

They disperse to hide, allowing us to continue fleeing.

Raine puts his total trust in Xander as he runs without using his stick, guided by the elbow he's gripping hard.

We've passed several buildings and found the path that leads to the southern side of the grounds when the first shots ring out. Undeniably real. My pulse ratchets—we're being fired at in broad daylight.

"Fucking guns?" Raine shouts. "What are they thinking?"

"They don't care anymore!" Lennox yells behind me. "Go, go, go!"

The world whizzes past me in a blur of fear and shock. As more patients pour out of the manor, fleeing into the grounds to escape the onslaught, I catch a flash of auburn hair from a distance.

"Rae!" I shout helplessly.

Before I can skid to a halt, I'm shoved forward.

"Don't you dare stop," Lennox barks into my ear. "I'll throw you over my shoulder if I have to!"

He pushes me again, forcing me to continue running. The brief sighting of Rae vanishes as we're swallowed by dense trees. Harrowdean's gothic outline melts into the forest's shadows.

"The perimeter is through here." Xander slows a little to help Raine dodge a tall juniper tree. "Stay close."

Not even the forest that encases the institute in mist-soaked mystery can silence the sounds of destruction. Shouts, screams and distant cries for help still reach our ears, carried by a cold wind.

"They can't just kill patients indiscriminately." Raine puffs in exertion. "Surely?"

"Who's going to dispute the lies they'll spin?" Xander replies curtly. "The corporation has total impunity. It always has."

"Not anymore," I pant back. "We are going to shout the truth so loudly, the world will have to listen to us."

I'm so focused on Raine and the death-grip he holds on

Xander's elbow that I don't see the huge tree root jutting out of the ground until it's too late. My foot catches, sending me tumbling forwards.

Before I can smash face first into the mossy forest floor, two strong iron bands capture me from behind. I hang suspended, cinched tightly by tanned biceps. There's a low, disapproving rumble from behind me.

"Watch your step."

Lennox pulls me upright, setting me back on my feet. He doesn't release me at first. Instead, his arms squeeze tighter, holding my back to his broad chest. I feel his breath stirring in my hair.

"Thanks," I mutter. "You can let go."

In all the madness, his scent still registers. It's rare that I'm close enough to drink in its intoxication. Lennox smells like summer campfires and musky, burning wood, carried into my senses like curling smoke.

His one unbandaged hand is balled into a fist above my stomach, making the scar tissue that disfigures his knuckles stand out. He twists the front of my t-shirt before blowing out a tense breath.

"You need to be more careful."

Releasing my t-shirt, Lennox's arms vanish. I immediately miss the firm press of his steel-carved muscles around me. The same arms that held me close the last time we faced death.

"Come on!" Xander bellows at us.

I look up at Lennox, his vast height towering above me. Two pale-green orbs stare back, the ever-present, burning hatred now awash with more concern and mind-bending tenderness than I can fathom.

"Look where you're going," he grumbles. "Now move."

With a far gentler push, Lennox encourages me to continue following. There isn't time to consider my actions. I reach down and grab his huge hand, forcing his fingers to wrap around mine.

Nostrils flaring in surprise, he glances at me. I stare back for a prolonged moment, allowing him to see my warring emotions.

Perhaps this is all we'll ever be.

Simply each other's means of survival.

Rushing to catch up, we find Xander and Raine as the trees begin to thin out. The cloudy morning sky emerges once more, penetrating the thick canopy overhead. With it comes the sight we've been searching for.

Glinting barbed wire. Sharp spikes. The metal monstrosity stretches at least ten feet tall, topped with deadly razor points and an array of security cameras. I don't have time to worry about whether they're working.

"Shit." Lennox comes to a halt.

"Yeah," Xander replies tersely. "It's high."

"Can we even climb that?"

"We have no choice," I answer them. "Be thankful it isn't electrified with the power still out."

"Hate to be the voice of doom and all," Raine vocalises. "But I can't climb shit. Not without being able to see it."

Glancing between us and the fence, Xander taps his lips, falling into deep concentration. Our options are limited. We climb or stay. Run or surrender. Die falling or die kneeling. That damn fence can't stop us now.

"Xander goes first with Lennox." I eye the towering fence. "He's still one-handed. Then I'll support Raine on this side. Xander guides him down the other, and I'll climb last."

"Forget it," Xander snarls.

Lennox glowers at me like I just suggested something utterly insane. "We are not leaving you standing here alone."

"Agreed," Raine parrots.

"We don't have time to argue!" I look around the circle. "This is the only way it'll work. So climb!"

They exchange grim looks. Raine remains silent, but eventually, Lennox and Xander both stiffen as they seem to reach the same conclusion. It's this or nothing; we don't have time to find another solution.

Xander's subsequent choice of curse words raises even Lennox's eyebrows. Resolving himself to this decision, the iceman goes first, peering up at the individual chain-links and looming spikes.

"Wait!" I quickly pull off my green parka to hand over. "Tie this around your waist. You can cover the spikes."

He accepts the thick coat, quickly looping it around himself. Xander hoists the backpack higher on his shoulder then begins to deftly hoist himself up, link by link, causing the fence to groan.

At the top, he drops the backpack over the other side. It lands with a hollow thunk. Xander braces himself in place to spread the parka over the spikes, offering some minor protection.

"Alright," he calls down. "Nox."

Stepping up, Lennox follows his lead. It's a torturously slow process, heaving himself up each inch with his bad hand curled into his chest. I internally panic each time he falters, almost losing his grip.

Halfway up, Xander stretches out a hand, intending to grab him. Lennox tentatively raises his injured limb, allowing Xander to snag his wrist above the bandage and pull.

"What's happening?" Raine asks anxiously.

"Xander has him. They're almost over."

The pair tackle the top together, Xander guiding Lennox over the spiked barbed wire, now hidden beneath feather-filled fabric. Lennox grunts when a sharp tip pierces through the coat and catches his inner leg.

"A few steps down then jump," Xander advises from his perch. "I've got Raine."

Knowing that's my cue, I nudge Raine forward. "You're up."

He folds his guide stick then tucks it into his waistband,

taking small steps forward. I help him hook his fingers into the criss-crossed metal and locate his first foothold.

"Go slow. Xander will grab you, alright?"

"Sure," Raine chirps. "Fucking brilliant."

"I'll catch you if you fall."

"I'd crush you, guava girl."

"I'd let you do that too."

With a tiny, forced smile, he starts to move. The process of feeling out each slot to nudge his foot into is painstaking. Raine has to blindly locate each metal link all while finding where to put his hands.

"Higher," I call to him. "Left foot."

"Almost there," Xander adds, still teetering up high.

When Raine's foot slips and he begins to fall, the scream trapped in my chest surges to the forefront. My vision narrows to the sight of him plummeting.

"Not so fast!"

Grabbing a covered spike for better balance, Xander swoops his top half low to reach Raine. I watch his mouth contort in an agonised grimace. He just manages to grab the scruff of Raine's t-shirt to steady him.

"Raine!" Lennox bellows.

He dangles for a horrifying split-second until his feet miraculously find a hold. Raine flattens himself against the security fence, gulping down air.

"Move," Xander shouts in a strained voice. "Now!"

I can see blood pouring from Xander's palm from here, the bright-red spill trailing down his forearm and elbow in swirling ribbons. He's clutching a spike to stop Raine from falling.

Lennox's face drains of colour as he watches in clear horror, unable to intervene. We can only stand and fret as Raine resumes climbing, step by treacherous step.

"Are you bleeding?" I hear him exclaim.

"Climb over, dammit."

"I can smell your blood, Xan!"

"Just hurry!"

At the top, Xander braces Raine to allow him to hook a leg over the barbed wire. My throat closes up as I watch both of them teetering, narrowly avoiding any further cuts or injuries.

My attention is dragged away from them by the sound of raised voices, leaking from the woodland directly behind me. It sounds a lot like orders being screamed.

"Incoming!" I cry out. "Get down, now!"

Encouraging Raine to drop down the other side, Xander watches him descend then drop to the grass beside Lennox. He barely spares his bleeding hand a second glance as he starts to descend after Raine.

"Ripley!" he thunders.

"I'm coming!"

I secure my backpack tight, already climbing up the same route the others took. The fence flexes and bends beneath my weight, the metal protesting at the violation. This is harder than it looks.

My fingers ache, pain slicing into my joints from the pressure caused by gripping such thin, inflexible metal. It's slick too, making me slip several times, barely clinging on for dear life.

"Faster, Rip," Xander calls from the bottom. "I see movement."

"I'm coming! Go take cover!"

"Take Raine and run!" Lennox shouts at him. "I've got her."

"No," Xander roars back.

"Go! You need more time to guide him!"

Xander reluctantly grabs hold of Raine and makes a beeline for the woodland that surrounds the institute. Raine tries to fight against him, shouting my name, but fails to break free.

Reaching the top in record time, I swing my legs over the barbed wire then toss the torn parka down to Lennox. He catches it, checking to verify that Xander and Raine have made it to safety.

"Go!" I scream down to him.

"Not without you! Shift your ass!"

I quickly drop the backpack to free up my movements. Just a few more steps down and I can jump the rest. Preparing to move, my blood freezes into a solid mass in my veins when a voice calls out.

"Ripley Bennet!"

Teetering, I almost lose balance at the sound of the familiar sneer. I find my next footing, risking a look over the other side of the fence. Four men have broken free from the forest.

Elon's smarmy grin hasn't changed. It still sits proudly on his face beneath gunmetal eyes that hold no mercy and his stern, military-cut hair. The sick fuck's even freshly shaven for the occasion.

He cups his hands around his mouth. "Long time no see, inmate!"

The three men with him are all dressed like something out of a prison escape movie. Thick, padded black clothing and stab proof vests. Holsters loaded with weapons—batons, tasers and guns. They came prepared.

"You look awfully uncomfortable up there," he jeers. "Fancy hopping down to have a little chat with me and my friends?"

My grip on the chain-links tightens. "Alternatively you could go join your other friend, Harrison, in the Z wing. I heard he's floating in a tub down there!"

The smirk wipes clean from his face. Elon clenches his stubbled jaw, a hand resting on the gun slotted into his holster.

"Fun's over, Ripley. I have one job today and not a whole

lot of time to do it. You're on my list of loose ends to clean up."

Below me, I can see Lennox still lingering. He should've run to safety and joined the others. Instead, he looks up at me imploringly, his hands spread wide in a clear message. I watch his lips move.

Jump.

The metallic click of a gun causes my head to snap back up. Elon has released his weapon and holds it aimed at me. His lascivious smile makes his intentions crystal clear.

"I'm under no obligation to bring you back alive," he gloats. "Though I'm sure the boss will be disappointed that he won't get the chance to deal with you himself."

Looking back and forth, my options are shitty. Fall and pray that Lennox catches me. Stay and get shot. Surrender to Elon and his sycophants. Karma is truly kicking me in the ass with these choices.

"Come on, Rip," Elon cajoles. "You know we will always find you, no matter where you run."

"Good luck with that, asshole!"

"You're a part of this. The world wants your head too."

"Don't listen to him," Lennox clamours.

It's too late to stop the seed of doubt from blooming. We may be jumping from the frying pan into the flames. The outside world holds no more safety than Harrowdean's crumbling ruins.

I'm their enemy too. Society will never understand the horrors we've endured. We don't fit into their cookie-cutter reality. Staying here to scream our innocence until we're quietly killed isn't happening, though.

"You're right!" I reposition myself, legs spread apart and shoulders squared. "I'll be labelled as a monster when the truth comes out. The world will burn me right alongside the corporation."

My grip on the chain-links loosens.

"But the least I can do is destroy the evil I've enabled before that day comes. I can atone."

Trees, clouds and four shocked faces become a fast-moving blur. I'm airborne. Free-falling. The ground rushes up to meet me, approaching in rapid flash frames.

BANG. BANG. BANG.

The feel of a bullet whooshing past me registers in drunken slow motion. Rushing air. Loud popping. Something else sails past me. But the third and final bullet doesn't miss.

I don't process the fierce bite of being shot at first. Not until the burning sensation becomes a deep, excruciating laser beam carving into my flesh.

The thin air doesn't cushion my fall.

Something else does.

Our bodies audibly smack together. Faintly, I hear someone bellow loudly in pain as we both crumple. I should feel the impact more, but all that exists is the radiating agony in my inflamed thigh.

More vision-blurring pain slams into me as I'm jostled in a pair of thick arms, the muscular cushion beneath me attempting to shift. Crackling bonfires and woodsy smoke filter into my nostrils.

Lennox.

"Fuck," he wheezes. "That hurt."

Yelling voices feed back in. We need to move, but for the life of me, I can't lift a single limb. Not with my body succumbing to weakness. I'm barely able to hold my eyelids open as adrenaline pours out of me.

"Xan! Help us!"

Reality keeps flashing in and out. Lennox's body trapped beneath me shakes, attempting to wrestle his way up with the new bruises I've given him. When the world reappears, I feel myself being lifted.

"Give her to me."

"No." Lennox's tone is strained. "I'm carrying her."

"Nox—"

"Let's move!"

More darkness. An inky pond pulling me into its all-consuming depths. Light eventually filters back in, and this time, I can tell we're running fast.

Wind whipping and voices bellowing. More bullets. Distant shouts. Crunching footsteps. Birch trees reappear all around us.

I'm cradled safely into a firm chest.

Broad. Warm. Adorned with military dog tags.

I'm… safe.

"Hold on, Rip," Lennox whispers raggedly. "I've got you."

CHAPTER 11
LENNOX
IN YOUR ARMS – CROIXX

RIPLEY'S round curves are featherlight in my arms. She's too small. Dainty. A delicate, tattooed shell holding so much beautiful fury. The same fury I've tasted first-hand.

I still wonder how such a tiny body can hold all that rage. What I wouldn't give for her to peel open her angry, hazel eyes and curse me out right now. I'd take any insult she wants to lash me with.

She can beat me black, blue and every shade of the fucking rainbow if she so pleases. As long as she's awake. As long as she's alive. Then we can go back to hating each other. I'll give her that.

"Is it clear?" I heave in exertion.

Xander peers through a dirt-streaked window, the thick cobwebs obscuring our view of the other farm buildings we stumbled across. We must've walked for miles before exiting the forest and finding signs of life.

"Helicopter still overhead."

"The same one?" Raine asks tiredly.

"Looks like it. They're circling the area."

Cradling Ripley close, I keep my uninjured hand clamped on her upper thigh. The bleeding has slowed to a sluggish trickle. Xander tore up one of our spare shirts to tie a tourniquet before bandaging his own hand.

She's still lost a considerable amount of blood, enough for her to keep dropping in and out during the hours we've been stealthily moving. I can feel it sticking to me, saturating my already filthy clothing.

"It's been hours." Raine rests nearby, keeping a hand on Ripley's pulse. "They'll give up soon."

"You think Incendia cares about a private helicopter bill?" Xander ridicules. "That wanker Elon said it himself. We're loose ends."

Back pressed against the wall, I glance down at Ripley again. Her sweetheart-shaped face is ashen. Waxy. The bullet passed straight through—I found the exit wound. That doesn't make blood loss any less deadly.

It's a miracle we escaped at all without catching another bullet. They sure fired enough of them after us before attempting to scale the security fence. I caught a glimpse of an over-confident guard falling on his ass before we made a run for it.

I have no doubt they eventually followed. On foot as well as in the air. The near-impenetrable woodland that keeps Harrowdean Manor secure from the outside world did us a favour. It was easy to lose their tail.

But now that we need to find safety? Not so great. We also need food, water and medical attention. Our varying degrees of mud-streaked skin, unkempt hair and drawn faces will scare anyone off.

"We need to find a doctor. A pharmacy. Anything," I fret anxiously. "Her wound needs treating."

Xander abandons his watch to approach us. The juicy vein throbbing at his temple betrays his anxiety, even if he's plastered his steely mask back in place for the sake of remaining calm.

He isn't fooling me.

Tension he can no longer suppress pulls his skin tight across sharp angles and defined bones. While he uses his ethereal looks to his advantage when hunting prey, he looks more like a starved ghost than a model right now.

"We're in the middle of nowhere." He studies Ripley's slack face. "Harrowdean is deep in the countryside, miles from the nearest town or city."

"Yeah, no shit," Raine drawls.

I jerk my chin towards the odd buildings scattered outside. "Someone must live nearby. Or there's another farm close. It can't be that much farther."

"You're forgetting that we're fugitives now," Raine interjects. "Who would help us? They'll just call the police."

"We don't know what the public's been told," I reason, trying to cling to some calmness. "Blackwood already fell before the riot. Now Harrowdean. People know we're victims now."

"Do you really believe that?" Xander laughs coldly. "No one gives a fuck about us."

"Now is not the time to debate hypotheticals, Xan. No one knows our faces or our stories. We can use that to our advantage."

"What about Sabre Security?" Raine shifts uncomfortably against the wall.

I want to facepalm even though he can't even see me to appreciate the sentiment. This is where our levels of optimism differ greatly.

The asshole Ripley thinks is her friend either got himself killed or abandoned us to die. I'm not about to bet anything on this mysterious company coming to our rescue any time soon.

We're all quiet while deep in thought. The sound of beating rotors seems to be moving farther away, giving me a small sliver of hope. They're searching a wide radius. The woods stretch on for miles behind us.

"We keep moving," Xander decides in a firm tone. "If Incendia's searching for us, they haven't been dismantled yet."

"And we're still in danger," Raine concludes.

"As long as they're operating, we will never be safe. I'm all for running, but unravelling criminal conspiracies can take years. We'll have to stop running sometime."

"Says who?" I retort.

His icy-blue eyes flash to me. "Be realistic."

"I am! We are not surrendering to those bastards!"

"Nobody is suggesting we surrender." Raine fidgets with his folded guide stick. "Right, Xan?"

"Not to the corporation," he clarifies. "But if Sabre really is investigating and planning to shut down all the institutes, cooperation may be our only chance."

My mind whirls as I catch on to his plan. Warner didn't come through for us. So what, Xander wants to contact his team himself? We'll be feeding ourselves to the wolves—just under a different guise. I don't trust any of these corporate suits.

"We need to get back online." Xander sighs wearily, buckling under the weight of the day. "I can swipe some phones if we find a town or city."

"You can?" Raine wonders aloud.

"Sure. Easy."

I know a little about Xander's criminal past. He was sent to Priory Lane for some elaborate embezzlement scheme, and he's happiest with his fingertips touching a keyboard. I know he has a talent for theft. The rest is a mystery, much like the man himself.

"I don't trust anyone but the people in this room." I blow out a leaden breath. "We're not surrendering, cooperating… whatever the fuck you want to call it. We keep running until it's safe to stop."

Our gazes locked, Xander seems determined to freeze me out. The way he glowers at me chills my internal organs. But

I'm not afraid of him. The time for him to call the shots is over. We all have a stake in this.

I look back down at Ripley.

Her.

Even if I've done a terrible job of showing my intentions so far. Every time I see her, I just get so wound up. She knows exactly how to push all the right buttons to drive me fucking insane.

"I can't hear the helicopter anymore." Raine tilts his blonde head, listening closely. "Are we clear to move?"

Xander drops his stare then returns to the window. I shift Ripley in my arms, cracking my neck to loosen the kink that's formed. Her dried blood pulls at my skin, adding to my unease.

"I hate this," Raine mutters. "We're sitting ducks."

"Me too. How's her pulse?"

I watch his fingers tighten on her wrist.

"Thready but strong. She's exhausted and lost a lot of blood. I think it's normal for her to dip in and out. You need to keep her warm, though."

"Yeah, I'm on it."

His thumb circles her skin in a loving, affectionate caress. We're facing life and death, but I can't stop my mind from flashing back to the moments before we ran for our lives. It's seared into my memory.

The powerful look on her face as she drove my friend to ecstasy with her filthy mouth. The way Raine flexed beneath her, so perfectly in tune to her body. Ripley swallowing his load before proudly licking her damn lips.

I've never considered the possibility of sharing a woman before—no matter how much I love the family I found in the shittiest of times. Fuck, I never considered touching Ripley until recently. At least not consciously.

But in that moment, it took all my self-control not to bend her over Raine, strip her tight ass bare and sink into her cunt while he fucks her smart mouth. I wanted to take that powerful look she wore and obliterate it.

Needing to earn Ripley's forgiveness is one thing—I can chalk it up to a guilty conscience—but this possessive need to protect her, to love and to hold her... That's something I never anticipated. Not even when we kissed in the padded cell.

I thought if I kept my distance, used cruelty to hide these strange new impulses... they would go away. My secret would be safe. But the longer we're trapped in this together, the harder it's becoming to battle my desires.

I want her.

Us.

Any tiny fucking scrap she'll give me.

"Nox!" Xander snaps me back to reality. "We're moving."

"Right. Coming."

Shifting Ripley higher against my chest, I push off from the wall. Raine may own her heart right now, but I have something he doesn't. Something he'll never have. And that feels so fucking good.

Their love will never compare to the addictive intoxication of our hatred for each other. I have the real power here. Namely, the sole ability to fix what I once broke. Only someone intimately familiar with her pain can ever hope to ease it.

I'll happily be her enemy.

Her own personal monster.

As long as I can also be the one to keep her safe. Perhaps even hold her the way that Raine does. Touch her. Comfort her. Fucking *matter* to her.

"This way." Xander leads us outside.

The late afternoon sunshine has broken through the thick cloud coverage. We plough on in a loose formation, Raine walking independently behind Xander with his stick swinging.

My leg muscles protest as the miles trickle by. I fall into a rhythm, my attention focused on the skies above and the path ahead. I almost startle when I feel ice-cold fingers pressing into my face.

"You don't suit the white knight stereotype, Nox."

A pulse of adrenaline shoots through me when I find Ripley's semi-open eyes. "You're awake."

"Is that what this feeling is?" she groans in pain. "Feels a lot like hell to me."

Her hand lowers, fastening on my shirt collar instead. She fists the bloodstained fabric, tiny whimpers slipping past her lips with each step.

"Sorry for ruining your t-shirt."

"You owe me a new one."

"Add it to my bill," she gasps.

"You've lost a lot of blood. Please don't die in my arms before settling up." I pause to enjoy her look of surprise. "Plus I don't want to be responsible for burying your body."

"Ever the charmer." Ripley rattles out a laugh. "Or should I say asshole?"

My mouth twitches in a smile. "More appropriate."

"Where are we?" she wheezes.

"We're going to find some help."

"In a field?"

"You're in no position to complain."

Xander suddenly halts, his exhausted shoulders straightening out. He's spotted something ahead. We've been passing fields of bleating livestock for at least an hour now. Perhaps we've finally escaped the farmland.

Barren fields have shifted to cobbled-stone pathways turn and wind-stripped fences, the grass massively overgrown. When I spot the first dated-looking structure ahead, the urge to laugh bubbles up in my chest.

"Seriously, Xan?" I call to him.

He glances over his shoulder. "You got a better idea?"

"What is it?" Raine taps his stick in a wide circle.

"Imagine the most British holiday you can think of."

"Uh… pass." He chuckles to himself. "My parents were a bit too concerned about shooting up to take me on holiday."

We're approaching a run-down resort, the front gates leading to rows of retro mobile homes. The place appears to be deserted in the late spring sunshine. We stop in front of the peeling welcome sign.

Golden Oaks Holiday Park.
Open July through November.

"Anyone against a little breaking and entering?" Xander asks after finding the gate locked.

There are no complaints.

"Good. Keep watch."

He pokes around the entrance, locating a loose, round stone on the roadside. Xander returns to the gate, contemplating for a moment before slamming the stone into the rusted padlock.

After three hits, the busted lock hits the ground. He pulls off the chain, allowing the gates to creak open. We all shuffle forward, tentatively entering the desolate park.

"Does this place look as spooky as it feels?" Raine whistles.

Squeezing Ripley close, my head swivels from side to side. "Pretty much."

"Kinda glad I can't see it, in that case."

Surveying the vacant homes, Xander guides us to the very back of the resort. The silence is fucking eery.

"This will do," he decides, gesturing ahead.

Shaded, net curtains hide the interior of the mobile home he's chosen. The garden is a wild jungle, indicating the months of closure during off-season.

"I'll see if there's a park office or something. They must have first-aid supplies. Can you get us in, Nox?"

"Leave it to me."

Xander nods, vanishing to keep searching. I approach the

mobile home then crouch down to lower Ripley onto the moss-speckled, plastic steps. Her pained grunting cuts deep into my chest.

"Easy," I murmur.

She hisses, releasing my t-shirt. "Son of a bitch."

"You're welcome."

With Ripley safely deposited, her leg stretched out in front of her, I check Raine is at a safe distance then look around for something to use. The door is made of two frosted-glass panes. If I can smash the top one, perhaps I can flip the inside lock.

"You reckon these things have alarms?"

Ripley grimaces. "Doubt it. This one looks ancient."

Buried in weeds and grass tufts, I spot my target. A stone garden gnome covered in crusty fungus. I pick it up with my good hand. The ugly bastard will do the job nicely if I get the swing right.

Backing up to a safe distance, I swing the gnome hard, letting it sail into the glass pane. The resultant crack pierces the silence like a gunshot. A huge split marks the pane in complex spiderweb patterns.

"Shit, Nox," Raine shouts from below. "Could you make more noise?"

"Feel free to come do it yourself, dick."

Still using the lump of slick stone, I repeatedly smash the cracks I've created to chip away the glass. With the pane destroyed, I'm free to reach in to feel for a lock. My fingers catch on smooth metal.

"Gotcha," I whisper. "Please work."

Click.

Thankfully, the lock is cheap and crappy. It flicks open, allowing me to flip the handle. The door swings open, granting us access to the mobile home. My momentary relief dissipates as I move forward uneasily.

"Let me check to make sure it's clear."

Ripley attempts to shift, her teeth gritted. "Need backup?"

"You're in no state to help."

"I can walk," she protests.

"No. You can't. Just sit still."

"But—"

"I mean it," I cut her off. "Sit fucking still."

Relieved when she deflates, not daring to protest more, I step inside. Stale air and dust register first. Then the stench of old, musty furniture. Anyone coming here for a holiday better have low expectations.

I check each room—a cramped living area, peeling kitchenette, single bathroom and two bedrooms with matching double beds. The old linoleum squeaks with each step I take, mirroring my rapid heartbeat.

"Nox? You good?"

Following Raine's voice, I step back outside. "It's clear. Probably best you can't see the '70s shag carpet and bright-orange kitchen. This thing is old as fuck."

"Awesome," Ripley quips.

"Raine? You good to follow?" I study him.

He waves my concern off. "I've got this. Go first."

Helping Ripley stand, I throw her arm around my shoulders. Raine follows us in, using his stick to feel his way up the narrow steps. I set Ripley down on the kitchen counter, outstretching her leg on top.

"So much dust." Raine wrinkles his nose in disgust. "I can literally smell the '70s grandma vibes in here."

"I'd like to think '70s grandmas had more style than this," I reply distractedly. "Who buys an orange refrigerator?"

"If it meant I could see it, I'd take a neon-green kitchen. Count yourself lucky."

"Buy a green kitchen, and I'll disown you."

"Well, that's you uninvited from the housewarming," Raine snarks.

"Thank fuck for that."

"Pack it in," Ripley snaps at us. "It's a roof over our heads."

Creaking footsteps interrupt our conversation. We all startle before Xander's dirt-flecked face quickly appears in the doorway.

"Room for one more?" He sighs.

"Welcome to the five-star hotel," Raine jokes.

Slapping a turquoise box down on the table, rattling the contents, Xander deposits his backpack next. He's practically sagging with fatigue, still covered in dirt and grass stains from our escape.

"First aid kit." He rubs his face tiredly. "There was a small shop in the office too. No CCTV cameras. They're not concerned about security out here."

"Anything good?" Raine folds up his stick.

"Some long-life cereals, a bag of peanuts, a few chocolate bars and a cheap bottle of whiskey."

"That's a gourmet dinner." Ripley winces when she tries to laugh. "No pain relief?"

"Nothing." Xander shakes his head.

"Then someone crack open that booze."

"Hand it over," I offer.

Xander passes me the backpack. "I'll sort out the medical supplies."

With my bandaged hand, I fumble with the zip until I get it unfastened and locate the sealed bottle inside. Once I've cracked the seal, Ripley immediately snatches it from me.

"Woah." I pull the bottle back to stop her chugging. "You haven't eaten or slept, and you nearly bled out. Go easy on the hard liquor."

"Fuck off," she retorts, reaching for the whiskey.

"Nice try." I pull the bottle behind my back. "We agreed you wouldn't die on my watch, remember?"

"I don't remember that." She grimaces, a pained whimper

slipping past her gritted teeth. "My leg feels like it's on fucking fire."

Reluctantly handing her the bottle, I watch her take another few mouthfuls before I intervene again, managing to wrestle it back. She pins me with the stink eye, a red flush already creeping into her cheeks.

"We need to do this now." Xander clicks open the first aid kit to search inside. "Bring Ripley here."

One arm sliding around her waist, I decide to take advantage and lift her off the counter by her ass. "My bad."

"Don't use your mangled hand as an excuse to grope me," she hisses out. "You're still on my shit list."

"Then I'm good to grope you, right? If I'm already on the shit list."

"Good luck getting off it with that attitude."

I carry her over to the kitchen table, gently laying her down across the tacky surface with her bleeding thigh on Xander's side. He takes one look at the mess and begins rifling through the box.

"Jeans off," he orders.

"Raine," I call out. "Come help me."

"You're both going to strip me?" Ripley asks incredulously.

I'm not sure if it's the booze or an actual blush staining her cheeks now. Raine laughs under his breath. I swear, the motherfucker knows exactly what's running through my mind.

"Any scissors?" I ask with forced neutrality.

Xander scours the kitchen, banging drawers and cabinets. "Nothing."

"Great." I study her splayed-out form. "Alright, this isn't gonna feel great."

With my good hand, I pick at the knotted t-shirt to untie the tourniquet before tugging her jeans down as gently as I can. Raine slowly pulls the denim over her ankles.

"That hurts," she spits through gritted teeth. "Go slow."

I try my best to carefully ease the denim down when we reach her thighs. The jeans are stuck to her skin and take some manoeuvring, each inch causing her to curse bloody murder.

"God-fucking-dammit!" Ripley lashes out. "I am going to put a bullet in Elon's fucking face. Fuck!"

"I think cheap whiskey breaks her cuss filter," Raine mutters.

"Did she ever have one?"

"Fair point."

"I can hear you both!" she bellows. "Fucking assholes."

Raine smirks to himself. "Case in point."

With the jeans removed, an inflamed, ragged mess is revealed. Thankfully, the thigh wound itself is small, maybe five or six centimetres wide. She's lucky they only had handguns.

"Lift her leg." Xander snaps on a pair of blue medical gloves. "I need to check the exit wound."

Slowly raising her leg, I avoid looking at the agony that's carved into her clammy features. Xander moves fast, ducking low to inspect the back of her thigh before straightening up.

"Clean shot, minimal damage. We need to flush the wound then pack it."

"Stitches?" I frown at him.

"Not yet. Got to rule out an infection first. Re-evaluate in a few days."

"A few days?" Ripley croaks.

"You're going to rest while we scout the area." Xander keeps his instructions clipped, leaving no room for argument. "We're secure here for the time being."

I lower Ripley's leg back down. "What about a hospital?"

"Right now, we don't even know where we are. We'll get her stabilised then make a plan."

Lining up sealed packs of bandages and swabs, Xander

quickly scans the label on a bottle of clear liquid. Behind me, Raine is shifting on his feet in clear agitation.

"Ankles," I order him. "You can hold her legs straight."

"You sure this is a good idea?"

"Have you got a better one?" Xander asks distractedly.

"Just feels a bit back-street clinic, you know?" Raine gnaws on his cheek.

"We're not giving a false name and paying in cash." I move up the table to stand at Ripley's head. "Make yourself useful."

Both moved into position, Xander unwraps several packs of cotton gauze. He uncaps the liquid, leaning over Ripley's injured body while wearing a displeased expression.

"This may sting," he advises with a quick glance. "We don't need company."

"Meaning?" Ripley grates out.

"Try not to yell too loud."

Without ceremony, he douses her leg in antiseptic. I watch the clear liquid run red, filling the bullet wound before spilling over in a crimson flow. Ripley's back arches as a shrill scream erupts from her mouth.

"Fuuuuuck!"

"Nox," Xander barks. "Cover her mouth!"

Cursing rapidly, I slam a hand over Ripley's O-shaped lips. Her tortured howls now muffled, she bucks and writhes on the table like we doused her in petrol then lit a flame.

"Stop it, Xan!" Raine frets in a high-pitched screech. "You're hurting her!"

"Less than a blood infection will," he hits back. "Let me do my job."

Using cotton gauze, Xander begins to dab and clean, his jaw locked tight. I can feel the tears pouring from Ripley's eyes soaking my hand. The huge, green-brown pits stare up at me like I'm responsible for carving her heart out.

It's a sight I once craved. Dreamed about. Fantasised over.

I wanted her tears, freshly spilled and bottled like nectar. Her grief and heartache helped ease my desire for revenge after she had us thrown in the Z wing.

Considering all the regret I feel now, that craving has packed up and left the fucking planet. My sick need for revenge drove me to the brink of insanity.

I'd do all manner of insane things to protect my family— she can attest to that—but somewhere down the line… my brain moved her into that same category. *Fuck!* When did that happen?

"Stop!" she shrieks behind my hand.

Xander tuts under his breath. "Not yet. We have to clean the wound."

"I'm sorry." The words tumble freely from my mouth. "I'm so sorry. Just hold on."

When Xander douses the gunshot wound again, her wails intensify, chest pumping and body trembling beneath a sheen of glistening sweat. I lift my hand so she can gulp down shuddering breaths.

"P-Please." She swipes at her wet cheeks. "Take m-my mind off it."

"How?" I ask desperately.

"Anything… Tell m-me something… A story."

Now finished flushing the wound, Xander resumes swabbing it to remove any debris. If that vein in his forehead throbs any harder, I'm worried it's going to explode. He fucking hates this too.

"I… I don't know any stories."

"Your sister," she whines through her pouring tears. "Tell me about her."

My gaze snaps to hers. "Uh, now?"

Slamming her mouth shut, Ripley shrieks again through tightly sealed lips. Raine looks on the verge of passing out too, his face white as a sheet as he continues to hold her legs straight.

"Shit, okay," I rush out. "She... She practiced ballet. Some free program for ex-service families. Our grandfather signed her up."

Ripley's eyes screw shut. Her skin has lost its alcohol flush and turned almost translucent. Determined to stop her from shutting down, I search for something happy amongst heart-wrenching memories.

"Every single day after school, I'd take the A7 bus to pick her up from class. It was a rattling hunk of junk. If I had enough money, we'd stop for an ice cream cone on the way home."

She mumbles weakly, her eyes flickering. "Ice cream?"

"Yeah, that boring vanilla kind. Bright-yellow and full of additive shit. But she enjoyed that damn cone so much. I loved seeing her smile, even if I had to scavenge pennies just to make it happen."

Tossing aside bloodied handfuls of gauze, Xander locates fresh bandages next. He nods to me in encouragement.

I smooth sweaty hair back from her forehead. "One time, the shop closed early. Daisy stared up at that closed sign, and the look on her face fucking killed me. I hadn't realised how much our little ritual meant to her."

Ripley's eyes flutter open and lock on mine. Her tears are pearlescent rivers staining her skin. Skimming her cheek with my thumb, I wipe them away.

She lets out a thready breath. "What d-did you do about it?"

"You know me too well."

"Yeah." Her laugh is weak.

"I snuck around back and broke into the storeroom. Stole two tubs of that shitty ice cream then took it home. Daisy had a bowl every night until it ran out."

Directing Raine to lift her injured leg, Xander packs the wound with sterilised cotton then begins to tightly bandage it.

Ripley's vibrating so violently, I wonder if she'll pass out again. I seize her shaking hand.

"Hey," I bark at her. "Eyes on me."

Her muddled gaze flicks back to my face. "I h-hate vanilla."

"You want to know a secret?"

She nods loosely.

"Me too. I only ate it to make Daisy happy. I don't have a massive sweet tooth. Though if pushed, I'd go for chocolate every time."

Xander applies medical tape to hold the bulging bandage in place. Panting roughly, Ripley interlocks her fingers with mine. I run a finger over her knuckles, studying each laboured breath.

"I went back to the ice cream shop after she died," I blurt before I can stop myself. "I guess I wanted to feel close to her again. All her stuff at home was gone by then, and it felt like she never existed."

Lowering Ripley's leg, Xander casts a critical eye over his handiwork before nodding. He starts to clean up the medical detritus. There's blood and bandage wrappings spread everywhere around us.

I didn't get the chance to hold Daisy's hand like this. I couldn't give her the love she needed. The protection of her big brother—the one person in the entire world who was supposed to keep her safe.

I failed her.

But I'll never fail my family again.

"It was gone." The truth is a raw whisper that I can hardly vocalise. "Boarded up and gutted. Some little shits even graffitied the exterior. Daisy died, and everything she loved died with her."

"Not you," she replies weakly.

"The Lennox she knew did. He was weak. Blind to the truth. Pathetic. He didn't protect her."

I ignore the other two paying close attention to our whispers. I'm focused solely on Ripley's face, wrinkles smoothing out and muscles relaxing. Her septum piercing is crooked again.

I gently straighten the silver ring. "Rest, baby."

She mumbles an unintelligible protest.

"It's okay, Rip." My vocal cords spasm, causing my voice to break. "I'm right here. I promise I'll keep you safe."

Because that's what family does, no matter how much they beat, bruise and hate each other. There's no stronger bond on Earth than that. Not all of us are lucky enough to have biological family left.

But the connections we create can be stronger than shared DNA.

We're living proof of that.

Ripley demonstrated her worth to me the day she avenged her best friend's death. She was defending her family. The family we took from her. Beneath all that goddamn beautiful rage, we're just alike.

Together, we could be unstoppable.

Our rage will burn the whole fucking world.

CHAPTER 12
XANDER
ROSES – THE COMFORT

THICK BLACK HOODIE flipped up to offer me protection, I stare straight ahead at the bald guy in front of me. He's distracted, intently studying the coffee menu on the wall while flipping his car keys in his hand.

Clueless.

The perfect mark.

Spending the better part of a decade in foster care teaches you life skills. Just not ones that are necessarily advertised. When you're competing with twenty plus kids for basics like clothes and toys, the art of stealing becomes second nature.

"Next!" a haggard barista calls.

Before he's even moved to place his order, I've already pulled my hand from his back pocket. I stuff the loot into my hoodie and quickly turn to leave. The sour-faced teenager wearing headphones behind me pulls a face.

"Changed my mind." I shrug at her.

The trick is to walk away slowly—with confidence and like I have all the time in the world. Baldie's in for a shock when he attempts to pay for his overpriced sludge. The idiot shouldn't stash his valuables in his back pocket.

I melt into the morning crowd, happily going about their daily routine. Dog walkers. Postmen. Delivery drivers dropping off boxes of newspapers and fresh produce to the numerous corner shops. The picturesque scene makes me fucking sick.

I'm headed for the outdated internet cafe two streets over that I spotted earlier on. None of us escaped Harrowdean with our belongings, let alone mobile phones. We've been totally cut-off from the world.

Using a walking map I pilfered from the holiday park's office, I volunteered to find the nearest town and get us back online. We already needed food, clothing and more medical supplies—requiring me to swipe some cash.

Before I set my sights on greater targets in my early twenties, I honed my skills as a street thief. I don't care what kind of person that makes me.

The rich take from the poor all the livelong day, and we don't kick up a fuss. Why shouldn't it work in reverse?

"Morning." The cafe's owner waves me in. "Just here for coffee, or you want internet?"

I adjust the heavy backpack on my shoulder. "Two computers. Half an hour should do."

The fact that this place exists at all speaks to the elderly demographic in the town it took me two hours to find. I haven't heard of anyone using internet cafes like this in the last decade. I was convinced I'd be stuck using the public library.

"Two?" he repeats.

Nodding to his plugged in phone, I slide an extra note over. "Your charger as well."

His grey brows raise. Sighing, I add another note. He palms the crisp twenties, any further questions drying up. I accept the charger then follow his pointed finger to the back of the cafe. Two monitors sit next to each other.

Sinking into the chair, I fish the two phones I've managed

to lift from my hoodie. Baldie wasn't my first mark; I had already targeted a distracted parent wrestling two kids from her flashy Range Rover outside the supermarket. It was easy to lift her phone and cash.

I keep the screens angled slightly to prevent any prying eyes. It's child's play to commence a hard reset on both phones. I snap the SIM cards in half before sliding in new ones I purchased earlier.

Two working phones.

We're in business.

While the phones reboot, I pull up the search engine on my second computer. Ripley and Lennox were itching to join me, even though she can barely walk. The least I can do is report back with news.

I quickly tap in *Harrowdean Manor* then watch the breaking news stories populate. We holed up for two nights, until the food ran out. That's long enough for word to spread.

As I suspected, the official story is vague in the extreme. Details are sparse enough to satisfy the public's demands for action but conceal the truth about how the riot came to an unceremonious end.

> ***Deadly riot at psychiatric institute ends
> in violence.***
> ***Hostages rescued, multiple casualties
> reported.***
> ***Sir Bancroft II to make a public
> statement as criminal investigation
> gathers speed.***

Scoffing under my breath, I scan through the final story. The silver-haired son of a bitch will soon charm the media. He always does. Even with the evidence pouring out of Blackwood, it took Harrowdean revolting to get the world talking this much.

Yet he's still a free man.

And there's still no justice.

The mention of Warner's employer, Sabre Security, catches my eye. I don't expect a full breakdown of an active criminal investigation, but these Sabre people seem to be kicking their feet.

There's some crap about cooperating witnesses from Blackwood but nothing more. It's infuriating. Why do we accept the existence of evil so quickly but discount the truth just as fast when it stares us in the face?

Because it's uncomfortable.

It's a mark of failure as humans.

We treat the truth with contempt when it doesn't tell us what we want to hear. It's far easier to turn the other cheek, to pretend like suffering doesn't exist all around us. We keep scrolling, drinking down the easy to stomach content we're drip fed instead.

At the bottom of the article, there's a number for a tip hotline. I type it into the first now-unlocked phone then study the half-empty cafe while waiting for the line to connect.

"Sabre Security," a perky voice chirps. "You've reached Operation Nightshade's tip line. Tara speaking."

"Tell them to print the truth," I whisper angrily. "Some of us don't have time for your investigation to gather speed."

There's a brief pause.

"Who am I speaking to?"

"And tell your idiot boss to look beneath Kingsman dorms."

"Sir, if I can just—"

"Each institute has a Zimbardo wing. You need to tear them all apart."

Loaded silence. I've got her attention.

"Priory Lane. Blackwood Institute. Harrowdean Manor," I lay them out, one by one. "All gone. You have the evidence you need to shut the remaining institutes down before Bancroft decides to clean house."

A scrabble on the other end makes me pause before hanging up. They're probably tracking the call. No matter, I'll be gone soon enough.

"This is Theodore Young," a new voice announces. "Your call has been escalated to me. Tell me, what might we find beneath Kingsman dorms?"

"Ask the pink-haired bitch who tortured my friend. She knows all about it."

The sudden intake of breath is curious. I have no clue who the woman that saved Ripley and Lennox is, only that she works for the prestigious security firm. We only have jagged pieces of a much larger puzzle.

His breath rattles down the line. "We've had plenty of hoax calls. Prove to me you're trustworthy."

"Trustworthy?" I check to ensure that no one is listening. "What about the trust put in a faceless corporation to protect the unwell? Or the trust put in you to bring them to justice? Don't talk to me about fucking trust."

"I'm in a position to help if you have information," he tries to placate. "This is a fast-moving situation, and I understand several patients from Harrowdean remain unaccounted for. Are you one of them?"

"What, amongst the dead bodies Incendia has piled up?" I laugh hollowly. "They're hunting us with helicopters and guns. How do I know *you're* trustworthy?"

His sigh stretches across several seconds. Bad day at the office, clearly. If Theodore is looking for a shred of sympathy, he better not hold his breath. I'm willing to cooperate, but only for the right price.

"We can offer protection," Theodore replies. "Will that earn your trust?"

"Empty words won't. We've heard this spiel before, and it amounted to nothing in the end. I need assurances this time."

"I'm not sure I can give that to you over the phone. We should arrange to meet at a rendezvous point. My superiors will want to hear your testimony."

"So you can hand us over to Bancroft and take his hush money? I'll pass."

His voice drops to a low whisper. "Off the record, that evil bastard Bancroft is going to get what's coming to him. I'll personally see to it. The pink-haired woman? She's dead. He's going to pay for that."

Ah. His reaction is an emotional one. Curious indeed. That would've repulsed me before. Now I find myself wondering how I would react in similar circumstances. If Ripley's death would impact me so viscerally.

Agony constricts my lungs at the thought.

Grief? Fear? Regret?

It's exhausting, telling all these emotions apart.

"I have others who deserve to be included in this decision," I eventually concede. "We will discuss your offer. How can I reach you?"

Theodore rattles off a phone number, different from the public line I found online. I quickly tap it into the spare phone and end the call before he can utter another word. Another SIM card snapped and discarded.

Shoving everything into the overflowing backpack, I haul ass to leave the internet cafe. If he's committed to earning our trust, Theodore won't follow the location my call inevitably gave his team.

I make it back to our hideout far quicker than my trek into the nearest town, skin prickling with the need to lay eyes on the three people I left behind.

Shoulders aching from the weight of the goods I'm hauling back, the holiday park is still deserted when I arrive. It will be for another month or two. Even though we boarded over the smashed window with several cardboard boxes I found, we can't stay much longer. It's too risky.

I knock on the door three times then twice more. There's a wait as footsteps move inside. The curtain twitches, showing Lennox's tired face before he clicks the lock to allow me inside.

"Fuck, Xan. You've been gone for hours."

"It's not exactly around the corner," I grumble while stepping in.

"We were getting worried."

In the cramped living area, Ripley lays on the retro, flower-print sofa with her legs stretched over Raine. He's fiddling with those ridiculous sunglasses he wears, the pair clearly mid-conversation.

"Xan," she breathes a sigh of relief. "All clear?"

"Yeah, no trouble. Just a long walk."

"Did you find what you need?"

"Enough to restock and get us online."

I reach into the full backpack to pull out a grease-stained paper bag. Ripley squeaks when the paper bag sails through the air and collides with her chest. The smell of baked goods permeates the cramped space.

"What is this?"

Avoiding her stare, I resume pulling items out. "For you."

I lay out more bandages and gauze. Pain relief. The phones and charger. A few clean shirts and miniature toiletries. Sanitary towels. And as much food as I could feasibly carry.

"Wait." Raine holds up his hand. "It's… Hmm, I smell sugar. Fresh dough. Maybe icing? Oh, I know! I know!"

"Cream-filled doughnuts," she tells him. "Good guess."

"Good nose," he corrects.

Ripley pulls out a golden doughnut, casting me a very suspicious look. "Apparently, Xander is an excellent guesser too."

I clear my throat, organising the packs of dried ramen. "No idea what you're talking about."

Lennox leans against the bright-orange cabinets, looking between us both. "What am I missing?"

"Apart from the fact that this man has made it his mission to stalk me relentlessly ever since he arrived at Harrowdean? And probably months in Priory Lane before that?"

My mouth tugs up in a satisfied smile. I wasn't sure she'd realise my choice of flavour was deliberate.

"I hate doughnuts," Ripley explains. "Apart from one kind."

"Cream-filled?" Lennox guesses.

With everything laid out on the table, I finally level her with a look. "Your choice of doughnut flavour is relevant information to me. And I dislike the unknown."

"Is that the stalker's manifesto?" Raine smothers a laugh.

"I'd say so." Lennox rolls his eyes.

Ripley sighs. "I suppose I've heard worse justifications."

Her voice is laced with sarcasm, but the tiny, reluctant smile tugging at her mouth screams of amusement. It makes my thundering pulse do all kinds of strange things.

"There weren't even any doughnuts in either institute." Raine frowns at the bag placed in his hands. "So how did you find that stupidly specific information out?"

"Trade secret," I deadpan. "Check the *manifesto*. I'm sure it's in there."

They all burst out laughing. Unable to stop myself, I join in. It's an odd feeling—one that pulls at my belly and abdominal muscles in an unfamiliar way. I haven't used those muscles for this purpose much.

"Xander's worrying tendency to overstep every boundary known to man aside." Raine pulls out a doughnut. "Did you find anything out?"

I take a seat at the kitchen table. "It's as we thought. The story's all under wraps. Whispers about the investigation but nothing solid. Bancroft's still preening for the cameras and spouting shit."

"You lifted these?" Lennox gestures to the phones.

"Yeah, wiped and ready to go. There are more SIM cards in the bag. Cash too."

Nodding, Lennox takes one of the phones to start fiddling with. "Good."

I removed the thick bandages around his hand yesterday, applying a lighter pad with gauze instead. The dressing on his face is gone too, leaving a fresh, pink slash across his cheek behind.

"I called Sabre Security."

My words cause Raine to drop his doughnut. He curses to himself while Lennox sets the phone down so he can give me his full attention.

"Why?" he growls.

"Testing the waters. We need to know what our options are."

"Xan, I thought we agreed—"

"I didn't cut a deal or make any agreements with them. The person I spoke to offered a secure rendezvous to exchange information. The same protection offer. I've got his contact number."

"Who was it? The director?" Ripley asks.

"No, someone called Theodore."

"Theo?" she repeats, eyes narrowed. "I know that name."

We all wait for her to cycle through her thoughts. Ripley dusts off her sugar-speckled fingertips, the doughnut now discarded.

"In the Z wing…" She shakes her head. "The woman, Alyssa. She was communicating with her team. I heard her call his name. Theo."

"So he's legit," Lennox concludes.

"Seems so." I focus on Ripley. "She's dead."

Ripley's eyes snap up to mine. "What?"

"The pink-haired mole. She died." I shrug nonchalantly. "Sounds like this Theodore character has some personal stake in taking Bancroft down. He seemed committed to helping us."

"I bet he did!" Lennox explodes in frustration. "You know that Incendia has their claws in everyone! Government. Private companies. Investors. They're probably bankrolling these Sabre pricks too!"

"No." Ripley turns to face off against Lennox. "Warner works for them. I trust his judgement."

"Some anonymous guard who ditched us? Great plan, Rip."

"I'm telling you, he's on our side, Nox!" she argues back. "Would it kill you to have some faith for once?"

"Yes! It could kill us!"

Anger tattooed into every line of his expression, Lennox pushes off from the kitchen cabinets and disappears deeper into the mobile home. I wait for one of the bedroom doors to slam shut before speaking again.

"That was a rather short honeymoon period."

"Fuck off, Xan." Ripley clenches her eyes shut. "His trust issues are going to get us killed."

I'd like to point out the irony that she's demanding trust from the man she tried to frame, but something tells me it wouldn't go down well. Besides, the pair seem to be putting their differences aside, if Lennox's heartfelt display in the kitchen was any indication.

"He has a point," Raine says quietly. "You of all people know how deep the corporation's ties run. We should be cautious."

Ripley stares down at her bandaged leg, the white cotton revealed by the long, oversized tee she wears with panties.

"Care to fill me in?"

Raine's head tilts in my direction, but he doesn't answer. I wait for Ripley to gather herself, watching her chest rise as she takes a deep breath.

"Bancroft. Incendia's president."

I nod in response. "We were acquainted in Priory Lane."

"Well, I met him before the Z wing." Her nose scrunches with a look of revulsion. "Incendia Corporation controls a huge portfolio of assets. Including two major investment firms in London."

I'm aware that her richer than sin uncle is an investment banker. Apparently, he's embroiled in all this too. He dripped with entitlement and wealth during his trip to the medical wing when Rick carved her up.

I overheard his brutal disownment speech. The man holds no love in his heart for the orphaned, mentally ill niece he was lumped with. Something inside Ripley broke that day when he walked away.

"You're sure he's involved?"

"I know he is," Ripley confirms, rage forming lines that bracket her mouth. "After Harrison beat the shit out of me over that business card… Bancroft paid me a visit. Told me he had my uncle's consent to repurpose me."

"Repurpose?" Raine asks breathily.

"It's what the Zimbardo program does." I swipe a finger over an old stain on the table. "Dehumanise, manipulate and torture until the mind breaks. Then it can be reformed."

"To what end?"

"Incendia creates mindless killing machines by destroying the vulnerable, one brain cell at a time." My lip curls at the thought. "Then they sell their creations off to the highest bidder."

Raine grows even paler than Ripley. "Jesus Christ."

We've shared enough of our past for him to understand. It was never a secret—hell, he was our customer once. But the real purpose behind the institutes is a tough pill to swallow.

"If I can't even trust my own flesh and blood… I can't trust anyone." Ripley pinches the bridge of her nose. "I hate it, but Lennox is right."

"Don't tell him that. It'll go straight to his head."

"Not funny, Xan. What the hell are we going to do?"

Staring at the phone left behind on the table, I can confidently say I have no fucking clue. We're completely alone out here with nothing but the clothes on our backs and the truth we carry with us.

Telling it may just set us free.

But it may also get us killed.

CHAPTER 13
RIPLEY

SAILOR SONG – GIGI PEREZ

RAIN HAMMERS against the mobile home's thin roof, creating a deafening roar. It's like we're trapped in the belly of a moving aeroplane. I stare up at the ceiling, unable to sleep. Each falling droplet too closely resembles the patter of gunfire.

It doesn't matter that we're taking turns to keep watch while the others sleep. Nor does it matter that we've seen no signs of life in the holiday park for the last few days while recuperating and weighing our options. It's as secure as anywhere for now.

That doesn't eliminate the fear, though.

There are still targets on our heads.

Carefully rolling over, I study Raine's face. Even though it's the middle of the afternoon, he's asleep. I have no idea how with his hypersensitivity. Even I have a headache from the pounding rain.

I run my finger down his straight, perfectly proportioned nose. There are slight indentations on either side that I never noticed before, evidence of him constantly wearing glasses. He still wears the aviators everyday like they're his proudest possession.

Without them on, I can see his thick black lashes, framing the brilliant, honeyed orbs that he keeps hidden from the world. I trace my fingertip over his cupid's bow, the defined dip exaggerating his full lips.

We're running dangerously low on his withdrawal medication. He puts on a brave face for our sakes, but I see the constant trembling, cold sweats and how he barely eats anything.

The methadone alleviates most of the withdrawal symptoms but not all of them. Without it, there's no telling how he'll react. Getting clean from years of opiate use is a long and extremely difficult process. Not to mention the impact his returned cravings would have.

With all the attention on Raine and his dwindling supply of pills, I've managed to keep my own ticking time bomb quiet. I know Xander sees everything, but out here, there's nothing he can do to help.

The insomnia can be explained away. We're all stressed and bone-deep tired. It's the constant agitation and unmanageable mood swings that are taking me to a dangerous place.

I screamed at Lennox yesterday for eating the final stale doughnut before bursting into violent sobs when he offered me the last bite. It was safest to barricade myself in the rear bedroom until I could think straight again.

"Rip?" Raine mumbles.

"You're supposed to be sleeping."

"As are you."

"How do you know I'm not asleep?"

"Besides the fact that we're talking?" He cracks a yawn. "Your breathing. Short and fast. Not exactly conducive to REM sleep."

"I don't think I like it when you spy on my body with your weird, Batman hearing."

"Sorry."

Moving my fingertips to his closed lids, I stroke the soft skin, following the curvature of his eyes. In the small bedroom, filled with late afternoon sunlight filtering through net curtains, it's easy to pretend we're the last two humans alive.

Part of me likes the idea of Raine having no one else, no matter how fucked up that is to admit. He'd never be able to abandon me if we were the last two humans. Not like everyone else has. I'd be his sole reprieve.

Love didn't stop my parents from dying, leaving me an orphan. It didn't stop my uncle from keeping me at arm's length until he cut all ties with me. And it didn't stop Holly from following them all on a fast-track course out of my life.

"You were sleeping so peacefully," I whisper.

"I think I was dreaming."

My soft touches still. "Can I ask you something personal?"

"Are we still at the stage where we ask for permission?" He smiles gently.

"I guess not. Think we've moved past all formalities at this point."

"So what's the question?"

I smooth the light creases around his left eye. "Can you still see in your dreams?"

Raine runs a hand over my curled-up body. "Sometimes I see visual images. Memories from before I lost my sight. Other times it's flashes with more sensory input like smells, textures, even tastes."

"What does that look like?"

He thinks for a moment, his caramel eyes now open and bouncing around. "I guess… a messy, colourful patchwork quilt."

The fact that he explains such a complicated concept with open-hearted honesty is what I admire the most. Raine has his demons, but he also has something not many can relate to.

The purest of souls.

That's a rare commodity.

"Can I ask you something else?"

"What is this, question time?" he jokes.

"I can stop."

"It's fine. Lay it on me, guava girl."

Snuggling closer, I take a deep breath of his salty, citrus scent. "Can you see me in your head?"

"I… have an impression of you." He cups my cheek.

"How?"

"It's made of fragments pieced together from touch. I guess I can tell you how your appearance feels to me. The image is a little more unclear, though. It's half imagination and half my best guess."

Equal parts confusion and curiosity draw my brows together. "So it's not an actual image?"

"Probably not in the same way you see me in your head. Images look different to me now. More textured and amorphous."

His inability to see me doesn't take away from the intense bond we've formed. Raine was the first person to worm his way inside my heart in a very long time. He did the impossible.

"Does it bother you?" he asks worriedly. "The fact that I can't see?"

"God, no!" I rush out. "Of course not."

"Then what's on your mind?"

"It's just… I thought it was safer to be alone. That's why I kept you at arm's length for so long. I feel like I wasted a lot of time by doing that."

"And now?" he urges.

"Now I'm glad we're in this together. It makes no sense, given what we're facing… but I've never felt safer than when I'm with you."

Raine listens intently, but his silence fires my uncertainty.

"Am I going insane?" I laugh.

"No." He tenderly brushes a hand through my short curls. "You're not."

"I want us to work, Raine. I want everything I was scared to even consider before. That fear has gone. We could be killed or thrown in prison at any moment, and I'm tired of wasting time."

The smile that blossoms on his lips is breathtaking. I just wish it didn't make my stomach curdle when my thoughts stray to whether I'll ever see a smile like it on Xander or Lennox. If they're even capable of it.

"But…"

"But… the others," he finishes for me.

"They're important to me. Even if I don't understand how or why, I know that much."

"You still don't get it. Do you?" Raine asks after a beat.

"Get what?"

Shifting closer, his nose brushes mine as he crowds my personal space. "I've accepted their place in your life."

"You… uh, have?"

"Because I don't have an image of your looks, and I don't need it. I'll never need it."

"I'm not sure I follow——"

"Just listen," he interrupts

I seal my lips, waiting for him to explain.

"I know your soul, Rip. I know your voice. Your scent. Your breathing patterns. Your intonations. I have the incredible privilege of seeing intimate, invisible, even unconscious details about you. I'll never have to share that privilege."

Numbly, I wonder if he can sense my heart soaring right now, racing at breakneck speed. Raine's self-satisfied smirk tells me he's all too aware of what his confession is doing to me.

"That's why I don't care how Xander obsesses over you," he continues. "Or how Lennox can't even comprehend the depths of his feelings because they're so overwhelming. I don't care if my brothers love you too because what we have will always be unique."

My toes curl when his lips press against mine.

"They can own their individual pieces of your heart, but what we have is just ours. And that's enough for me."

Too shocked to respond, I let his kiss linger. It's deep and passionate, our mouths familiar enough to fall into a tempo that feels natural. Raine kisses the hell out of me then rests our foreheads together.

"You… love me?" I murmur.

He chuckles. "Is that the only part you heard?"

"I mean, it kinda stood out."

His sigh sweeps across my face. "Yes, Rip. I love you."

"Can you say it again?"

"I love you so fucking much, I'm willing to give you this because I know you need them too. And hell, they need you. We all do."

A loose tear trails down my cheek. That single droplet encapsulates a lifetime of grief and loneliness. All the hope for a different life I imprisoned long ago when I realised that love was unrealistic. It dies and life goes on.

I didn't think I wanted it.

I didn't think I needed it.

But for the first time, I feel like my heart is beating wholly in my chest. I'm not just the lonely orphan, misunderstood by the world, finding solitude in her oil paints and immoral choices.

I'm loved.

Raine actually loves me.

Slanting my mouth back over his, I pour all that grief into my kiss. Every sleepless night spent sobbing into a pillow. The hole in my heart that formed as I grew up without a parent's love or touch. The rejection and self-hatred my condition created.

Sometime during those empty years, I stopped waiting for someone to love me. I stopped trying to love myself. It was enough to escape this world through my art, longing for the next life… where someone might love me instead.

Feeling his lips move against mine, I wonder how I made it this far on my own. Sheer determination and will to survive alone, I suppose. For the longest time, it was enough.

Not anymore.

I don't want to just survive by any means necessary. To live a solitary existence, taking comfort in the inanimate and protecting my heart from any further hurt. I want the whole fucking world. A future. A goddamn life. And they're all in it.

Fingers fisting in his sandy-blonde hair, I take it all. Every last drop of commitment and devotion his kiss has to offer. He lets me push my tongue into his mouth and taste each dark corner, needing to commit this moment to memory before it floats away.

"Ripley," he gasps into my lips. "Fuck, babe. I want to touch you so badly, but these walls aren't exactly soundproof."

"I don't care if they hear."

"The guys—"

"Can mind their own business," I finish his sentence.

After pushing him onto his back, I sit up, tugging my baggy shirt over my head. I'm left in panties and the slightly thinner bandage on my thigh that Xander applied last night.

"You're still hurt." He worries his lip.

"Not enough to change my mind. I need to feel you inside me."

"Rip…"

"Just strip."

Shimmying my panties off, I watch him deliberate before eventually tossing his clothing. He was sleeping in boxers and one of the clean shirts Xander brought back, his jeans nearby in case we need to move fast.

Raine lays back on the bed, a hand pumping his stiff

length. For a second, I leisurely watch him. How his muscles clench and pull taut. The smooth curves of his pectorals. Flat stomach and tapered hips.

"I can feel you watching me," he teases.

"That isn't actually possible, you know."

"I can assure you it is."

"Well, sue me. I like the view."

He smirks proudly. "Bring your gorgeous ass to me. Just go slow, alright?"

I carefully lift myself on top of him, keeping the weight off my leg. "How would you know my ass is gorgeous?"

"Call it intuition."

His touch skims over my hips and waist, each teasing brush electrifying my nerves. When his hands move to cup my breasts, I arch my back to push my chest into them. Raine makes a low, satisfied noise in his throat.

He squeezes my mounds, his thumbs sliding over my aching nipples. Each brush causes them to harden into sensitive points. Everything is tender, heightening the twinges of pleasure.

I grind myself on him, feeling his shaft sliding against my pussy lips. It feels more intimate somehow, now that we've laid all our cards on the table. This isn't just sex anymore. We've become more than the shallow labels I insisted on.

"I can feel how wet you are," Raine marvels, lightly pinching my nipple. "Were you soaked when Lennox watched us the other day?"

"Yes," I admit.

"You wanted to make him jealous, didn't you?"

Sliding a hand down my body, he locates my pulsating clit. I gasp when his thumb circles the sensitive bundle of nerves, causing my skin to tighten with pins and needles.

"Ripley," he says sternly. "Answer the question."

Between his length sliding back and forth in a torturous

taunt and his thumb pressing down on my clit, I have no hope of keeping the truth to myself. It spills out in a low whine.

"Y-Yes."

"I bet he was dying for a taste of your sweet cunt." He grins wolfishly. "And furious when he couldn't have it."

Pleasure rolls over me. I love the thought of driving Lennox insane with lust. Especially when I'm touching Raine. He spent so long trying to tear us apart, it felt right to tease him with his failure.

"You know, I imagined what it would be like if he joined us," Raine admits as he flicks and circles my bud. "How I'd feel if he touched you while I rode your mouth."

The mental image is enough to make the heat within my core boil over. I push myself against him, begging for any amount of friction. All I want is for him to sink inside me and ease the hollow ache.

"Can you imagine it, Rip?"

"It crossed my mind," I whimper.

"Did you imagine him bending you over and pushing inside you? How would it feel taking us both, do you think?"

"Fuck, Raine." My pussy clenches, weeping with unmet need. "Please."

"It's not something I've tried before. I wonder if he has."

The dirty-minded bastard is going to kill me off with all these mental images. Sure, I wanted to piss Lennox off. Perhaps I even considered what it would feel like, having them both inside me. But Raine's bringing the fantasy to life with each filthy word he whispers.

Reaching between us, I seize his shaft, tired of playing games. He's hot and pulsing in my palm, a bead of shining pre-come gathering on his tip. I slick the moisture with my thumb, watching his breath catch.

"You want to know what I imagined?"

"Fuck yes, babe. Tell me."

I languidly work his length up and down. "I imagined

Lennox bending me over while your cock was deep in my throat. He'd be rough. Angry. Determined to prove himself."

Raine breathes raggedly in time to each squeeze. I don't care if it's messed up to be talking about his friend while straddling him like this. None of us have to answer to anyone. If it feels right, I'm doing it.

Circling my entrance with his tip, I hold him at the precipice of satisfaction. An inch from heaven.

"I imagined him shoving himself inside me," I tease breathlessly. "Taking me hard and deep like he wants to fuck the fight out of me. You'd ride my mouth while he fills me from behind."

"Such a dirty little angel," he groans. "Why does this turn me on so much?"

"I think you have a sharing kink, Raine."

Nudging him inside me, I slowly sink down, inch by excruciating inch. He stretches me so perfectly, filling me to the breaking point as he bottoms out. I watch his golden eyes roll back in his head.

"Shit, babe. I think you're right."

Gasping at the intensity, I savour the burn. "I'm all for exploring it. Keep that in mind."

Lifting my hips, I push back down on him. It's an awkward manoeuvre that tugs at my thigh wound, but in the heat of the moment, the pain only amplifies my acute pleasure. We've talked ourselves into a frenzy.

I move slow and steady, taking him deep with each thrust. His cock pushes against the sweet spot buried within me that makes stars burst behind my eyes. Already, I feel overwhelmed with sensation.

"You feel so fucking good, babe. So good."

He ruts up into me, matching each stroke with one of his own. Raine's always been acutely in tune to my body. His ability to see the unseen comes into play when we fuck. He's as attentive as he is passionate.

We're perfectly synchronised, reading each other's needs without words. Each time I press down on him, Raine slides up into my cunt with a low groan. I clench tight around him, my walls hugging his length.

Footsteps halt outside the bedroom, making my heart patter harder. My ears straining, each clash becomes harder, more frantic. Raine's muscles clench, his burnt-toffee orbs swallowed whole by expanded pupils.

"Please," I mewl, letting him slam into me. "I need to come."

"Take it, babe. Show me how well you fall apart."

Hands splayed on his chest, I throw my head back. I'm close to exploding. My climax hangs on the cusp of overwhelming me, magnified by the knowledge that those halted footsteps haven't moved away.

When Raine finds my clit again, lightly tugging the tingling bud, all rational thought vanishes. My release hits hard and fast. I don't know if it's exhaustion or the imbalanced chemicals swamping my brain, but the orgasm is blisteringly intense.

"Yes!" I moan loudly.

Raine eases to a slow roll, his hips shifting up into me. He's breathless too, but I haven't felt him finish. He's still thick inside me, holding my climax in suspension as aftershocks move in.

"You're bleeding, Rip."

"Hmm?"

His movements slow. "Your leg."

Glancing down, I find the thin bandage speckled with blood. I didn't even feel it. We ruled out an infection when Xander stitched the wound yesterday, but it's still tender.

"We should stop."

"No!" I writhe on top of him. "Don't you dare."

Grasping my hips, Raine gently manoeuvres out of me. I cry out at the sudden loss. I'm about to chew him out when he lays me down, feeling for my legs then spreading them wide so he can settle between them.

He doesn't say a word as he slides back into me, assuming the position of power. I greedily accept his forceful thrust, my blood pumping like liquid caramel through my veins after my first release.

"You drive me insane, Rip. I want to take care of you, but instead, I'm fucking you senseless because you don't know when to take no for an answer."

"You're right. I don't." I stare up at his unfocused expression. "So shut up and fuck me senseless, Raine. Give me what I want."

"So demanding."

His grin tells a different story. Secretly, he loves it. The explosive way our bodies collide. The sense of control it gives him in a world determined to take his autonomy away. With me, he can take a piece of himself back.

As he begins pounding into me faster, it feels like Raine is determined to prove a point. I've given him free rein, and he's damn well going to take it regardless of who may be listening nearby.

My mind fantasises about the possibilities. I know Xander has no respect for boundaries, that's old news. He'll happily munch his popcorn while listening to us if he so pleases. The man doesn't care about social graces.

Lennox… He's the question mark.

Our dynamic is changing, morphing from raw hatred to bitterly reluctant infatuation. I don't know if the new, softer Lennox would dare interrupt our privacy. He's an unknown to me.

Raine's continued thrusting shows how little he cares too. He hasn't just accepted the others' place in my life; I have a sneaking suspicion he actually fucking loves it.

"I want you to give me one more, babe."

With lust snaking through me, I fist the tangled bedsheets. "Yes."

"That's it. Give me everything." He urgently ruts into me, chasing his own climax. "Show me that you love me too, Rip. I need to feel it."

I'm sure I don't imagine the barely audible curse emanating from outside the bedroom door. I don't have the mental capacity to question it as Raine ducks down to kiss my chest, sucking a nipple in between his lips.

The cramped bedroom is a blur all around me. Raine's silhouette fills my vision, dappled with sparkling sunlight. Stray hair falls across his slick forehead, the sunshine accentuating every taut muscle in his neck and shoulders.

He licks and sucks my nipple, his teeth scratching against the peak. His playful bite sets off sparks in my mind that catch alight and spread, filling my whole body with delicious heat.

"I can feel you clenching around me," he marvels. "I know you're close, babe. Let go."

"Oh god," I whine. "Raine!"

"Let them hear you scream my name."

The heat inside me reaches its apex. Everything seizes, my nervous system knotted so tightly, it's just begging to be unravelled. All he has to do is shove me into that downward spiral.

Raine draws my breast into his mouth, pulling on my skin so firmly, I know it'll leave a bright mark. An indelible reminder of all we've shared. I still can't quite believe it.

He loves me.

And… I think I love him too.

I know I do.

My second climax hits harder than the first, the blistering cloud of pure euphoria sweeping everything else out. I'm a sputtering wreck, my entire body shattering into a thousand unrecognisable shards.

Raine bellows in time to me crying his name again. I feel

him judder inside me, his release filling me up with a rush of heat. The feeling stretches out my orgasm until it's echoing on in tortuous waves.

Slumping, he hides his face in my neck. I can feel how violently his heart is beating through his skin. Raine breathes hard, his hair tickling my face as I pant for air too.

When my brain decides to function again, I realise how much my thigh is screaming at me. The discomfort didn't matter in the moment. Now I know I've pushed myself too far. Worth it, though.

"Raine," I whisper throatily. "I need to go clean up."

He groans, half-awake. "Are you okay?"

"Yes. More than okay."

Lifting himself off me, he collapses to the side so I'm free. I move stiffly, grimacing at the blood-soaked bandage around my thigh. Xander's going to chew me out if I've popped a stitch.

Raine catches my arm. "You're not okay."

"It's just a bit of blood. Stay here."

"I can help—"

"I've got this."

Teeth gritted, I stand up. I'm headed for the door to find the bathroom when something stops me. I look back at Raine in the bed, his attention fixed on me, even if his eyes aren't.

"Raine?"

"Yeah, guava girl?"

I smile at the silly nickname. "For the record, I love you too."

A stupid grin spreads across his face, softening his pink-flushed features. I leave him smiling like an idiot. Limping out of the bedroom, I'm thankful the corridor is empty. Our voyeur has vanished.

I'm so focused on avoiding being spotted in my naked, messy state, I don't look up as I enter the bathroom. The sound of harsh breathing and low, guttural grunts only filter in when I've closed the door.

"Oh," I squeak.

One hand braced on the sink, Lennox has his jeans around his ankles, the other hand fisting his thick, vein-streaked cock. My eyes bulge at the sight, cataloguing not only his ridiculous size but the blazing desire written all over his face as he jacks off.

"Am I interrupting?" I ask slyly.

Jaw locked, his gaze swings to me. Touching everywhere. My breasts. Raine's love bite. My swollen pussy, slick with our come. Lennox rubs his cock faster, hand flashing up and down, unashamedly drinking me in.

And I let him.

It's a liberating sight.

My feet carry me forwards without command. I hold his stare as I reach in to push his hand away. Lennox sucks in a ragged breath when I take over, cupping his shaft and delivering a slow squeeze.

"Did you like listening?"

His tongue darts out to wet his lips. "I wanted to break the door down and take you for myself."

"What makes you think I'd let you?" I rhythmically stroke his cock.

"I know you feel it too, Rip." His stubble-smothered throat bobs. "I know you're struggling to fathom how the person you once hated most can become the very thing keeping you sane."

"You drive me insane," I correct.

"Which one of us looks insane right now?"

My lips spread in a satisfied smirk. "You."

"Exactly."

"Since we're being honest, I enjoy the thought that I've driven you to this. I want that power. In fact, I want you on your knees, begging for the chance to fuck me like Raine does."

"That's what you want?" he grits out.

"Yes. I want you grovelling on your fucking knees, Lennox Nash."

"Then when the time comes, that's what I'll do."

Grabbing a handful of my hair, he pulls my mouth to his. Lennox kisses me above the hot flush that Raine left behind. His lips are firm, devouring the memory and replacing it with a brand of his own.

I can feel them both on me. Claiming. Marking. Possessing. But in my mind, they're distinct. Even Xander has his own little patch of neurons dedicated just to him. There's no competition.

Working Lennox's length over, I call the final victory. His huge cock jerks in my hand, mirroring his sudden grunt into my mouth, and I feel sticky ribbons hit my lower belly.

We separate, his lips rapidly pecking mine when I steal a final taste. I love how closely his pale-green eyes resemble a seaborne storm right now. Unruly and uncontrollable.

"I look forward to it," I purr, releasing his dick. "Preferably away from prying ears. My roommates seem to have no sense of privacy."

Snorting, he looks down in embarrassment. That's when he notices the saturated bandage on my thigh, now leaking thin trails of crimson.

Lennox pierces me with a glower. "What the fuck?"

"Erm… it was an accident?"

"Raine!" He pushes me away from him even as I start laughing. "I'm going to fucking kill him!"

CHAPTER 14
RIPLEY

HATE ME NOW – RYAN CARAVEO

TIME PASSES DIFFERENTLY when you're running for your life.

It's broken flashes.

Disjointed. Rapid.

Staring out the window at the dreary, grey sky hanging over the hotel, I breathe a matching cloud onto the glass and watch the condensation drip down. The droplets fall slowly, sluggish and tiresome.

It's a total contrast to the energy burning me from inside out. I thought it would've fizzled out after several sleepless nights in the crappy hotel we moved to. That usually does the trick. But not this time around.

The door beeps on the other side of the double room before it clicks open. I recognise Lennox's thudding footsteps. He stomps around like he's determined to shake the earth with his weight alone.

"That son of a bitch turns my stomach," he hisses as the door slams shut.

I turn around to check him over. There's a hollow ache in my stomach that triples at the sight of the food bag clutched in his hands. Lennox offers me a tense smile, pulling his healing facial cut.

He heads for the small table opposite the bathroom. "We're lining his fucking pockets just to keep his mouth shut."

Focused on the newspaper clasped in his hands, Xander lounges on one of the double beds. He spares Lennox a dismissive look over the lines of typed ink that have held his attention for the past hour.

"We're paying over the odds in cash for the hotel's discretion. No IDs and no questions asked. Suck it up, Nox."

"The owner is rinsing us for every goddamn penny!"

Xander shrugs. "We can cover it."

"With more stolen cash?" he retorts.

"If you'd like to offer an alternative solution, be my guest."

With that, Xander disappears back behind his apparently fascinating newspaper. The man's living on a different planet if he thinks the answers to all our problems are printed in that thing.

The media is still acting like we're the bad guys for inciting the riot. All the limited coverage we've seen has been unfairly biased. Apparently, unstable patients overtook Harrowdean. Unprovoked and with the intent to cause maximum destruction.

What's worse is the fact that people are actually swallowing it. Even with rumours of medical malpractice and abuse running rampant. The narrative that we're the instigators is a more palatable truth.

There's been no mention of Rick, Rae or the others in the media. The official public line is that all remaining detainees in Harrowdean have been secured and transferred elsewhere. I'm sure Rick didn't make it that far, though. Like us, he knows too much.

Lennox drops the paper bag on the table. "I know we had to move on at some point, but holing up so close to the city feels like an unnecessary risk. We should pack up and leave."

"Derby is twenty miles away." Xander remains focused on the newspaper.

"Close enough! What if we're recognised?"

"By a greedy hotel owner? Or his half-deaf cleaner?" he harrumphs. "Doubtful."

I turn back to face the window. They've spent the better part of the last week bickering. As the days have passed, it's been harder for me to decipher exactly what about. Something to do with a phone call, I think.

The running shower halts in the attached bathroom. Raine must be nearly done. He's having a rough day, barely able to keep food or water down between fitfully sleeping.

"How is he?" I hear Lennox ask.

"Spent an hour throwing up. I've located a public library with decent computers. So I can forge a paper prescription slip given enough time to fabricate the details and a false ID."

"You can get that stuff on prescription?"

"I've done some research. Rehab patients take it in the community too. I should be able to make something convincing enough to get refills."

Tuning them out, I focus on my breathing. In and out. Chest expanding. Oxygen spreading. If I break the process down in my head, I can fool myself that I'm still the one in control.

My hands shake at my sides, shattering the illusion as quickly as it's able to form. Too much is going on. My defences are shot to pieces right now. I can't control the haywire thoughts invading my mind like I usually can.

I've been turning over what superpower I wish I had for the last ten minutes or so. If I could go incognito, I could slip past the men eyeing me like a ticking bomb and run free. Invisibility would be a cool power.

It would feel so good to run as fast as my little legs can

carry me. Strip off my clothes. Sprint into the threatening rain. Or perhaps oncoming traffic. I can see the main road to the city from here.

I wonder if my incognito powers would kick in to stop me from becoming a human pancake if I were struck. I'd like to try—I bet they would. Not even fast-moving cars can slow me down.

Don't they know who I am? I'm Harrowdean's whore. The ultimate stooge. I'm untouchable. Invincible. Not even a high-speed, fatal crash could stop me from running for the hills right now.

"Rip!"

A touch on my shoulder is an unwelcome shock. I jump out of my skin, quickly falling into fight-or-flight. Grabbing the paw-like hand, I tug hard, throwing my assailant forward.

They don't even fight back, allowing me to floor them in record time. How dare they touch me? I don't belong here. Not in this shitty room. Not with these people. Not on the run. This wasn't the plan.

What was the plan?

I can't quite remember.

"Ripley! Hey!"

"I'm invisible!" I roar angrily. "You can't see me!"

Kneeling on the cheap hotel carpet, Lennox peers up at me with concern. "It's me, Rip."

Blinking rapidly, I stare down at him. Lennox Nash. Funny to think he scared me once. Both he and Xander did. I'm not sure why since I can turn invisible. Perhaps if I try hard enough right now, I'll disappear in front of him.

"Talk to me. What's going on in your head?"

"Can you still see me?" I ask in frustration.

Lennox blinks, still on his knees. "Uh, yes. I can."

"Goddammit!" I tug at my hair. "Why isn't it working?"

His newspaper discarded, Xander stands up to approach us. "Why isn't what working, Ripley?"

"I hate it when you look at me like that," I snap at him. "I'm not a zoo animal."

Eyebrows drawn together, Lennox stands up. "No one is looking at you like that, baby. You're not eating or sleeping. What's going on?"

At the mention of food, an embarrassingly loud growl erupts from my stomach. I slap a hand over the offending organ. Why is it making such a fuss? I ate… hell, a few days ago. Maybe?

It doesn't matter. I don't have time to eat or sleep while I'm plotting my grand escape. I'll never master my new superpower if I'm too busy resting like they're always insisting upon.

"Have you ever seen her like this?" Lennox whispers.

Xander shakes his head. "Not to this extent."

"What do we do?"

"No idea. I'm not a damn psychiatrist."

See, this is exactly what I'm talking about. I may as well be invisible. They're talking about me as if I am. Unless… Has it finally happened? I look down at myself, pinching my tattooed forearm to check.

"Stupid!" I hiss impatiently.

Someone is touching me again—Xander. Cursing him out, I attempt to peel his fingers from my bicep. He's trying to direct me over to the bed. I don't want to lay in that again.

"Don't touch me!"

"Ripley," he scolds. "You need to rest."

"I'm not tired. I need to keep working!"

"On what?" Lennox follows us.

"My superpowers, obviously. You can still see me. How can I disappear if you can see me? I have to disappear!"

Lennox's shoulders slump as he turns back to his best friend. "I think we need to forge more prescriptions. How did we not see this coming?"

"I did." Xander exhales. "The signs have been there for a while."

"Why didn't you say anything?"

"We've been a little busy running for our lives, Nox."

I'm still trapped by his grip. It feels like he's scalding me. When I pull free, Xander bands his arms around me, cinching me tight like a straitjacket. I'm strong-armed, bucking and protesting, over to the bed.

"Xan, I don't think—"

"I'm trying to get her to rest," he justifies.

"You shouldn't physically restrain her, though!"

"Do you have a better idea? I'm all ears."

The bathroom door opens on their continued arguing. Spotting Raine, damp and redressed, I cry in relief. I know he'll understand. Maybe he'll help me practise my invisibility.

Raine is safe. Warm. Familiar. He never hurt me like these two did. I didn't have to forgive him because he's been nothing but genuine and respectful towards me since day one.

"What happened?" He tilts his head, listening closely.

Lennox clears his throat. "We're concerned Ripley's having a manic episode."

"Help me, Raine!" I blurt out in panic. "He's trying to make me sleep. I don't want to sleep."

One hand outstretched to feel for obstacles, Raine follows the sound of my whimpers. I sob in pure relief when he eases me from Xander's imprisonment and wraps me in a warm, citrus-scented hug.

"It's okay, guava girl. No one is going to make you sleep if you don't want to."

Arms thrown around his neck, I break down in hysterical tears. Raine lets me cling to him, covering his fresh shirt in moisture. If I could share my invisibility, I'd extend it to him. He can run with me.

"What were you thinking?" he mutters above my lowered

head. "She needs to feel safe and supported. We have no idea what's going on inside her head right now."

"I'm trying to help!" Xander booms.

"By scaring her? Great plan."

"I just thought…"

"No, Xan. She's a person. You can't take her choice away even if you think it's for the best."

I'm grateful when they all shut up. The frenzied voices yelling in my head are making it difficult to focus.

"Come on," Raine coaxes, clutching me tightly. "Did you know I had panic attacks for months after I lost my sight?"

"N-No," I stammer.

"My sensitive hearing made it feel like the entire world was screaming at me. The trauma centre assigned me a therapist. He told me to picture a giant ocean wave crashing over me when I was panicking."

"I'm not… This isn't… I'm not panicking! I just don't want to rest!"

He rubs up and down my back. "I know. You don't have to. But I do want you to try and calm down."

His fresh scent is seeping into me, drawing me into the dream of a warm summer's day on the beach. Sipping orange juice and dipping my toes into the salty ocean. Content. Invisible. Free.

"The waves I imagine sparkle in the sunlight," Raine murmurs soothingly. "And I sometimes picture dolphins dipping in and out of them."

"Dolphins?" I whimper.

"Why not? It's my imagination. You can picture a massive pink unicorn swimming along if that's what you want. Give it a try."

Ignoring the sounds of heavy breathing and moving footsteps behind us, I desperately yank together my mind's frayed strands. I can do this for Raine. It's just a silly game.

Hands fisting in his t-shirt, I screw my eyes shut. The

blackness of my closed lids fades as my vision takes shape. Shimmering, aqua waves, topped with a light-white froth. Gleaming sunshine. Squalling seagulls.

"Let the wave roll over you," Raine encourages just loud enough for me to hear. "Feel the water. The bubbles. The current carrying you along."

"W-What if I drown?"

"You won't. It's perfectly safe to let yourself bob along, floating on the water. Let it crash over you and wash everything else away."

The sobs ripping out of me slowly begin to ease as I picture calm waves falling over me. The water feels like silk. It kisses my skin and warms my bones, pushing out the intense energy that's been tormenting me.

"That's it." Raine strokes the back of my head. "Deep breaths. Did you see the unicorn yet?"

"A whale," I breathe out unsteadily. "Beluga."

"Okay, we can work with that. Keep going."

His hand moves rhythmically over my spine. Each stroke mirrors the waves that have filled my head, swelling up and undulating with the swirling current. White, pearlescent whales pop their head up and squeal.

I'm not sure how long we stand there for, lost in our heads and ignoring the entire world. Long enough for terror to set in when I realise how out of control I'm feeling right now.

"I… don't f-feel so good," I hiccup.

"I know." Raine blows out a long breath. "Tell us what you need."

"I want to go. We have to run."

"We're going to keep you safe, Rip. I promise."

No. Nobody can.

The sound of the other two talking filters back into my awareness. They're exchanging urgent whispers elsewhere in the hotel room.

"How long will it take you to forge a prescription? And do you know what she takes?"

"Of course, I do," Xander responds. "Stay here."

"Take a phone. Be careful."

Hearing Xander grab something and leave, I immediately pull away from Raine. He can't leave. I didn't mean it. I'll share my invisibility with him—he shouldn't go out alone. It isn't safe.

"Rip!" Lennox calls out. "I brought something back I think you'll like."

Skidding to a halt, I look between him and the door. "But, Xander…"

"He'll be back soon," Raine rushes to assure me. "I smell food. Are you hungry?"

I shake my head, reluctantly turning away from the door. Lennox has started emptying the bag he brought back, laying out takeaway cartons. That gnawing in my belly is back. Tiny ravenous butterflies.

"Come and eat something," he encourages.

"I don't have time to eat!"

"Then I can't show you the other thing I got." Lennox raises an eyebrow. "Food, Rip. I need you to eat something."

Tiptoeing closer, I follow Raine over to the table. "What's the other thing?"

"Something that will help. But food first."

"Come sit with us," Raine adds with a smile.

They both sit down, passing plastic cutlery between them before digging into their food. The salty, savoury scents assault my nose. Spices. Herbs. Something rich and fragrant. The butterflies are going berserk now.

"Mmm." Raine chews his mouthful. "Sure we can't tempt you, Rip?"

I stare at them, conflicted.

"This is so good," he continues with exaggerated

enthusiasm. "We've been living off crap for so long, I forgot what real food tastes like."

"Enjoy it while it lasts," Lennox responds, though he keeps an eye on me.

I've inched within touching distance of a carton. I can see herb-studded rice and a vibrant sauce with chunks of meat. My mouth waters. All the fizzing energy that's distracted me narrows in on that carton.

Nudging a plastic fork closer, Lennox moves it to the edge of the table. I have my hands on the carton and the fork in my mouth before I can draw a breath. Exotic flavours explode on my tongue.

"S'good," I moan.

Lennox looks down at his food, smiling to himself.

Finishing in record time, I snag a few triangles of bread then move back to the window to munch in peace. Their attention in the past few days has been suffocating. It's why I wanted to disappear in the first place.

The sound of eating dissolves as I zone back out. The clouds have broken now. Big, fat raindrops hammer down from the sky. It obscures the busy road running alongside the budget hotel.

A woman with auburn hair rushes to safety from the falling rain, holding a soaked magazine over her head. The bright-red waves linger in my mind, taking me back to our final moments inside Harrowdean.

Is Rae alive?

Did she make it out?

The bread in my mouth turns to ash. I abandoned her. All of them. People I hurt to bolster my own position. People I equipped to hurt themselves. Rae deserves to be free, not me. She's the innocent one.

"Ripley?"

Lennox stops next to me without touching me this time.

He peers at my face, a frown forming between his dark-brown eyebrows.

"You're crying again."

I numbly touch my cheek, finding it wet. "I don't deserve to be invisible."

"What's that?"

"That's why my superpowers aren't working. The world wants me to be punished for what I did in Harrowdean. It won't let me disappear."

"Oh, Rip." He shakes his head. "Can I touch you?"

When I don't reject him, Lennox moves closer. He clasps my cheek in his huge, calloused hand, the rough skin making my face itch. His thumb travels through my falling tears in a wide arc.

"You've been punished enough," he whispers emphatically. "Just being locked up in there was a punishment. You did what you had to. The world could never begrudge you that."

"But… I left Rae behind."

His gaze fractures with sympathy. "You barely escaped with your life. That's a bit different."

Eyes closing, I lean into his touch. It feels more welcome this time. I know it's Lennox. Not the Lennox that exists in my memories, but the Lennox I recently discovered. Protective. Loyal. Firm but gentle when needed.

"Now, I can't help with this superpower issue." He strokes a thumb over my parted lips. "But I have something that may take your mind off it. Want to come see?"

I nod, reopening my eyes. "Okay."

He releases me to take my hand. Raine still sits at the table, surrounded by their empty takeaway cartons. Lennox guides me into his vacated chair as he locates the backpack he also brought back.

"Found a small art shop on the walk back to the hotel," he

explains while reaching inside. "It's been a while, right? I heard this helps you cope with stuff."

Lennox stacks two sketchbooks, a pack of charcoal pencils and a miniature watercolour set with sealed brushes in front of me. For several astonished seconds, I just gape. It's been so long since I saw paint or brushes.

"These are for me?"

"Well, yeah." He shrugs, his teeth digging into his bottom lip. "If they're not right… I can go back."

With still-shaking hands, I pick up the watercolours, clicking the tin open to inspect the colours. The familiar scent of paint feels like walking into my childhood home and accepting a perfume-scented hug from my mum.

Tears well back up. "I don't know what to say."

"Reckon you could show me some of those famous skills while we wait for Xander?" he requests, locating a bottle of water to fill a glass. "I haven't seen much of your art before."

Flipping open the sketchpads, I run my fingertips over the paper. It's good quality, thick and well-grained for watercolour work. The charcoals are all perfectly sharpened. He chose these supplies thoughtfully.

"Just like old times in the studio." Raine laughs before quickly sobering. "God, I miss my violin. I really hope she survived the riot."

Lennox takes a seat, pushing cartons out of the way. "We'll get you another."

"Not the same. She was perfect."

Ignoring their conversation, I dip the flat brush into the water he poured and begin mixing colours. Just seeing the brilliant swirls kickstarts the creative fever that always sets in when I sit down to paint.

It's a living, breathing thing, stirring deep inside my gut. The world just fades away. I've never felt more at peace than when I'm creating. In these moments, I can control the emotions running rampant in me.

I test each brush and colour, familiarising myself with the equipment before sketching an outline with a thin charcoal. The image comes out of nowhere.

My hand steadies with each stroke and flick. The excruciating energy that's kept me on the verge of a breakdown since we escaped pulls tight inside me. I'm uncoiling it, taking back control from the violent force and stretching it to breaking point.

Vivid blacks. Deep, burnished greens. I mix red and blue to form bubbling, purple storm clouds around the landscape that's spilling from my brush. Using my pinkie finger, I blend the paint to create the perfect, fluffy shapes.

The persistent ache in my neck tells me hours have passed when I finally sit up, looking down at the scene I've crafted. It's not the image I thought I was painting. Somewhere along the way, it changed.

When I look at Lennox and Raine, both slumped in their chairs, I realise I'm no longer shaking. I can breathe again. Think again. The coil has snapped and withered, leaving me to float back down.

I push the sketchpad over to Lennox so he can take a look. He picks it up, his expression neutral as he studies the scene closely for several long seconds.

"What is it?" Raine asks curiously.

Sliding the sketchpad back to me, Lennox keeps quiet to let me answer. I look back down at the watercolour sketch. Stormy, threatening skies. Smoking ruins. The destruction entombed in a woodland sarcophagus.

I've recreated the institute we fled. Harrowdean Manor in all its grandiose monstrosity—stained glass, gothic stone, the wrought-iron gates and ivy-wrapped crest pronouncing the letters *HM*.

Only the manor no longer stands.

Harrowdean has been demolished.

I refocus on Raine. "The future."

CHAPTER 15
LENNOX
BLEED – CONNOR KAUFFMAN

PACKING the supplies we've gathered over several cautious trips, I set the third and final backpack at the end of the double bed. I'm straining my ears for any sign of Xander and Ripley's return. They've been gone for two hours.

We decided to take the plunge and test his counterfeit skills before moving on. Raine collected his medication yesterday without issue. Now it's round two.

After working tirelessly to forge fake IDs and prescription slips, Xander has taken Ripley to collect her medication today. It can't come a moment sooner. She's been semi-lucid since the first manic symptoms manifested.

"They've been gone for too long." Raine folds and unfolds his stick, obviously agitated. "How long does it take?"

"He's taken her to the pharmacy in the next town over. We don't want anyone asking questions about Xander's forgery."

"How long can we continue hiding like this? Living off scraps and stealing to survive?" He sighs. "We need help, Nox."

"We're not trusting those Sabre people."

"Then who can we trust?"

"Ourselves." I glance over the packed supplies again. "We just need to keep moving. I'm not letting any of us get taken back into custody or worse."

"And if this situation rumbles on for years to come? If the investigation doesn't find Incendia at fault or clear our names? What happens then?"

Ignoring him, I perch on the bed and watch the door. When they get back, we'll set off. Xander found a sleepy bed and breakfast in a small town farther east. It's a mammoth trek, but we can't risk public transport right now.

"Lennox! I'm talking to you!"

"I don't know, alright?" I bark at him. "I have no idea how this ends. My concern right now is getting through each day. We can't think beyond that."

"We can, and we should. This is untenable."

"What do you suggest, Raine? Hand ourselves over to the authorities? Let them quietly execute us? I suppose you'll be okay. They may ship you off to one of the other institutes and just kill us three."

He slaps his folded stick down on the bed. "That's not fair. We're in this together."

"Are we? I don't remember you dealing contraband, killing the fucking warden or breaking out of the Z wing."

"No," he replies hotly. "I suppose I just *accidentally* tagged along on this little trip, right? The same way I *accidentally* chose to go all in with the three of you. I do hope they let me off easy."

Head bowing, I press the heels of my palms into my eye sockets. Escaping Harrowdean feels like a lifetime ago, yet the infinite nightmare has also passed in a terrifying flash. None of us can live like this much longer.

"I'm sorry," I croak. "That wasn't fair."

"You're damn right it wasn't fair."

"I said I'm sorry, alright?"

"Don't turn on the people who love you most." Hurt laces his words. "Not when they're all you've got left."

Regret swamps me, provoking a burst of honesty. "I just feel so powerless."

The bed shifts as he shuffles to the end to sit with me. Raine bumps his shoulder into mine.

"You're doing the best you can."

"It sure doesn't feel like it."

"Look, I know you don't trust these people. I don't think any of us do. But we're running very low on options right now. This could be our last play."

"We can't risk ending up back there, Raine."

He whooshes out a sigh. "Bouncing from place to place, hoping we're not spotted or tracked down, isn't exactly a long-term plan either."

Lifting my head, I look down at my mangled hand. It's healing, a shiny, puckered scar forming. The discoloured skin reminds me of the horrors we escaped every day. And what I'll do to keep my family from enduring them again.

"Footsteps," Raine announces.

"Jesus, man. Your hearing really is creepy."

"You're starting to sound like Ripley."

Right on cue, the woman in question storms into the room. Xander follows behind, a baseball cap tugged low to cover his ash-white hair. We decided he needs to be more inconspicuous, given how many supply runs he's been making.

Ripley doesn't even spare us a glance as she marches straight to the bathroom and slams the door shut, the lock snicking into place. Pulling several medication boxes from his hoodie, Xander tosses them on the bed.

"Well?" I prompt.

"We got everything." He gestures to the boxes.

"Then… what's the issue?"

"We need to get moving. There was a slight complication."

"Slight?" Raine repeats apprehensively.

Xander runs a hand over his pale face. "Ripley was a bit agitated and got upset. The pharmacist took her into a side room. I wasn't allowed in."

Dread blooms in my gut. "Why?"

"Concern for her safety, I guess. We had to play along."

"Then what happened?" Raine asks.

"She won't say. All I know is we left behind a pharmacy tech with a broken nose on the phone with the police. I managed to swipe the meds before we hauled ass."

"Shit!" I exclaim. "Were you followed back?"

"No. There was CCTV, though."

Frowning at the soft vibrating coming from his pocket, Xander pulls out one of the stolen phones. I walk over to the bathroom door and tap, my ear pressed against the wood to hear Ripley's response.

"Rip? Are you okay in there?"

"Go away," she fires back.

"What happened?"

"Leave me alone, Nox!"

"Please, open up. Let us help."

Silence.

Shit, this isn't good. She's been hanging on by a thread. If this tech did something to trigger her paranoia, it's lucky they didn't get worse than a broken nose.

"Raine. Can you talk to her?"

Turning around, I find him tuned in to the voices emanating from Xander's phone. They're both totally immersed. My scalp prickles uneasily as I stop at Xander's side to look over his shoulder.

"What is it?"

"Another press conference," he mutters. "I just got the notification. But it's not Bancroft dolling out more professional lies this time."

"Then who is?"

Bloodthirsty journalists gather on the live feed. It's being shot against a professional backdrop, the pedestal and microphone set up next to an oversized easel with a board positioned on it.

The floor falls away beneath me when I realise whose face is printed on that board. She's younger. Hazel eyes filled with innocence. Smiling. Arms tattoo free. Tawny-brown curls pinned back with two criss-crossed paintbrushes. No septum piercing in sight.

Ripley.

"What is this?" I gasp.

"Some kind of missing persons' appeal?" Xander laughs without humour. "This is a new low."

The hum of voices on the live feed falls silent. Striding over to the pedestal, a broad-shouldered man takes the stage. His smooth skin is tanned, like he's been sunning himself on a tropical island recently.

Dark-brown hair that doesn't seem to match his age belies an expensive dye job. Even his beard is well-trimmed without a hair out of place, complementing his crisp, pinstriped suit.

Businessman, clearly. From his confident walk to the way he holds his head high with self-importance, his entire persona screams extravagant wealth and power. Already, I hate him.

"Who's the suit?"

Xander exhales loudly. "That… is Ripley's uncle."

"Oh, shit," Raine mutters.

On the screen, journalists lean forward in their chairs, notepads poised and questions ready. This is another staged show for the world's media to gulp down. I have a bad fucking feeling.

"Good afternoon. My name is Jonathan Bennet."

"Weren't her mum and dad married?" I question. "He's the maternal uncle, right?"

Raine braces his elbows on his knees, listening closely. "This dickhead made Ripley change her surname when he took custody. I gather he was more concerned about his public image than being a parental figure."

"Be quiet," Xander orders.

He turns up the volume on the phone. We all lean closer.

"I'm appealing for information about the disappearance of my beloved niece, Ripley Bennet. She was undertaking a rehabilitative program at Harrowdean Manor until the recent violence broke out."

Jonathan actually manages to look concerned. It makes my skin crawl.

"Ripley is unwell and has serious, long-term, mental health needs that require ongoing treatment. She's vulnerable. I'm very worried about the delinquents my niece has gotten caught up with."

I guffaw at his choice of words. "We're delinquents now."

"Been called worse," Xander grumbles.

"Delinquent is a damn compliment for what you are, Xan."

"Hey, idiots," Raine redirects our attention. "Why is he going public now? Minimal information has been coming out of Harrowdean for weeks."

Xander studies the asshole wiping away his fake tears. "He's Bancroft's new mouthpiece. It's probably just another tactic to hunt us down. They're getting desperate."

"Ripley, please." Jonathan bleats emotionally. "The riot is over. You don't need to run from us. Let us provide the help you need."

"He's actually convincing." I shake my head. "Fucking hell."

"I know you didn't mean any harm… Please come home. We only want to help."

"This piece of shit never wanted to help Ripley," Raine viciously snarls. "He's treated her like damaged goods ever since she was diagnosed. The man disowned her!"

"But now his investment is in danger." I watch the

journalists throw up their hands to ask questions. "This is the performance of his career."

The first journalist takes hold of the microphone. "How does a renowned investment banker and respected public figure like yourself justify bankrolling a criminal enterprise?"

A nasty, red flush creeps up Jonathan's neck, spilling from his pressed collar. "I have full faith in the important work Incendia Corporation is doing in the private medical sector."

"That's a non-answer, Mr Bennet. Does that work include illegal human experimentation and abuse?"

"Most certainly not." Jonathan's sneer is a very brief crack in his façade. "You shouldn't believe everything you hear, Miss Moore."

He turns his attention to the next journalist, his picture-perfect smile back in place. The slick bastard's been media trained to within an inch of his life. Though I recognise a snake when I see one.

"Sir Bancroft announced the death of Harrowdean's warden, Abbott Davis, in his latest update. Does the disappearance of your niece and several other patients relate to his passing?"

"Son of a bitch." I roll my head over my tense shoulders. "I can't believe they dared to ask him that."

Xander keeps his lips sealed shut. Cool as a cucumber. The warden's death was publicly announced not long ago— we caught that news while moving to this location. So far, no information is being released as to the circumstances.

Xander assured me he wasn't seen and the killing can't be traced back to him. I'm sure all manner of violence that took place during the riot is being investigated, like the multiple guard deaths.

I can't help worrying that this will come back to haunt us. We're being drip-fed updates while management scrambles to make sense of the destruction we left behind. That doesn't mean there won't be consequences.

"Warden Davis's death is a senseless tragedy," Jonathan replies calmly, his fingers steepled in front of him. "One that is being actively investigated. I am confident that justice will be served."

The questions keep coming, prying for any updates into the riot, Harrowdean's now closed doors and the increasingly serious allegations facing Incendia. I watch Jonathan's cool, PR-perfect mask falter again.

"Ex-patient of Blackwood Institute, Brooklyn West, has publicly accused the corporation you support of medical malpractice and negligence. Tell me, has your niece fled for the same reasons?"

"Oh, killer." Raine excitedly pumps his fist. "Please tell me the asshole is melting into a puddle right now."

"More like a purple-faced ogre," I respond.

"I will not be commenting on media speculation and the false accusations of unwell individuals." Jonathan keeps his reply curt. "I'm only interested in locating Ripley and bringing her home where she belongs."

"How can he say that?" Xander spits in disgust.

"Because he only cares about the money."

We all turn at the sound of Ripley's flat voice. Focused on the screen, we didn't hear the bathroom door reopen. She stands in the doorway, chest heaving and eyes shining, her hands curled into white-knuckled fists.

"Ripley." I start towards her.

"Uncle Jonathan would throw his own mother under a bus if it scored him a pretty penny." She steps past me, heading for the medication.

The press conference wraps up as Jonathan stalks off. Apparently, his patience for uncomfortable questions has expired. The comparison to other escapees was the final straw for him.

Xander tosses the phone aside, turning his focus to Ripley. She's unpacking various boxes, checking over the names and dosages. We watch her line up a handful of different pills—methodical and oddly calm.

I grab a bottle of water to hand over to her. "Got it all figured out?"

"I wasn't always locked up in a fucked up psych ward run by corrupt maniacs," she replies dryly. "I know how to organise my own medication."

Ripley takes her pills, one by one. It's the calmest I've seen her all week. I guess part of her understands she has to do this, the same way a type one diabetic takes Insulin every day. Mental health is no different.

Repackaging the boxes, she neatly stacks them up. It almost seems like a calming ritual. I thought we'd have to beg her. She's been fluctuating up and down faster than a goddamn yo-yo recently.

"You want to talk about what went down in the pharmacy?"

She shudders. "I just got muddled up, that's all."

"On what, exactly?"

"The woman was asking me all these questions. I couldn't think straight."

"Did you hit her?"

Ripley frowns, glancing down at her fist. The knuckles are red, marked with a shallow abrasion. She studies the evidence, her brow crinkling.

"I just wanted to get out of that room." She exhales slowly. "It felt like the walls were closing in on me. I couldn't see Xander. I was scared it was a trap."

Honestly, it's hard to tell where the manic paranoia ends and legitimate concern for the insanity we've found ourselves in begins. If we weren't running from a criminal conspiracy, I'd be concerned about her justification.

Taking her hand, I trace her swollen knuckles. "It's time to move."

Ripley glances between the three of us. Her freckle-dusted

features are filled with apprehension. Biting down on her lip, she seems to think something over.

"What is it?" Xander prompts.

"Are you sure you want to take me with you?" Her chin drops, eyes pinned to the ground. "I'm a proven liability. The police could be on their way here this very second because I couldn't keep my shit together."

This fucking woman.

I'm such an idiot for ever making her doubt us.

I want to crush her to my chest and forcefully strangle it from her mind. Her demons aren't liabilities. We started this journey together, and we're going to finish it together.

Before I can do just that, Xander strides over to us. He snatches Ripley from her chair, trapping her chin between his thumb and forefinger. I watch her visibly gulp as his darkening gaze bores into her.

"You are not a liability, Ripley. Say that about yourself again, and I'm going to take you over my knee."

Her mouth opens, and he promptly clicks it shut.

"Priory Lane. Harrowdean. On the run. Dead in the ground. I don't care where we are. You will stay right by our sides. Where. You. Fucking. Belong."

Something about Xander's emotive growl feels so right. Ripley has become our nucleus without even trying. She's transformed the chaos and suffering we've endured together into an opportunity.

A chance to belong.

A twisted, toxic, perfect family.

Releasing her so she can respond, Ripley sucks in a breath. "I want to stay with you. I just… I don't want anyone else to get hurt because of me."

"That's our choice," Raine speaks up. "We're choosing to stand by each other. Whether we get hurt or not is irrelevant. It's our decision to face the danger as a united front."

I nod in agreement, gaze locked on her. "If we get hurt, then we do that together too. It wouldn't be the first time."

Ripley flashes me a knowing look. We've witnessed far too much of one another's pain. Caused plenty of it too. My motivations are different now, though. We're standing together on the right side of the line this time.

I swore to myself that I'd make right on all the damage I've caused. If she thinks I'm giving up so soon, she's in for a real surprise. We're only just getting started. I'm going to stick around and fix what I've broken.

"Let's go, then." Her lips lift ever so slightly.

Picking up his stick, Raine unfolds it. "That's our girl."

CHAPTER 16

RIPLEY

SEE YOU IN HELL – BEAUTY
SCHOOL DROPOUT

THE CHECKOUT IS fast and impersonal. Our favourite hotel owner barely spares us a second glance now that he's milked us dry for an extortionate hush fee paid in cash. We step out into the daylight and follow Xander's directions.

Each one of us has dressed to blend in, wearing dark colours and casual t-shirts. Raine is unrecognisable beneath his aviators and the indigo hoodie he pulled on. Don't get me started on Mr Polo Shirt now wearing a baseball cap. Xander's sleek style is long gone.

Tensions are high as we leave the town behind, walking along a concrete underpass that snakes beneath the main road. We're moving away from the Derby vicinity now that we have supplies and medication.

Xander doesn't release my hand as the miles sluggishly trickle by. He's holding onto me so forcefully, I wonder if he thinks I'll float away like a helium-filled balloon. Or start rambling about my incredible invisibility again.

The time between holing up in the holiday park and the hotel is worryingly disjointed. My episodes often leave me confused and left to pick up the damaged pieces my manic self has scattered around me.

It's an exhausting cycle.

Not many stick around afterwards.

Part of me can't believe they're all still here and didn't take me up on the offer to leave me behind. I wouldn't have blamed them. I'm an unstable element. A liability. No one wants that on their team.

"About the press conference." Xander draws my attention.

"It doesn't matter, Xan."

"Doesn't it?" He quirks a brow. "That snake is still your uncle."

"Trust me, I've long stopped believing he's going to wake up and suddenly give a shit about me. That was just further proof of how little he cares."

My words are bitter and caustic.

"You don't need him," Xander spits out.

That was never the issue.

It wasn't a need. It was a *want*.

As we walk, our surroundings filter between rundown council estates to half-empty high streets. Families pass us on the way home from the school run, carrying bicycle helmets and glittery book bags.

The scene makes my heart ache with loss. I never had that. A chauffeur handled the school runs throughout my childhood while the housekeeper my uncle employed performed the role of caregiver.

I didn't have the normal, workaday familiarity of a warm family home. I'm sure some kids would trade their lives for the luxury and privilege I had, but to me, it was nothing but hollow grief. A reminder of all I'd lost.

All my life, I wanted a family.

I wanted to be loved.

All I got instead was sickness and disgust.

"We'll make them pay, Rip." Xander keeps his voice down. "All of them."

"How?" I laugh quietly. "We're penniless and on the run.

Up against wealth and corruption the world barely believes. Not even the authorities can see the truth."

"Then we make them see."

"We both know it isn't that simple."

The destruction we left behind wasn't the smoking gun Harrowdean's patients hoped it would be. It won't be that easy to dismantle the lies pushed by money and privilege.

"Comfort break?" Raine taps his stick in an arc. "We've been walking for ages."

"It's been two hours." Xander scoffs. "Suck it up. Daylight's fading."

"Not a problem for me. You seeing folk may struggle, though."

I resist the urge to smack him upside the head. "Do you want us to get lost?"

"Isn't the human satnav leading the way?" Raine retorts.

Xander flips him the bird over his shoulder. "I have a name."

It takes me by surprise. I never thought I'd see the day he loosens up enough to laugh and joke with us. Raine chuckles when Lennox translates the gesture to him.

"Up yours too, Xan. Ripley's leg is still healing, you know."

"I'm fine," I splutter.

"No thanks to the stitch you caused her to tear," Xander adds acerbically. "I didn't think you had it in you, Raine. It must've been some spectacular sex."

Fucking kill me.

"Hey!" Raine cuts over him, visibly incensed. "I've said I'm all for this weird dynamic we have going on, but don't insult my ego, man."

"Not sure your ego was his target," Lennox claps back.

"I was aiming for his sexual prowess." Xander's tone is matter-of-fact. "I've always assumed you were a vanilla pushover, not a closeted freak in the sheets."

Bursting into laughter, I can hardly walk straight. Lennox yelps at the hard smack delivered to his arm. His blow delivered, Raine lowers his guide stick back to the ground, lips smashing in a grimace.

"What the hell did I do?" Lennox whines.

"You encourage him! Did I get your head?"

He rolls his eyes at us. "Not even close. Better luck next time."

"I never want to hear Xander say the words *freak in the sheets* ever again."

"Honestly, me neither," I agree.

We pass a sign denoting our destination, informing us that the small town of Keyworth is still six miles away. We've graduated back to narrow country roads, the winding bends sandwiched by drystone walls and fields of munching cows.

As the last of the sunlight fades, Xander pulls a flashlight from his backpack. They stocked up on batteries on the latest supply run. The yellow beam lights the road ahead, leading us deeper into the countryside.

"How much farther?" Raine groans exaggeratedly.

"Probably two or three more hours." Lennox pulls a cereal bar from his coat pocket. "Here. Eat this."

Raine stretches out his hand for him to place the food in it. Lennox almost drops the bar when the sound of a rumbling engine breaks the quiet nighttime. We haven't seen a car for miles now that we're back in the sticks.

"What's our excuse here?" I scan the road ahead. "Out for a pitch-black hike?"

"We haven't seen a local for ages," Xander replies. "Let's take cover."

Snagging Raine's sleeve, Lennox guides him over to the side of the road. We deftly scale the wooden fence, one by one. The field beyond is completely dark, pierced by the occasional mooing sound.

The distant rumbling grows louder. Safely ducked inside

the farmer's field, Xander clicks off the flashlight, plunging us into complete blackness.

"It sounds like a van," I whisper.

A huge, familiar hand engulfs my leg, offering a reassuring squeeze.

"Delivery truck maybe?" Lennox guesses.

"In the middle of nowhere?" Raine replies.

Headlights illuminate the thick rows of hedges we've ducked behind. The engine slows, idling for a second before crunching tyres pull up. I hear Xander quietly curse as heavy-sounding doors slam.

Come on. Please.

Be here for someone else.

Lighting the flashlight but covering the beam with his hand, Xander gestures for us to creep after him. He keeps down, ducked close to the wet grass before he begins crab-walking as silently as possible.

"Stay low," Lennox murmurs.

Grabbing hold of Raine's hand, their grips interlock, ensuring he won't get lost in the shadows. Xander moves ahead with us following, away from the road. With any luck, it's a taxi driver taking a leak.

I almost falter and faceplant when another door slams and high-pitched sobbing permeates the night. Xander looks back with a questioning look, also searching for the source.

"Go ahead, sweetheart." A familiar, male voice rings out. "Call for your friend."

Ice blooms deep within me and crystallises in my bloodstream. The darkness must be playing tricks on me. There's no way that voice has followed us all the way out here, far from the subterranean hellscape we left it in.

"Do it!" he thunders.

Stretching to his full height, Xander motions for us to run. "Go!"

But paralysing fear holds me captive. A clammy chill

sweeps over me, causing beads of cold sweat to trickle down my spine. My breath comes in short gasps as I hear the weeping voice scream out again.

"N-No! I won't do it!"

"Rip," Xander hisses under his breath. "Move!"

Lightning cracks through the night, causing us all to startle. Only it isn't an electric crackle but a gunshot. The boom disturbs sleeping birds and livestock, echoing endlessly in the nothingness all around us.

"Next shot won't be a miss," the man yells. "Do it!"

The sobbing intensifies.

"Ripley! Rip!"

Realisation comes in an awful trickle, burying its pincers deep in my chest. I know that voice. Xander pulls off his backpack to search inside. He then tosses something shiny and metallic to Lennox.

"Here," he mouths.

Lennox catches the folded switchblade. It has a stainless-steel grip, the slightly curved blade flicking out with a deadly snick. Xander locates his own pocketknife. A surviving relic from our Harrowdean days.

"We're not here to mess around!" the deep voice rattles through the air. "Let's make this quick and easy, shall we? It's been a long few weeks for us all."

Xander tsks. "Is this joker for real?"

"Come on, stooge. Show yourself. I don't think you want Red here to take a bullet."

Red?

"No," I whisper in horror, my suspicions confirmed. "Please, no."

"It's the one who tortured us, isn't it?" Lennox stares at me imploringly. "Harrison?"

"He's… He's got her."

"Who?" Xander demands.

"Ripley!" a petrified wail answers his question.

Tossing my head back, I clench my eyes shut. "It's Rae. He has Rae."

"Show yourself, Ripley!"

That evil bastard can't be here. It isn't possible. Excruciating memories rush to the surface before I can staunch the traumatic flow.

Harrison's fists and feet delivering each punishing blow, beating my organs into a paste in an attempt to find the truth. Him tossing me around like a bag of bones. Being cruelly stripped and hammered with freezing water.

It is Harrison.

He's here.

The sadistic motherfucker is supposed to be dead. Rick told me himself—he left him floating in an ice-water tub. Stupid me dared to believe Harrison was dead. He must've been down there for the whole riot.

Who survives that?

"Next bullet's going in her stomach!" Harrison shouts gleefully. "There's no one around to hear your pretty friend's wails as she bleeds out."

Dropping my backpack, I snatch the flashlight from Xander's hand. "I'm getting Rae."

"Ripley, stop!" Lennox bellows. "He'll kill you."

"She doesn't deserve this! I'm not letting anyone else get hurt because of me!"

Silent and deadly, Xander pounces on me. The flashlight is knocked aside as he weighs me down in the damp field, the pocketknife an inch from my eyeball. I recoil from the cold determination on his face.

"I'll knock you out and throw you over my shoulder if that's what it takes," he warns starkly. "Don't test me."

"Xan! Please!"

"No, goddammit!"

Bucking wildly to throw him off, I freeze dead when another shot rings out. The resultant howl sets my teeth on edge as hot tears prickle my eyes. All I can picture is the blood pooling around my friend.

"No! Rae!"

She's screaming in agony… because of me. All I've ever done is put her through hell. She's going to bleed out on the side of a fucking road because I'm too weak to save the people I care about.

"Who should get the next bullet?" Harrison calls out.

I want to face the son of a bitch who hurt my friend head-on. But Harrison's next threat causes sense to win out.

"Your little blind friend?" he cackles. "Or one of his two guard dogs?"

"Screw that." Lennox pulls Xander off me. "Let's fucking move!"

My breath escapes me when I'm plucked from the ground and shoved forward. The paralysing numbness that's seeped in prevents me from fighting them. I can't watch Raine or the others get hurt.

"There!" someone screeches. "They're running, sir!"

Xander snatches my hand. "Go!"

Lennox is half-dragging Raine, the pair hot on our heels. We're straying deeper into the field, slick grass quickly turning into tall, ripe maize stalks.

As shouts pursue us, the world narrows into rapid snapshots. Crops whipping our arms and faces. Flashing lights carried on the breeze. Pain pulsing from my still-sore thigh, matching the stitch forming in my stomach.

Tears blur my vision as an arctic defeat settles in my heart, turning my entire body to ice. We're running into literal blackness with a futile hope of escape.

"There they are! Fire!"

Voices overlap more gunshots. Bullets sizzle past us in a fast stream as we all duck low to avoid being hit. Lennox hisses a curse, pulling Raine with him, the pair taking cover amidst swaying crops.

"Stop! We need her alive!"

During a brief pause in firing, we throw ourselves forward. Evil is snapping at our heels. Fleeing for your life is a horrifying pressure like none other. I can almost feel death breathing down my neck.

"Argh!" Raine howls.

Tripping over, he flies onto the dirt ground. Lennox is pulled down with him, the pair landing in a tangle. I tug Xander to a halt, my pounding heart on the verge of spewing from my throat.

Yelping in pain, Raine grabs fistfuls of dirt. "Shit!"

"What is it?" Lennox picks himself up.

"My ankle." He tries to stand and immediately falls. "Fuck it. Leave me!"

"Never!"

Scooping him up, Lennox throws Raine's arm around his shoulders to carry him onwards. We've lost precious seconds. The pounding footsteps sound closer than ever as light swings above us.

I shriek Lennox's name when a red beam slices through the crops, marking a target in the dead centre of his chest. Noise is exploding all around us, creating a dizzying effect. I've lost track of direction completely.

"Lennox!"

He skids to a halt, looking down at the red glow. "Oh, fuck."

"Move another muscle and the big guy gets it." A balaclava-clad figure emerges through the stalks, carrying an assault rifle. "You're done."

Two others follow with flashlights while the third carries a small weapon. None of us dare breathe, let alone take off. That red dot hovers just above Lennox's heart, his gaze fixed on the man threatening to end him.

Xander steps forward, his hands spread. "Let's talk about this."

"Silence!" the assailant snaps. "We're here for the girl."

"You've got me!" I throw my hands up. "Lower the weapon."

"And let you take off again? I don't think so."

Breaking through the maize forest, a face I never thought I'd see again emerges. Harrison is sweaty, an ugly flush reaching his buzz cut. His once-bulky frame has slimmed down since he delivered me to Professor Craven.

He still wears an unhinged grin that promises all manner of ungodly sins. If he didn't have a screw loose before, it's safe to say his entire brain is untethered now. He's looking at me like I'm a fucking Christmas present.

"As much as I enjoy a chase, I promise to shoot the next person who moves a muscle." He smiles maniacally. "It's over."

"How are you alive?" I blurt.

Harrison lifts his arms, showing off welts and healing abrasions that circle his wrists. "Courtesy of our mutual friend."

Looks like Rick was telling the truth about shackling him in the same barbaric tub he'd been imprisoned in. The sick fuck survived the riot, handcuffed in the darkness. I don't want to imagine how.

"I'm afraid to say Rick's dead now," Harrison chortles without remorse. "A little apology present from the boss for all that I endured."

"You didn't suffer enough for my liking if you're still alive and breathing."

"Charming." He hooks up an eyebrow. "It felt like Christmas had come early when I heard you'd been spotted in a pharmacy. It wasn't hard to track you from there."

Harrison flicks his eyes to Lennox, lip curling in a sneer. I take the chance to make eye contact with Xander who shakes his head infinitesimally. *Don't move.* We're outnumbered.

"I'm surprised this tool survived Craven's lair." Harrison

chuckles derisively. "Perhaps I underestimated your plaything, Ripley."

"Fuck you," Lennox seethes.

"I have no qualms about shattering your skull, Mr Nash. Your life is forfeit now. Watch your mou—"

"What's the play here?" I cut across him. "A quiet little execution?"

"Originally, yes." Harrison sniffs in mock disgust. "A waste if you ask me. However, my orders have changed. You should be glad."

"Changed?" Xander parrots.

"Our management structure is rather complicated right now. I'd hate to bore you with the details. Suffice to say, for the trouble she's caused, the price for Ripley's safe capture has tripled."

In my periphery, I can see Xander clenching the pocketknife in his palm. He keeps his hand angled so it's tucked out of sight, allowing him to finger the blade. Rage radiates off him in waves.

"Where is Rae?"

"The redhead?" Harrison smirks. "I'll take you to see her body if you'd like. She may still be alive."

Nausea flushes over me, setting off light-headed prickles. Harrison's lying. He has to be. Surely, they haven't stooped so low as to shoot innocent people in plain sight. Not in public, at least.

"Surrender, and we'll kill your other friends quickly."

"She's going nowhere with you!" Raine shouts back.

Harrison casts a withering eye over Raine, Lennox and Xander. "You're protecting a monster, boys. Think about it. The Z wing program wouldn't run if each institute didn't have a willing stooge."

"Because you're so much better than me?" I snarl at him.

He shrugs, grinning ear to ear. "I'm just doing my job. It's a generous pay cheque. What excuse do you have?"

The lunatic actually thinks he has the moral high ground. This is the same man I saw attaching spike-laden handcuffs to Patient Three. His fucking pay cheque is saturated with spilled blood.

"Ripley stays with us." Xander strokes his blade.

"Is that your final answer?"

"Yes!" Lennox roars.

A sinister grin curls Harrison's lips. "Very well. I played nice."

Clicking his fingers, Harrison gestures for his men to advance. I'm preparing to throw myself in front of the rifle's scope to protect Lennox when Xander strikes.

Like a coiled python going in for the kill, he glides through the air with graceful precision. The pocketknife strikes faster than a whip as he jams it into the first assailant's shoulder.

The scream that spills from the man's lips is ear-splitting. He drops the rifle, the red glow spinning out of control. Xander pulls the blade free and sinks it into his exposed neck before the others can react.

Lightning fast.

Savage.

Deadly.

Blood erupts in a tidal wave, spitting out of the wound and spraying across his face. Xander continues to jab over and over. Wet, stomach-turning stabs that turn smooth skin into shredded flesh.

"Take them!" Harrison jumps into action.

Stepping in front of Raine, Lennox holds his own glinting blade. He faces the two men coming for him, elbow cocked and switchblade poised. His wide shoulders hunch in preparation.

I can't step in to help him before I'm faced with my own attacker. Harrison has set his sights on me. Perfect. I'll be the one to kick the shit out of him this time around. Retribution for the beating he doled out.

"Afraid to face me now that I'm not handcuffed and half-dead?" I taunt.

He pulls a baton from his belt. "On the contrary, I'm going to enjoy this. I don't mind losing a few thousand for turning you over in bad condition."

Ducking the baton's swing, I surge at him. Harrison grunts when I slam into his midsection, throwing him backwards.

It's easier than anticipated to throw Harrison off his feet. Being confined in his own filth has dissolved much of his strength. I follow him down, my fist cracking across his gleeful face.

Blood and spit somersaults from his mouth. My pleasure is short-lived as he rolls us, the inflexible metal of his baton smashing into my back, sending pain shooting up my spine.

As the breath flees from my lungs, he rolls to crush me beneath his weight. The baton sails towards me, but I dodge at the last second, causing him to strike the ground.

Frantically searching for anything to defend myself with, I seize a handful of wet dirt. He curses when I throw it in his eyes, buying me precious seconds to punch him in the throat.

"You should've died in that basement!"

Harrison clutches his throat, gurgling beautifully. I shove him off me, searching around for the others. The gloomy night clamours with punches, cursing and yelps.

Raine is still on the ground, cupping his ankle. In front of him, Lennox is able to put one guy in a headlock while the other rolls around at his feet. I follow the heavy scent of blood to the culprit.

Oh my god.

Xander is doused red, locked in a hand-to-hand knife fight. He discards the still-bleeding corpse of the first man he disarms, turning his focus on gutting his current opponent.

I'm dragging myself up to intervene when a hand latches around my leg. Yanked backwards, I fall on my chest, nails painfully digging deep into the ground. Grunting tells me who's got me ensnared.

"Little bitch." Spittle blasts past Harrison's lips, his amusement spent. "You never could obey."

Something sharp slams into the middle of my back. Any retort dies on my tongue at the instant rush of blistering pain. My entire body is gripped by a violent electrical current, causing every muscle to lock up.

I'm being stabbed by a thousand needles all at once. The convulsions take over, assaulting me with rapid bursts of excruciating electricity. My heart threatens to explode as disorientation sets in.

"That's better." Harrison relinquishes the taser from my back. "I prefer you like this. Whimpering like the pathetic stray you are."

My silent howls wrap around me. I'm trapped by aftershocks, each spasm causing more tears to leak from the corners of my eyes. For good measure, Harrison stands and boots me hard in the stomach.

Heat radiates through my belly. I cry out, unable to move a muscle or curl in on myself. His steel-capped boots strike over and over, sending me plummeting back into the past.

I'm back in the Z wing, stripped bare in a padded cell. Covered in my own blood. Tears. Sweat. Taunted by his cackling while beating me to a semi-conscious pulp. This time, he'll kill me.

"S-Stop," I beg.

"Now you want to behave, huh? Where was that attitude when I held a gun to your cute friend's head?"

Blood bubbles in my mouth, forming a hot, foaming pool. I feel it streaming from my lips, mingling with stinging tears. Everything around me is swimming in the dropped flashlight's glow.

I couldn't save Rae.

I can't even save myself.

"Step back." The command is delivered in a monotone voice. "I'd prefer not to cover Ripley with your innards."

Peering through cracked lids, I can make out the shadow looming behind Harrison through a beam of light. Lanky. Blood-streaked. Hair unkempt and eyes cold. Harrison sucks in a surprised breath.

"Now." Xander nudges the back of Harrison's head with the rifle. "I quite fancy testing out your friend's gadget. You can be my guinea pig."

Slowly, Harrison raises his hands, the baton clattering to the ground beside me. I watch his gaze harden, but my lips won't move for me to warn Xander. They're still numb and slippery.

"You know how to use that thing, son?"

Xander sighs in a long-suffering manner. "I'm disappointed at your lack of confidence. Though I appreciate the chance to make good on my threats."

With the speed of a trained thug, Harrison snatches a sheathed knife from his belt. The black-handled blade slashes in a circle as he spins. I'm powerless, forced to watch everything unfold in slow motion.

The knife.

His secret smile.

Xander being sliced wide open.

Only the blow never comes—just in my petrified imagination. Before Harrison can land his shot, the thunderous burst of the assault rifle marks his fate. The muzzle flash temporarily blinds me.

I have to squint through my tears to take in the aftermath. Terror grips me at the sight of the body sprawled out amongst crimson-soaked crops. Except he doesn't have bright-white hair and calculating eyes.

The corpse is Harrison.

Mouth open in an eternal scream. Chest caved in from a bullet delivered at point-blank range, tearing straight through his heart. His cruel eyes stare at the night sky, empty and lifeless.

Teeth bared, Xander drops the gun. "Ripley!"

He looks like an avenging angel, saturated in our enemies' blood as he steps over his final victim to reach me. Xander falls to his knees, yanking out the taser darts then sliding an arm beneath me to lift me into his lap.

"You hurt?"

"I hate tasers," I cough out. "Fuck, my ribs."

His almost-black stare bores into me. "I'm sorry."

Blood trickles from my mouth. "Why?"

"I promised no one would hurt you again." His neck muscles spasm. "Yet the son of a bitch laid his hands on you."

My eyes stray to Harrison's body. "He p-paid the price."

"I'll tear his corpse limb from limb!" He wipes the blood from my chin.

With a heavy thump, Lennox spits out a curse nearby. He's got the final perp subdued, a knife pressed against his jugular. The three other men are dead, watering the earth with their life blood.

"One move and I'll give you a new smiley face." Lennox digs the switchblade in deep. "You wanna join your friends?"

He's rewarded with a groan.

"That's what I thought." Lennox looks over at us. "Rip?"

Breathing deeply, I force my lips to move. "I'm okay."

"Jesus, Xan. Did you have to go full Hannibal Lecter?"

"We need to get out of here." Xander eyes the bloodbath all around us. "Can you walk, Raine?"

"I think so," he utters quietly. "Christ, all I can smell is blood."

Struggling to his feet, Raine winces as he puts weight on his ankle, but he manages to stay upright this time. His stick has vanished somewhere in the melee. All of our supplies are scattered in the dark.

"What should we do with this one?" Lennox nods to his captive.

"Kill him." Xander isn't fazed.

"W-Wait," I stammer. "We can use him."

"For what?" Lennox frowns.

Raine catches on, looking panicked at the thought of even more death. "Leverage. He works for Incendia."

Sighing in disappointment, Lennox lowers the blade to tuck it in his pocket. "Pass me the gun."

I work on flexing my muscles, attempting to regain control of them while Xander tosses the rifle over. Lennox trains it on our new prisoner's back, ensuring he knows the deal.

"Let's get you up." Xander pulls me to stand with him. "Easy."

I cry out at the throbbing heat wrapped all around my middle. The entire area is tender, pulsing with deep, shooting pain. Xander braces me against his side, a hand clasped on my waist.

"Can you move?"

Lips smashed shut, I nod curtly.

"Let's get the fuck out of here, then."

"What about the bodies?" Lennox asks.

"Leave them for Bancroft to find."

With each step, the internal fire roars hotter. Still, it falls short of the fear knotting my windpipe at the thought of what we'll find. Or rather *who*. We ran into the night while Rae was still screaming.

Retracing our steps is a harrowing dance in the dark, hobbling along in faint light, all panting and exhausted. Lennox still guards his stumbling prisoner.

"Hear anything?" Xander asks apprehensively when the road comes into view.

Raine tilts his head, still favouring one foot. "Ticking engine up ahead."

"I'll go first with this one." Lennox digs the rifle into the man's spine. "Just in case."

Blood surges in my ears, creating a vehement roar. Xander has to help me over the fence, his face crumpling as he struggles to remain stoic. The still-running van's lights illuminate the deserted road.

Hesitating, Raine's steps slow. "Rip... maybe you shouldn't look."

I can already hear the words he doesn't want to say. He can sense what lies ahead. Shrugging off Xander's support, I stumble towards the vehicle, a relentless fist locked around my lungs.

There's a delusional slither inside me that hoped I'd imagined it. Maybe Harrison found a way to trick us. Those sounds were recorded, or he used someone else... Or... Or...

No.

Life isn't that kind.

It's hard to tell where her vibrant auburn hair ends and the puddle of blood spilling from her stomach begins. A crimson river paints the tarmac, glistening in the headlights. Surrounded by her deathly halo, Rae lays still.

The discomfort from slamming to my knees fails to compute. Her blood is still warm as it slides across my palms. I wade closer, uncaring of the mess. Rae feels boneless in my arms when I hug her body close.

"No," I weep helplessly. "I'm so fucking sorry, Rae. I'm so sorry."

All I want is for her arms to hug me back. She could crack a smile or drop one of her sarcastic jokes. Tell me I'm forgiven for leading her to this place. But that doesn't happen. It's too late.

She's dead.

And it's all my fault.

Sobbing senselessly, I cuddle her close until I have nothing left to give. Not a single tear. Soul-destroying grief boils into smouldering rage. It hits hard and fast, sweeping in and obliterating my self-control.

I slacken my grip to look at her face. Ashen. Waxy. Slack. Blood smears across her freckled skin as I stroke her hair back, lowering my lips to her forehead.

"I'll make it right, Rae," I vow fiercely. "All of it."

"Ripley." Raine awkwardly crouches down near me. "She's gone. You need to let her go."

"It's my fault. She didn't deserve this."

"I know," he whispers sincerely.

"I was so cruel to her, Raine. Unnecessarily. She just wanted to be my friend, and I kept pushing her away. I was scared to let her get close."

"She didn't see it like that, babe." His voice is thick with emotion. "Rae wanted to be your friend. She knew you needed one."

"And where did being my friend get her?"

His nostrils whistle with a long sigh. "You can't take the blame for all the world's evil. This isn't on you."

Smoothing her red waves a final time, I gently lay Rae back down. My fingertips leave two matching streaks on her eyelids as I slide them shut. Like this, I can convince myself she's asleep. Peaceful and safe.

By the time I look up, my decision is made.

"No more running scared," I declare firmly. "We're taking the fight to them."

"How?" Raine questions.

Looking up at Xander, I implore him with my gaze. "Call Theodore. Tell him we have a hostage for them. I want a rendezvous by dawn."

"Rip," Lennox attempts.

One look in his direction silences him. I'm kneeling next to my friend's corpse, covered in her blood. Death and defeat are scattered all around us. We've fled. Schemed. Bargained. Killed.

Enough.

No more cheap hotels or breaking and entering. No more stealing cash to buy enough food to keep us alive. No more hiding our faces and praying death doesn't come knocking. I'm done being scared.

"Make the call." My words come out steadier than I feel. "That's final."

Xander pats his pockets, searching for the stolen phone kept on his person at all times. A startling ringtone erupts before he can find it, only the noise isn't coming from him. We all glance around in shock.

Our captive moans weakly. Eyebrows knitted, Lennox reaches into his bulletproof vest, pulling out a clunky-looking burner phone. He frowns down at the lit screen.

"Boss," he reads.

The ringtone halts, leaving us in crushing silence. It quickly starts up again with a second call.

I lift a trembling hand. "Here."

Lennox pauses, clutching the device. "Sure you want to do this?"

"Yes."

His mouth pursed, he tosses the phone underhand towards me. I numbly catch it, stabbing down on the green button before holding it to my ear.

"Why is no one else answering their phones?"

My hand tightens into a vice, creaking the cheap plastic.

"Hello? Is it done? Do you have her?"

Summoning my voice, it sounds alien to my own ears.

"Hello, Uncle Jonathan."

CHAPTER 17
XANDER

JERK – OLIVER TREE

PRESENT DAY

THE SHINING lights of Central London blur all around me in the drizzly morning rainfall. It paints a saturated, kaleidoscopic world, busy with suit-clad workers, dawdling taxis and bright-red tourist buses whizzing past.

Normality is a thin veneer painted over the truth I know lies within. A transparent film, invisible to the naked eye, concealing the reality that few are unlucky enough to ever uncover and live to tell the tale.

London—the heart of power and corruption in a lawless land.

I hate this fucking city.

It's not so much the people. I've learned to tolerate them. And I only truly pay attention to those I care about. Like always, everyone else is irrelevant. Inconsequential. Undeserving of my limited empathy.

No, my qualms with this dirty, sweaty hellhole are far more pertinent. It's the secrets this city holds so dear. So much exploitation, hiding in plain sight behind glittering tourist attractions and gilded palaces.

What if those in power cared?

Would we still have suffered back then?

Even if the bigwigs behind the corporation that stole our lives from us harboured a mere speck of humanity, we earned our places in Harrowdean Manor. Perhaps it's only fair that we bore the brunt of their scientific curiosity.

No.

That isn't true at all.

Sure, some of us earned our place there. You only have to look at the long list of convictions that were quickly doled out when the world started the lengthy process of assigning blame for what unfolded.

Not everyone deserved to be hammered with society's hatred and disgust, though. Regardless of what they did, and the innocents they harmed, to ensure their own survival. Which is exactly why I'm here today.

"Mr Beck?"

Wrenched from my musings, I look over my shoulder. "Mr O'Hare."

His morning coffee in hand and a tan, leather satchel slung over his shoulder, Elliot O'Hare blends into the crowd on his morning commute. I've memorised his routine well enough. The investigative journalist is a creature of habit.

"What are you doing here?" He jostles on his feet to keep warm.

I push off from the wall. "Waiting for you."

"You're alone."

Staring at him, I lift my shoulder in a shrug.

"Changed your mind about that interview?" Elliot fishes.

The anticipation gleaming in his eyes turns my stomach. I've denied enough media requests over the years. None captured more than a split-second of my attention. But I'm not here for me.

It isn't selfishness that's led me to lurk outside his place of work at eight o'clock in the morning, waiting for the nosy reporter to show his face. I swear, the fucking lengths I go to. Yet I'm labelled obsessive and controlling.

When I don't immediately answer, he scans his security fob to open the door. "How about a cup of coffee?"

Fuck yes, you leech.

Nodding, I follow him inside the fancy skyscraper, escaping the lightly-misting rain. Elliot has a quiet word with the security guard manning the entrance before he's handed a visitor's pass that's then passed to me.

My body clenches tight with paranoia as I watch the guard absently wave us past. His eyes are glued to his morning newspaper. Thank fuck he didn't insist on doing a search.

"Right this way," Elliot chirps. "I'm glad you're here, Mr Beck."

I have to grit my teeth to maintain my blank expression. He thinks he's scored a big fish. To get to where I need to go, I have to keep it that way. Lips pursed, I follow Elliot over to the elevators and we ride upwards.

"What changed your mind?" he asks.

"Irrelevant."

Elliot chuckles softly. "Believe it or not, we're on the same side."

"And what side would that be?"

"The side of the truth."

Welcome rage swirls in my chest, a vortex spewing sulphuric ash that quickly heats my veins. "No one has ever cared about that."

"Well, I do."

"I'm sure."

Slipping the lanyard over my head, I smooth a hand down my pressed, white polo shirt, tucked into plain black jeans. In my periphery, I can see Elliot trying to subtly look at my toned forearms.

Pale skin stretched over corded muscles, both arms are layered with years' worth of meticulous horizontal lines. They haven't faded since I first inflicted the marks as a sullen teenager, fascinated by the pain that accompanied seeing myself bleed.

I'm not ashamed of the silvery lines covering me. In fact, I never have been. Why should I? It's my body. My blood. My pain. If I wanted to take myself apart to study the pieces, that was my prerogative.

Now at thirty-six years old, those marks have evolved to mean something more to me. Not evidence of my experimentation with cheap razor blades as a child. Nor a survivor's badge of honour, even if the battle was fought against my own mind.

No.

These marks are a reminder.

A reminder of who I once was—and who I'll never be again.

Because of her.

My eyes ping-pong as we weave through desks bearing half-awake employees, camera gear, desktop screens and steaming cups of coffee. I'm surprised by the size and gravitas of it all.

This is an industrial-scale operation, filming episode after episode of documentary footage, ready to be churned out. When it airs… I predict a toxic media frenzy. And I refuse to see that shit play out again.

"What are you trying to achieve here?"

Stepping into the studio, Elliot holds the door for me. "There are still many unanswered questions about Harrowdean Manor and the other institutes. The world needs to know."

"You're reporting on them all?"

"Yes, we're unravelling the whole story. This documentary series has been in the works for the last decade." He smiles proudly. "It will be my life's work."

Inside the studio, two folding chairs sit in the centre of the room. It's clear I've caught him with his pants down—lackeys rush in to begin setting up tripods and cameras, and an assistant is urged to make fresh coffee.

Elliot flips through several stacks of notebooks. I get a glimpse at the covers while he searches for the correct files. Each is carefully labelled with the names of the interviewee attached to their relevant institute.

They've spoken to a whole pool of people. Countless names I recognise. I've followed the lengthy criminal investigation and subsequent years of media reports ever since those horrific days.

My eyes brush over the labels denoting the five other institutes until he lands on *HM*. Harrowdean Manor. The sixth and final institute. We got our own file. How organised. But beneath those letters? There are names.

Ripley Bennet.
Lennox Nash.
Raine Starling.
Xander Beck.

"Ah, here." Elliot hums as he plucks the file free. "Truthfully, I didn't think you'd come around to this interview. You've caught me rather unprepared."

"Clearly."

My gaze is locked on that file. I want it. The tapes. Notes. Documents. Photographs. I want every fucking scrap of salacious gossip he's got piled up in there so I can build myself a nice little bonfire.

The truth isn't some ray of light shining on those who've spent their lives downtrodden. How could it be? Nobody values truth anymore. Not even when it's printed, played or publicised. We're wilfully ignorant as a species.

That doesn't mean I will allow our lives to be sold off for profit. I don't care how healing this bullshit is supposed to be. Some stories shouldn't be repeated, and ours is one of them.

"We've been given a great deal of information from Miss Bennet. Perhaps you'll be able to fill in some gaps for us."

Jaw clenching, I fight to keep my voice even. "Of course."

Elliot casts me a look. "She was rather tight-lipped about what became of your... uh, relationship. I wonder if you'd care to shed some light on that."

"Alternatively, you could mind your own fucking business."

Elliot grimaces, his crow's feet deepening with the movement. "I don't get paid to mind my business, Mr Beck."

"Or to respect people's privacy, it seems."

"Unfortunately, not in this line of work."

The coffee appears right on time, carried by a bumbling, early-twenties lad who seems eager to impress. Elliot appraises me while I accept the hot drink.

"You know, we had journalists stalking us for years," I state casually. "Hacking into our email accounts, accessing medical records, reading therapy notes. Even picking through our trash. We were hunted."

"Harrowdean was a sensational story." He shrugs like the lifelong invasion is a mere inconvenience. "It still is."

"And this tell-all documentary series... That's going to settle the score, is it?" I chuckle. "You're going to create public spectacles of us all. The last decade will have meant nothing."

Elliot takes his own coffee. "I believe the public reaction will be one of sympathy."

"When have they ever been sympathetic to people like us, Mr O'Hare?"

He opens his mouth to answer but can't find a response.

"The ignorance of the world is the reason Incendia Corporation and its six institutes went unchecked for decades." I stare at him without mercy. "The public is culpable here, not us."

His gaze ducks to my white-knuckled grip on the coffee

mug. There's a flash of apprehension in his eyes, like he can tell I'm wrestling the urge to dump it over his head.

Did no one else give him a hard time? I have no idea how many people he's sat down with. Only one matters to me. One I made a promise to protect ten long years ago. I intend to keep my word.

"Excuse me?" A dawdling employee sneaks into the room. "Elliot, security would like a quick word. It seems you have another visitor."

"Of course." He clears his throat. "Mr Beck, make yourself at home."

Placing his notebook down, Elliot scuttles from the room, taking his lackey with him. Pathetic. It shouldn't be this easy to play him, but I've never had much trouble bending the will of others.

He's so desperate for his scoop, he'll do anything to capture our stories on tape. Including letting the wolf into the sheep's pen. I have to stop this. He'll regret ever dragging the past back up.

Setting the untouched coffee down, I know I have to move fast. This place is prestigious enough to have a full security team and countless levels of staff, offices and more. I won't have long.

Scanning the room, my determination hardens, steeling my muscles with staunch focus. This has to be done. I'm the only one who sees this exposé for the threat it really is.

Opening my jacket, I pull the canister of lighter fluid out. I'll have to aim for the important stuff. Documents, cameras and records. Anything that can be used against us. Secrets that should never see the light of day.

My foot connects with a tripod, sending it flying. I douse the motherfucker in fluid then turn my attention to the other cameras. It's easy enough to pop the memory cards out, each marked with date stamps.

RB. Interview Three.

Seeing Ripley's initials causes a lump to lodge in my throat. She's done a brave thing. I want her to find peace. Salvation. Whatever the fuck she's still looking for after all these years. This just isn't the way to do it.

But she chose this.

Can I take that from her?

Unable to burn the memory cards, I tuck them into my pocket. I'm not chickening out. These files will remain in the one place they'll be safe: my possession. I'll protect Ripley's secrets with my life.

The cameras are smashed then added to the pile of metal gathering in the room. I don't have long before the dickhead returns. There's still so much to destroy before I can calmly rest again.

Grabbing as many of the labelled notebooks as I can hold, I toss them into the mix, dousing everything in fluid. One lands on top, spelling out another recognisable name written beneath the words *Compton Hall*.

Colour me surprised.

I never thought they'd get that nutcase to sit down.

Not even I would risk that conversation.

The pungent scent is thick in my nose as it fills the room. I've turned the studio into a tinder box. I take a moment to enjoy the scene before pulling a cigarette lighter from my jeans.

Elsewhere, Harrowdean is being ripped down for the final time. Bricks pummelled and secrets burned. I'll burn its legacy here and finally set us all free. We need to forget. It's the only way to start living.

Flames leap from the lighter's tip. All emotion drains away as I drop it onto the pile of rubble. The effect is instantaneous.

Fire engulfs the stacks of evidence, setting noxious fluid alight in bright-blue flames. Black smoke curls from the smouldering pages, setting off multiple fire alarms.

Yet not even the blaring racket can rouse me. I've zoned

out, staring deep into the flames, watching our history vanish for the last time.

I thought I'd be relieved.

Defeat settles like ash instead.

I can't burn the memories. Years of suffering. Lives destroyed, by our own hands and theirs. Indelible scars left behind on skin and soul alike. Truthfully, nothing can erase that lifelong trauma.

"No!" The studio door cracks open. "Stand back!"

I'm manhandled from the room, now billowing with thick smoke. Bodies swarm, and footsteps pound. The screeching alarms add to the escalating panic, and in the mayhem, I summon a smile.

"You!" Elliot stops in front of me, spitting with anger. "You did this!"

"Correct." I seize fistfuls of his cheap dress shirt. "Our story is not your life's work. It never belonged to you."

Grabbing my hands, he tries to prise free. The alarm on his face is enough satisfaction for me. I haven't hurt anyone for a long time, but that side of me is still in there. I can bring it forward if he doesn't let this selfish pursuit of fame die.

"Xander! Put him down immediately!"

My scalp prickles, a flush racing all over me. I release Elliot, setting him back on his feet, and look over his shoulder at the lilting voice spelling my name out with utter disbelief.

Ripley stomps closer, her weary, hazel orbs trained on me. "You had no right."

I lick my suddenly dry lips. "I had every right."

She looks between the fire being tackled with extinguishers and Elliot scuttling away from me, shouting down his phone at an emergency responder. My little toy's anger still tastes the sweetest.

"This was my choice," she screams at me.

"I'm protecting you! You have no idea what this will unleash!"

Ripley stops in front of me, our faces almost touching. The years have softened her sweetheart-shaped features and lightly-freckled skin. She still wears her septum piercing after all these years.

"I'm choosing to unleash it." Ripley's furious eyes scour my face. "I need to speak up. I can't spend another year hiding in the flat, painting the pain away until it returns come daybreak."

Hand spasming, I take her cheek into my palm. Despite her fury, she leans into my touch, a ritualistic behaviour that's stood the test of time. Years haven't diminished the intensity between us.

"It's killing me," she whispers. "I want to live, but I can't until I face the past."

Unwelcome guilt infects my cells. "Don't make me watch you get hurt again, Rip. We barely survived."

She rests her hand over mine. "And we're still not living. Not really."

Foreheads meeting, I push my lips on hers. Each time we kiss, it's like the first time all over again. Back then, I was manipulating her. Ensnaring the touch-starved orphan with the attention she craved in order to achieve my own goals.

Yet another story I'd like to erase.

One the world won't get.

So much of our history doesn't bear dredging back up. I wish our family had been forged under better circumstances. That we hadn't spent so long hurting each other or found our strength when it was too late.

No one will understand. Love like ours isn't fit for public consumption. They'll judge our shared darkness. Ridicule the bond we formed. I didn't want to silence her—I just wanted to protect her. To protect all of them.

"I need to do this." Ripley releases my hand. "Burn whatever you'd like. I'll keep doing these interviews until the truth is out there for everyone to hear."

She steps to the side, giving me a view of who's behind her. Of course, she didn't come alone. None of us have been that for a long time. Harrowdean took everything from us. But it didn't take our family.

Gripping his white guide stick, Raine stares off to the side, listening to the whooshing extinguishers. Lennox loosely holds his bicep, exchanging urgent whispers with our mutual friend, Hudson Knight.

"Come home, Xan," Ripley pleads.

I look away from her to the mess I've made. The fire has been extinguished. Elliot stands in the doorway, shaking all over as he studies the destruction. His staff are scattered in varying states of shock.

"You should give him these." I reach into my pocket, reluctantly pulling out the memory cards. "I kept them for you."

Shaking her head, she takes the small handful. "One day, you'll stop being the obsessive psychopath with no boundaries who made me fall in love with him."

"Is that really what you want?"

Peering up at me beneath her lashes, a small smile curves Ripley's lips. "I wouldn't still be here cleaning up your messes if I did."

I watch her walk over to Elliot to hand over the remaining memory cards. He's gesticulating angrily, losing the professional persona that makes him so slyly amicable. This wasn't a total waste, then.

Strolling over to me, Hudson pulls a cigarette from tucked behind his ear. "If you'd like tips on how to be a successful psycho boyfriend, I offer private tuition."

The black-haired bastard pins me with a hard stare. I bite back an eye roll. Like that's ever worked on me.

"Fuck off, Hud." I punch him in the shoulder.

"The offer stands. It's an art I've perfected over the years."

Hudson snakes an arm around my neck to lock me in a

playful headlock. Snarling, I knock the unlit cigarette from his hands.

"This was your plan?" Lennox shakes his head, approaching with Raine in tow. "Great plan."

"I did this for her." I lower my voice. "For us. Nobody knows how our story ends. Do you really want them to find out like this?"

"Of course not! But it's Ripley's decision!"

"We did what we had to, Xan." Raine's eyes shift behind his round, blacked-out lenses. "It's nothing every other person in our situation wouldn't have done."

I hope the world sees it that way.

Because surviving cost us everything... Including our souls.

CHAPTER 18
RIPLEY

STRAY – JXDN

TEN YEARS EARLIER

OAKHAM AIRFIELD IS NESTLED between a smattering of sleepy villages in the rural midlands. By some miracle, there are no passing motorists on the quiet roads. I've no doubt anyone who spots us would run away screaming.

We're all filthy, struggling to walk and utterly exhausted. Even after doing his best to clean with water and old napkins found inside the van, Xander is covered in bloodstains.

The others haven't fared much better. Lennox has a rapidly swelling black eye while Raine limps with a bad ankle that we've concluded is sprained rather than broken. I'm covered in Rae's dried blood. We're all done.

After a lengthy debate, we decided not to risk driving the van straight up to the private landing strip, allowing us to be tracked. Leaving Rae's body behind with our captive when we parked the vehicle miles back was devastating.

Xander holds me braced to his side. "The airstrip is coming up."

Hobbling along, Raine clutches Lennox's sleeve. "See anything?"

With his guide stick still lost somewhere in a maize field, he's reliant on Lennox to move safely. We couldn't locate any of our supplies either before we had to flee, leaving a bloodied graveyard behind.

Lennox scans the distant buildings. "Not yet."

"Theodore said to meet here," Xander grumbles unhappily. "He better turn up."

"He will," Raine croaks.

I'm leaning almost all my body weight on Xander. Hours of sleepless travel have made an already pitiful situation worse. I haven't stopped to look, but I can feel how badly bruised my tender stomach and ribs are.

If the mysterious Theo doesn't show up, I'll march down to London and tear down Sabre's front door myself. No matter what happens, the running ends today. We've already lost too much.

"Ripley?" Lennox calls my name. "You still with us?"

I feel Xander peer at me, his arm curled around my back. I've been silent since my beloved uncle swiftly hung up the phone upon hearing my voice, leaving us stranded with several corpses and a half-alive hostage.

"She's okay," Xander answers for me.

I'm grateful. I don't have any reassuring words for them right now.

"Raine's ankle is the size of a fucking balloon." Lennox guides him forward. "We can't go much farther."

"The airfield should be just up ahead," Xander replies.

In the rising dawn, our rendezvous point is eventually revealed. It's an exclusive, members-only landing strip in the middle of upper-class suburbia. Probably home to all manner of sleazy politicians' private jets.

Bonus? It's deserted.

Sabre chose carefully.

The office buildings appear empty at this hour, but the two blacked-out, armoured SUVs pulled into the car park make my hackles rise. Our desperation doesn't make this last-ditch effort any less risky.

We've been alone since escaping Harrowdean. Pinning everything on total strangers is a tall order after everything we've endured. But regardless of the lies Warner previously told, I trust his intentions.

"Eyes open," Xander orders curtly. "Two vehicles parked up."

"This is a shitty idea," Lennox mutters.

Raine hisses in pain. "We're out of options."

"Doesn't mean I have to like this."

"When do you ever like anything, Nox?"

Tentatively approaching the car park, we linger outside the gates. The two SUVs are tinted, concealing their occupants. Birds chirping is the only sound for several tense seconds. No signs of movement.

It feels like we're locked in a tense Mexican standoff. Someone has to make the first move. I shrug off Xander's support, swaying on my feet for a moment before steadying.

Xander creeps behind me with each step I take, refusing to let me move more than an inch from his side. He hasn't let go of me since we clambered into the van and fled for our lives.

A car door cracks open, two booted feet hitting the gravel. My pulse races at lightning speed, almost knocking me straight off my feet. When the heavy door closes, I recognise the face that appears.

Thank god.

Overwhelming relief makes my knees knock together. It takes all my mental resolve to hold still instead of melting into a puddle.

"Ripley!"

I stare into Warner's rich baby blues. "Hey."

Hand braced on a gun holster, he rushes across the car park to meet us. I've barely managed a step before I'm pulled into his arms. Not even my smarting ribcage can stop me from hugging him tight.

"You have no idea how good it is to see you."

"Yeah." My throat is thick with emotion. "You too."

Leaning back to examine me, his mouth turns down in a grimace. When his gaze travels to the other three standing nearby in varying degrees of distress, that grimace morphs into a look of abject horror.

"What on earth happened?"

I wave for Xander and the others to approach. "Long story. We have some catching up to do. What happened to you?"

He shrugs with a strained smile. "Even longer story. I got caught up in the violence and had to hide so I didn't get taken hostage like the real guards."

"Well, I'm glad you're alive."

Warner squeezes my shoulder. "I'm sorry we got separated. I searched for you once the authorities moved in, but you were already gone."

"We managed to escape."

"So, what happened?" he repeats.

I brush his question off. "Later. Is your team here?"

"Yeah, we're all here." He shakes his head in disbelief. "I couldn't believe it when I heard you'd made contact. Thought I'd never see you again."

"We contacted Theodore a while back, but things have escalated."

"So I can see."

Surveying the guys, Warner offers them a tight nod. I shoot Lennox a glare, silently urging him to behave. He's glowering at Warner like he can melt the skin from his bones with his mistrustful stare alone.

The sound of more car doors slamming interrupts our reunion. We all tense as several figures emerge from their

SUVs and stroll towards us. Every single eye is locked on our motley group.

Walking ahead, a truly intimidating mountain of a man leads the way. He's built like a fucking house, exuding strength and aggression. I try not to gawp at his massive frame, stacked with corded muscle.

The moment his glowing, amber eyes land on me, the most peculiar shift happens. This terrifying, raven-haired beast... offers me a little smile. Peculiar. Though it does soften his harsh features.

Behind him, a slimmer man walks fast to keep up with his colleague's strides. He's hugging a laptop to his flannel-covered chest like it's a safety blanket. His messy blonde ringlets are denser than mine.

They're flanked by security—two men and one brown-haired woman, all wearing holsters and matching black clothing. I count several weapons, though I have no doubt more are concealed.

"Warner," the giant rumbles deeply. "Care to introduce us?"

"Right." He steps back to wave them forward. "This is Ripley, Xander, Lennox and Raine."

"The missing patients." Blondie looks up at us.

Past the wire-rimmed frames he wears, intelligent blue eyes several shades lighter than Warner's hold deep apprehension. I recognise his voice from Xander's earlier phone call. This is Theodore Young.

"That's close enough." Xander inches in front of me. "Who are you?"

"Bloody hell." The woman's eyes are wide as saucers. "You walked here looking like that?"

If looks could kill, she'd be adding her blood to Xander's splattered state with that comment. He looks none too pleased about her attitude.

Warner clears his throat, gesturing to the huge man first. "Enzo Montpellier. Second in command of Sabre Security."

Scanning us up and down, Enzo narrows his bright-amber eyes. "You're all looking rough."

"Charming, aren't they?" Raine snorts to himself.

"Trust me," Lennox whispers back to him. "If you could see us, you'd agree with them."

Enzo gestures to his glasses-wearing colleague. "You've been speaking to Theo. Head of Intelligence." He turns to wave a hand at their security detail. "This is Becket, Ethan and Tara. Warner's teammates."

With pleasantries exchanged, I run out of patience. It takes a moment to moisten my mouth enough to form words.

"There are bodies behind us," I rasp. "Just outside Keyworth. Look for the maize field."

"How many?" Enzo doesn't even bat an eye, his attentive stare still locked on me.

"Four." Xander eyes him suspiciously. "And another in the van we ditched several miles back. An unconscious hostage all trussed up too. He works for Incendia."

Murmuring to each other, Warner's teammates seem to be formulating a plan.

"Rae." I glance at Warner, vision swimming with burning tears. "They killed Rae."

"Oh, Rip." His gaze fractures with sympathy.

"Harrison shot her. He tracked us down in the middle of the night." My voice cracks. "We ran for our lives. They had weapons… an assault rifle. We barely escaped."

"Are you injured?"

I contemplate our sorry states. "A little. Raine has a sprained ankle. And all our stuff is gone… Meds, clothes, everything. We lost it all."

"Don't worry; we can sort all that out and arrange immediate medical attention. What about Harrison? Is he alive?"

"Not anymore." Xander lays a possessive hand on my shoulder.

I push past my grief, sucking in a deep breath. "Rae's body is in the van. I couldn't just leave her in the field. She deserves better."

Cataloguing that information, Warner nods. "I'll take care of her, Rip. I promise."

He turns to his teammates. Weirdly, Warner defers to the older blonde guy, Becket, who seems to be presiding over the small group. I reluctantly match the smile he shoots me.

"We can locate the vehicle," Becket assures me. "And it's… contents."

Theo clutches his laptop. "You'll need help disabling the tracking software. I'll accompany you." He looks at Enzo. "Are you taking them back to HQ?"

"Hunter has a safe house lined up," Enzo responds. "Brooklyn and the others are still at HQ. We'd like to keep witnesses separate to avoid evidence contamination."

I perk up at the familiar name. The escapee from Blackwood. She's still working with them. These people seem to be collecting Incendia's strays faster than we can escape.

"Just hold on a minute." Theo and Becket turn back at Lennox's deep timbre. "Why should we trust you?"

"Nox," Raine chastises.

"In the last twenty-four hours, we've been hunted down, shot at, threatened, beaten and damn near killed. I respect Ripley's choice to make this call, but I still want assurances that my family will be safe."

My head jerks in his direction, a swarm gathering in my stomach. *Family.* Lennox fucking Nash wants his family to be safe—including me.

His pale-green gaze snaps up as if he can feel my surprise. For a breathless second, we're alone. Isolated by our locked eyes. Hatred bled into attraction a long time ago, but right now, it feels like something more. A destructive force.

The kind that ruins people.

In the best possible way.

"Unravelling Incendia's complex criminal web is painstaking work." Enzo sizes him up. "It may not look like it from the outside, but we've been battling these people for years."

"Are you expecting some kind of praise?" Lennox laughs.

"No. Just a little faith."

Whispering a curse, Xander tilts his head up to the sky like he's searching for patience. The analytic in him doesn't ascribe much to faith. Every move he makes relies on cold, hard logic.

"We will make a move on Incendia Corporation and its assets soon," Enzo proclaims, his gaze fixed on me. "When we do, your testimonies will join the countless others we've helped."

"To what end?" Xander growls.

"You'll have the chance to earn your freedom."

They may not be able to have faith right now, but I can. I don't have much choice. I've got nothing else to give. Pulling Xander's hand from my arm, I move to Lennox.

His deep-lidded eyes are pinched with tension, watching me approach. "Don't even start—"

"Can you give us a moment, Raine?" I speak over him.

Raine releases Lennox's sleeve, taking a limping step away. "Sure."

"Thank you."

I stop in front of Lennox, laying a hand on his broad chest. He paces backwards, putting some distance between us and everyone else. His expression is caught somewhere between apprehension and intrigue.

"Ripley, I'm just—"

"I can't run anymore," I interject. "Not from this. We need to take a stand."

"I know," he agrees. "But I need you to be safe."

Newfound warmth curls around my heart. Not the same warmth that Raine's honesty and soft affection provoke. Nor the toxic warmth I hold for Xander and all his complexities.

This feeling is different. It's been there for a while, escaping in brief moments ever since our shared trauma in the Z wing. Even when he's driving me insane or I'm plotting his death, I still feel it. The inescapable draw.

Lennox brings out the worst in me. I want to taunt him. Punish him. Break his mind the same way he broke mine. Yet I also want to reassure him. Gain his trust. Put the broken pieces in his brain back together.

"Don't look so surprised." Lennox smiles wryly. "I'm aware that I fucking suck at… well, this. I've never felt the need to fix my mistakes before."

"Must be nice."

"It was." His teeth pierce his bottom lip. "Until you."

This isn't the time or place, but honestly, we need to lay it all on the table. We almost died last night with all this unfinished business.

"And now? What do you feel?"

"I've been trying to figure that out." Lennox shifts from foot to foot.

"When we go with these people, I don't know what's going to happen. What they'll demand from us. We have to be able to trust each other… fully."

Seeing him so uncertain would be funny if it didn't take us almost dying to get here. I suppose it couldn't have been any other way. Only facing pure evil could force us to put our old hatred aside.

"You flipped my entire world upside down in that basement." He pauses for a breath. "I finally understood your actions. We hurt your family."

"And you were protecting yours."

"I'll always hurt someone else before I let the people I love suffer. I want to protect you, Rip. I want to make up for all the cruel shit I've done. The pain I've caused you."

In the spirit of honesty, I gather my courage.

"We've almost died more times than I can count, but these past few weeks… Fuck, I've never felt so whole, Nox. Even while on death's door. You all make me feel that way."

My hand still resting above his heart, I can feel how out of control it is right now. Stuttering with each hard pound, the organ is pleading with me. Begging for this clean slate.

"That's why I'm willing to have faith right now." I smooth his bloodstained shirt. "Because I know you'll protect me. Just like you'll protect Raine and Xander. I trust you."

Reaching up, Lennox pushes a matted curl behind my ear. "You do?"

"Perhaps against my better judgement."

His mouth quirks. "I've learned to ignore my judgement. It's led me down the wrong path too many times."

"And now?"

"Now… I think it was wrong all along. I'm where I need to be." His knuckles gently stroke down to my jaw. "I'll spend every waking moment ensuring your trust isn't misplaced."

I take Lennox's hand from my face, his grip firm and reassuring. It feels right clutching mine. His fingertips dance over my skin, leaving butterfly kisses that raise my gooseflesh.

"Ready?" I ask him. "They won't wait forever."

"No. I'm not ready. Not yet."

Grip tightening on my jaw, he leans in to touch his lips to mine. It doesn't matter that we're standing in broad daylight, surrounded by strangers. Coated in blood. Beaten and broken down.

Because Lennox is kissing me.

He's holding me close.

Giving himself to me.

Unlike previous kisses, this one is tender. A slow, delicate touch of the lips. He's hesitant at first, mouth lingering on mine before he pecks me again. Harder. Breathing vulnerability and hope into the vacant space I've carved for him in my heart.

Everything about Lennox is intimidating. His harsh demeanour. Acid tongue. Propensity for violence. Inability to forgive. But I'm starting to realise this isn't the real Lennox at all. Like Xander and Raine, he played a role.

We all did.

It's how we survived.

This is the real Lennox. Kissing me so softly, I almost wonder if the man who knocked me unconscious and left me for dead in a flooding pool ever really existed. Back then, I was just another threat.

The kiss ends, and I gulp down air.

"Now I'm ready." He plants a final kiss on my forehead. "Let's go see what these fuckers want from us for their stupid protection."

"You don't have to sound so thrilled."

"I'm struggling to contain my enthusiasm, really."

"I can tell."

Fingers interlinked, we turn to face the others. Xander's holding Raine upright to relieve his bad ankle, while Warner's team is pouring over a map pulled up on Theodore's laptop.

Enzo glares around with his thick arms folded. The hard-faced grump can't fool me. I saw that smile earlier and all it entailed. He's a fucking teddy bear.

We walk over to Xander and Raine. Standing as one united front, even in our pathetically dishevelled state, I've never felt so powerful. Perhaps we can do this. Face the evil hunting us and end it, once and for all.

I want the future I became the stooge for.

And I want it with them.

CHAPTER 19
RAINE
PULL THE PLUG - VOILÀ

SHAKING the pills from the plastic bottle, I count out each dose. I'm determined to do this alone, hands sliding over each sleek kitchen cabinet as I search for a glass.

I've barely familiarised myself with the two-bedroom apartment we were deposited in by Warner and his superiors. They instructed us to get cleaned up and rest while they handle the fallout of the mess we left behind.

After being driven down to London and checked by the doctor waiting, we were ready to pass out. First, we had to wait for medications to be delivered. Sabre must have serious money if they can summon controlled substances with a click of their fingers.

They left quickly, promising to return with updates and more essentials. Warner assured us that security would remain outside for our protection. They're taking no chances after our close call.

Feeling something cool knock against my fingers, I feel for its texture. Curved edges. A glass. Triumphant, I pluck it from the cupboard. With the pills in one hand, I can attempt to locate the sink.

Clang.

My foot smashes into a hard piece of furniture, causing my still-painful ankle to flare. The sudden collision unsteadies me, and before I can stop it, the glass slips from my hand.

"No," I yelp, trying to catch it.

The shattering blast of it smashing on the kitchen tiles will certainly draw attention. Sighing hard, I rest against the sink, my fist curling around the pills.

Bloody useless.

This is why I always kept my room precisely organised, down to the inch. I hate new environments. It always takes time to adjust. And right now, I don't even have a guide stick.

"Raine! Where are you?"

"Kitchen, Xan."

Hurried footsteps bang through the apartment. I don't bother attempting to move. Xander announces his arrival with a loud exhale.

"Ah."

"Yep." I pop the P exaggeratedly. "Figured you'd slept enough."

Cracking a yawn, he steps closer. "You should've just woken one of us up."

"It was just a dumb mistake. I hit my ankle."

"Alright, stand still."

I remain frozen while Xander cleans up the broken shards then fills another glass with water to hand over. Knocking back the pills, I swallow the powdery mouthful then hand the glass back to him.

"How long did we sleep for?"

I hear the glass make an impact when Xander deposits it in the sink. "Fifteen hours. Must've needed it."

"Christ. Those guys will be back soon to start taking statements."

"Yeah." He sounds groggy and half-awake. "I'll get Lennox up. Can you find your way back to Ripley's room?"

"Erm…"

Xander chuckles. "We'll get you another stick. Come on, take my arm. You shouldn't be walking on that ankle."

"It's fine, the swelling is down."

Gratefully accepting his elbow, I let him steer me through the unknown space. Once I commit the layout to memory, I'll be fine. In the meantime, I despise being so dependent on others.

"Good luck with the snorer."

"Thanks," he drawls sarcastically.

"I'll wake Ripley up."

Easing the door open, I keep a hand stretched out to avoid any more collisions. Ripley's stirring in the bed. She was exhausted when we arrived, passing out immediately once the doctor cleared her and she'd showered.

Finding the double bed, I crawl back underneath the cheap, scratchy duvet. Being roused by turbulent shaking and nausea twisting my gut wasn't a pleasant awakening. She slept through it, though.

"Mmm," Ripley moans.

Snuggling up to her back, I hold her in a close spoon. "Just me."

"Where did you go?"

"To take my meds." Her scent is an unfamiliar perfume, not the papaya fragrance I'm used to. "I don't like the shower gel you're using."

Laughing sleepily, she presses her back into me. "It was a bar of soap. This place is sparse."

"What's it like?"

"Bare." Ripley pauses to yawn. "Kinda like a cheap London rental but unfinished. I don't think anyone's been here for a long time."

"I guess safe houses aren't supposed to be luxurious."

"At this point, I would take a cardboard box on a street corner if it's safe." Her back vibrates with a laugh before she curses. "Ouch."

We all heard the doctor declare her stable, though she'll be multicoloured for a while. Thankfully, there's no permanent damage from Harrison's beating and the brutal tasing she received.

"How are the bruises?"

"Delightful," she groans. "I can't believe that bastard didn't break a rib."

"You got lucky."

"Some didn't."

Ripley falls silent, and I know she's thinking about Rae. Whenever I interacted with the girl, she was open and warm. I liked her energy.

"I'm sure Warner's teammates have taken care of Rae."

"I don't even know if she had family," Ripley replies thickly. "I know what type of razors she liked. How often she'd reorder. What she was willing to pay. Nothing actually important or meaningful."

Unable to alleviate the guilt she's overwhelmed by, I do the only thing I can. I hold her close, her spine aligned with my chest as I rock her gently. Her sobs are barely audible when they take over.

"How did Harrison even know we were friends?" she weeps. "It's my fault. I let her get close. He used Rae against me."

"Stop, Rip. Her death isn't on you. Letting people get close doesn't mean you're sentencing them to death."

"Doesn't it?" She releases a miserable-sounding laugh. "I let her matter to me, and she's dead."

"Because a lunatic killed her. Did you ask him to?"

"No," she whimpers.

"Did you want her to get hurt?"

"No, of course not!"

"Are you happy she's gone?"

Ripley shrugs away from me, awkwardly twisting in the bed. "What the fuck, Raine?"

"I'm proving to you how the rest of us see it. Rae's death is a tragedy. She didn't deserve what happened to her, but that doesn't mean it's your fault. You have to stop taking on all this guilt."

"But—"

"No buts, Rip. It stops now."

Finding her shoulder, I slide my hand up and behind her neck to knead her skull. Ripley draws in a heavy breath, curling up into my chest. I can feel her tears sliding against my skin with each hiccup.

"It's okay, babe. Let it all out."

In many ways, I feel lucky to experience this side of her. Not many people know the real Ripley. The fact that she's willing to let herself fall apart in front of me is a privilege I'll never take for granted.

Holding her tight until her sobs turn to quiet sniffles, I let Ripley work through her grief. Sometimes, words are unhelpful. Providing a safe space to acknowledge the grief and let it come pouring out is far more powerful.

"Did you go into the kitchen naked?" She breaks the silence after a long time.

"I have boxers on."

"What about the smashing sound?"

"Erm, I dropped a glass. Need to map the place out in my mind."

Her hand splays across my lower back. I tune into the rhythmic strokes, each touch taking me to a familiar place where I don't need sight. Not with her. With Ripley, I feel perfectly whole.

We drift for a long while until the sounds of stirring echo from outside our bedroom. Kissing the top of her head, I gently peel her from my chest.

"Ready to face the music?"

"Not really." She sighs.

"We can hide here if you need more time."

"As much as I appreciate that, we can't. We'll have company soon."

"I'll happily barricade the door for you."

Ripley pecks my cheek before I feel her sit up. "I love you."

I never thought three simple words would mean so much to me. Perhaps I never thought she'd say them back. In a matter of months, my entire existence has shifted. It used to revolve around the next hit.

Now, it's her.

A far more intoxicating drug.

Dragging myself from the bed, I feel around to locate the sweats and crumpled t-shirt I discarded before climbing into bed. They hang loose on my frame, but for clean clothes found in a pinch, I won't complain.

Ripley uses the bathroom then pads back out, the ruffling of clothes being pulled on evidence of her stiff movements. She clasps my arm, leading me from the room.

"How's the ankle?"

"It feels a lot better. The ice pack helped." I hesitate, sniffing the air. "Oh, smooth."

"Huh?"

"Xander's demonstrating his obsessive knowledge once more."

As she pulls me into what I think is the open plan living and dining area, I hear Ripley gasp. It's a weirdly happy sound. That alone makes me smile.

"Is that…"

"Not me," Xander volunteers. "The snorer was already up and dressed."

I sense movement accompanying Lennox's signature heavy thuds. I'm convinced he's incapable of walking quietly. He fiddles with something before approaching us.

"Joint effort," he explains. "Xander knew your coffee order."

Ripley snickers. "Of course, he did."

"Here. Macchiato, right?"

The satisfied groan she releases can only be described as sexual. Seriously, I'm concerned about what she's planning to do with that coffee.

"You went out?" Ripley takes a loud slurp. "Oh, holy shit."

Lennox laughs under his breath. "Yeah, I wanted to check out the security we've been assigned. There's a coffee place across the street."

His rough fingertips brush my hand, passing me a Styrofoam cup. I won't tell Ripley that I'm a tea before coffee kinda person. She'll probably decapitate me with her macchiato in hand.

"Security still outside?" I take a hot sip.

"Five of them."

"Armed?" Ripley asks.

Lennox sniffs loudly. "Yeah."

Seems they're taking the meagre information we've offered seriously. Warner and his colleagues don't even know half the story yet.

We all listen to Ripley make increasingly disturbing sounds as she drinks. You'd think the woman hasn't tasted decent coffee in years… Which isn't far from the truth, thinking about it.

"Here." There's a rustle before footsteps near. "Eat before your heart gives out from all the caffeine."

"Xan," Ripley warns sassily. "Touch my coffee and I'll drink it from your skull."

A choked cough comes from Lennox. "He'd probably enjoy that."

"No." Xander is quick to protest. "I wouldn't."

"That's an outright lie." I savour another sip.

"It's not!"

"You totally would enjoy it."

"Raine's right." Lennox harrumphs in disdain. "Tell the truth."

An audible sigh.

"For fuck's sake… Yes. I would probably enjoy that."

Xander joins our laughter—begrudgingly, from the sound of it—as he helps me walk over to what feels like a kitchen table. Measuring the space between the chairs with my foot, I begin to form a mental image.

Lennox passes around breakfast pastries crammed full of thick, sugary jam. I recognise the taste and texture on my tongue. We eat peacefully, sipping our drinks, until he breaks the silence.

"Do you think he meant it? That Enzo bloke?"

"Meant what?" Ripley chews loudly.

"What he said about cutting the head off the snake," Lennox clarifies. "Are they going to make a move on Bancroft?"

"Are we even sure he's the real threat anymore?" Xander slurps his drink. "Harrison hinted at management changes. Then there was that phone call."

I hear someone put their food down.

"You can say it. My uncle."

"Yes. He clearly sent those men after us," Xander says, blunt as ever. "Your uncle put a hit out on us."

"That goes a bit beyond mere disownment." I wince at my own words. "Sorry, Rip."

"Don't be. We can't tiptoe around this." She sounds resigned. "I think his role goes beyond being an investor. He's more deeply embroiled in the conspiracy than I realised."

"We have to tell them," Lennox chimes in. "Bancroft is still a threat, but they need to get eyes on Jonathan. Perhaps he's pulling the strings while his boss is under fire."

"That seems likely," Xander agrees.

Finishing up our breakfast, we remain at the table, gulping down our hot drinks. Ripley's leg pushes against mine underneath the table—she's sitting on my right side. I drop a hand to her thigh.

"So we tell them everything." She covers my hand with hers. "In exchange for what? Protection?"

"We need to negotiate for immunity," Xander responds. "For the riot. The contraband. All of it."

"You really think we'd face prosecution?" Nausea spikes through me.

"Warner told us criminal charges were on the table for other escapees."

My mouth pulls down in a grimace. "And if Sabre doesn't have that power? Or won't help us avoid charges?"

Xander doesn't answer. Fantastic. That really gives me a vote of confidence.

"Shit, Xan." Lennox breaks the long pause. "You can't tell them about… You know…"

The silence is frustrating. I strain my ears, trying to understand what's happening.

"Lennox is miming," Ripley whispers to me. "Throat cutting, to be specific."

"Thanks. Can we really keep that a secret?"

"Nobody saw me," Xander says nonchalantly.

"Are you absolutely certain?" Lennox counters.

His silence is telling. Nope. He's not.

"Then lie!"

There's a loud boom, and the table shakes as Lennox must slam his fist down onto it.

"Tell them what happened, but say the warden threatened you. Anything. It'd be your word against a dead man."

Something has really gone wrong if I'm sitting here, trapped in a safe house, discussing how best to cover up a grisly murder one of my best friends committed. It's a far cry from my old life.

"We aided and abetted the experimental program by

selling contraband." Ripley changes the topic. "I doubt the law will look upon that leniently."

"Then we have a bargaining chip." Lennox snaps his fingers. "Our inside information will fast-track years of investigative work. We can tell them everything. We sell them on that."

Someone drums on the table's surface. I can taste the boiling tension. We've sided with the good guys, but that doesn't mean we're off the hook. The world doesn't work that way.

"And if it's not enough?" Xander eventually asks. "Lennox, we both have criminal convictions. Who's to say we won't be sent to an actual prison this time?"

"They wouldn't do that, surely?"

Just the thought has anxiety vibrating beneath my skin.

"This will turn into a blame game. Throwing us in jail with a nice guilty label will be an easy win."

The thought of them being ripped away from us is too much to bear. While a violent episode landed Ripley in Harrowdean Manor, I know she was never charged. Like me, she was among the percentage incarcerated without a criminal conviction.

The rest—patients like Lennox and Xander—took their rehabilitative sentence to avoid prison. That's not to say their mental health wasn't a deciding factor. Ultimately, no one in the institute was altogether sane.

I rub my aching temples, a headache forming. "Why does it sound like we're screwed either way?"

"No." Ripley's leg presses harder into mine. "We just have to play this smart until the investigation concludes with Bancroft and his associates behind bars."

"Or six feet under," Xander adds.

Lennox makes an agreeing sound. I trace circles on Ripley's loose sweats, the cotton rough and cheap. No matter what role he's played, Jonathan is her last living relative. She has to be struggling.

"I know he's your uncle, but…"

"He won't stop," she finishes for me. "Jonathan is relentless. Focused. If he wants something, he'll pull every trick in the book to get it."

"In business," I point out. "This is different."

"I was always a business transaction to him. It's no different now. He's a core investor in Incendia Corporation, and we're a threat to that. To his entire livelihood and reputation."

Her words hang ominously. She's right. To him, we are a threat. An erasable one. That's why he sent those men to capture or kill us. Jonathan is far more than the heartless bastard we all took him to be.

He's dangerous.

And we're on his hit list.

CHAPTER 20
RIPLEY

ANOTHER ONE – TOBY MAI

TAPPING a ballpoint pen against his notebook, Enzo Montpellier stares me down. His attention is a precisely-aimed blowtorch, intending to incinerate any lies he detects. He's terrifyingly perceptive.

I'm holding my own against his harsh glare, even after several hours of his carefully worded questions. The others were removed from the apartment under protest to be interviewed separately.

Xander had to be threatened several times to get him to leave for his own interview. It took a lot of pleading for him to eventually relent for the sake of getting this done.

"Why do I feel like you don't trust me?" Enzo deadpans.

Shifting, I fold my legs. "Because I don't."

"We're on the same side."

"No one is on our side, Mr Montpellier. Ever."

"Enzo is fine," he tells me for the fifth time.

Piercing amber eyes sweep over me. We've been talking for hours, running through every single detail. Years of information from my first day in Priory Lane to scaling the security fence at Harrowdean.

I never thought I'd be laying out my life story in brutal

black and white for a total stranger. One whose job is to judge whether I'm deserving of his help. After all I've done, I wouldn't be surprised if Enzo threw us back out on the street.

When you're drowning, it's easy to justify pushing other heads beneath the water so you can stay afloat. It's necessary, right? They'd do the same to you. Only in the aftermath does the price of evil come knocking.

"I have one more question." He snaps his notebook closed, placing the pen on top.

"Shoot."

"Why'd you do it? Become their stooge?"

"Do you ask all Incendia's victims this?"

"Most of them were admitted into the program by force." His mountain-sized shoulders lift in a shrug. "I have one guy who even worked for them before he was imprisoned and tortured for several years."

Acid swarms in the back of my mouth. "So I'm the bad guy for choosing to do what I did?"

"Do you deny it?"

Focusing on the coffee table, I avoid his stare. "No."

"Why, then?"

"I've done things I'm not proud of." I lace my hands over my roiling stomach. "A lot of people have gotten hurt because of my actions."

Looking down at the battle wounds decorating my arms, I struggle to find the right words. The events that have led me to this sofa, recounting a tale too harrowing for most to fathom, feel alien.

Did I do all those things? I hold the memories. Bear the scars. It must've been me.

I spent so long detached from my morals, I didn't care who I was hurting. At least part of me didn't. Peddling management's agenda became second nature. I fanned the flames so they could study us all.

Sick, right?

I'm under no illusions.

It's an old cliché. Hurt people, hurt people. Is it the same for those who've been abandoned? Do we dole out cruelty to ensure our own survival at all costs because no one else is coming to save us?

No one has ever helped or been there for me. Not since Holly. I've done everything myself, starting with getting revenge. Leveraging my grief into power was nothing more than a calculated business move.

"Every time I sold pills to an addict or blades to a cutter, I knew what I was doing." I swallow the lump in my throat. "It was just... inconsequential. I needed the power. The control."

Listening attentively, Enzo doesn't look judgemental as I expected. The gentle look of understanding is back, crumbling his gruff exterior. I'm surprised he hasn't run for the front door yet.

"Their pain guaranteed my freedom," I try to explain. "Doing things that made me sick meant I would live when Holly didn't get to. It was a desperate trade off."

He nods in acknowledgement. "In my experience... desperation is the source of most evils."

"Don't excuse what I did."

"I'm not." Enzo smiles sadly. "Perhaps it was simply an inevitable side effect."

How this towering pillar of strength can hold so much soft-hearted concern, I can't quite understand. He isn't what I expected from Sabre's second-in-command.

Despite his tactics, I hold the full, unfiltered truth back. Enzo is playing the good guy, but I've fallen into that trap before.

"I'll take your testimony back to our director, Hunter."

"Warner mentioned others were facing criminal charges." Panic flutters behind my breastbone. "I need to know what I'm looking at."

He appraises me, the crinkles around his eyes making him seem conflicted. "I don't know, Ripley."

"That isn't good enough."

"We're negotiating charges with the Serious Crimes Unit. Your cooperation will help your case."

"I have more information. Inside knowledge that can help you dismantle their entire operation."

"If you're all willing to cooperate with the investigation, perhaps a plea deal can be made. Hunter will take your case to the authorities to make a decision."

"He doesn't want to speak to me himself?" I ask in surprise.

"He's… preoccupied right now." Enzo worries his bottom lip. "We lost a member of our organisation recently. Someone important to us."

"Alyssa?"

The muscle in his neck twitches. "Yes."

"She freed us from the Z wing."

"So I've heard."

"What happened to her?"

Enzo releases a world-weary sigh. "The night we entered Harrowdean, we were undertaking a rescue mission. Alyssa lost her life in the crossfire."

"If it weren't for her, we would be dead or worse. I'm sorry."

"Yeah." He clears his throat. "Me too."

Feeling like I've poked a sore spot, I decide to look away. "What happens now?"

"You'll remain in protective custody here at the safe house while we take this information away. The security detail won't let anything happen to you."

"Bancroft will plough straight through your men."

Enzo gathers his things, rising to his full height. "Bancroft won't be a problem for much longer. Until then, we will keep you safe."

"You're not going to tell me anything else. Are you?"

Humour sparkles in his molten eyes. "No."

Frustration burns through me, but I hold it at bay. We've barely survived a few weeks in the firing line. This man helps run a multimillion-pound business that operates under enemy fire. This is his fight.

Before showing himself out, Enzo glances back at me, looking like he wants to say more.

"What?" I prompt.

"You remind me of someone. She's feeling guilty right now too."

When he pauses, I wait for him to gather his thoughts.

"I told her healing is hard."

"Why do you say that?" I can't hold the question in.

"Well, it's a constant battle between your inner child who's scared and just wants to feel safe… your inner teenager who's angry and wants justice… and your current self. The one who just wants peace."

Gaping at him, I'm too surprised to form a response. Enzo drags a palm down his rugged face, his gaze now averted.

"I don't know if that helps. Good to meet you properly, Ripley. We'll be in touch."

With that wise pearl delivered, he turns and leaves. Enzo Montpellier could rival Lennox with his aggressive stomping around, but I doubt anyone could match the heart of gold he seems to have.

Silence drapes over me, broken by the distant ticking of the clock hanging on the wall. Now that I'm alone, all the shameful secrets I've just revealed leave me feeling dirty.

Perhaps the different parts of me have been fighting all along. Orphaned Ripley. Angry, grieving Ripley. Abandoned Ripley. Now tired Ripley. In that battleground, I lashed out, creating so much collateral damage.

A layer of blood and tears coat my soul, and short of digging the thing out with a rusty spoon, I'll never be able to get it clean. Not after all I've done to be sitting here today.

The invisible fist in my chest squeezing, I head for the shared bathroom, quickly stripping off the clothing I was given to wear. More essentials and toiletries were delivered this morning.

Studying my bruised torso in the mirror, I poke the sensitive flesh. It could be worse. The pain meds are working. I locate the new shampoo and shower gel we were given before stepping into the shower.

Not so long ago, I stood in a shower and scrubbed the memories of Xander and Lennox from my skin. Life has changed so much since then. I feel lost without the guys all around me now.

Head ducked, I brace my hands on the tiled wall. Water sluices over me, and in the spray, I fail to realise I'm not alone until the bathroom door clicks shut.

"Wha…?"

My exclamation dies on my lips. Leaning against the bathroom door, Lennox watches me through the steamed-up glass. A million warring emotions dance in his eyes beneath ruffled, thick-brown locks.

"You're done?"

He shrugs. "That Ethan guy didn't have any more questions. I guess the other interviews are taking longer. Xander and Raine aren't back yet."

"I see."

Continuing to wash myself, I lather my body with foaming shower gel. Lennox's throat bobs beneath dark stubble overdue for a shave. His chest stretches the bounds of his shirt, the defined muscles making my toes curl.

"What did you tell Enzo?"

"Enough to take to the authorities." I tip my head back to rinse my hair. "Kept some details brief."

"Like?" Lennox challenges.

"Like you zip tying me in a swimming pool, for one."

His gaze lowers, flitting over me unashamedly. "I see."

A column of heat gathers between my legs, the long slow burn gathering into a raging furnace. I like the way he looks at me. Powerless and hungry. Like he'd beg for a mere touch.

After washing the shower gel from my body, I turn off the spray and step out. Water clings to me, trailing over my curves as I disregard the towel I laid out. The sore bruises and bright-pink gunshot wound on my thigh suddenly feel inconsequential.

Lennox holds stock-still, watching me pad towards him. I stop mere inches away, completely bare. His attention dips to trail over me, greedily drinking in every inch.

It isn't the first time he's seen me naked, but we're not imprisoned in a cell now. He can do whatever he likes.

"Don't you want to know what I told them?" he asks thickly.

"Not right now. No."

Nodding, Lennox's tongue darts out to lick his bottom lip. "So what do you want?"

Pent-up desire has emboldened me. We've exchanged heated whispers and the odd kiss since escaping. Yet he refuses to take that next step. I'll take it for the both of us if I have to.

"For you to keep your word."

"My word?" He tilts his head.

"I recall you promising to do something."

His eyes widen in understanding. "I thought you were injured."

"And I wouldn't be asking if I couldn't handle it."

Without touching me, Lennox holds eye contact as he steps away from the door. I watch him sink to the bathroom floor and land on his knees.

The almighty Lennox Nash is fucking kneeling in front of me. My hand knots in his soft brown hair, giving it a hard tug.

In this position, I feel utterly invincible. The man who

vowed to ruin me is cowering on his knees, a million miles from the person he once was.

"Is this what you want?" he purrs.

Feeling brave, I lower my other hand between my legs. My fingers meet slick warmth. I'm wet, my swollen clit aching. Lennox watches me push a hand over my folds, spreading my arousal.

I slide a finger in my pussy, my thumb rotating above my clit. His rapt attention on me is exhilarating. He hasn't even touched me. This is all about surrender after months of our futile war for revenge.

"Yes," I answer breathily. "This is what I wanted."

"What if I tell you that you are the most infuriating, confusing, frustrating person I've ever met?" He hesitates, nostrils flaring. "But also the most beautiful woman I've ever laid eyes on?"

Slipping in another finger, I scissor the digits inside me. My back arches, pushing my cunt closer to his face. Still, Lennox doesn't move an inch, determined to give me all the control.

"And for the longest time, I was terrified of admitting how drawn I felt to you. How you infiltrated my dreams. My thoughts. My fantasies. I was scared to love the very thing I hated."

Working myself over for his perusal, I fist the hand still knotted in his hair. "Are you still afraid?"

I watch Lennox nod, pulling in fast breaths.

"Of me?"

"No. Now I'm scared of losing you."

Triumph fills my every cell.

"I want you to forget it all, Nox. Everything we've done to each other. And I want you to prove to me how much you want this. Right here, right now."

Anticipation blazes in his seafoam orbs. "Are you sure?"

"I won't break. I need you to touch me."

The tentative Lennox dissipates. All it took was that verbal admission. He knocks my hand aside, sliding my fingers from inside me. Hunger pulses between my legs when he sucks the glistening digits into his mouth.

Lennox swirls his tongue over my fingers, sucking them clean. Then he lowers his mouth to the apex of my thighs, dead set on one target. Placing my other hand on his shoulder, I buck into his face.

When his lips meet my core, I mentally rejoice. The man who tried his best to kill me is now on his knees, worshipping my body. I've taken his hatred and turned it into pure lust.

He devours my pussy like a starving man, his tongue dragging over my tingling clit. I continue rocking against him, encouraging each lick. Sparks are zipping up and down my spine in fast succession.

"I can't wait to feel you, baby."

When he thrusts a finger into me, I can't help but cry out. Lennox fucks me with his hand, mouth fastened on my bud with each pulse. The combined effect has my knees weakening.

He pauses for a breath. "You taste so fucking good."

"Is that all you've got?"

"Fuck no. I'm dying to fill this sweet pussy, but I need to prep you first." His heated gaze flashes to mine. "I don't want to hurt you."

I suppress a smirk. The eyeful I got of his package in the bathroom was intriguing. He's far bigger than any man I've been with, matching his stacked height. Part of me wants to push my own limits.

"I want you to come for me, Rip." His fingers pump into me, hard and fast. "I'm begging you to give me an orgasm. Cover my hand in your juices."

"Yes," I moan.

"You like that, huh? When I beg on my knees?"

Squirming, I ride the hand driving me wild in time to his

ministrations. My climax is approaching, making my skin tighten and tingle like I've been wired with electrodes.

"God, Nox. I like it."

"What if I beg to throw you on the bed and spread your legs wide open so I can see your glistening, pink cunt?"

"Yes! Oh, fuck. Yes."

"And what if I beg to sink my cock inside you and stretch this tight little cunt to breaking point?"

"P-Please."

My vision swims, an electrifying wave washing over me. His dirty words are heightening my arousal to the point of being overwhelmed. I'm going to explode if he keeps going.

"And what if I beg to fill every inch of your spent pussy with my seed? Just so I can see it dripping out of you and trailing down your legs?"

All it takes is a final thrust and I'm erupting all over his hand. My orgasm hits all at once, core spasming and body trembling. I dig my nails into his shoulder, riding out the wave.

Removing his hand, Lennox ensures I'm watching as he slowly sucks each soaked digit, just like he did to mine. His expression is downright predatory. I wonder if I'll even survive his begging.

"Such a perfect girl," he croons. "May I stand up now? I'd like to do everything I just said and more."

Christ.

Everything clenches tight.

"You may," I pant, my heart galloping. "Take me to your bedroom. Right now."

Finding his feet, Lennox sweeps me into his arms. I grunt when I'm tossed over his shoulder, the pain flaring through my stiff body only serving to heighten my arousal.

His palm smacks against my bare ass as I'm carried from the bathroom to the room he's sharing with Xander. The king-sized bed has been neatly made. God forbid the iceman ever leaves a single thing out of place.

As soon as he places me on the mattress, he's yanking his t-shirt off. I lay back, thighs pressed together to alleviate the intense pressure his words have created.

Naked Lennox is a sight to behold. Barrel chest carved with stacked muscles, his abdominals, pecs and shoulders resemble chiselled marble. Unlike Xander, his skin is bronzed and smattered with dark hair, a trail leading into his sweats.

"Spread your legs, baby. Show me everything."

I follow his instructions, spreading myself wide open so I'm utterly on display. Lennox's piercing attention scours over me, drinking in the view as he strips off the rest of his clothes.

The faintest crack of doubt inches in at the sight of him. As I remembered, he's fucking huge. His shaft is thick and girthy. I'm doubting whether he'll even fit.

Lennox fists his cock, slowly pumping it. "Don't look so scared, Rip."

I squirm on the bed. "Are you going to hold me in suspense?"

Prowling closer, he kneels on the bed above me. The anticipation is heady. I wasn't ready to give myself to Lennox before, but now I want him to take everything. All I have left to give.

He braces himself over me, moving down to plant open-mouthed kisses across my chest. His lips lock around my right nipple, sweet pain flashing through me when he pulls it deeply into his mouth.

Releasing my nipple, he sucks and bites a path to my left breast, leaving a constellation of red marks. I wriggle beneath him, pleading for any amount of friction.

"So impatient." His words warm my already scalding skin.

"Nox," I whine.

"Easy, baby. I want to take my time with you."

Hasn't he waited long enough?

Playing with my nipples, he seems determined to cover every part of me in tiny bites. I don't know if it's some kind of branding in his mind, a statement to the other men allowed to touch me. I think I like that idea.

"Please," I try again. "Stop teasing me."

Lennox lifts his head. "How can I get you to shut up?"

My mouth falls open in protest.

"Ah." He quirks a thick brow. "I know."

Pulling me upright, he sits back on his haunches between my legs. Lennox threads his hand through my hair, pushing my head down towards his proud cock.

"I'll fuck your throat if that's the only way to teach you patience."

He pushes himself past my lips, holding my head in place. The rough handling only makes me hotter. I take his length deep into my mouth, bobbing up and down on his shaft.

His grip on my head guides my moves, allowing him to set the pace. Lennox doesn't deny himself, pushing down fast so he can roughly ride my mouth. Each time he hits the back of my throat, tears spring up in my eyes.

"That's it." His praise is guttural. "Get me nice and wet so I can slide into that dripping cunt."

Tongue swirling over the velvety tip, I suck him deep once more, feeling moisture springing from my eyes. I can't take all of him—he's too big to fit into my mouth even while relaxing my jaw.

"Yes, Rip. Perfect. Let me fuck that mouth, baby."

I could fall apart from his enthusiastic praise alone. It's making my pulse thrum, struggling to hold the excitement building within me. I had no idea he'd be so vocal.

He ruts into my mouth, over and over. Pushing deeper each time. Forcing me to suck down more of his huge length until I'm gagging on his cock and loving every intense second.

"God, how I want to pour myself down your throat. You are everything, Rip. Fucking everything."

Before he can finish, Lennox eases himself from my

mouth. I sit up with streaming cheeks, my chin soaked by strands of saliva.

"Lay down," he commands. "Now."

I'm shaking so hard, it's a relief to slump back on the bed. He retakes his position, pushing my thighs farther apart until my bones ache to fit his wide frame.

The head of his dick slides through my folds, swirling heat and moisture. He teases my slit with it, only entering me the smallest amount before withdrawing and sliding himself around my entrance again.

"More!" I beg shamelessly.

Each slow tease is torture. I want him to surge into me and take me as roughly as he did my mouth. We may not be enemies anymore, but I'd happily let him fuck me like we are.

"Please… Oh god. Please give it to me."

"Are you this demanding with the others?"

Writhing beneath him, I don't answer. Lennox bares his teeth and pushes farther into me, his girth straining my walls. We both groan at the same time.

"So goddamn tight."

He withdraws before I can fully adjust, sliding out before nudging back inside. The agonising dance goes on and on with him giving an extra push then snatching it away each time.

My mind is starting to fray. He's barely entered me, and it already feels like too much. I'm not a shrinking violet. I've slept with my fair share of guys. None that rival Lennox, though.

Giving me more of his cock, he rocks into me. The shallow thrusts make me stretch to accommodate him. I couldn't take him if I wasn't so frenziedly turned on right now.

Each time he pushes forward, I take a little bit more. Adjusting to the pressure is excruciating in all the best ways. It feels like my mind is set to split in half before I can orgasm again.

"Nox," I whimper, overwhelmed.

"It's okay, Rip. You're doing so good. Can you take a bit more, baby?"

He moves faster, retreating and thrusting back in enough to make me moan loudly. It's too much. I'm so full. Stretched to my limits. Lennox is filling every part of me, mentally and physically.

"Just like that," he hums. "Good."

"Oh f-fuck. Nox!"

"That's it. You can take me. I know you can."

When he bottoms out, we're both struggling for air. Lennox shifts his hips, finding the perfect angle to glide into me with steady strokes. I'm over-stimulated, my skin slick beneath his weight above me.

"You're so fucking perfect."

Lennox palms my breast, squeezing tight as he jerks into me. The burst of pain is welcome. It cuts through my mind's fog and gives me something to latch onto amidst all the warring sensations.

He pistons into me, switching between shallow thrusts that stoke my building climax and deep pounds, delaying my release each time it nears. Just as I feel it within reach, he slows his pace, holding me on the brink.

It's like he can read my body, translating each tremble and whimper to determine exactly when to restrain himself. Lennox is determined to break me open and take my shattered pieces for himself.

"You take me so well," he grunts in exertion. "So damn well. It's like you were made for me."

I gasp and moan, my body slick with our combined sweat. I wonder if the others have returned and they're listening to everything Lennox is saying. Their friend's mouth is filthy.

Feeling my core tense, I'm ready to finish. My bruised

body is taut, desperate for relief. The cusp of my orgasm rises, on the precipice of consuming me, when Lennox abruptly pulls out.

"Not yet."

I scream loudly, slamming my clenched fist against his chest. "Fuck! Lennox!"

"You know, Xander warned me you're a little brat. I may have begged, but now, you're going to come when I say so."

"Goddamn you!"

"And not a moment sooner," he adds, ignoring my outrage.

He stands, seizing my ankles to pull me to the mattress edge. I'm a boneless pile as he turns me over, my stomach meeting the bed and face burying in the warm sheets.

Lennox lifts my hips, positioning me like I'm a limp doll. When he surges inside me from behind, I come back to life. My hands twist in the sheets, needing something to hold on to.

I distantly hear him spit before it hits my ass, sliding down into my crack. I startle at the impact, surprised by his fingers pushing the saliva farther down until he's circling my asshole.

My whines reach a fever-pitch.

"Have you ever taken a man here before?"

I'm not going to tell him about Raine finger-blasting my rear while he fucked me during a depressive episode. We need at least some boundaries.

"I was jealous, watching Raine ride your mouth." Lennox's fingertip enters me. "But I also wanted to join in."

He pushes in deeper, listening to my muffled wails. I'm already full to the brim. Just when I think I can't take anymore, he finds a new limit to test.

Working his finger in and out of my backside, Lennox resumes fucking me. His timing is perfect, breaching each hole simultaneously. My stolen orgasm comes soaring back within reach.

"Easy, baby. You're tensing up."

"Because you won't let me come!"

He chuckles behind me. "Do you have any idea how long I've waited to do this? You can hold out a little longer."

Digging my nails into the bed, the room is filled with the sound of our bodies smacking together. It's reaching intolerable levels. I'm far too full to cope with his thrusting much longer.

"I hate you!"

Pain sizzles across my scalp as Lennox seizes my wet hair. He manages to twist the short curls around his fingers, forming a tight leash. My head is wrenched back, pulling my torso upwards.

"Say that again," he hisses. "I dare you."

I'm suspended mid-air by his grip on my hair alone, his cock still plunging into me. It's a dominating move, inflicting pain to silence me while he's still fucking me into oblivion.

Breasts pushed out, I think he's going to finally relent. Only for him to still again when I don't respond, denying me right before I can fall apart. My throat is raw from crying out.

"Well?" Lennox tugs on my hair.

Panting, I can't string a response together. Lennox slides his finger from my asshole to deliver a punishing spank. It leaves a fiery brand on my skin, already sensitive from his constant teasing.

"Do you hate me when I've got my cock in you?"

"No," I moan helplessly.

"Then don't lie. Or I'll keep you hanging for an eternity."

"Please... Nox. Let me come. Please."

He swats me again, right above my soaked asshole. "No."

"Please!"

My ass is still tingling from his penetration, the feeling intensified by him striking me. Shockwaves roll over me, exploding in every limb.

"I want something from you."

"A-Anything," I whimper.

Lennox pushes back into my slit, nudging the hidden spot inside me that makes stars burst behind my eyes. A strangled sound erupts from me. I can hear how soaking wet I am from so many denials.

"I told you how I feel, Rip." His voice is rough, like he's trying desperately not to finish. "Now I want to hear it from you."

Another hard slap causes his grip on my hair to tense. The white-hot pain blurs with everything going haywire inside me. It sends my system into a cataclysmic meltdown.

"Hear what?" I bleat uselessly.

Lennox swaps to a slow roll, his hips jerking. "I heard what you said to Raine. You love him. I won't begrudge you that, Rip."

He delivers another loud smack, causing me to cry out his name.

"But I'm a selfish bastard. I need proof that you've forgiven me."

His tempo increases again, slapping our bodies together. I'm going to slide off the bed in a boneless puddle if he doesn't stop this game.

"I want to hear that you love me."

The son of a bitch.

He's trying to tear the truth out of me. Fuck me until I have no fight left to give and steal my affections before I can change my mind. But worst of all?

I want to give it to him. He wants proof. Fine. I'll hand over the signed confession he needs to finally move on. We've come too far to stop before the final hurdle.

"Lennox." The six letters strain my vocal cords. "You're a sadistic motherfucker."

Spank.

"Argh! Fuck! But I do… I do love you. God, I fucking love you."

Spank.

"Again!" he commands.

"You insane asshole! I am in love with you!"

Spank.

The sheer intensity has tears saturating my cheeks. I can no longer tell exquisite pain from pleasure anymore. I've melted into him, too weak to withstand his onslaught.

Spank.

"Now," Lennox orders. "Come all over my cock, baby."

It's all the permission my mind needs. It splinters apart, the individual lobes rupturing behind my skull. The howl pouring from me doesn't sound like my own. I've become something unrecognisable.

My climax is so intense, I faintly wonder if I'm going to black out. It feels like too much to hold inside. Every part of me is quivering, exhausted by his relentless teasing.

The hot burst of his release surging inside me makes my own deep pangs roll on and on. Lennox roars through his climax, hands clamping on my hips so he can pour every last drop into me.

"Take it all." He thrusts furiously. "Milk me dry, baby."

"God! Yes!"

I shout out through each iteration of blissful agony. I've fallen flat onto the soaked sheets, unable to hold myself up any longer. Lennox pulls out and slumps, lifting me so I can rest on his chest.

Beneath my head, his heart rate is a racing symphony. Warmth slicks between us as our essences mingle. I feel utterly spent, every part of me wrung-out.

"Fuck," he gasps.

My eyes are sealed shut. "That was… intense."

A hand drags up and down my sweaty spine, rough fingertips pausing on the healing punctures left by the taser.

As we both struggle to catch our breath, I hear the faint words he forces out. It takes all my strength to raise my head to look up at him.

"What?"

Blazing lake water eyes flick over me. "Nothing."

"I heard you, Nox. Just say it again."

His mouth crooks in a tired smile.

"I love you."

Lowering my mouth to his, I press our lips together. Lennox kisses me passionately, his tongue gliding over my lips to seek entrance before filling my mouth.

He's everywhere. Tongue brushing mine. Hands wrapped around my hips. Chests glued together. For a man who once couldn't stand the sight of me, he's now practically living in my skin.

"I love you," I reply simply.

"You meant it?" His smile is wide. "Not just a mid-sex confession?"

"I mean, you did torture it out of me. But that doesn't mean it isn't true."

Resting our foreheads together, I feel the final pathetic wall stacked around my heart crumble to ruin. The inevitable destruction feels like fucking nirvana.

I've opened my heart to them all. Accepted the possibility of grief for the chance at something more. A future without emptiness and heartache. Perhaps a happy ending.

I'll do anything to get that.

Even if I don't deserve it.

CHAPTER 21
LENNOX
SPIT IN MY FACE! – THXSOMCH

EARLY SUMMER in London used to be my favourite time to visit the city. I grew up east of the capital in a working-class town but visited on occasion. Once for my grandfather to collect his military pension.

Now the glass skyscrapers, towering office blocks and crammed tourist buses glisten in the warm sunshine. Through the window of the tinted SUV, I watch the morning chaos go by undisturbed.

It's funny how even when your own life is hanging by a thread, the world still turns. Oblivious and undisturbed. People stroll past stacks of newspapers, emblazoned with headlines that lose impact after a while.

"Headquarters is up ahead." Warner indicates to move into a different lane. "The SCU have already arrived—they're interviewing other witnesses today too."

"They took long enough to decide what to do with us," I grumble.

In the passenger seat, Xander nods in agreement. It's been a tiresome week, hiding in Sabre's safe house, uncertain of our own fates while the SCU deliberates over our fates.

After our interviews, Enzo and his team agreed to

negotiate any charges. We're not so worried about Raine. He was little more than a bystander. But for myself, Xander and Ripley, all bets are off.

Each of us have aided and abetted Incendia's criminal activities over the years. Then there's the grisly murder that Xander owned up to, though he claimed self-defence. Not to mention the altercation in the maize field. We've racked up a list of possible charges.

"Yours are the first to be agreed on." Warner huffs. "The Blackwood inmates are still being questioned. So be glad it didn't take months."

"Why is it taking so long for the others?" Ripley frowns.

"Their situation is a little more complicated."

The curved point of Ripley's jawline clenches tight. I know that in her mind, we deserve whatever lies ahead. She's feeling the guilt of all we've done to make it this far. I see things differently.

For every bad deed we've done, we prevented the suffering of our loved ones. Sometimes ourselves. Evil is justified if it's to stave off something worse for those you want to protect, right?

While I don't relish what we did to Holly, I also don't feel guilty. She was a stooge too. Culpable and heartless in the name of her own survival. But I do regret what it did to the woman who's fast become ours.

"What about Bancroft?" Raine speaks up from between us. "We can't hide in a safe house forever."

His lips sealed, Warner remains silent.

News reports appear daily about Incendia's worsening legal troubles. Aside from that, we've been kept in the dark. The evidence appears stacked against them and calls for the remaining institutes to close are growing.

Ripley rests her head on Raine's shoulder. "We swapped one prison for another."

"You're safe, fed and have around-the-clock security."

Warner stares at her in the rearview mirror. "That's a damn sight more than those trapped in other institutes or transferred from Harrowdean."

"Hey," I snap at him. "She's allowed to feel frustrated."

"We're doing the best we can. This is a complex investigation."

"You need to do better."

The dick doesn't deign to respond.

Merging through the dense traffic, we're deep in the business district, surrounded by cloud-kissing buildings on all sides. Bystanders wear pressed business suits and carry extortionately priced coffees on their morning commutes.

It's places like this that gave birth to Incendia Corporation. All the country's wealth and power concentrated into a handful of streets and buildings. Millions of lives dictated by the select few privileged enough to rise to the top.

"Jonathan's firm is half a mile from here, in Canary Wharf," Ripley observes.

"My team is monitoring your uncle personally," Warner attempts to reassure her. "If he steps even a toe out of line, we'll know about it."

"Comforting," Xander chuffs. "Because none of these people have done anything criminal under scrutiny before, right? They'll stay on the straight and narrow now."

His sarcasm aside, Xander makes a good point. Surveillance isn't enough. We've warned them about Jonathan Bennet and his connections to the conspiracy they're attempting to unravel.

"Look." Warner sighs audibly. "We're up against decades' of corruption here. This conspiracy goes right to the top of the government. You need to be more patient."

The monstrously huge building he drives up to silences our conversation. I'm gawping at the sky-high slab of polished steel and impenetrable tinted glass as the SUV slows to pull in.

Countless burly security officers surround the building, all wearing dark sunglasses and visible earpieces to match their stern expressions. Warner waves to one as he stops for a retinal scan before entering the underground parking garage.

We all pile out together on high alert. Raine unfolds his new white guide stick then takes Ripley's arm with his spare hand. Resting a hand on her lower back, I follow Xander and Warner over to the elevators.

The ride up to discover our fate is fraught with nail-biting silence. We're all balancing on a razor's edge, instinctively closing ranks in the small space. Ripley and Raine end up sandwiched between us.

I have no idea how many witnesses are cooperating with their investigation but given that we haven't been hauled in front of the authorities until now, Sabre must be combing through countless interviews and testimonies.

"What if they want to prosecute?" Raine whispers.

Considering his question, I study the back of Warner's head. It'd be easy enough to knock him out. I doubt we could take his whole team or their reinforcements, though I'd give it a damn good shot.

"We handle it." Xander's voice is impassive, betraying nothing. "Like we always have."

Translation—he goes full feral and butchers anyone standing in our way. Xander's ability to switch his humanity off would terrify anyone else. For us, it's like having our own personal army.

"Great plan." Ripley scrubs her face.

"I'm aware."

"Sarcasm, Xan. You need to rein in the stabby attitude."

I snort at her words. "Like that's gonna happen."

The floor we arrive at is brightly lit with plush carpets and numerous rooms off the long corridor, hidden by frosted glass. Warner gestures for us to follow him, tucking the special black pass he scanned in his pocket.

We're taken to an empty conference room fitted with a

long, wooden table and several chairs. Ripley steers Raine to the nearest seat, glancing up to ensure we're following. I brush her shoulder as I pass.

"Wait here." Warner ducks from the room.

Arms folded, I lean against the wall, unwilling to relax. Xander moves to stand beside the window, studying the impressive skyline beyond. We're high up, enough to see the wispy clouds.

"What's the play here?" I question. "I'm not seeing anyone get taken to prison."

"That won't happen." Ripley somehow sounds certain.

"You trust these people that much?"

"I trust that they know an opportunity when they see one. We have inside information. The only way to get us to cooperate is to guarantee our freedom."

"Think they'll go for that?" Raine wonders.

Ripley huffs out a tense breath. "They have to."

Remaining silent, Xander stares into the distance. He's been characteristically quiet. That never leads to anything good. It's the kind of silence that precedes a violent explosion.

We're not held in suspense for long. The door reopens, allowing two suits flanked by Warner and Enzo into the room. I recognise the final person from the newspapers—Hunter Rodriguez. Director of Sabre Security.

He scans two dark-chocolate eyes over our group, his steely frown pulling a scar bisecting his eyebrow taut. Tall and well-muscled, he wears an expensive, three-piece suit and a flashy watch that befit his position.

"Let's begin." Hunter's tone is smooth and impersonal. "Please take a seat."

The two suits, one male and one female, sit at the other end of the table. Hunter moves to take a seat opposite Ripley and Raine, sparing them both curt nods while Enzo leans against the wall beside me.

"This is Agent Barlow." Hunter gestures to the female suit.

"And Agent Jonas. Our representatives from the Serious Crimes Unit."

None of us offer a greeting.

"Well, then." Agent Barlow clears her throat. "Let's not beat around the bush."

"Our clients have provided written testimony to my team," Hunter explains crisply. "They have invaluable information that will aid your investigation. And they're willing to cooperate."

Agent Jonas laughs coldly. "Undoubtedly to save their own skins. This is quite the rap sheet of crimes you've compiled for us."

"Our clients are under no illusions about their culpability. Regardless, they're willing to act as cooperating witnesses. Their knowledge could shave years off the criminal investigation ahead of the SCU."

Drumming her nails against her chin, Agent Barlow stares straight at Ripley. I hate the way she's making her squirm under the spotlight. I move to step forward, but Enzo rests a hand on my shoulder, giving a head shake.

"Ripley Bennet."

She looks up at the female agent. "Yes?"

"You stand accused of severe crimes. It won't be hard to trace back the history of patients' deaths in Harrowdean's custody resulting from your dealings."

"Ripley was just doing her job," Raine protests hotly.

"Hurting people?" Agent Jonas counters.

"The real monsters are those manipulating desperate patients into doing their dirty work! Those profiting on exploitation and abuse!"

"Raine." Ripley touches his shoulder.

"No. You can't be blamed for this!"

"It's okay."

"Nothing about this is okay."

"I know what I did was wrong, and I'm prepared to accept

the consequences. But there are people out there still trapped and suffering. They need our help."

The two agents listen to their exchange, both seeming to contemplate the best path forward.

"You're barely keeping the media on our side right now." Xander turns from the window to address the agents. "Government incompetence has allowed an exploitative regime to torture and experiment on the mentally unwell for profit."

A smile tugs at my mouth.

Here he is.

"We have plenty of uncomfortable details that we'll happily take to the press. Gory, unpalatable information that will impede your efforts to tame this raging fire. You don't want us as enemies."

"You're threatening to go public?" Agent Jonas laughs. "Why would that impact us, son? We're not Incendia."

"Perhaps not, but I'm sure the names of government inspectors who were paid a tidy profit share to ignore our dealings would cast an unpleasant light on a public-funded department such as yours."

The agent's smile quickly morphs into a glower.

"In fact, I saw a rather fetching photo of Sir Bancroft accepting his knighthood after a quick online search not so long ago. Plenty of politicians and public figures in attendance."

Xander's musings are silky-smooth. Even my hairs are standing on end. The entire room is focused on him.

"Perhaps we could talk about the man who watched us being whipped, beaten and psychologically tortured then ordered us to become his stooges when we refused to break. A man you've failed to catch."

"Making the media storm worse doesn't benefit you either." Agent Jonas draws his silver-grey brows together. "You'll be dragged over the coals."

"Less than you will be for allowing this to go unchecked. Bancroft's out there right now, getting his feet rubbed by countless political heavyweights and business leaders. That's on you."

"What do you want?" Agent Barlow intervenes.

Xander shrugs. "We're not asking for clemency, we're demanding it. Agree to a plea deal, and we'll cooperate. Prosecute and we'll cause the biggest public outcry you've ever seen. Enough to make your jobs hellish."

Leaning back in his chair, Hunter looks mildly impressed. He scrapes a hand over his trimmed, chestnut beard, seemingly appraising us in a new light. I doubt any other witnesses have been so bold as to make threats.

"We can tell you everything." Xander lands the final blow. "Supply routes. Contraband stashes. Key players in the institute's power structure. Criminals you'll never prosecute without our testimony."

"With all due respect—"

"Prosecute and you'll never hear a word from us again," Xander cuts the male agent off. "Not so much as an ID verification when you round up a few culprits after decades of investigative work."

Their stunned silence causes Enzo to chuckle under his breath. "He drives a hard bargain, doesn't he?"

"This bullshit calls for it," I whisper back.

"Not disagreeing with you, Mr Nash. I don't believe anyone should be blamed for the fucked up stuff that went down in the institutes."

"We'll need a moment to discuss and call our superiors." Agent Barlow rises. "Excuse us."

The pair shuffle out, their heads hanging. I can't believe our futures are being decided by a pair of government stuffed suits. Ones who didn't see rampant corruption staring them in the face all this time.

As soon as they've left, Hunter turns his attention to us. "Bold move, Mr Beck."

Xander glares back, unrepentant. "If you had bothered to interview us yourself, you would know that we'll do anything to protect each other. No one is going to prison."

I bite back a laugh. The look on the famous Hunter's face is like he's bitten into a sour apple and spat the innards out. The man clearly isn't used to his authority being challenged.

Stepping into the room, Theo's familiar face causes everyone to release their held breath. He offers a two-fingered wave with his laptop in hand, the door clicking shut behind him.

"All wrapped up with Hudson?" Enzo asks.

Theo nods. "His final interview is done."

"Tell Brooklyn and the others I'll be out soon," Hunter tells him.

Anger curdles in my gut. We've spent all week locked behind bolted doors, fearful for our lives. Not so much as a goddamn whisper about when this nightmare will end. I've had it.

"I suppose some witnesses are more valuable than others, right?" I look between Theo and Hunter. "While we're being left to fend off fucking prosecutions for surviving something unimaginable."

"Nox—" Raine begins.

"No! Enough of this! Why are we being treated differently?"

"You're not," Hunter replies flatly. "But your cases are vastly different."

Ignoring his shitty excuse, I stare at Xander. "I told you we shouldn't trust these people."

Enzo attempts to grab my shoulder. "Look here—"

"Lay a single hand on me, and it won't be attached for much longer. I'm getting my family out of here before you pull out the cuffs."

Marching over to Raine and Ripley, I'm hellbent on yanking them both up when the conference room door opens again. Agents Barlow and Jonas sidle back in with matching grim expressions.

Nope. Fuck this.

If we can get out of here, they'll never see us again. We never should've come here. They're going to take my fucking family from me, just like all the other times I've lost the ones I love. This is all my fau—

"You have a deal."

The panic dies a sudden death within me.

"For all of us?" Xander asks.

Sighing, Agent Jonas wrings his hands. "Full clemency for Ripley Bennet, Xander Beck, Lennox Nash and Raine Starling. No charges relating to the contraband, deaths or riot."

My breath is still held, waiting for the punchline.

"In exchange, you'll give us absolutely everything you know about Incendia Corporation's dealings. Names. Dates. Locations. The lot. You'll remain as cooperating witnesses until we deem your roles fulfilled."

"And if the investigation takes years?" Xander pushes.

His shoulders rise dismissively. "Then you'll certainly earn your freedom, won't you? When this is over, you can have it."

Lips parted, Xander looks at each of us. Weighing our reactions. We're talking about signing our souls over to the authorities for an undefined period of time. Snitching on every last person doing dirty dealings in Priory Lane and Harrowdean.

But we'll be free.

We could have a future.

Her fingers clenched tight around Raine's hand, Ripley does her own sweep over us all before facing the two agents. Hunter, Enzo and Theo all keep quiet. None dare to speak for us.

"We want witness protection until this is over," she calmly demands. "Our lives are already at risk. This will paint an even bigger target on our backs."

Agent Barlow looks over to Hunter, communicating something silently. I watch the formidable director nod once, signalling his agreement. Neither Enzo nor Theo protests the decision.

"Do we have a deal?" Agent Jonas drones.

This is my chance to protest, but I don't say anything. No matter the mistrust and paranoia brewing inside me. I trust Ripley, and if this is her decision, then I'll respect that choice.

She rolls her shoulders, looking at the agents without fear.

"Yes. It's a deal."

CHAPTER 22
RIPLEY

AGAIN – NOAH CYRUS (FEAT. XXXTENTACION)

WATCHING the breaking news slogans filter past on the TV screen, I'm only half-heartedly paying attention. Balled-up, failed sketches are scattered all around me. I can't focus long enough to create anything decent despite my return to a medicated equilibrium.

We had the chance to request items via Warner and his colleagues. I've since learned they're one of several investigative teams within Sabre Security. He's part of the Anaconda team, who've now been assigned to us.

The charcoal pencil clenched in my hand leaves a black smear, staining my fingertips. I shouldn't be watching the news. If Xander were here and not having his brain picked at HQ, he'd unplug it at the wall.

"Incendia Corporation's president, Sir Joseph Bancroft, had this to say to our reporters this morning."

The exaggerated voice of the newscaster catches my attention. I can hardly stomach seeing Bancroft's wizened, wrinkle-linked face and sagging jowls take up the screen.

He wears a fine, navy-blue suit, the deep silk accents showing off his diamond tiepin. Behind him lies a disgusting display of wealth. His vast, old money estate is hidden deep in the Cheshire countryside.

"Blackwood Institute will be open again soon after significant refurbishments to repair the damage. We hope to return to normal operations at Priory Lane and Harrowdean Manor in the near future too."

Pain lances my hand. Startled, I look down and find the charcoal pencil snapped, the sharpened tip digging into my palm. Unclenching my fist, I flick my eyes back up to the TV.

The obnoxious flash of reporters snapping photos fills the screen as Bancroft climbs into the back of a fancy town car. Their yells are unanswered. He doesn't address the accusations thrown at him and the chauffeur service drives him away.

I attended a lavish fundraiser at his country estate once, forced into a hideous velvet gown by my uncle's stylist. The thirty-bedroom monstrosity was bustling with famous faces and well-lined pockets that night.

It turned my stomach even then.

Now it's fucking intolerable.

A click draws my head up as the news report switches off. Standing behind the sofa I'm curled up on, Lennox peers at me in an assessing way. He places the remote control down.

There's something different about him today. He looks heavier somehow, a sad kind of darkness making his pale irises appear dull in a sharp contrast to the shiny, vibrant pink scar on his face.

"Are you okay?"

Rolling his lips, he glances over me. "Would you come somewhere with me?"

"Like... go out?"

Lennox nods.

"Is that allowed?"

"I've cleared it with the team. Warner's guy, Ethan, will drive."

Unlike Xander, Lennox doesn't lock his emotions away when he doesn't want anyone to see them. He's always been an easy read, it's just the only story his face ever told before was one of gut-punching anger.

Now there's a tale of grief written across his slumped facial features and bag-lined eyes. Even his clothing is gloomy today, an all-black shirt and fitted sweatpants combination that makes his golden skin stand out.

He has washed and styled his hair, though, like he wants to make some effort. The messy brown locks are pushed behind his ears in a semi-tidy pile, revealing the silver ring in his left ear.

"What's going on?"

"It's… my sister's birthday today." He slowly trails a finger along the back of the sofa. "I've never been able to visit her on her birthday. Figured I may go."

"I'm so sorry. I had no idea."

Canine sinking into his pillowy lip, Lennox looks away. "I just don't feel like going alone."

Setting my sketchpad and charcoals aside, I sit up on the sofa so I can lean over and reach him. Lennox keeps his gaze averted as I wind my arms around his neck to tug him closer.

"You don't need to be scared to ask, Nox. If you want me there with you, I'll be there. No questions asked."

Daring to make eye contact, he appears relieved, the tense lines around his mouth evening out. I stroke a hand over his trimmed stubble, trying to wipe away any doubts.

"Where is she?"

"About an hour or so from here." He pulls my hand into his. "You sure? We've all had a lot on our minds since that meeting."

"Yes, I'm sure. Let's go."

He pulls me up, leaving the failed sketches behind. We call out to Raine, washing the city off himself in the shower. He was escorted out to see Sabre's medic for a check-up and meds refill earlier on.

"Be careful!" he yells back.

Escaping the apartment together, one of Sabre's blacked-out SUVs is parked on the curb outside. Ethan leans against it, studying the quiet neighbourhood.

The safe house is surrounded by copy and paste apartment blocks with little character. We're far enough from Central London to grant us some privacy from the usual hustle and bustle.

"Hey." Ethan offers us both a professional smile. "Ready?"

Lennox opens the back door for me. "Yeah. Did Warner give you the location?"

"He did. I've got a couple extra security officers following in a second vehicle to be safe, but they'll keep their distance. The rest will remain here with Raine."

Nodding to him, I climb into the SUV. Lennox joins me in the back and clips my belt in place for me without thinking. The small gesture makes my cheeks warm.

"Where did you grow up?" I pull his hand into my lap.

Lennox settles into his seat. "Near Colchester."

"I don't know much about your childhood."

"There isn't much to tell. We were raised by my grandfather. You know he was a retired army vet. Mum died shortly after Daisy was born from birth complications. Neither of us had dads we knew about."

The silver chain peeking out of his t-shirt collar is even more visible against the black fabric. I've never seen him without it. Even when we were running for our lives without a single belonging, he kept it safe.

"You've never been to see her? Daisy?"

"I was arrested not long after her burial. You know why. I haven't seen her grave since."

It's no secret that Lennox was facing a hefty sentence for

first-degree murder before he took the plea deal to attend Priory Lane. He burned down his childhood home with his abusive grandfather still inside.

I can't imagine the pain of burying a sibling, let alone in those circumstances. It was hard enough saying goodbye to my parents. Throwing dirt on your baby sister's coffin must be a whole new level of agony.

Holding his hand tight, the journey passes fast once we escape London to find the main road heading east. The cramped apartment blocks shift into vast green fields with clustered neighbourhoods.

Lennox doesn't speak again until we turn into a small town just outside Colchester, but I can feel his legs quaking underneath our linked hands.

We wind through twisting streets sandwiched with in-bloom summer florals to reach the graveyard. It's tucked away in a quiet spot, the church car park empty when we pull in with another SUV loosely following us.

"We'll remain here in the car park, but don't wander too far," Ethan announces, turning his head to us. "We're not taking any chances."

I offer him a tight smile. "Thanks, Ethan."

"Of course. Take your time."

Dragging Lennox's silent self from the car, we face the graveyard together. His feet seem rooted in the gravel when I try to encourage him to start walking. He's eyeing the scene with a look of mild panic.

"I left her alone for all this time," he croaks.

"That wasn't your choice."

"None of this was, Rip. Doesn't change the fact that I haven't been there for her."

Linking his arm with mine, I squeeze tightly. "You're here now. And you aren't alone."

Taking a deep breath, he nods and begins to walk into the

graveyard. Sunshine beats down on us, bouncing off polished marble headstones adorned with dried and fresh flowers.

We walk all the way to the back where the newer graves are located. Lennox's tentative steps slow beneath a tall apple tree, laden with unripe fruit. He stops in front of a moss-speckled stone, third from the left.

My eyes water as I read the inscription.

Daisy Nash.
Our beautiful angel.

The dirt streaks on her headstone and lack of flowers break my heart. There's been no one to visit Daisy for a long time, not while Lennox has been serving his sentence. Her grave is unadorned.

I release Lennox's arm. "Wait here."

At the base of the apple tree, a cluster of wildflowers have sprouted. They aren't much, but I gather up the colourful pops of indigo blue, yellow and vibrant purple.

He raises an eyebrow when I walk back over. "Here."

"What are they for?"

"You can lay them on her grave."

Taking the picked flowers from me, Lennox studies the makeshift bunch for a moment. He then splits them into two halves and passes one back to me.

"Do it with me?"

I take the flowers, my chest twinging. "Of course."

Together we lay the tiny bunches in front of Daisy's gravestone. The natural sprigs immediately brighten up the sad scene. Lennox remains kneeling while I shuffle back to give him space.

"Sorry I haven't come by for a while, Dais. I... uh, made some choices. Got myself in a bit of trouble. I'm okay, though. Don't worry about me."

He runs his hand over the inscription, tracing her name.

"Happy birthday, squirt. I miss you every day. I'd give anything to feel you yanking my sleeve and begging to go for ice cream one last time. I never should've taken those moments for granted."

Lennox's head lowers, shielding his face. I can hear his quickening breathing, matching each time his shoulders shake. The remains of my heart splinter at the sight of him crying for his baby sister.

I've come to realise it's a misconception that bad people don't feel pain or regret. Oftentimes, those who've been forced to make the most awful decisions do so from a place of immense pain.

Lennox is no different.

All his choices, even the most morally questionable ones, have come from such deep-rooted trauma, it's a wonder he's alive at all. His fierce protective instincts have led him to many dark places.

"I don't blame you for what you did, but I wish you'd talked to me." His sonorous voice breaks. "I'd have gotten you out, Dais. I would've protected you from him."

Kneeling beside him, I wrap an arm around Lennox's broad back. His head presses against my shoulder, the sound of his quiet sobbing filling the warm breeze. There's nothing I can do but hold him.

"I failed her," Lennox whispers brokenly.

"No. This cruel world failed Daisy. Not you."

"She needed someone to save her, Rip. I didn't do it."

The silence stretches on. Helpless tears prickle my eyes.

"I fucking failed her," he rasps. "I'll never forgive myself for that. What good was my revenge when she's still lying dead beneath the ground?"

Licking my lips, I decide to speak my mind. "I know I'm not supposed to say this… but you did right by her, Nox. You got rid of the monster who hurt her so badly. And that man can't hurt anyone else now."

"It was too late for her."

"Yes, it was," I agree sadly. "But it isn't too late for you to start living your life for her. She wouldn't want you to carry around all this guilt forever. You have to live in her name now."

He vibrates with barely silenced sobs. "How?"

"However you want—that's the point. She'd want you to be happy, living a life you've chosen for yourself. Not one full of regret for something you didn't choose and can't ever change."

Holding him tight, I let him cry it all out. The grief. The guilt. Every toxic emotion and traumatic memory that's carved Lennox from immovable steel into the complex man he is today. A man borne from pain but holding so much capacity for unconditional love.

My muscles are protesting from sitting frozen for so long by the time Lennox lifts his head. I trace my thumb across his cheek, smoothing the faint, silvery trails that have soaked into his stubble.

"Better?"

He puffs out a long sigh. "Yeah. Thanks."

"It's okay to rely on others too, you know. I get that you want to protect us all, but we care about you. And you can lean on us when the burden gets too heavy as well."

With a faint smile, he presses a kiss against my hair. "I'll bear that in mind."

"Please do. I'm a mess half the time anyway. I'll happily share that title with you."

"How generous."

Rising, I offer him a hand up. "That's me. Such a giver."

Lennox clambers to his feet, clutching my hand in his huge paw. We both look back down at Daisy's grave. He curses, leaning down to clean the stone with the hem of his shirt and remove the moss speckles.

"I should book one of those grave cleaners." Lennox

brushes off his tee. "You know, when we have actual lives and freedom again. She deserves for it to be sparkling clean."

"We'll make it happen."

"Ripley!" someone bellows. "Lennox!"

Both startled, we turn simultaneously to look back at the car park. Another tinted SUV has pulled in, the interior shaded from sight. No one drives vehicles like that around here without having a good reason.

Terror blooms inside me, quickly growing into a spiky ball that fills my stomach. Ethan's backup is another man I don't recognise, and Tara, the brown-haired agent we first met.

They've both pulled out their weapons. The guns are aimed at the driver's side, but it's the passenger door that opens to release an occupant.

My breath catches. "Shit."

"Is that…?"

"Yes."

Brushing off his smart trousers and designer polo shirt, my uncle casts a withering glare at the agents training their guns on him. It's rare he's seen out of a full suit. Apparently, he views this as a social call.

I watch the agents reluctantly lower their weapons, though they are kept drawn. Right now, Sabre has no jurisdiction to threaten my uncle. Harming him would cause a huge scandal.

Lennox keeps me slightly tucked behind him as we walk back to the cars. Their voices grow louder. Three men exit the SUV behind my uncle, all stacked with muscle and wearing fearsome scowls.

"I'd just like to speak to my niece." Jonathan shows his palms placatingly. "There's no need for weapons."

"That isn't going to happen," Ethan retorts.

"Now now. Your hostility isn't required."

"Jonathan," I call out, approaching the tense scene. "What are you doing here?"

"Ah, Ripley." He trains a picture-perfect smile on me. "I

thought it's time we had a chat. You've been laying low for some time now."

"Keeping an eye on me?"

"Much like you've been monitoring me, I assume. Your new friends didn't spot us coming today?"

Ethan's eyes connect with mine, full of apologies. I shake my head at him. They can't be expected to follow his every move, twenty-four hours a day. Not when his team is spread thin like it is today.

"Can we talk?" Jonathan's request draws my eyes back to him.

"You had the chance to talk before you ended that phone call. Now I have nothing to say to you."

He audibly sighs. "Always such a difficult child. Come on, Ripley. Spare me a few minutes."

"Like you spared my friend's life when your men killed her in cold blood?"

"That was not their instructions," he explains like it's obvious. "These mercenary types... They do get carried away, I'm afraid. The girl's death was unfortunate."

"Unfortunate?" I glare at him.

"We've all made some regretful decisions of late. I'm here to simplify matters."

Lennox cinches his arm around me. "She isn't going anywhere with you."

"Ah, Mr Nash." Jonathan turns his attention to him. "You know, my niece can do a lot better than a filthy criminal such as yourself. Do release her before I'm forced to take action."

Laughing hard, Lennox doesn't budge. "You're funny. I see Ripley didn't inherit anything from you. Thank fuck for that."

His eyes hardening into cold diamonds, Jonathan takes a step forward. The lowered weapons all around him suddenly raise, again pointed at him. In turn, each of his men pull their own guns, aiming them at Ethan's team.

Great.

We're all going to die.

"See, this is the fuss I hoped to avoid." Jonathan huffs with a head shake. "Ripley, walk with me. No one needs to get hurt."

Releasing Lennox, I try to inch away from him only to be held back by his thick arm. He stares at me with fierce disapproval, his glower firmly fixed in place. Damn. I haven't been on the receiving end of that for a while.

"Not a chance," he growls through his teeth.

"Would you prefer for us all to get shot in some bullshit Wild West standoff? Come on, Nox."

"He's playing us!"

"And killing me in broad daylight would be just as bad for his public image as Sabre shooting him would be. We're out in the open. I'll be fine."

Cursing colourfully, Lennox eventually surrenders me. I pat his arm before gesturing for my uncle to follow. He orders his men to remain behind and follows me into the churchyard, away from Daisy's grave.

Once we're far enough from prying ears, he slows his steps.

"You're looking well, Ripley."

"Cut the shit. What do you want?"

"Am I not allowed to check in with my beloved niece?"

"I didn't feel very *beloved* while running from assassins in the dead of night. We almost died."

"Unfortunately, desperate times sometimes call for a blunt instrument. I can assure you, it was merely a business decision to round you up and prevent any further damage to our operations."

Laughter spills out of me. "In that case, I do apologise for foiling your plan. I'm sure it would've been more convenient for us to die in a maize field."

We circle several crumbling statues of well-known saints,

coming to rest at a wooden bench. Jonathan gestures for me to take a seat. Eyeing him, I reluctantly sit down.

"I'm seeking a quiet resolution to all this bother, Ripley. It's bad for business."

"I have no idea what you're talking about."

He sits down next to me. "I'm sure the plea deal you signed with the authorities to act as their informant has already slipped your mind."

How the fuck does he know about that?

Jonathan waves dismissively. "Before you ask, I'm not inclined to reveal my sources. You've squandered the trust I once had in you. Now you've become a problem."

In the distance, I can see Lennox keeping a wary eye on us, pacing with his arms folded in front of him. He looks ready to bolt over here and pummel Jonathan into the ground if he dares to try anything.

"I want you to come home, Ripley."

I jolt in shock, staring at my uncle. "Excuse me?"

"You've proven your point. Good show, very dramatic. But we both know you're knee-deep in this. Your new friends cannot be trusted. I'm offering you a lifeline."

I thought he was just a stone-cold, power-hungry asshole, but I'm starting to wonder if my uncle is certifiably insane.

"We can weather this storm together," he continues, laying on the faux concern. "I'd hate to see you blamed for all that has transpired. Let me help you."

"Help me?" I scoff. "You can't even help yourself! You're backed into a corner along with your dickhead boss, Bancroft, and all his associates. Silencing me won't save any of you."

"I raised you to make smart decisions," he tries again. "I'm offering you a chance to avoid any further bloodshed. Take it."

Unable to stand our close proximity for a moment longer, I quickly stand, turning to shoot daggers at him. Jonathan remains seated, a leg casually crossed over and his hands clasped.

"You didn't raise me, Jonathan. An endless parade of hired help did. I've been alone ever since Mum died."

"Always so ungrateful. I took you in!"

"And treated me with disgust and contempt for my entire life!" I don't bother trying to remain calm any longer. "You hated me before I was diagnosed and couldn't stand the sight of me after."

Creases form on his forehead as he pinches the bridge of his nose. "You had a chance to rule in Harrowdean, dear niece. Who gave that to you?"

"I sold my soul to survive an evil regime you helped fund."

"And were you not safe? Protected? Able to live a privileged life behind bars?"

"You're fucking insane! Nothing about that was privileged!"

He tuts condescendingly. "You're still a child. Spoiled and selfish. I've given you everything, and this is how you repay me?"

"No, this isn't." I take a breath, unclench my fists then stare into his clear gaze. "I'll repay you by tearing down Incendia Corporation and ensuring the trail of money leads straight back to you. Then we'll be even."

"Careful," he warns.

"Or what?"

"Or your position as my niece won't keep you safe from what's to come, Ripley. I've been gracious thus far."

In my periphery, I can see Lennox jogging over to us. He's run out of patience. I'm glad—this was a huge mistake. Every second spent entertaining Jonathan's psychosis is just wasted breath.

"I don't care how long it takes for the investigation to tear your empire down," I lash out. "I'll give them every single detail to ensure you rot behind bars for the rest of your life."

Instead of fear, Jonathan merely smiles. Cold and unaffected.

"Very well. You've made your choice."

"I have." I inch away from him. "We won't speak again."

His fake smile remains fixed in place. "If that is your wish."

When Lennox skids to a halt, eyes scouring over me in search of any signs of harm, he's red in the face. Jonathan rises to his feet, but his attention is now fixed on Lennox.

"You've tied yourself to a sinking ship, Mr Nash. I'd advise you to get far away from my niece before she takes you down with her."

Lip curling, Lennox casts him a look that would terrify even the most steadfast of men. I know something has well and truly broken in Jonathan's brain when it only makes his sick smile widen farther.

"I count my blessings that your niece even gives me the time of day," Lennox replies unequivocally. "Threaten her and you'll have a hell of a fight on your hands."

Jonathan snickers. "Why should I be afraid of a scumbag convict like you?"

Approaching him, Lennox's shoulders pull back, his head held high. Not a single flinch or hint of embarrassment for his past.

"Because I've proven the lengths I'll go to for my family. That includes Ripley now. Consider the kind of people you're threatening before running your mouth."

I relish the look of surprise on Jonathan's face when Lennox snaps his curled-up fist out. The punch hits him square in the nose, a powerful blow that elicits a loud crack. Jonathan shrieks in pain.

Lennox shakes his fist out, knuckles now covered in fresh blood. My uncle is doubled over, cupping his bleeding nose.

"Us *convicts* aren't afraid to play dirty to win the game,"

Lennox hisses. "Enjoy explaining that at your next board meeting."

Still dripping in my uncle's blood, he seizes my hand. I let him tow me away, wrapped up in his campfire-scented warmth. This time, I'm walking away from Uncle Jonathan. Leaving him afraid and alone.

And I'll never look back.

I don't need him anymore.

CHAPTER 23
RIPLEY
VIDEO GAMES – GOOD NEIGHBOURS

SUMMER RAIN PATTERS against the bedroom window, blocking out all light. The storm rolled in overnight, ending the brief hot spell that's encapsulated England's capital city. London sucks in the heat.

I'm grateful for the reprieve while tucked up in bed, limbs laden and immovable. Despite being stabilised on medication prescribed by the doctors who attended to us, it doesn't stop the inevitable cycles from continuing.

Soaring highs and crushing lows. At least in this state, I'm not rambling about turning invisible. I've had stranger delusions during manic episodes, but even for me, that was a weird one. It could've ended far worse.

"Rip?" Raine pokes his head inside the room.

I peek out of my blanket pile. "Yeah?"

"You're awake. Reckon you can try getting up for me?"

Burrowing deeper into the snarled-up covers, I ignore his pleading. "I'm fine, Raine."

"We all want to help, guava girl. I hate seeing you like this."

"It'll pass. Just leave me alone."

I hate crushing his hopefulness, but when the depressive episodes that keep me immobilised hit, it's easier to wait them out. Their lingering around and attempts to force food down me are wasted. I want to rot alone.

"Come on, babe." He steps into the shaded room, stick in hand. "Don't you remember the agreement we made before?"

"No."

"I know you do. Don't give me that crap." Raine stops next to the bed. "We agreed you'd give me a signal on the bad days. I need to know what I can do to help."

God, that feels like ages ago. Raine dragged me out of the eternal misery I was drowning in when my uncle left me in the medical wing in Harrowdean. He refused to let me wallow.

"We never did agree on a code word." I sigh tiredly.

"How about papaya?"

"That's ridiculous."

"Ouch! Shot down. You're bad for my ego, Rip. Papaya it is."

The brief smile that touches my lips feels like seeing sunlight after a long, dreary winter. Snagging his shirt sleeve, I stroke my thumb across his forearm, the small touch offering me an anchor point.

"Raine?" I murmur.

"Yeah, babe?"

"Papaya."

Straightening, he pulls his arm away. "I'm on it."

Tapping his way from the room, Raine disappears into the corridor. I can hear voices conversing. The other two left me in peace after we returned from our latest interrogation with the happy twins—what we've started calling Agents Barlow and Jonas.

At this point, we're barely scratched the surface of gory information. They're methodically picking through every last detail, documenting our inside knowledge for the investigation. We're being fucking dissected.

When Raine returns, I can hear footsteps leaving the apartment. We've been granted a little more freedom now, though security still follows us everywhere. He returns to the bed to tug my covers off.

"Arms around my neck, babe."

"Where are we going?"

"I'm going to take care of you while Xander and Lennox gather some stuff. Then we'll ride this out together, alright?"

Reassurance trickles through me. "Okay."

I wind my arms around his neck. Raine lifts me from the bed, holding me curled up against his chest. He taps a path to the bathroom, only stubbing his toe once while carrying me.

Thrusting the stick out, he maps each bathroom fixture until he locates the tub. It echoes with a hollow thunk. Raine carefully deposits me on the edge, tossing the stick aside so he can feel for the taps.

"You're going to have to read the bottles for me." He laughs to himself. "Unless you fancy a shampoo bath."

While he adjusts the flowing water, I read the various products lined up on the bath's edge. I wonder which member of the Anaconda team purchased marshmallow-scented bubble bath.

"Who do you think went shopping for us?"

"Why?"

"Just curious. These scents seem very specifically chosen."

Raine runs his hand beneath the stream of water. "That Ethan dude is a total softie. I heard him chatting to some guy called Ryder on the phone the other day. They were flirting like crazy."

"Do you think it was his boyfriend?"

"Early days, I think." Raine shrugs. "Sounded like a long distance love affair."

"That's kinda cute. I pegged him for the bachelor, secret agent type."

Uncapping the bubble bath, I hand it over to Raine and

gape when he dumps the whole bottle in. He raises an eyebrow at my chuckle, but I don't dare tell him. Not when he's making an effort to help.

Once the bath is three quarters full and overflowing with bubbles, I reach over to turn off the taps. The last thing we need is to flood the bathroom. He kicks off his jeans and tee then reaches for my shirt.

"Oh," Raine chortles. "Mind if I come in?"

"Looks like you've already made that decision."

"Sorry." He smiles cheekily. "I just assumed."

"It's fine. Some company would be good."

I let him help me out of the baggy t-shirt I've worn for the past few days. I'd feel embarrassed, but I know he isn't judging me. If I could choose otherwise, I wouldn't be this way.

"Hop in, Rip."

"Can you help me?"

"Of course, I can."

Letting him steady my trembling legs, I climb into the steaming bathtub. The sweet smell of marshmallows curls around me in the rising steam, inviting me deeper into the warmth.

I sink down in the middle, leaving space for Raine behind me. He runs his hands along the edge, estimating how high he needs to lift his legs before clambering in. I shift to let him settle at my back.

"This feels like a lot of bubbles."

I hold back a laugh. "You were pretty generous."

"Well, shit."

Slender arms slide around me, pulling me flush against him. Raine places gentle kisses along my shoulders, pushing matted curls aside to reach my neck. I lean into him, taking the comfort he's offering.

"You haven't spoken much since Lennox took you to the graveyard."

"There's nothing to say," I reply quietly.

"You don't need to pretend, Rip. I'm sure the situation with Jonathan is painful. If you want to talk about it, I'm here to listen."

"He's made his choice. That's it."

Raine doesn't respond right away, pouring water over my arms and chest. "Okay."

"Okay?"

"I'm not going to pry. If you've come to terms with it, then I trust you'll reach out if you need to. Just know I'll be here if anything changes and you need to vent."

I relax at his easy acceptance. He knows when to push but also when to back off. That's a skill most people aren't capable of.

"Shift forward and lean your head back." He gently nudges my hips. "I won't shampoo your face this time."

"Promise?"

"Now, I wouldn't go that far."

Smiling, I do as told and give Raine access to my head. He takes the shampoo I place in his hand, wetting my curls with bathwater and lathering them up. His touch is slow, coaxing. I always feel so revered in his arms.

"Can I ask you something else about your trip with Lennox?"

"Like what?" I feel my muscles tense up.

"Xander told me he's stopped wearing that necklace. It's vanished."

"Wait, what?"

"Yeah." Raine begins rinsing my hair with handfuls of water. "He took it off."

In the depths of my latest episode, I hadn't noticed that detail. Lennox has been curling up in bed with me each night, pleading with me to eat small bites of food or watch a movie with him.

It's a gentler approach than Xander's threats to hogtie me in a kitchen chair and shove food down my throat if I don't look after myself. I'm sure that comes from a place of love, just Xander-style love.

"Has Lennox said anything?" I ask him.

"Nah, nothing. He seems different, though. Lighter, I guess. Whatever happened at the graveside has changed something."

Weirdly, it gives me a slither of pride to think that I helped Lennox put some stuff aside. Even if it's the tiniest amount. He's carried this burden alone for so long, I want to help him.

After conditioning my hair, Raine takes his time washing my limbs, even as I protest. He completely ignores me, reaching around me to lather up my arms and legs, ensuring I'm clean.

"Does that feel better?" he asks once done.

"Yes. Thank you."

"I'll soap you up anytime."

We relax in the water for a while, enjoying the comfortable silence. I feel better after getting cleaned up, but his touch is making the real difference. I wouldn't have peeled myself from the bed on my own.

The water is almost cold by the time I feel more like myself. The internal smog is still there, but it's receded enough for me to see the light shining through. Raine has dragged me back to the surface.

"Is that them?" I listen to the apartment door opening.

"Most likely. Shall we climb out?"

"Not yet. I want more time with just us."

Raine presses a kiss to the top of my head. "You can have as much time as you need, guava girl. Forever if you want it. I've got no plans."

My heart rate spikes. "Do you think about forever?"

"Sure. Who doesn't?"

"I guess we haven't had much time to plan the future,

between dodging bullets and escaping psych wards. When this is all over… I don't know what I'll do."

He smooths wet hair from my neck. "You know we'd all follow you anywhere."

"I can't expect you guys to do that. You have lives."

"Sure, we do." Raine laughs shallowly. "Mine is laying in my arms right now. And if you think Xander or Lennox are going to let you out of their sights, you're in for a shock."

Relief settles behind my breastbone, silencing the rapid beating that fills my ears. For so long, I was focused on getting out of Harrowdean and returning to my life. That doesn't feel so important now.

My home isn't a stale apartment in Hackney, full of dusty belongings. It isn't the paint or canvases I replaced human connection with. Nor the state of quiet existence I'd made my peace with long ago.

I feel at home curled up in Raine's arms. Breathing in his citrus, sea salt scent. Arguing with Lennox. Drowning in his watered-down green eyes. Touching Xander and dragging a smile from him on the days he closes himself off.

Somewhere along the way, they became my home.

I don't have to be alone anymore.

It doesn't feel terrifying to rely on them. Raine has proven he'll love me through my depressive episodes. Xander's communicating more, opening himself up to me. Lennox has relented, and now I can't seem to get rid of him.

We've gone to hell and back together.

While our current arrangement isn't ideal, and it's exhausting to continually relive our pasts, this will buy us a future. One where we can start living instead of just existing.

"Raine?" I vocalise.

"Hmm?"

"When this is all over, I want forever too." Certainty steels my words. "The four of us. I don't care where, but I want us to be together."

"Took you long enough, babe."

Turning my head, I reach up to press my lips to his. The kiss is sweet and simple. An honest declaration. It causes the numbness that's fallen over me to recede the last few inches.

When that darkness feels overwhelming, I know I won't have to face it on my own. It's easy to forget that until they remind me. My illness still hasn't scared them off.

Raine fervently kisses me back, his lips moving against mine in a tender exploration that still makes butterflies erupt inside me. I'll forever be falling for the tortured musician I found in the dark, stroking his violin strings.

He didn't just heal me.

Raine brought *them* back to me.

He's the glue holding us all together. The positive ray of light in a band of broken individuals. Without his determination to worm his way into my heart, I don't know if we'd all be here today.

I pause for a breath. "Have I mentioned that I love you?"

"Once or twice. I'm always happy to hear it, though."

"Forever, right?"

He kisses between my eyebrows. "Forever."

Resting our foreheads together for a moment, we hold still, embracing each other tightly. The sound of banging in the kitchen indicates the others are up to no good, and we should probably intervene.

"I'm turning into a prune."

"My entire body feels shrivelled up." Raine chuckles. "And I'm cold. Let's move on to phase two."

Climbing out the bath on legs that feel significantly stronger, I pluck a towel off the hook. "What?"

Raine stretches to his full height, accepting the towel I hand him. It's a struggle to keep my eyes averted. I could drink in his gorgeous body all day long without getting bored.

"Get dressed and find out."

"Suspicious much?" I ask sceptically.

"That's us."

We both return to the bedroom to throw on clothes. Pulling on one of Xander's spearmint-scented shirts I stole from his room, I finger-brush my dripping curls into some semblance of order.

Raine takes my hand, leaving his stick behind. I guide him down the corridor into the open plan living room where voices exchange conspiratorial whispers. An odd scene greets us.

Xander is obsessively arranging something on the coffee table while Lennox supervises. The pair are trading arguments, their entire attention focused on whatever they're doing.

"Guys?"

At Raine's prompt, both snap upright, wearing sheepish looks. It's a change after Xander's aggressive approach to caring for me. They've drawn the curtains and lit a handful of cheap tea lights throughout the room.

"Um, ta dah?" Lennox spread his muscular arms wide.

Xander smacks the back of his head. "Have a bit more showmanship, for fuck's sake."

"You want to take over?"

Clearing his throat, Xander gestures around the room in a weird, awkward way. "Well, we realise that none of us had a real first date with you."

I take in the candles, the dimmed lights and an array of different snacks that have been laid out. Including several of my favourites and a multipack of chilled beer. An old sci-fi movie is already loaded on the paused TV.

"This is a first date?" My hand flies up to cover my mouth.

"Safe house edition." Lennox shrugs. "We realise it isn't much."

I'm too surprised to fathom a response. Xander curses while studying my reaction. Raine shuffles on his feet. Hell, Lennox's chest is heaving so hard, it looks like he's on the verge of a fucking panic attack.

"You hate it. Shit, Xan! She hates it!"

"I told you to get the double chocolate chip cookies, not the plain kind!" Xander snarls at him. "You had one job, Nox."

"You're the one who chose the shit movie!"

"You're both useless." Raine shakes his head.

"Hey! We got beer!"

"Guys!" I shout above them, trying hard not to laugh. "This… This is everything. It's the best first date I've ever seen."

Their arguing halts, all fixing their attention on me. Xander visibly relaxes. Lennox runs a relieved hand down his face. Raine chuckles, nudging me forward with a touch to my lower back.

"My idea," he whispers proudly.

I take a seat on the sofa before they can start bickering again. Lennox hands out cracked open beers, fighting to hold back a grin. I study his neckline, finding his silver chain is indeed absent. It really is gone.

"Guys?" Raine clears his throat. "The first date gift?"

"Fuck." Lennox fists his hair agitatedly. "Xan!"

"Chill out. I've got it."

Plucking a small box off the coffee table, Xander presents it to me. Eyeing him, I accept the wrapped gift, feeling all kinds of confused. They're really not the type to go in for grand gestures.

"We figured flowers are average," he says with a slight smile. "And not your style."

Looking down at the box, I slip the lid off. Inside rests a delicate, black bracelet made of miniature chains welded together. I finger the smooth metal. It's lightweight and totally unique. I've never seen a bracelet like it.

"This is for me?"

Lennox stares at me. "Do you like it?"

"Yes." I lift the light chain, finding it's the perfect size. "This is so beautiful."

Xander snags the seat next to me, a huge pile of snacks stacked in his arms. He dumps them on the side of the sofa, finding a comfortable position where he can lay his head in my lap.

"Want me to fasten it?"

Nodding, I hold out my wrist for him. "Please."

The chain slips easily around my wrist, fitting like it was made for me. I'm still a little flabbergasted. No one has ever bought me jewellery before, and this is exactly my style.

"Perfect." Xander fastens the small catch. "Now you're shackled to us for life."

"Is this some kind of proposal?" I laugh.

"No." He rests back in my lap. "Just a reminder."

Smiling to the others, I murmur my thanks. They both take seats, their expressions pleased. I bury my fingers in Xander's hair, gaze focused on the unique present.

The simplest of gestures mean even more coming from him. It was worth getting out of bed just to see his features soften and his eyes slide shut now that I've approved of his gift.

Sighing as he relaxes, it's clear that Xander is perfectly content with me touching him. Lennox watches his best friend's behaviour with a perplexed look.

"Well that's just fucking bizarre."

Eyes still closed, Xander flips him off. "Fuck off."

"Since when did you become a cuddler, Xan?"

"Since now, shithead."

I try not to disturb Xander with my silent laughter, accepting a beer from Lennox. He and Raine are sharing the other sofa, clinking their beers together.

"I'm not sure when I last had a drink." I lift my own bottle. "This is going to taste so good."

"You literally doled out contraband for over a year." Lennox frowns at me. "You never drank any of it?"

"Well, no."

Raine sighs in pleasure as he sips his beer. "Seems like a waste of power to me."

"Agreed." Lennox nods.

"Neither of us should be drinking on medication," I point out.

Raine swallows his mouthful. "I don't care right now."

Taking a long draw, I savour the lightly fizzing liquid. I've never been much of a drinker, but something about this feels triumphant. Like we're celebrating living long enough to share a pack of beers.

"Did you get the sour cream pretzels?" Raine asks.

Without answering, Xander plucks them from our pile of snacks and tosses them at Raine. They hit his chest. He hums happily, tearing into the snacks with gusto.

"So freaking good," he mumbles around a mouthful.

Lennox wrinkles his nose. "That's the worst flavour."

"Then I don't have to share with you. Win-win."

Lennox starts the movie, but I'm too focused on the silky-soft tresses weaving through my fingers. I comb through Xander's hair before repeating the action, measuring and studying each platinum strand.

Having him so relaxed around me feels like a privilege. A couple of nights ago, he even slithered into bed with Lennox and me. The three of us tangled together without uttering a word. It felt so natural.

"Have you ever been on a first date before?" I whisper to him.

"No."

"Ever?"

"Do I look like much of a dater, Ripley? Not exactly the relationship type."

"You never… ah, romanced your toys before?"

"I'm sure they didn't need romancing after being referred to as toys," Lennox butts into our conversation. "Who wouldn't fall for that?"

"Watch it, swimming pool. You aren't winning awards for romance either."

He falls silent, glowering at Raine when he starts laughing. I tune them out, focused on Xander.

"I never wanted more than a brief physical connection before," he explains slowly. "I didn't care about their feelings or wellbeing. This is all new for me."

"Well, I'm glad to be your first date."

Candlelight flickers in his navy irises, highlighting the varied tones of blue melting into a dark, inviting hue. Xander lifts a hand to run his fingers over my chin.

"Me too."

The sounds of the movie play in the background. Lennox is explaining it to Raine, describing the dystopian future where robots have taken over and all but eradicated the human race. The pair are laughing together like idiots.

"So you're a sci-fi fan?"

"Does that surprise you?" Xander is still watching me.

"It seems fitting. You love technology."

"I like computers. That's all."

"Right. I heard you've been making friends with Theo at HQ."

"He showed me his set-up in the intelligence department." His pitch lightens, seeming to radiate excitement. "You wouldn't believe the tech they have in there. Incredible."

He's so touchy about admitting he enjoys something, but the clear passion in his voice reveals the truth.

"Did he let you touch his computer?" I tease.

"Not yet. I'll convince him, though." He looks away, deep in thought. "Or offer to break his skull."

"You can't manipulate everyone with threats of death or

violence. I'm happy you're excited, but we should perhaps talk about managing these new feelings."

"What's to manage?" Xander sniffs. "I'll simply befriend the flannel-wearing nerd and convince him to let me use his tech. That or I'll find a new home for my pocketknife in his gut."

I stifle the urge to facepalm.

Xander is a work in progress.

CHAPTER 24
RIPLEY
HIGHER – CROIXX

I WAKE to weak morning light, far too warm and comfortable to move. Credits roll in the background, accompanying the sound of heavy breathing and snores. I must've dropped off after the fourth movie.

Something hard and wiry is sprawled out beneath me. I've turned Xander into a human mattress, my face tucked into the crook of his neck, legs spread either side of his waist and chests flush together.

On the other sofa, Raine is resting in Lennox's lap. Both fast asleep. None of us survived the sci-fi marathon we ended up undertaking after watching the first movie Xander put on.

"No, stop," Xander begs beneath me.

I quickly sit up to shake him. "Xan. Wake up."

"No… Please."

"Hey, hey. It's me."

"S-Stop."

"Xan!"

With enough shaking, he finally rouses. "Argh!"

The sleepy fog that fills his eyes whenever I wake him from a nightmare clears faster than usual. Xander looks over me then the room, verifying his surroundings. He hasn't had a dream like this for a while.

Throat bobbing, he slumps back on the sofa, drawing in uneven breaths. I push damp hair from his face. He's feeling clammy and looks even paler than usual.

"You okay?"

"Yeah," he pants. "Fine."

"Just take deep breaths. You didn't wake the others."

He works on breathing slowly while I continue smoothing his hair.

"You're safe with me, Xan. You can come back."

It takes time for him to calm down, his eyes now at half-mast. The dawn sun splatters across his porcelain skin, highlighting curves and angles sharp enough to slice me wide open.

Xander hides his face in my chest, his hot breath warming my skin. I keep him close until the sound of birdsong leaks into the living room, and my neck aches from holding it at an odd angle.

I'm not sure if he's gone back to sleep. We've been cuddled together for what feels like forever. When I try to move, his hand quickly bands across my back to hold me in place, answering that question.

"Xan," I whisper. "I need to stretch."

His only reply is a low moan of protest, face tucked into my throat. I squirm at the feel of his lips teasing my neck, skipping higher until he finds my pulse point and lightly nips.

The arm keeping me trapped against him tightens, flattening me on his chest. My breasts are pressing into him, the baggy shirt I stole from his stash riding up to reveal my hips and thighs to the air.

A hand sneaks down my body, coasting lower until he slides it into the back of my panties. I gasp when Xander grabs a handful of my right ass cheek and squeezes hard.

"I could get used to you waking me up from bad dreams looking like this," he purrs into my throat.

His tight grip on my rear causes me to buck, accidentally pressing into his growing erection. I want to stand and move away, knowing what woke him up, but he won't release me.

"Xan, wait—"

"Keep squirming," he rasps. "I'm not letting you go."

"We shouldn't…"

"Shouldn't do what?"

His hips press upwards, rocking his hardness into me. I'm straddled right above his crotch, giving him the perfect position to rub himself on me. I can feel how my body on his is affecting him.

The hand infiltrating my panties cinches again, making my skin burn. He's squeezing my backside like he wants to flip me over and take out all his emotions on my body.

"The others," I gasp.

"Trust me, we've heard about Raine's sharing kink," Xander murmurs back. "He's discussed it at length with us."

"Oh."

He chuckles beneath me. "Surprised?"

"A little. Do you guys… erm, discuss what we do together?"

"No, never. But Raine wanted to broach the subject. I was surprised by how on-board Lennox was. He's changed his tune, hasn't he?"

That may have something to do with the mind-blowing sex we had during their interviews and the multiple times he's made me shamelessly beg for an orgasm since. The man has a passion for edging.

"Want to test the theory?" Xander teases.

Simmering heat pools between my thighs, created by his hard cock pushing up into me. Each move makes my skin tighten and constrict. I feel like I want to tear myself apart just to get more friction.

"How?"

"You're going to follow my instructions, little toy. Word for word."

Hips surging upwards, his hard bulge meets my clit. It throbs beneath my panties, the thin cotton quickly becoming soaked.

"I want to watch them fuck you." Xander's lips touch my ear. "And I want you to keep your eyes on me when they fill you with their cocks."

"Fuck, Xan."

"You like the sound of that, don't you?"

More warmth swirls through my veins. "Yes."

"Go on, then. Wake Lennox up with your mouth. I know he'd like that."

Releasing his arm, Xander pushes me away from him. I slide off the sofa to find my feet, drinking in his desire-laced gaze. He actually wants me to do this.

Fine. I'm not scared to take what I want.

Padding over to the other sofa, I kneel in front of Lennox. He's asleep in an odd position, almost seated normally but with his head laid back and Raine's head resting on his left leg.

I stroke a hand up his other leg, feeling each rigid muscle in his bulging quads and thighs. When Lennox stirs, I halt briefly, my eyes locked on his face. His breathing evens out, and I continue upwards.

Lifting Lennox's shirt, I place featherlight kisses along his abdominals. My lips leave a light trail, causing his already firm bulge to grow. He's sporting morning wood.

Easing the front of his sweats down, I splay a hand over his lower belly and use the other to rub his cock through his boxers. His huge length strains against the fabric, barely trapped inside.

"Are you staring at it?"

The quiet voice almost scares me until I realise it's coming from Raine, his head resting inches from where my attention is focused. His eyes are still closed.

"No."

"Then do as Xander asked, babe."

"You really want to hear this?"

"Fuck yes, I do."

I slip Lennox's dick from his boxers, taking it in my hand. The thick steel fills my palm, hot and throbbing as a deep sound rumbles from his chest.

In their own ways, both Xander and Raine are observing me now. Neither moving nor speaking. Ducking my head, I pull Lennox into my mouth, swirling my tongue over his smooth head.

Muscles tense beneath my other hand. I draw his cock in deep, bobbing up and down on his length to coax him awake. Lennox stirs with a groan, his hand moving to rest atop my head.

"Wha…? Rip?"

Hearing his voice, I suck hard, taking him to the back of my throat. Lennox's fingers tighten in my hair. Easing back, I tease his shaft with my tongue and move my eyes up to his.

Yep. He's awake.

Wild-eyed with surprise, Lennox stares down at my mouth latched around his dick. Raine hasn't moved, though his unfocused, golden eyes are now open, and he's breathing a little harder.

"Raine," Lennox says gutturally. "Get off me so I can fuck our girl's face right now."

Raine pulls himself upright. "Be my guest."

I watch his hand move to cup the straining bulge between his legs as Lennox repositions himself, his grip still firm on my hair.

"Whose idea was it to wake me up like this?"

I blink up at him innocently.

"I have a few guesses." Lennox looks at the two others. "Do we all want to do this?"

When there's no complaints, he ruts up into me, pushing his cock deeper into my mouth. His thickness skates against my tongue, nudging my throat until I make a faint choking sound.

"Shall I show them how rough we like to play?" Lennox strokes my head.

God, I have no idea how either man will react. Xander loves to mix pleasure and pain. Raine's game for just about anything, but Lennox smashes past my limits like it's a personal vendetta.

I let him set the pace, using my mouth as if I'm little more than an inanimate doll. It's freeing to let Lennox take control and be rough, even with his friends in the room.

When he yanks on my hair to lift me off his cock, I gulp down air, feeling thick strands of saliva pull from my mouth. Lennox glances to the side before refocusing on me.

"Raine," he grumbles. "Get down there, and tell me how wet our girl is for us."

Raine pulls himself off the sofa to land on the floor next to me. He uses his hand to feel for my position, identifying where I'm placed on the carpet before I sense him settle behind me.

He lifts Xander's loose shirt to locate my panties, gliding the elastic over my hips but leaving it around my knees. Air kisses my bare backside and pussy, now exposed to the room.

I'm bent over to reach Lennox's cock, leaving me wide open. Violin-roughened fingertips dance across my hips, back and ass cheeks in a taunting rhythm. When he slides them over my wet folds, I can't hold back a moan.

Lennox's nostrils flare. "Quiet, Rip."

He silences me by shoving his cock deeper into my mouth, cutting off any further noises. I swallow down his length, still focused on the feel of Raine torturously circling my entrance with two fingers.

"Our dirty girl is fucking soaked," he announces, running his thumb over my aching clit. "She likes being watched. Don't you, Ripley?"

I'm unable to defend myself with Lennox rocking into my mouth, filling it at a steady cadence. Each nudge against my throat makes the backs of my eyes burn.

"Taste her," Lennox demands.

A wet tongue slides over me, clit to pussy, making me spasm. Raine sucks my bundle of nerves into his mouth, applying just enough pressure to make my spine curve.

"Focus, Ripley." The knot of desire in my core tightens at Lennox's commanding tone. "You have a job to do."

Tightening my lips around him, I move in time to each of his upward thrusts. Saliva runs down my chin, causing wet, sliding sounds to spill from where we're connected.

Hearing his throat clear from across the room, my eyes dart to Xander. He's still watching, now sitting up on the sofa, one leg braced on the other. Yet he doesn't touch himself. All his attention is on me.

I whimper when I feel Raine's tongue spear my slit, pushing inside me. It's a welcome intrusion, causing my pussy to pulse and contract. I can imagine how his face looks, smeared in my juices.

"Problem, Rip?" Lennox fists my hair tight. "Is he fucking you with his tongue?"

Blinking up at him, my eyes are swimming. Raine pulls his tongue from my entrance long enough to push two fingers in, circling them inside my cunt. I let them both fill me, keeping my gaze locked on Xander as power unlike anything I've ever felt floods me.

Eyebrow cocked, he gestures for me to move. I know what he wants to see. This is all a tease. Pushing against Lennox's hand, I remove him from my mouth.

"Xander wants a show," I explain shakily.

Breathing ragged, Lennox looks at his best friend. "Is that so?"

Xander shrugs. "She has her instructions."

He looks between us then back at Raine, still positioned behind me. He's pulled his fingers from my pussy, now resting at my backside and awaiting his next order.

"Well, I wouldn't want to get in the way of that." Lennox snickers, tongue dancing slowly along his bottom lip.

I kiss his inner thigh before shuffling around to face Raine. After pulling off my panties the rest of the way, he lets me push him down to the carpet in the space between the sofa and the coffee table, putting him on his back.

Grabbing the waistband of the pyjama pants he pulled on yesterday, I tug them down, pulling his boxers with them. Raine braces a hand behind his head, content to let me take control.

Each guy has their own dynamic with me. We trade power in unique ways in the safety of the bedroom. I'm not sure what the combined result will be, but my quivering pussy is ready to find out.

Settling above Raine's hips, I keep my attention fixed on Xander as I seize hold of his cock to position it at my entrance. Raine grunts beneath me, his hands finding their way to my hips.

"What are you waiting for?" Xander asks impatiently.

I narrow my eyes at him. "Nothing."

Then I push down on Raine's steel, allowing him to bottom out inside me. I don't need any more prep after having his fingers and tongue. I'm itching to feel him stretch me open.

He groans loudly, fingertips digging deep into my skin. I've found the perfect angle to take him fully inside me. Still, my focus is split between all three of them.

Xander's stare. Lennox watching me take Raine. The

moaning violinist caught in the middle, letting me ride him. Even outnumbered, I feel in control. They're all here for me.

"Shirt off," Lennox orders. "Let us see those perfect tits bounce."

Pulling it up and over my head, I toss the shirt at him. "Here."

He catches the balled-up fabric then throws it onto the sofa. With my free hand, I seize my breast and squeeze, adding to my own pleasure. Lennox watches me flick and twist my nipple until it stiffens.

"That's better. Now ride him, baby."

I hungrily slide up and down on Raine's shaft. He's still gripping my hips, allowing him to drive into me each time I thrust down. The result has me moaning loudly, over-sensitised by all the eyes on me.

I've no idea how Xander is still just sitting there, drinking in his fill. Lennox is pumping his cock as he watches us perform in front of him. But the iceman is content to observe for now.

"Yes, babe." Raine surges into me, his blazing caramel eyes darting in all directions. "God. You feel so fucking good clenched around me."

Pinching my nipple tight, I throw my head back, rising and falling on him at a quickening tempo. My breasts jostle with each move, the heavy mounds pushed outwards for their perusal.

"Fucking gorgeous," Lennox praises. "Right, Xan?"

He nods in approval. "She is breathtaking."

"She feels it," Raine adds throatily.

Their compliments only make me feel bolder. I drop a hand to my pussy, working my clit in fast circles in time to Raine surging up into me. He's panting on the carpet, chasing each movement to make our collision even more intense.

In my periphery, I can see Lennox rising to circle us. Anxiety prickles my body. I can't possibly take them both—

not with Lennox's size. I have a feeling he'd be all too happy to try, though.

When he halts on my right side, hand curled around the base of his cock, I know what he's seeking. My mouth opens, accepting his length back. Lennox glides past my lips to fill me.

"That's my perfect slut." He cups the back of my neck. "Taking us both so well, aren't you?"

My only response is a hum from my chest, barely audible.

"I'm going to fuck your pretty throat while you make Raine come." Lennox slams into my mouth, over and over. "Let him fill your cunt up, baby."

I'm already clenching around Raine's length, hugging his cock in a vice. Between all the stimulation, I'm ready to climax. But I want Raine to fill me first. I want them to see me dripping in it.

Controlling my sucking with his hand on my neck, Lennox quickly drives into my mouth. Each hit pushes my tolerance to the limit. I can feel the moisture sliding down my cheeks from his roughness.

"Come for me." Raine replaces my hand with his so he can strum my clit. "That's it, babe."

The feel of him jolting inside me is so exquisite, I let myself fall apart. My orgasm hits in an intense rush, rolling in with little warning. My muscles pull tight, holding me in suspension between them.

"Fuck!" Raine bellows.

Heat rushes into me, spilling from his cock. I slow my movements, undulating my hips in a circle to pull every last drop of pleasure from him. He grunts underneath me, thumb stilling on my clit.

Lennox pulls out before he can finish, rubbing his thumb over my bottom lip. Seeing that Raine is spent, he slides his hands underneath my arms to pluck me up like I weigh little more than air.

"Sorry, man. You wanted to share, though."

"Fair." Raine wipes a bead of sweat from his forehead.

I'm carried to the sofa, but Lennox doesn't deposit me on it. Instead, he bends me over the curved armrest, nudging my legs open with his knee. He lifts me by the hips so he can access every part of me.

"Look at all this mess," he grumbles roughly. "Your perfect cunt is glistening, baby. I hope Raine didn't tire you out."

"Not yet," I gasp. "Please… More."

"You beg so beautifully for me. I love the sound of it."

I cry out when he nudges against my entrance, teasing my sensitive slit. I'm not sore after riding Raine, but I know I will be by the time Lennox is through. He loves to make me work for it.

"Easy, Rip. We both know you can take me, and Raine's got you all relaxed."

He clearly doesn't care that I'm soaked in another man's fluids. Noted.

"That's it," Lennox praises, nudging himself inside me. "Legs open for me, baby."

Bent over the armrest, I have a perfect view across the room of Xander. Still unmoved. The strain tenting the jeans he slept in must be uncomfortable. Why won't he touch himself?

Holding his eyes, I let him see every iteration of bliss that having Lennox inch into me creates. Just when I don't think I can take anymore, he withdraws and slides back in, pushing me that little bit further.

I feel the moment he's fully sheathed, his balls slapping against me. Hell, it's intense. Even after an orgasm from the man still sprawled out on the floor.

"Dammit." Lennox moves behind me, our skin slapping together. "You've already got me so worked up."

It's a hedonistic thrill to know that Lennox is struggling to hold it together. I don't know if he can feel my satisfaction, but the harsh spank he delivers feels more like pleasurable punishment than praise.

"You like taking us all, don't you?" he grunts. "Letting three men fuck your sweet pussy."

"Yes." I can't suppress the loud moan that escapes me.

"After all this time… You got what you wanted. We're all gone for you, Rip."

Contracting around him, I love the way it makes Lennox turn feral. The first time we slept together, I could hardly sit down afterwards, he'd hit me so hard.

I loved feeling the bruises twinge each time I moved. Even if I was already black and blue from Harrison's beating, it felt good to have Lennox's handprints on me, erasing the unwanted touch.

With each pump into me from behind, Lennox spanks me hard on the ass. Fire ants race over my skin, making me cry out at each impact. His strokes are long and broad, sparing no time.

I catch sight of Xander moving the slightest amount. He unfolds his legs, tongue darting out to wet his lips. The psychopath still hasn't touched himself. Not a single stroke.

"Patient, isn't he?" Lennox puffs. "Half the pleasure is watching you like this. Sweaty and stripped bare, covered in our come."

"Oh, Nox."

"Should we relieve him? He looks rather lonely sitting over there."

Slapping my ass hard, Lennox abruptly pulls himself out. I shout his name louder, feeling myself overflow with trickling warmth. The sudden change sends me reeling.

I'm lifted from the sofa, my midsection burning from being bent over the stiff fabric. I let Lennox carry me, taking a second to look at Raine. He's upright now but still on the carpet, listening.

When we stop in front of Xander, something is silently

communicated between them. Xander shifts on the sofa to strip his bottom half off. Lennox holds me mid-air, planning something unknown.

"You're going to ride him backwards," he murmurs into my neck. "Fold your legs beneath you then lower yourself onto him."

"I can't—"

"Yes, Rip. You can."

Lowering me onto Xander, Lennox gives me a moment to fold my legs. I end up kneeling on the sofa cushions, a leg either side of Xander's thighs so I'm braced above his prominent erection.

Lennox stands in front of us, his dick at eye-level with me. He fists his length and begins to stroke, jerking the shaft in fast pumps.

"Take him." He tilts his head towards Xander. "I want to see what it looks like."

My core clenches tight, loving the remaining boundaries between us being smashed down. Xander's hand stroking up and down my spine leaves gooseflesh. He takes hold of my breast and twists, causing pain to hum through me.

"Shy, little toy?" His soft purr sweeps over me.

I find my balance over him. "I'm not fucking shy."

"Prove it."

Finding his shaft, I guide him inside me. Xander slots in like lock and key, taking full advantage of my sweat-slick state. I'm a mess, but he doesn't complain. Not when I accept his full length without protest.

"Good." Lennox continues to work himself over. "That's perfect."

"You like watching me take another man?"

His eyebrows draw together. "Surprisingly, yeah. It's hot as fuck."

Despite my burning thigh muscles, I lift myself on Xander

and ease back down to take him inside me. I have enough energy to see this filthy game we've begun through.

It takes some adjusting, riding Xander from this position. I can't see him or gauge his reaction, but in some ways, that makes it hotter. All that exists is the pressure of him pressing into me.

Teeth sink into my shoulder, causing me to yelp. Xander presses his canines down, breaking skin. He ignores my whimpers. I can feel warmth trickling from where he's drawn blood.

"Help Lennox." His tongue glides over my skin, licking up the red spill. "Now."

Biting my lip, I reach out to cup Lennox's balls. His teeth are gritted, face flush with exertion. I know he's close. Massaging the softness beneath his shaft, I help him towards the finish line, watching for his reaction.

"Open your mouth," Lennox growls out.

Still fondling him, I spread my lips. He fists his cock, inching closer to hold the engorged head over my mouth. When his eyes screw shut, I accept the hot strands of come that shoot onto my tongue.

He shifts after a second, letting his fluids cover my face too. I can feel stickiness hitting my cheeks and parted lips, leaving me stained with his juices.

"Christ." Lennox gapes, wide-eyed. "That's a fucking sight."

Watching him, I lick my lips and swallow the seed that made it into my mouth. Lennox smirks through his laboured breaths, squeezing his cock as he wrings out his climax.

I'm still rolling back and forth on Xander, letting him slide deep inside me. Seeing my task is complete, his mouth lifts from cleaning the wound he's inflicted to touch my ear.

"Such a good toy," he whispers indulgently. "Next time, I'll let him finish inside you while I fuck that beautiful mouth of yours."

"Xan…"

"Yes?"

"P-Please… I… I need…"

"What do you need, Ripley?"

Between all of them, I don't know which way is up anymore. They've all marked me in some way. The salty fluid all over me and blood streaming down my shoulder are evidence enough.

"I hate it when you make me guess." Xander's slim arm circles me. "You're to answer when spoken to."

The hand that finds my throat isn't even a surprise. I may be on top of him, but Xander will only entertain my desire to control him for so long. His grip on my throat proves his patience has fizzled out.

And I let him. He can do as he pleases. They all can. I'll let them live out their fantasies with my body while I relish in mine. That's what trust is. We surrender ourselves to the mercy of those we love most.

I drag in a deep breath, prepared for his hand to close. He's gripping my throat, fingertips piercing my skin with each stroke of his cock. Every time I push down on him, Xander's hold tightens.

"I'll give you the air to answer me, little toy. But this time, I want to hear words."

Frantically, I bob my head.

His hand loosens, granting me a precious sliver. "Speak."

"I… I—"

"No." He doesn't let me finish. "Too slow."

Unable to cry out in frustration, I'm forced to succumb once more. Xander chokes me again, his short nails cutting into my skin. While Lennox observes with parted lips, Raine listens intently to each small sound.

What did they expect?

Xander fucks exactly how he loves.

Intensely and all at once.

My lungs sear, lit with invisible fire. The room is blurring, morning light piercing my vision. Still I ride his length, pushing past the pain to seek the release I'm so desperate for.

"Try again." Xander quickly lets go of my throat. "What do you need, Ripley?"

"To c-come."

"Good. Now ask me nicely."

Sadistic fucking bastard!

Eyes streaming, I work myself on his cock, chasing my climax with each rough surge of his hips. My body is on the verge of giving out, but I need a release for all the tension coiled inside me. It's becoming unbearable.

"Please, Xan. P-Please let me come. Please."

"I can see the appeal in making her beg," Xander comments to his best friend, still watching us with saucer-like eyes.

"Told you," Lennox retorts.

Lowering his hand from my throat to my swollen nub, he pinches it hard. More pain crackles over me, setting alight numerous nerves that are already stretched thin.

Xander circles my clit, rubbing it over in a rhythmic pattern. He pistons upwards from the sofa, grinding into me when I begin to falter. I've reached my limit. I want to fall into oblivion in his arms.

"You can finish," he finally relents, slapping into me. "Show them whose cock you love the most."

The evil son of a bitch's whispered command travels directly into my mind, pulling the trigger on an orgasm that's been threatening since Lennox bent me over. I screw my eyes shut, head thrown back and lungs constricted.

The release barrels over me. Eruptions inside me sap all my strength, adding it to the fire that's crisping my insides until it feels like I'm being burned alive.

Xander announces his own climax with a roar, holding me clamped on top of him. If it wasn't for him, I'd slump over in a lifeless pile. My body is beyond exhausted and awash with sweet pangs.

His forehead connects with my shoulder blade, soft hair tickling my skin. I sag backwards into him, letting Xander take my dead weight.

It takes great effort to peel my heavy lids open to take in the scene. Still on the carpet, Raine is repeatedly opening and closing his mouth, trying to find appropriate words.

"Um, in case anyone is keeping tabs… I definitely have a sharing kink. That was so fucking hot, I think I came twice."

"Gross," Xander mutters breathlessly.

Lennox shrugs, legs crossed to cover his manhood. "Raine called it. Hot as fuck."

"Oh my god." I let my head fall back onto Xander's shoulder. "You're all insane."

CHAPTER 25
XANDER

BRAIN STEW – GREEN DAY

WE'RE SITTING SILENTLY with morning coffee when the news comes in. Our entire group has been on tenterhooks since we received word that Sabre is making its move on Bancroft. Just in time for his grand reopening of Blackwood Institute.

It's been splashed over the airwaves for days now, deafening any other news reports. His last-ditch PR effort to fix Incendia's public image is a newly refurbished institute with reformed measures and security practices.

What a crock of shit.

Naturally, Enzo and his team kept details limited, citing unearthed concerns about the SCU's trustworthiness. Not like we hadn't figured that out long ago when Ripley's deadbeat uncle knew far more than he should.

Nursing my black coffee, I watch Ripley fret over the commentators tearing the story to shreds. Overnight, hours' worth of interview footage was leaked to blow the cover off Incendia's lies once and for all.

"This is insane," Lennox grumbles. "I can't believe this has all been leaked."

Remaining silent, I watch the reports drag on.

None of us have been mentioned, but the elusive inmates from Blackwood feature in all the snippets we've seen. The blonde-haired ex-patient, Brooklyn West, is being ripped to pieces live on air right now.

Another short video clip rolls.

"Blackwood and all the other institutes like it harbour a dark secret." Brooklyn's slate-grey eyes stare dead into the camera lens. "One bought and paid for by this country's wealthy elite."

Newscasters flick back on to the screen, dissecting every word and tearing apart Brooklyn's recorded testimony. It's a character assassination. This leak has rocketed the investigation back into public awareness but at great cost.

"This is what they'll do to us in time," Ripley mumbles lifelessly. "Drag up our pasts, throw every last mistake we've ever made in our faces and tell us to be silent once more."

"They're just chatting shit for the views." Lennox is trying to placate her, though his voice lacks any hope.

"We can never go public."

"Rip…"

"No matter what I threatened my uncle with." She ignores him. "If we aren't silent for the rest of our lives, we'll face the same public lynching as these patients."

None of us can offer Ripley any comfort. Not when the irrevocable proof of what she fears is staring us all in the face. The regime that ruined our lives is falling apart at this very moment, but it changes nothing.

We're still outsiders.

Misfits. Rejects.

That's all we'll ever be.

"Do you think we'll be free now?" Raine changes the topic.

Sitting next to him, Lennox is pushing cold toast around his plate. "That seem likely to you?"

"Well, I don't know. Bancroft is the head of the snake. If

Sabre is apprehending him, the rest of his empire will follow, right?"

"It isn't that simple," I butt in. "We have other enemies."

"But if the truth is being dragged into the light, they can apprehend everyone who funded Incendia's evil for so long," Raine states like it's simple. "Including Jonathan."

In theory, that's how it should work. Yet we all know the wheels of justice turn slowly, and in the case of mass-scale corruption and decades' worth of high-level bribery, they turn even slower.

Laying a hand on Raine's arm, Lennox's stare is fixed on Ripley. She's twisted in her seat at the table to see the TV better, her charcoal-stained fingers drumming nervously on her folded arms.

We're all on edge, but she's worryingly calm. Her only anxious tic is the twitching of her fingers. It's like she's waiting for the other shoe to drop. I don't trust this supposed ending, but Ripley trusts it even less.

Hours pass sluggishly without an update. Lennox cleans up from breakfast, wasting time making endless cups of tea and coffee that sit untouched while Raine has coaxed Ripley onto the sofa to rest.

"Now let's take a look back at the history of Britain's privately-funded psychiatric care, commencing in 1984 with the opening of…"

"Enough," Lennox snaps, grabbing the remote. "We can't listen to this crap all day long."

"Stop!" Ripley shouts at him.

"Come on, Rip. This isn't healthy."

"What else do you expect me to do? Sit here and wait for news?"

"I expect you to stop digging yourself a mental hole!"

Knocking pounds on our front door, making us all collectively freeze. The loud banging comes again. Louder.

More frenzied. Someone is trying to break our goddamn door down.

Lennox drops the remote, his posture stiffening as he launches into battle mode. I shove back the kitchen chair to stand, my eyes focused on the corridor leading out of the apartment.

"Stay with Raine," I bark at Ripley. "We'll see who it is."

She moves to Raine, fists clenched. "Be careful."

I bend over to roll my jeans up, pulling the stashed pocketknife from its hiding place. Lennox raises an eyebrow before quickly moving to pull a meat cleaver from the kitchen block.

I gape at him. "Are you for real?"

"What?" He shrugs.

"This isn't a horror movie. Why the cleaver?"

"Shut up, Xan. A knife's a knife!"

Together we creep through the apartment, following the sound of the obnoxiously aggressive knocking. When Lennox leans in to check the peephole, his wide-set shoulders still don't relax.

"It's Warner."

I remain poised, mirroring his suspicious stance. "Alone?"

"Yes."

Ripley trusts him far more than we do, and if recent accusations are anything to go by, Bancroft has moles planted all over the place. Warner hasn't earned my unequivocal trust yet.

"What do you want?" Lennox yells.

Warner braces a hand against the door. "Let me in, Nox. It's urgent."

"Then tell us urgently."

"Not here."

"Then we're not opening the door," I fire back.

"For fuck's sake! Let me in. I think your location may be compromised."

We exchange glances, both wavering. I make a fast judgement call and open the door, allowing Warner to step inside. His eyes blow wide at the sight of us clutching weapons, but he quickly nods.

"Good. You're prepared."

"Prepared for what?" Lennox demands.

"Where are Ripley and Raine?"

I gesture down the corridor. "Kitchen."

"Let's talk together. Hurry."

We return to the living area where Ripley is still standing in front of Raine. He's been backed into the corner beside the TV. She visibly relaxes at the sight of Warner, red-faced and jittery in our doorway.

To be fair to him, my least favourite agent looks rough. His blue eyes are bloodshot, face sagging with tired lines and his clothing rumpled. Even his gun holster is fastened lopsidedly.

"Warner!" Ripley rushes towards him. "You're okay."

He waves her concern off. "No time. Sabre raided the Blackwood reopening last night. Bancroft is dead. His known associates are being arrested as we speak."

Surprise stiffens my muscles, holding back the barrage of questions I intended to hit him with. Bancroft. Dead. The man who hurt us all so badly and forced us to flee for our lives… is gone.

Why don't I feel relieved?

This is what we wanted. But the emotion never comes. It can't be me because I'm still feeling all kinds of fucked up about what's driven Warner to our door. My brain is trying to tell me something.

Bancroft's death may have kicked the hornet's nest. There're plenty more below the head of the snake. Far more harrowing secrets will come to light now that he isn't here to hold them back.

"That's… good, right?" The uncertainty in Raine's tone is palpable.

"It was." Warner swallows hard. "Until I got word that Jonathan Bennet's bank accounts, the legit and offshore holdings we've identified, were emptied at eight o'clock this morning."

I connect the dots faster than he can explain. "Shit."

If Jonathan is shuffling funds, he's planning to disappear. With the amount of money that bastard holds, he could vanish off the face of the planet in no time.

Something tells me he isn't the type to cut and run without tying up loose ends. Especially not after his altercation with Ripley and Lennox. He knows we'll keep talking. The authorities will never stop hunting him.

Even if he can escape, tuck himself away on some bought and paid for tropical island under a false identity... he'll live the rest of his life as a fugitive. It's far from the luxury he's used to. That won't do.

"You think he'll come for me," Ripley surmises.

"I think he's going to be angry and desperate." Warner shifts on his feet. "He made it clear that he's had you under surveillance. To be safe, I want to move you to a new location."

"Move us?" Lennox glares at him. "That doesn't sound safe at all."

"It's a necessary precaution."

Warner doesn't seem like a man who'd act as a mere precaution. Moving risks exposure, but if our location is compromised, staying would be far riskier.

"Why are you alone?" I ask, the hairs on my arms standing at attention.

"The teams are dealing with last night's raid." He fidgets again, failing to contain his nerves. "Sabre is preoccupied right now. Everyone's guards are down."

"But not you." Lennox scrutinises him with his head inclined. "You came to get us."

"Just call it a hunch, alright? I'm worried about the timing.

Jonathan isn't the type to scuttle away with his tail between his legs. I need to make sure you're safe."

Observing him, I decide to heed his warning. Warner didn't have to come here. It would be stupid to ignore his instincts, even if I still loathe the bastard.

"Pack your bags," I order them all. "We're leaving."

"But Xan—" Lennox starts.

"That's final."

Mouth slamming shut, he throws his hands up in frustration then stomps off towards our room. Raine presses a kiss to Ripley's cheek and leaves the room too, a hand outstretched to feel for the layout he's memorised.

Crossing my arms, I level Warner with a stare. "What else happened last night?"

For a moment, I don't think he'll respond.

"Bloodbath," he eventually admits, pinching his nose with his thumb and forefinger. "There were multiple casualties including Bancroft. Enzo, Theo and Hunter are all safe. The other witnesses too."

"How did he die?" Ripley asks.

Warner kneads the back of his neck. "Does it matter?"

My temper flares. "He hurt us both. It matters."

"His... ah, throat was torn out, I believe."

Whistling under her breath, Ripley's mouth spreads in a smile. She looks up at me. I'm trying to puzzle out the thoughts I can see dancing in her eyes... Relief, satisfaction, maybe disappointment?

Did she want the kill for herself?

Our lives are inextricably interlinked by the monster who ensured our paths would cross. I can understand her thirst for revenge. That man caused untold damage to so many people.

"Good." She nods.

Appearing uncomfortable, Warner's eyes flit around the apartment. "We should move."

"I'll grab my things."

Leaving Ripley to find Raine and pack her essentials, I don't budge. Warner flicks me a glance.

"You're not packing?"

"I've got all that I need." I toss the pocketknife effortlessly up and down in my left hand. "Where are you taking us?"

"We have another safe house far from London. Closer to Oxford."

If Warner is a mole, he would've turned us over to Bancroft long ago. Or be fleeing to hide from the inevitable convictions that will now be doled out. Perhaps it's time I gave him some due credit.

"Listen, Warn—"

CRASH.

Glass daggers hurtle towards us as the living room window shatters. A projectile flies through the air, carrying sharp daggers. Warner lunges to shove me to the floor, landing half on top of me.

We hit the rough carpet with a thud, the impact jolting my spine. His weight pins me down, azurite eyes lit with concern. The brief second of silent shock doesn't last long.

CRASH.

A second projectile hits the carpet closer to us in a pile of scattered shards. It takes a moment for the round, dark-green object to register in my mind. Then terror sets in faster than I can bellow a warning.

"GRENADE!"

Warner kicks the grenade across the room before a flash blinds us. The detonation causes an almighty roar of crumbling bricks and broken glass. Smoke quickly fills the open plan space.

It's all we can do to cower. The explosion ripped a hole in the apartment, causing an almighty racket. When I lift my head in the thick plumes of dust that have filled the room, I spot the first projectile.

Another grenade, but it hasn't detonated. I'm not taking

any chances. Reason doesn't pierce the surface of my determination. We can't take another hit. Protecting those around me becomes my only thought.

"Xander! Stop!"

Warner hollers when I pick up the grenade and aim it towards the window, hoping it sails through the smoke to reach outside. For an awful second, I'm standing there with it in my fucking hand.

"Run!" I scream at him.

Thick, noxious smoke is billowing from the hole blasted in the side of the apartment. The first grenade flies through it, vanishing into the black cloud. I momentarily look at my hand. Huh. It's still attached.

"Go!" Warner bellows back. "Now!"

Dropping low, I follow him out into the corridor. The hollow smash of an exploding bottle reverberates throughout what's left of the room behind us. Crackling flames and the stench of ignited fuel chase us out the kitchen.

Is that..?

"Fire!" Warner roars.

Molotov cocktails.

We're being firebombed.

I point for him to find Lennox while I head towards Raine and Ripley's room, my panic narrowing into a pure adrenaline rush. We need to get out of here.

"Xan!" Ripley pulls Raine into the corridor, their bags forgotten. "What's going on?"

"No time! Out, now!"

They run for the door, leaving me to find Warner and Lennox. The pair stumble through the rapidly-increasing smoke, billowing from the burning kitchen. More cocktails must've been thrown in.

Grabbing Lennox's wrist, I hold onto him as Warner guides us to the exit. Raine and Ripley hang in the stairwell outside, waiting for us to follow. Throughout the building, fire alarms are wailing.

"We can't just go out there," Lennox shouts over the sounds of destruction. "We're under fire!"

"Service exit." Warner draws the weapon from his gun holster. "Second floor. Car's outside. Go, go!"

All clinging together, we race down the levels, passing other startled residents battling to escape. Chaos is fast unfolding. The apartment block is huge with countless lives now caught in the crosshairs.

Ripley almost trips in her hurry to get downstairs as fast as possible. I lunge to catch her before she can go flying down several flights of steps. She steadies in my arms, barely able to breathe.

"Shit," she wheezes in panic. "Xan!"

"Keep moving, goddammit!"

My grip on her bicep doesn't relent. We escaped the dense black smoke and flames only to run into herds of people flooding out, heeding the warning to find the nearest exit. I can't risk losing her in the melee.

"This is insane!" Ripley shrieks. "Why attack so blatantly?"

"Figure that out when we're secure!"

Warner darts ahead, waving for us to follow when we reach the second floor. While everyone else heads for the main exit below, we wind around the staircase to head deeper into the building.

Lennox is now hauling Raine each step, ensuring he doesn't hit anything. We follow closely, keeping a wary eye out for anyone who decides to infiltrate the building.

"There." Warner points towards a service door marked with a sign. "Should be steps leading down to the back of the building."

He wrenches the door open, ducking his head outside for a cursory glance. After a beat, Warner takes a tentative step outside with his gun raised, ready to fire off a round into the first person who stops us.

"It's clear. Follow me."

I hold Ripley back. "Bring up the rear behind Lennox and Raine. I'll go first."

"So you can get shot first?" she hisses back.

"If necessary, yes! Don't argue!"

Shoving her behind me, I step in front of them and follow Warner. Ripley has the good sense to heed my instructions, moving to the back of our group.

I step outside, surveying the concrete slab wrapped around the apartment block. It's littered with communal bins and broken down cardboard boxes that are piled up, set to be recycled.

Not a single assailant.

For now.

Warner gestures towards his SUV, clicking the key fob. "In! Now!'

The exit steps are made from thin, inflexible metal sheets. This door is clearly only used for building maintenance. It's a tight squeeze to fit us all as we rush to reach ground level.

"Let me help you!" Lennox insists, pulling Raine down the steep steps. "We don't have time."

Reaching the ground, we take a split second to check each other over before racing towards Warner's parked car. The sound of erupting glass and raging fire is deafening.

A quick glance up reveals that the flames have spread, now consuming several apartments surrounding ours. Our attackers didn't seem to consider the collateral damage of their firebombs. Or they simply didn't care.

"In the back!" Ripley throws open the door for Lennox. "Hurry!"

They both help Raine into the car. I climb into the passenger seat, all my focus fixed outside. Still nothing. Distant sirens are now wailing, adding to the mayhem rattling my brain.

Warner clambers behind the wheel, stashing his weapon in the door. He throws the car into gear then takes off in a squeal of tyres, causing us all to be slammed back in our seats.

"I didn't think Jonathan's surveillance was that sophisticated," he mutters to himself. "We should've moved you days ago, before the raid went down."

"You think?" I counter.

"We fucked up, alright?"

"No! It's not!"

"Stop, Xan," Ripley gasps. "This isn't his fault."

Warner drives like a man possessed, attacking sharp turns without an ounce of hesitation. Other motorists blare their horns, narrowly avoiding being mowed down.

"Shit." Lennox stares out the back window.

Black smoke billows into the sky behind us even after the apartment block vanishes. It must be visible for miles around. Their reckless attack is eating through the building's cheap cladding without mercy.

"All those people." Ripley stares out of the window numbly. "God, what about casualties?"

"Emergency services are en route." Warner hits the handsfree, pulling up a phone number. "We can't worry about them right now."

Ringing fills the car as he manoeuvres his way through the traffic winding out of London. The line connects to heavy, panicked breathing.

"Warner!" Becket's crisp voice booms. "What the fuck is going on? We're getting reports of a fire at the safe house."

"We need backup. I got them out. Track the car."

Curses spew down the line.

"We're half an hour out from your location. Goddammit!"

"Just find us, Beck. I'll keep them safe."

"Be careful."

The line disconnects. Gaze locked on the rearview mirror, I study the huge, black Range Rover swerving through other cars to catch up to us.

When it passes several cars to catch up, my suspicions grow. It can't be a coincidence. The windows are tinted too, showing a hint of multiple passengers.

"Behind us," I call out. "We have a tail."

"Bollocks." Warner bangs a fist on the steering wheel.

We almost career straight into the back of a rusted minivan as Warner slams his foot down on the accelerator. This road is cluttered with traffic. Horns blare all around us.

Swerving dangerously, the Range Rover gains on us. Warner spits another choice curse word, his eyes fluctuating between the road ahead and his mirror.

There are only two cars acting as a buffer between us, holding the Range Rover back from a hard collision. At this rate, they'll be hot on our tail in seconds.

"You know how to use a gun?" Warner glances at me.

I have the inappropriate urge to laugh. "No! I just guessed what to do with that damn assault rifle before."

"Well, you're gonna have to learn on the job. Those bastards are coming for us fast."

Gingerly accepting the weapon he passes me, I familiarise myself with the metal grip. Running a one-man, international embezzlement scheme from my keyboard didn't exactly call for much firearms practice.

"Aim for their tyres!" Lennox suggests, gripping Ripley's leg. "We need to get them off the road."

"Civilians!" Warner exclaims. "Hang on."

The engine revs, pushing the car to the max. We pull out in front of a dawdling estate car, taking a left to find a dual carriageway. The press of traffic thins out, leaving us to advance ahead in the fast lane.

I roll down the window, peeking out to evaluate how far the speeding car is behind us. I've no doubt they're also armed. I don't exactly fancy getting my head blown off while trying to defend our vehicle.

"Now, Xander! Fire!"

Aiming as best as possible, I squeeze the trigger. Pain ricochets up my arm from the kickback. The bullet hits the smooth tarmac then bounces off, missing its target.

"Shit." I blow out a tense breath.

"Again!"

Shifting my aim higher, I fire off another shot. This time, I'm prepared for the force that pulling the trigger creates. The shot lands in their front bumper, leaving a smoking, black hole.

My head smacks into the door's frame when Warner is forced to turn, the lanes merging into a narrower road. More cars sandwich us, forcing me to retreat so I don't hit anyone around us.

"Take the wheel," he instructs, clicking the car into cruise control to free up the pedals. "And pass me the gun."

"Seriously?"

"Yes! Now!"

I lean over the console, steadying the steering wheel. Warner takes his weapon and shifts closer to the window. Ripley screeches his name in alarm, watching him leaning outside to find his aim.

Before he can pop off a shot, something hard slams into us. The impact jolts the SUV to the side, shaking us all. Warner grabs the seat to steady himself, preventing himself from falling out of the fucking car to become a human pancake.

"There!" Lennox cries out. "Blue transit van."

A faded blue vehicle is swinging between lanes like the driver was mainlining heroin before deciding to drive. It swerves deliberately, bringing it back within range. The front rams into us, causing another rough impact.

"Xander!" Ripley screams in alarm.

I lose grip of the wheel, causing the SUV to slam into the railings. Sparks fly. Metal grinds, causing a horrific screech. Warner retakes his seat, abandoning his attempts to fire at our pursuers.

"Incoming!" Ripley shouts, trying to hold steady. "Swerve, swerve!"

But we're sandwiched against the railings, the blue transit van trapping us in place. With the Range Rover creeping up behind us, there's nowhere to go but forwards.

"Brace for impact!" Warner yells.

SMASH.

More screams come from the back seat. We're rammed repeatedly, each slam causing the tyres to slip. Warner pulls us into the middle lane before another impact can land.

"Hang on," he warns.

It's futile. Our pursuers ram their front bumper into the back of the car. It propels us forward, giving the van the perfect chance to hit us at an angle.

SMASH.

My stomach lurches when our tyres leave the tarmac. Reality slows to a crawl, hitting me in horrific jolts. The car is airborne. Warner desperately flails. We're going too fast to prevent the inevitable.

BANG. BANG. BANG.

Each time the SUV hits the road, flipping us over in a death roll, agony crashes over me. It feels like my bones are being pulled out and ground into a fine dust, unable to withstand each hit.

Blood pours down my face. Hot. Slippery. Something burns. The pain... It's overwhelming. Something else cracks. Distant wails sound dull in the weightlessness.

Head smashing on a surface, everything blackens. The crying and pained howling all around me feels like it's happening above surface while I'm sinking to the bottom of a frozen lake.

Forcing my eyelids to lift, all I can see is smoke. Crackling flames. Shattered glass. Twisted, unrecognisable metal. I think... I'm upside down. Pinned by the seat belt making my ribcage wail.

Beside me, a crimson-soaked lump of meat is trapped at an unnatural angle. Head slumped. Leg pinned. Warner's breathing is uneven, matching the sobs coming from somewhere behind me.

I dip in and out, too tired to hold myself in the present. The flashes return. Shouts. Car doors. Barked orders. Crunching footsteps. Someone is prising the back doors open.

"Ripley," I slur semi-consciously.

Hands grab her. Slicing seat belts. Wrenching her struggling limbs. No matter how much I shout internally, I can't get my body to respond. It's shutting down on me.

The sound of her screaming our names is the last thing I hear before the world disappears.

CHAPTER 26
RIPLEY

END OF A GOOD THING – CORY WELLS

I'M TRAPPED IN A NIGHTMARE. A terrifyingly realistic, lucid dream. One pulled from the depths of my traumatised memories. That's the only explanation for this scene. There's no way it can possibly be real.

Wrists chained above me, I battle to clear the fog from my struggling brain, hoping my surroundings will change once I wake up. I must be on death's door to be imagining this place.

A scratched, ancient, padded cell.

Blood streaks marking the concrete floor.

Dusty air vents high above me.

Alone and shackled.

Slamming my eyes shut, I will the nightmare to be over when I reopen them. It's no good. Nothing changes but the worsening ache in my head. It feels like it's on the verge of rupturing.

Small details filter in like trickling tar. Like the fact that I'm wearing the same clothes I had on while watching the news reports spill in over morning coffee. It's tacky with dried blood now. I'm covered in it.

Wiggling my toes, I try to decipher any injuries. The steady throbbing in my skull sure feels like a concussion. I can remember my head smacking into something hard when we flew through the air.

Fuck!

Realisation hits in a heady wave.

The car crash. Being rammed. Flipped over until our armoured vehicle was little more than cotton wool. Lennox slumped over me. Raine's shouting. Smoke and fire all around.

I was conscious when a balaclava-wearing figure wrestled me from the wreck. My neck aches as I shift, testing my theory. It's a familiar pain. The result of being jabbed with a syringe.

"No," I whimper in pain. "Fuck… Xan! Lennox! Raine!"

My shouts are pitiful, barely permeating the old padding that wraps my cell. This can't be happening. There's no way I'm back in Harrowdean, locked in a cell. The concussion is fucking with my head.

Yelling their names at the top of my lungs, nothing but abandoned silence answers me. The padded cell absorbs my cries, playing them back to me in a sickening taunt.

When I notice the tally marks that have been painted on the cell walls in crusted blood, my sobs turn to screams. This isn't the same cell I was previously in.

It's dirtier, scarred from years of battling to escape by any means necessary. Each day trapped in hell marked in mortality. Perhaps the same cell Patient Three and countless others were held in.

I cry myself to the point of almost throwing up, falling into petrifying hysteria. Any comfort that surviving my last trip here should offer is short-lived. Escaping the Zimbardo wing was a miraculous feat.

One I can't repeat.

And this time, I'm alone.

For a long time, I simply float. Exhausted and riddled with pain. When I find the energy to rouse myself again, I tug on the shackles pinning my arms above me at such an awful angle, it feels like my shoulders are being ripped from their sockets.

Solid. Immovable.

My tear-logged eyes catch on the black, chain bracelet still secured around my wrist. I haven't taken it off since that night —our makeshift first date. Not even to shower. Seeing it only increases my hysterical panic.

I have no idea if they're alive.

No. They have to be.

I don't want to live if Xander, Raine and Lennox aren't in this world with me. Not after all we've seen together. I'd die right here just to be with them before taking another step alone.

Time holds no meaning in the cell. Like before, it could be passing in minutes or hours, and I'd have no concept of it. I don't even have Lennox here to keep me sane this time around.

All I can think about is their twisted, broken bodies trapped inside that wrecked car. Lifeless and bleeding. The thoughts become reality in my solitude until I'm convinced the guys are dead.

Gnawing stomach pain degrades into nausea, but it fails to rival the fierce burn in my throat. I'm painfully dehydrated— the only measurement of time passing. My arms have gone numb too.

When the door to the cell opens, I don't move. I can't summon an ounce of will to defend myself against whoever has come to greet me. Revulsion stirs in me at the sneering grin worn by my captor.

"Isn't this a familiar scene?" Elon saunters into the cell. "Nice to see you again, Ripley."

Not real. Not real. Not real.

He crouches down in front of me. "You're looking a bit peaky. Can I get you a refreshment? Glass of champagne? We do like our guests to be cared for."

"E-Elon," I somehow manage.

"Yes, stooge?"

Licking my crusted lips, I draw saliva into my mouth. "Please…"

"Ah, the begging stage. Perfect. Please what?"

"P-Please…"

Smiling maniacally, he slaps me across the face. A dull throb radiates across in my jaw, causing my eyes to water. I blink aside tears to look into his cruel eyes.

"Do spit it out," he commands impatiently.

"P-Please… go f-fuck yourself."

His grin pulls down. "Always such a disobedient bitch. You never learn."

This time, he punches me in the face. My neck snaps to the side, wrenching agonisingly. The pain increases tenfold, racketing through my bones and teeth, making tears spill over.

Elon watches my reaction, his knuckles red from hitting me. The look of satisfaction on his face is fucking repulsive. He looks genuinely thrilled by my tears.

"You've been a monumental pain in the ass, Ripley. Running away to join the super spies like that… Tut tut. Poor choice. They couldn't keep you from ending up back here."

Rising back up, he brushes off his jeans and shirt. Seeing him out of his all-black uniform is unnerving. This isn't Elon the overpaid thug. I could handle him.

Now I'm dealing with Elon the rogue ex-con. Unhinged and without a master to answer to. All bets are off.

"Killing Harrison was a low blow but rather impressive, I'll give you that." He inspects the cell with a look of disgust. "Never thought I'd see that tough bastard get snuffed out."

"Like your b-boss," I cough out.

"We have your new buddies to thank for that. Though we all saw it coming. Bancroft got sloppy; he allowed too much evidence to slip past him. We were prepared for his demise."

"W-We?"

He nudges my leg with the tip of his boot.

"Turns out, there's far more profit in protecting the underdog. It's easy to sit atop an empire and dictate the world. But the real power lies in those who fund the man on top."

Dread sinks into me faster than a knife into butter. I knew we were in trouble the moment Warner turned up at our door. Blood is irrelevant when decades of wealth are burning all around you.

My uncle has millions tied up in this investment. There's no way he'd let all that money simply go up in smoke. To him, this madness is just another business decision.

"The boss wants you quiet and secure like a good patient for the plane ride." Elon sighs exaggeratedly. "If I didn't need this job, I'd happily slit your throat and call it done."

Pounding roars between my ears.

"P-Plane ride?"

Elon grins down at me. "We're all going on a trip."

"I d-don't understand."

"Killing you would create a martyr. Another evidence trail. You're going to take your medication and be a docile little freak."

With a sudden adrenaline rush, I buck and fight, attempting to reach him. If I can just slip these shackles, I'll fight my way out of here. Kick. Punch. Stab. Anything to escape.

Watching me struggle, Elon simply laughs. "You'll spend the rest of your life in a drugged-up haze until your brain cracks open like an egg. He needs you complacent, Ripley. Silent."

"No!"

"Now, now. No need to make such a fuss. I'll get your meds, hmm? That'll make you feel better."

Strolling from the cell, Elon hums a tune under his breath. The shackles tear into my wrists, reopening old scar tissue in my desperate attempt to pull free. Even if I have to dislocate my limbs to do it.

Blood trails down my forearms, joining glass shards buried deep in my skin, dirt and ashy streaks. The words carved into my skin are obscured, the eternal brand covered by my fresh blood.

"Lennox! Xander! Raine!" I wail helplessly.

Elon returns, a zipped pouch in his hand. "Oh, they're dead. Nasty wreck that was. I did tell my men to be gentler."

"You're a fucking liar!"

He rolls his eyes. "Again with the yelling. Let's get those lips sealed tight."

Elon unzips the pouch, pulling out a glass vial and hypodermic needle. I can't read the label through my swimming vision.

He moves onto one knee beside me, pinching the skin above the veins at my inner elbow. That goddamn humming. It's like nails scratching my brain apart as Elon draws clear liquid into the syringe.

"Stop," I beg uselessly. "Don't do this."

"Ah, now she changes her tune. It's too little, too late."

"No! I'll be good, I promise. I'll keep my mouth shut. Just… Please, don't do this."

"We have a long way to travel to meet your uncle, Ripley. This was just a pit stop. And I don't want to listen to you for the entire ride."

I scream out at the pressure of the needle slipping in, plunging deeply into my vein. Blood wells up, spilling around the entry wound. Elon doesn't bother to be gentle.

"You know, Craven once told me this is the good stuff," he says conversationally. "Trialled and tested by his colleague, Professor Lazlo. An old friend, I heard."

Elon depresses the plunger.

"Let's give it a go, shall we?"

I watch in terror as the clear liquid is pushed into my body, a chill quickly spreading through my vein. He squeezes out every last millilitre then tears the needle from my arm.

"No," I moan, my lips thick and rubbery.

"We may as well make use of their stash now that the institutes are toast." He stands back up, rezipping the pouch. "Consider it payment for your role in destroying all our hard work."

I frantically try to fill my lungs. For every second he watches me, I can feel my bodily functions slowing. Woollen numbness is rushing through me faster than a heart attack.

He squints while watching me. "How interesting."

My fingers soon stop responding. Not even a twitch. Then my legs and toes. My tongue becomes an immovable mass, trapped in my mouth. Even breathing shallowly feels like it takes great exertion.

"I believe the drug has a paralysing effect," Elon muses. "You can hear and see everything… but you're powerless to move. Can't even say a word. How fascinating."

No, I want to scream.

But my vocal cords have been severed.

Pinching my chin between his fingers, Elon peers into my eyes. Whatever he sees causes satisfaction to stretch his smile into a clown-like caricature.

All I want is to claw that fucking sneer from his face and leave him in fleshy ribbons. The will is there, but nothing responds. I can hardly blink.

My body has been stolen from me and locked in a mental cage, the key dangled out of reach. He could do anything. I can't fight back.

"I enjoy seeing you like this." He trails a finger along my jawline. "Immobile and trapped in your own mind."

Vomit swells in my belly and throat, unable to expel itself. Not even at the nauseating feel of his touch coasting over my face.

"No one is coming to save you. Harrowdean is

abandoned, and believe me, it's low on the list of priorities right now. We'll slip away while the world is busy arguing over blame."

The drug hasn't paralysed my tear ducts which seem to function perfectly well. Stinging rivers stream down my cheeks, making my skin ache where he punched me. Elon catches a tear and lifts it to his lips.

I watch him lick up the moisture, tongue flicking out to taste the proof of his victory. My stomach lurches again. I'd take choking on my own vomit over going anywhere with this maniac.

"I think we're ready to go."

His laugh bounces around the cell.

"This all could've been avoided if you'd just kept your mouth shut."

CHAPTER 27
RIPLEY

BURN IT TO THE GROUND – NICKELBACK

THE RUMBLING engine is my sole companion in the blackness. Discomfort long since stopped registering after my third hit of Elon's favourite weapon. Each time the numbness begins to lift, he doses me up again.

I've been carelessly tossed between vehicles every time he stops. The two men travelling with Elon seem determined to throw any potential tail, changing vehicles multiple times.

During our most recent stop, I didn't even open my eyes. My limbs had started to tingle and wake up, but I remained a limp rag doll. Enough to avoid another dosing to keep me placid.

Every part of me is still weak albeit coming alive. As the engine roars and infinite time slips by, more feeling returns to my extremities. I can make my fingers twitch now. I'm basically deadly.

No, Rip.

You're basically screwed.

In the pitch-black din of the car boot I've been tossed in, I construct a mental portrait of the faces I left behind. Adding brush strokes here, splashes of colour there. Creating realistic texture and nuance. Adding voices, touches, familiar scents.

God, I fucking miss them.

Raine is sunshine. Warmth dappled on my face. Summer barbecues on the beach. Orange juice freshly squeezed in the morning. All things love and light in a world awash with such despair.

By comparison, I see Xander as all dark. The violent, bubbling storm clouds that roll in when that summer day comes to a close. Yet it's still beautiful—all that destructive threat. Complex and purposeful. Storms are a necessary part of nature.

I'd paint Lennox as the undulating lake that lives in his seafoam eyes. That's the reality beneath his angry façade. A bottomless pit of water with a whirlpool at the centre. Holding us all firm.

The painting I first created of them in Harrowdean couldn't be further from the truth. I thought they were my demons. The villains lurking in the background, creeping ever closer with their foul intentions.

Now... I'd take the monsters I first encountered over whatever lies ahead of me. Given the chance, I would rewind the clocks, return to Priory Lane and do it all over again.

Every second of heartache and anguish. All the trauma, the grief, the regret. I wouldn't change anything. Even if it leads me right here.

If they're dead... I would know, right? I'd feel it in my bones. Gravity would shift, and the world would dim into everlasting night. I've waited so long to find a place to belong, and now it feels like it's being torn away with each mile that passes.

This can't be it.

I didn't survive all I did for it to end like this.

Ears straining when I feel the vehicle pull to a halt, I listen for any clues as to our whereabouts. These assailants are incredibly skilled. Jonathan must be expending a small fortune to secure my safe capture.

I don't know why he doesn't just kill me. Sure, it would play into the villain narrative that will form against him. He'd be forced to hide underground for the rest of his life. But isn't this far more effort?

Car doors slam, causing the boot I'm encased in to jolt. I close my eyes, forcing my tingling limbs to loosen. I'm far from being able to run for the hills, but I won't take another hit of those damn drugs.

"Sir," someone greets.

"Any problems?" a clipped, all-business tone responds.

"None. We're clear."

"Good. Get her inside."

Fresh nighttime air rushes in when the boot clicks open. Hands grab hold of me, lifting my torso and ankles between them. It takes all my self-control to keep my eyes shut.

My body is jostled between two people, the hands beneath my armpits carrying me a short distance. Multiple footsteps follow. I dare to crack open a lid the tiniest amount.

Black tarmac marked with stripes and landing strips. Curved metal fuselage. Circular windows. Spinning rotors. Golden embossing spelling out a familiar company name.

Langdale Investments.

I'm being carried onto a private jet.

If I try anything now, I'll be drugged and incapacitated again before I can get far. The pins and needles are still spreading, bringing sensation with them.

"Leroy will meet with us in Rio De Janeiro."

Uncle Jonathan. I recognise his voice.

"Very good, sir."

That motherfucker, Elon. I'll kill the son of a bitch.

"You'll be compensated for your assistance, Elon. I understand it has been a trying time, but we'll recover from recent setbacks and rebuild."

"Sir." Elon hesitates, shuffling his feet. "Is it wise to keep her alive? She's a proven risk."

Jonathan chuckles. It's a flat, ugly sound. A true reflection of the man who lies within his carefully choreographed exterior, clothed in luxury and false smiles to schmooze his clients.

"My niece can do far more damage in death than she'll do subjugated by my side. I will not allow her ramblings to destroy what assets we have left."

"But—"

"That's final," Jonathan cuts him off.

Elon sighs audibly. "Very well, sir."

I'm roughly deposited in what feels like a leather seat. Terror grips my lungs, almost causing my act to slip. I can wriggle my toes now. When my body obeys me, I'm going to tear these monsters apart.

Noise bustles all around me. Bags being heaved. Men huffing. Pre-flight checks accompanying the hum of the engine warming up. I sense someone stop in front of me before cool lips briefly touch my temple.

"Dear, dear niece. It didn't have to be this way."

"Please take your seat, sir. We'll be ready to depart soon."

His presence moves away, taking his expensive aftershave with him. The smell of it makes me want to gag. All the things that made my uncle seem like such an impressive deity when I first arrived in London as a scared kid are laughable now.

It was all a sham.

One I swallowed for too long.

His rejection and disgust used to hurt me. Enough to leave wounds that impacted every relationship I had since. But I didn't hate him. Not fully. Not until he showed his true colours and harmed those I care about.

Now I'm ready to end this, once and for all.

Bloodlines be damned.

Holding my eyes open as slits, I can safely peer around.

I'm sitting at the back of the jet, an incapacitated prisoner kept out of sight. Elon is barking at his guys, disregarding my unrestrained state.

Always so cocky. He hasn't even bothered to cuff me or fasten my body into the seat. The wanker clearly thinks I'm still dosed to my tits on his drug cocktail. I'll show him.

"In the distance! Headlights!"

Before I can move, shouts pour in from outside. Jonathan stiffens in his seat, sternly calling out for answers, but Elon waves him off.

"Stay seated, sir."

"Who is it?" he demands, angrily slamming a fist down on his armrest.

"Those Sabre pricks have tracked us down!"

I don't allow the blast of dizzying relief to change my mind. These men have harmed me for the very last time. I'm not going to wait to be rescued this time.

I carefully test my limbs. Still shaky. My legs respond, pressing my feet into the plush aeroplane carpet. Hands balling into fists, I can just about move my arms. It'll have to be enough.

My plan is simple—I have no fucking plan. Nothing but a last-ditch attempt to escape whatever unthinkable fate my uncle has cooked up for me this time.

I finally get what Xander meant as we fled Harrowdean. I'd rather die on my feet than on my knees. Even if that means throwing myself at the mercy of a suicide mission in order to escape this jet. They can shoot me on the runway before I let it take off with me onboard.

Numb fingers latching onto an empty crystal tumbler on the beverage cart next to me, I lift the leaden weight. Elon has moved to the front of the jet to continue yelling at his men, hurrying them along for take off.

My legs are like trembling spaghetti underneath me. I can hardly hold my own weight. Each step forward towards my uncle's occupied chair feels like running into the middle of a battlefield with a high probability of being shot.

He's watching the exit for any hints as to what's coming, sitting on the edge of his seat. Elon hasn't returned. It's now or never.

I lift the glass as high as possible, swinging it in an arc to meet the back of his head.

"Argh!" Jonathan cries out.

He slumps forward, falling from his seat. I react fast before we have company. My body protests at the sudden movement, carrying me to his fallen form.

"Fuck you!" I hit his head again, causing the glass to smash.

Crystal scatters between us, cutting his shocked face and forehead. Jonathan writhes on the carpet, trying to peer through the blood now pouring from the wound under his hairline.

"Ripley, stop!"

Instead, I launch myself on top of him, willing my fists to respond. The punches are feeble, borderline pathetic, but I pour all my will into each strike. Raining down every last scrap of fight I have left to give.

We wrestle each other, two opposing forces, both on the wrong side of the law. I may have earned this fate, but I learned to be bad from the best. He sank his evil into me long ago.

"Little bitch!" he screams out.

My fist slams into his cheek, causing spit to fly from his mouth. "You did this!"

"I saved you!"

"No." I hit his barely-healed nose. "You fucking doomed me!"

Shouts are fast approaching. I'll be tossed aside by his men soon. Snagging a crystal shard, I grip the sharp piece, raising it high above Jonathan's face. His eyes bug out, but he doesn't dare move or provoke me.

I don't think I've seen him afraid before. It's a pleasant sight. Empowering. For the first time, I hold the upper hand over him. I'm no longer a petrified teenager, handing over her diagnosis for his perusal.

"Ripley," he splutters. "We're… We're family."

"You were my family," I howl at him. "You were all I had!"

"Stop this!"

"Did you stop those doctors from torturing us? Experimenting on us? Killing without consequence?"

"You can still walk away," he pleads, eyes locked on the shard.

Years of hatred boil into a concentrated poison in my veins. Rage has been injected into my heart's muscle, pouring fuel on a fire that's long burned within me. The same fire that drove me to avenge Holly's death.

Injustice.

Pure abandonment.

Cruel, senseless fucking grief.

It all stares back at me in his terrified eyes.

I won't allow the world to hurt me ever again. I've given up enough. I don't need Jonathan's threats hanging over me any longer. I'm more than the orphan he beat down with his negligence.

"I don't want to walk away. I'm right where I need to be."

Jonathan bellows when the shard sails towards him. I numbly register that I'm screaming as I slam the pointed tip into the side of his throat, just below his jawline.

The glass easily tears through his flesh, parting skin and muscle like it's little more than butter left out on a summer's day. It buries deep inside him, slicing vital arteries, and I know I've paid the final price.

My soul.

It's truly broken now.

Pulling the weapon free from his throat, blood squirts from the wound and splashes all over my face. Beneath me, Jonathan's eyes are wide as saucers, a crimson spill pouring from him at an astonishing speed.

Still straddling his chest, I relax my hand, letting the crystal shard hit the carpet. Watching the life rush from him, taking with it a man who did nothing but hate the child he was supposed to love.

"You didn't silence me." I stare into his petrified eyes. "You just made me desperate. I'll never let you take my voice from me again. *Never.*"

Jonathan tries to clamp down on his throat to staunch the blood, but it's futile. I easily capture his wrist and pin it above him, stopping his efforts to save himself. I want to watch him die.

The guilt never comes.

Not as the light inside him begins to dim. Nor as the last remaining member of my family slowly fades before me, growing weaker with each second blood gushes from his neck wound.

He isn't my family.

Not anymore.

This monster doesn't deserve that title.

"You fucking lunatic!"

Movement over my shoulder is the only warning I get before Elon launches himself at me. I'm tackled to the side, thrown off Jonathan. We roll together in between the leather seats.

"Goddammit!" Elon's spittle wets my face.

Plastering on a smile that hopefully rivals his, I'm caught underneath him. "Did I foil your great retirement plan?"

"You killed him. Your own fucking relative!"

"No!" I screech back. "I killed a stranger!"

Surging my head forward, I slam my forehead into his

face. Elon yelps in pain, knocked off kilter by the hard blow that reignites my head wound. Before I can launch another attack, he lands a fast punch to the cheek.

The strike makes my teeth grind together, metallic blood bursting on my tongue when I accidentally bite down. I turn feral, bucking against his body and acting on pure instinct.

"Help me restrain her!" Elon roars over his shoulder.

Yet no backup comes.

When his men fail to make a reappearance after several long moments, he hisses in frustration, attempting to pin my wrists above my head so I can stop trying to claw his face.

"Stay still, whore!"

I'm pinned on the carpet, running low on viable options. I don't have the strength to buck him off or attempt another head butt. The glass shard is out of reach beside my uncle's still-gurgling body.

"I should've snapped your fucking neck when I had the chance." Elon's neck is mottled with red spots, a sheen of sweat shimmering above his lip.

"You should have," I snarl back.

"You've ruined everything!"

Bullets spray against the side of the jet, causing him to startle. He releases one wrist, trying to reach for his weapon. The split-second opening allows me to lash out, aiming my nails towards his eyes.

I don't have time to hesitate. It's a last ditch move. A final, desperate act. My fingers connect with his eye sockets and begin digging, tearing through wet mulch.

The wails that spill from his mouth feel like they're going to shatter my eardrums. I push past my revulsion, scratching deeply until blood soaks into my fingertips.

Oh, how he screams.

So fucking gloriously.

Elon clasps his hands over his bleeding face and falls backwards. I wipe my fingers off, ignoring the ruckus echoing from outside. Bullets have been replaced by stern shouting.

I'm hardly able to stand, bracing myself on a nearby seat. Elon lays flat on his back, writhing in pain. Too exhausted to smile, I loom over him, debating whether to slit his throat from ear to ear.

"People like you are the reason evil exists." I boot him in the stomach as hard as I can. "You enable it. Profit from it. Fucking create it. All from the sidelines."

A strangled howl is his only defence.

"I could kill you, but when the dust settles, the world will forget. You'll be wiped away. And I need everyone to remember what happens to snakes who profit from others' pain."

Curled up like a despicable worm, it's hard to imagine how this man spent a year taunting me. Forcing me to push product and hurt everyone around me. Ferrying innocent lives down to Craven and Harrison to meet their inevitable end.

He's a failure now.

The final pawn to fall.

Falling to my knees, the rush of extreme exhaustion almost drags me under. My adrenaline is waning fast. I have just enough energy to crawl back over to my uncle's body, lying deathly still in a puddle of blood.

His eyes are frozen open, pupils expanded to cavernous pits. Mouth slack. Tongue lolling. Throat gaping open. I reach over to slide his eyes closed, forever silencing his evil.

Footfalls clang against the jet's steps, indicating multiple arrivals. But my muscles can't hold out any longer. I lower my head to Jonathan's shirt-clad chest, forehead resting above his still heart.

That's how Sabre finds me.

Bloodied and limp.

"I'm sure I'll meet you in hell someday, Uncle Jonathan," I

whisper into his chest as my strength wanes. "Hold the gates open for me."

CHAPTER 28
LENNOX
S P E Y S I D E – BON IVER

THE INSCRIBED military dog tags weigh heavy in my hands, tossed from palm to palm. Back and forth. Over and over. The nervous tic mirrors my rapid heartbeat. I need something to focus on while we wait.

Sitting opposite me in a shitty hospital chair, Raine fiddles with the Velcro brace that encases his wrist. He's lucky to have escaped the wreck with minor injuries, mostly cuts and deep-purple bruises.

We were partially shielded in the back, leaving the front seats to take the worst of the impact. By the time I roused after being knocked unconscious, Xander was unresponsive. Warner screaming in pain. Raine yelling for help.

And Ripley… was gone.

All I felt was pure fucking terror.

The same terror that sunk into me and set up shop the day I found my sister's corpse. Blue and lifeless. I was too late to save her. Trapped in the back of that SUV, I couldn't save my family from this either.

The terror didn't abate even when we were cut from the twisted, smoking wreckage and blue-lighted to the nearest hospital. Nor did it ease when a still-unconscious Xander was rushed away to receive a CT scan.

"I hate this," Raine grouses, snapping the Velcro strap back into place. "We should be in there."

"We're not family, Raine."

"Bullshit! We are!"

As much as I agree with him, my last conversation with the medical team resulted in them offering to call the police to have me thrown out on the street. Apparently, violent threats aren't acceptable in hospitals.

Who knew?

We both fidget and stew until the sour-faced ward manager, Doctor Kilton, eventually makes a reappearance. He's a miserable fucker, far too old to still be working the midnight shift in a chaotic place like this.

My bones protest as I tap Raine's shoulder then rush to stand, tucking the dog tags into my pocket. Countless scratches, sore scrapes and bruises make my movements stiff. Raine stretches out the cheap blue stick the hospital lent him.

"Well?" I demand.

Doctor Kilton huffs at my sharp tone. "She's awake and ready for visitors."

"We should've been in there hours ago," Raine snaps at him.

"You are not listed as next of kin."

"Because she has none!" I try to retain a sense of calm. "Just take us to Ripley."

Waving tiredly, the weary doctor leads the way into the mixed ward. We both raced to the ward as fast as our battered bodies would allow when news of Ripley's arrival by helicopter filtered down to us.

We're escorted past several occupied rooms, accompanied by the sound of beeping machines and nurses bustling all around. It's a busy emergency department, taking the most severe triages from across London.

Doctor Kilton gestures towards the final room. "In there."

I don't bother to thank the old bastard. He could've bent the rules for us hours ago. We all know Ripley has no relatives or emergency contacts to call. He was just deliberately being difficult.

"You want to go first?" Raine asks me.

I snag his arm. "Together. Come on."

The frosted glass door clicks open, granting us access to a private booth. Hearing a fluttering heart rate monitor causes me to stride faster with Raine in tow beside me. We quickly round the corner to enter the room.

That's when the terror dissipates.

At last.

Sitting upright in a wide hospital bed, Ripley's propped up on several fluffy pillows. She watches us run in through one eye, the other blackened and swollen to the point of being closed shut.

Like us, she's covered in cuts and scrapes from the car crash, the deeper ones closed with stark white strips. I survey her body, searching for any other injuries. She's pale and rumpled, her septum piercing off-kilter, but she looks whole.

"Lennox. Raine."

"Rip," I gasp.

We both stop at her bedside, searching for anywhere to touch her. Raine finds one of her hands while I feather kisses across her mouth and face. Ripley's here. Safe. Alive. Fucking breathing.

We made it.

The sound of her crying reaches into my chest and rips out what's left untouched inside. There isn't much of me she hasn't sunk her claws into, but I'll happily surrender the rest to her now for the relief she's giving me.

"Oh god," Ripley hiccups, her face burying in Raine's chest. "You're both okay."

"Us?" I look at her quizzically. "What about you? Fuck, Rip. You were kidnapped!"

"I thought you were all dead."

She's sobbing, hands fisting Raine's shirt.

"We thought you would be too!"

Stroking her hair, Raine plants kisses on top of her head. "Nobody is dead. Everyone take a breath. We're all here safe."

Jolting in his arms, Ripley pulls back to look around behind us. The frenzied look in her one working eye matches how we've been feeling for the last fifteen hours, waiting for any updates from Sabre's teams.

They tracked us down as soon as emergency services attended the crash, assuming jurisdiction to prevent any further public spectacles. By then, Ripley was already gone. They were too late.

"Xander?" Her head hurriedly swings back to me.

"Hush," Raine soothes, still stroking her hair. "He's fine, Rip. Just had some sense knocked into him."

"What? Where is he?"

"A couple of floors above us being fussed over by nurses he keeps threatening to stab." I smile broadly. "Slight skull fracture, but unfortunately, still alive."

Tears well up and streak down her bruised cheeks, causing me so much fucking pain, I don't think I can take it. I gently ease her from Raine's arms to swipe the moisture away.

"It's okay, baby. We're all fine."

"I was so scared, Nox."

"I know. I'm so fucking sorry, Rip." The apology spills out of me in a jumbled rush. "I hate that you were taken from us."

Ripley's breath shudders, causing her gown-covered body to shake between us. We both sandwich her closer, offering gentle reassurances and touching her wherever possible.

It's a while before she can suck in a full, unobstructed breath again. The machine she's wired up to eventually calms, her heartbeat evening out and returning to a healthier, only slightly elevated rate.

"Are you hurt?" I study the fluids hanging above her bed.

Ripley leans back to shake her head. "Elon was injecting me with some drug cocktail. The doctors are just making sure it's all flushed from my system. I was pretty dehydrated too."

"Any other injuries?" Raine frets.

"Concussion." She winces at the sight of her bandaged wrists. "And rubbed myself raw trying to escape the shackles Elon put me in. No permanent damage."

"I can't believe he took you to Harrowdean." White-hot anger is a bitter weight inside me, causing my body to tense up. "What a fucking nut job."

"You heard?" Ripley glances up.

"The Anaconda team debriefed us," Raine explains, sitting on the bed. "They're the ones who caught up to you. Ethan, Becket and apparently some big, scary dude called Hyland from another team."

"Those were Enzo's words," I point out.

"Isn't he big and scary?" He laughs.

"I'm not answering that, Raine."

"That's a yes. You were intimidated."

"I was not!"

Ripley smiles, sinking into the pillows. "I don't remember any of that. I was fading fast by then."

Trying to gauge her mental state, I decide to rip the Band-Aid off. "Your uncle is dead, Rip."

"I know." She screws her eyes shut. "I... I killed him."

"It was you?" Raine arches a blonde brow.

"Yes. I stabbed him."

We're both silent for several seconds, processing the confirmation of what we suspected. The description of the crime scene on that private jet, mere seconds from taking off, didn't leave many other explanations.

I still wasn't sure she had it in her. Ripley is many things, but I know she's never taken a life before. Even if she's ruined plenty of them. Taking that step extracts a different kind of mental toll.

She shakes her head, bloodshot eyes flicking back open. "He wanted to keep me drugged up like some kind of zombie prisoner. I had no choice."

Raine clutches her hand tight. "You did what you had to."

"Does that make it right?" Her bottom lip wobbles.

"No," I reply honestly. "It makes it necessary."

"I've justified a lot these past couple years using that line." Ripley sighs with what appears to be bone-deep exhaustion. "I don't think I want to be that person anymore."

"We're free," Raine reminds her. "You can be whoever you want to be now."

"It's really over?"

I take her other hand, careful not to disturb the IV line feeding into it. "The investigation will rumble on, and we'll still have to cooperate... but the corporation is being dismantled."

"The institutes are all closing," Raine adds with a hopeful smile. "Everyone will be transferred to real facilities. No more experiments."

The back of my throat burns. Honestly, we haven't had time to process the news. Not while anxiously waiting for updates. There's still so much to be uncovered, but this is the first step towards eradicating Incendia's rule.

I'm not stupid enough to believe we'll be left in peace. Not after the deals we've all signed to act as informants to avoid any prosecution for our actions. Freedom has come at a steep cost.

"What about Elon?" She swallows hard.

"Alive," I answer. "Not sure he'll ever see again, though. He's been remanded into custody along with his men and countless others."

A relieved breath whooshes out of her. "Good."

"Did you really gouge his eyes out?" Raine scrunches his nose up.

"Um, a little bit."

"Damn. I feel like I shouldn't approve of that, you know?" He gestures to his own honeyed eyes. "But honestly, if anyone deserves to suffer, it's that son of a bitch."

"Seconded," I grumble.

"I half-expected it to be the police when you guys walked in," Ripley admits, chewing her bottom lip. "What's going to happen to me?"

Raine shrugs. "Jonathan's death was self-defence."

"With no witnesses?" she challenges.

"You've got a massive black eye, a concussion and were kidnapped after a hit and run," I list off. "I don't think there's a court in the world that would prosecute after all that."

"Fair point."

"Enzo says we're all free to go as long as we hold up our end of the deal." Raine caresses her bruised knuckles. "We won't be transferred with the other patients or taken back into custody."

"Fuck." She looks up at me, a glimmer of hope in her one good eye. "Seriously?"

"Seriously. The SCU will honour their word."

"We really are free." Ripley shakes her head. "I can't quite believe it. What now?"

Lifting her hand, Raine presses a kiss on it. "You remember that future we talked about?"

I look between them, eyebrows raised.

"It rings a bell," Ripley hedges.

"Well... perhaps it can be more than a far-off dream now."

"Am I allowed to ask about this inside joke?" I nudge Raine's shoulder playfully.

"Not an inside joke." Raine tilts his head in my direction.

"I told Ripley that when this is all over, we'll follow her wherever she wants to go."

"Xander and Lennox may not want that." Ripley looks down at her legs, covered by the thin hospital sheet.

Aghast, I stare at the most insane woman I've ever met. The vengeful bitch who jeopardised our lives. Instigated our torture. Stole our power. Then… our fucking hearts too.

"Nox?" Raine sighs. "Help me out here."

"I'm struggling myself."

"Then use your words! Fucking hell."

Releasing Ripley's hand, he picks up his new guide stick and walks away from the bed to give us a moment. I wait for him to tap his way to the window, weighing up my words.

For a moment, I just look at her. The one person I never expected to feel something so incredibly strong for beyond stone-cold hatred. For so long, I fucking loathed her.

My eyes catch on the black bracelet still secured around her wrist, above the bandages covering where she must have been shackled. Again. This time without me there to hold her close.

Fuck.

We almost lost her.

I can't lose her ever again.

"We had an unconventional journey to get here, didn't we?"

She chuckles under her breath. "Is that what we're calling it?"

"Sure."

"Then I guess we did."

"Six months ago, I never would've thought we'd be here. I had every intention of paying you back for the pain and torment you put us through. I wanted you dead, Rip."

"I'm aware."

I lick my lips, searching for the right words. "But I wouldn't change any of it. Do you know why?"

Ripley meets my gaze through one open eye. "Yeah, I think I do."

"Then you know what I'm about to say. All that grief, trauma, unthinkable torture… it led me here. To this crossroad. Staring at the most incredible woman in this fucked up world."

My voice has turned raspy, forcing me to stop for a breath. I'll scream in her face until I'm hoarse if that's what it takes for her to hear me. To believe what I know to be true deep in my soul.

"A woman I love," I add emotionally. "And who I hope will let me join her on this future train she's taking far away from all this heartache. If she'll have me."

"How could you even doubt it?" Her tears overflow, making her bruises shine. "You know I love you, Nox. Our future is what all this has been for."

"Then I guess I'm following you, baby."

Hands braced on the bed, I lean in to press a kiss onto her lips. Ripley responds fervently, proving her words with mere touch alone. There's no lie in the way she kisses me like I'm her life support machine.

Little does she know… she's mine. Always has been. Even when we despised each other and traded blows from afar, both determined to eradicate the other. That hatred kept me alive so I could love her to death now.

"Where are we going, anyway?" I laugh into her lips.

"You have a preference?"

"I don't exactly have a home to go back to. Hell, none of us do."

"I suppose we can figure it all out," Ripley decides with a tiny, hope-filled smile. "We've got our whole lives ahead of us."

Turning away from the window, Raine taps a path back over to us. "Now that's taken care of… how about a snack? I'm fucking starving."

"I saw a vending machine down the corridor." I consider him. "Need help reading the buttons?"

"Nah." Raine waves me off. "I'll leave it to chance."

Ripley snags his arm before he can leave. "Wait. How did Sabre find me so fast? Elon changed vehicles like a thousand times."

A hot, guilty flush creeps up my neck. I roll and pucker my lips, unable to provide an immediate response. Raine looks like he wants to laugh. He's barely holding it back.

"What?" She frowns at us both.

"Yeah, Nox. What?" Raine breaks out in laughter.

I rub the back of my neck. "Look, if we hadn't done it… We never would've gotten you back. Remember that."

"Done what?" Ripley asks suspiciously.

"It was just a precaution… Sabre helped set it up! Blame them!"

Chortling, Raine squeezes his stick between his hands. "Oh, this'll be good."

"And it came from a place of love," I add, feeling my panic spiral. "Nothing else."

"Seriously, Nox. What the fuck?"

My eyes skid back down to her bracelet. The one we gave her on our impromptu date. She looked so confused when Xander handed it over out of the blue.

I clear my throat. "Ahem. There's… erm, a tracker in your bracelet."

Ripley is silent for several seconds. It seems to stretch on endlessly. I'm preparing my escape plan before she can throttle me with her IV line when she finally spits out a response.

"You gave me a fucking tracking device as a fake gift?"

"Technically, it was a real gift," Raine jumps in. "And for the record, I knew nothing about it. All I suggested was flowers or something."

"Oh, let me guess!" she shouts in a rage. "I know exactly who's goddamn idea this—"

Click.

The door to her room swooshes open. Wheels roll across the tacky linoleum, preceding the appearance of a chair being pushed by an aggravated-looking orderly.

His ghostly face set in a scowl, Xander is seated in the wheelchair, demanding his carer hurries up. When they round the corner, his tired midnight eyes snap over to us.

The doctors decided that surgery wasn't required after his emergency CT scan showed a hairline fracture in his upper skull from the wreck. Much to our collective relief. Xander simply bitched about being kept on the ward against his wishes.

Before he can say a word, Ripley points a finger at him.

"You! Xander fucking Beck! What kind of psychopath gives his girl a damn concealed tracker on their first official date?"

Thin lips pressed together, he turns to look up at the orderly. "Turn me around and run, would you?"

The middle-aged woman snickers, parking him up right next to me.

"You've dug your hole, son. I could use a break from your complaining while she rips you a new one."

CHAPTER 29
RIPLEY
VIOLET HILL – COLDPLAY

AN OBNOXIOUSLY LARGE bunch of sunflowers clasped in my hands, I follow the signs to the male ward. I left Lennox and Raine in Xander's room while his discharge papers are signed and went on a hunt for flowers.

I know I'm in the right place when I spot two familiar figures outside a hospital room, both with crossed arms and hard scowls. Neither look like they've slept in days.

Ethan sees me first, arms dropping so he can wave. "Ripley?"

I adjust the flowers in my arms. "Hi."

At the sound of my name, Enzo straightens. I expected the rest of the Anaconda team to be here, but from what I understand, the whole of Sabre Security is facing months of evidence collection and investigating. They must be overwhelmed.

"Hey, guys."

"What are you doing here?" Enzo looks over me.

"Here to see the patient."

"It's good to see you in one piece." He smiles reassuringly. "Been discharged?"

"Not with a clean bill of health, but yes. I'm free to leave."

"You need a ride somewhere?" Ethan offers.

"Are you still our protection detail?"

"For the time being. While the investigation is ongoing, you'll have security."

Unease filters into my bloodstream. "Are we still in danger?"

"The main threats have been eliminated. We believe you're safe."

"Consider it a precaution," Enzo adds with a wink. "We're already working with the authorities to round up suspects based on your evidence."

"I'm not taking any more risks after what happened." I glance between them, offering a genuine smile. "So thank you."

"You gave us a scare," Ethan admits. "The car wreck was a complete disaster. And finding you passed out on that damn jet shaved ten years off my life."

"Sorry?" I pose it as a question.

"It's us who should be apologising. I'm sorry it took us so long to get to you."

"Apparently, I have the guys to thank for my rescue." Cool metal slides along my arm, reminding me of the bracelet I'm still wearing. "But thanks for coming to get me."

"Sure thing."

"Is Warner awake? Lennox told me he's here. I want to see him before we leave."

Enzo rolls his shoulders, working out the tension. "He's pretty heavily drugged right now. His surgery is scheduled for the morning."

"Surgery?" Anxiety explodes inside me.

Looking down at his feet, Ethan flinches. "His leg was crushed in the wreck. It cut off the blood circulation. The doctors have tried all they can to save it, but…"

"No," I whisper, horrified.

"It'll have to be amputated," Enzo finishes. "There's nothing else they can do."

"Shit. I'm so—"

"Don't apologise." Ethan cuts me off. "This isn't your fault. We understand the risks in this business, Ripley."

"Still, his leg?"

"He'll recover and live. Nothing else matters now. In time, he can return to work if he wishes."

Throat thick, I can't find anything else to say. I hitch the flowers higher in my arms and give them both nods. Ethan holds the door open for me to step inside the room filled with ticking machines.

Warner rests in a bed on the far side of the room, surrounded by countless machines. He's hooked up to several monitors with bags of sedatives and pain relief suspended from a hook above him.

I quietly pad closer, placing the sunflowers on the folding table pushed away from his bed. Above the crisp, white sheets, his injured leg is secured in a brace, holding the doomed limb prone.

It's hard to see through the stitched cuts and grazes that cover his face. I didn't recognise myself when I stumbled to the bathroom to shower, but Warner looks even worse. He took the brunt of the hit.

"Hey." I lightly touch his arm, scared to hurt him. "It's Ripley."

His eyes don't open.

"God, I'm so sorry." Guilt strangles my lungs. "All you wanted to do was help us. If you hadn't come to the apartment... I don't know if we'd still be alive. And look what thanks you get."

Beep. Beep. Beep.

"I heard about the surgery. We're all going to be here when you wake up, okay? I promise we'll help you through this. Just like you helped us."

Adjusting the covers, I smooth the wrinkles out, making sure he's securely tucked in. There's a stray lock of hair hanging in his closed eye, the dark-brown hue stark against his sickly pallor.

I swipe the hair away, pushing it back from his face. "Thank you for being my friend. Even when I was hurtful to you and determined to make it on my own. You didn't have to care about me."

Beep. Beep. Beep.

"I have the chance for a life now. I'm hoping you'll be a part of it. I could use a friend."

Determined not to start crying again, I take one last look at his face. For a whole year in Harrowdean, I took Warner for granted. Even when he did his best to provide the help I desperately needed.

I'll never do that again.

I'm not afraid to care now.

Connections are what make us strong, and if he wants a friend, I'll spend forever repaying him for doing his best to help. That's the kind of person I want to be. Not someone who hurts others for selfish means.

Someone who helps.

The kind of person my parents would be proud of.

———

"Stop here."

Pressing the brakes, Ethan pulls up at the curb. Aside from taking a phone call from his long-distance boyfriend in some faraway town, he's been silent the entire ride into Hackney.

I look over my shoulder. "You guys okay?"

Xander, Lennox and Raine are all seated in the back of Ethan's car. We're all a sorry sight, wearing donated clothes from the hospital, our bodies bearing the marks of all we've endured.

"Tired." Raine smiles sleepily.

"Cramped," Xander grouses.

Lennox elbows him. "Stop moaning."

"Ow. I'm injured."

"I'll give you a fucking injury if you complain one more time."

"Get him, Nox." Raine yawns.

Convincing them to get back in an SUV took some pleading on Ethan's part. I was busy fighting my own internal battle after making the decision that we would return to my home for now.

None of us have another place to go. It was this or a hotel. I have money tied up in various accounts, but Uncle Jonathan took charge of my affairs when I was shipped off to Priory Lane. I don't even know where my purse is.

"I called Theo," Ethan informs me. "He sent a team in to fit new locks and check the place for anything Jonathan may have installed. It's clear. You should be able to get in."

"Thank you."

"Pretty sure he also installed a security system with CCTV cameras." He casts me an unrepentant grin. "Sorry."

"Am I going to have secret agents turning up at my door every time someone dodgy walks past?"

"I'll keep them in check. Don't worry."

Placing my hand over his, I squeeze tight. "Thanks for everything."

"I'll be back tomorrow to take you all into HQ to be debriefed."

"Got it."

Ethan nods. "Theo told me he had the team leave a couple phones inside from the company stash. My number is programmed in if you need anything."

"Is this dude giving Ripley his number?" Lennox murmurs.

Raine huffs. "Did you miss him flirting with a guy on the phone?"

"Irrelevant," Xander quips. "Can I rip his spine out of his throat?"

I turn around in my seat to scowl at him. "Xander! Jesus!"

He tilts his head, deadly serious. "Is that a yes?"

"No!"

"Too bad." Shrugging, he glares at Ethan. "Well, the offer stands."

"Ripping out people's spines is not a proportionate response in any circumstance, and most certainly not when Ethan is trying to help us."

"See that's where we disagree," he deadpans.

Popping the door open, I clamber out before he can threaten to kill anyone else. The guys all follow with Lennox helping Xander to straighten. Ethan offers us a wave then pulls away from the curb.

With a calming breath in, I turn to face my building. It's an old, converted warehouse, swept up in London's gentrification. I bought it when I moved out, so I've owned the loft apartment for several years now.

"Home." I wave awkwardly. "Top floor."

"This is your flat?" Lennox asks, surprised.

"Yeah, there's an art studio combined with the living space. And I have a spare bedroom. Should be enough space for us all."

Leading the way up the slick stone path, the entry door swings open after I tap in the security code. Thankfully, it hasn't changed. Climbing the concrete stairwell proves to be a challenge for all of us.

As promised, my front door is unlocked, fitted with shiny new locks and a blinking camera strategically placed outside. I hesitate before pushing it open, feeling a sense of trepidation.

"What is it?" Xander drops a hand on my shoulder.

"I just… I'm not the person I was when I lived here. I don't know who I'm coming back as now."

"You're still you, little toy."

"Am I?"

His nimble fingers sink into me, providing a reassuring pressure. "Sure. Perhaps just a little rougher around the edges. A bit more scarred. But also a hell of a lot stronger."

Twisting my head, I look up at him. "I lived here alone for a long time. I'm coming back with something else too. Three something elses."

"That a problem?" His mouth hooks up.

"No." My hand moves to rest on top of his. "I love you, Xander. I want you to know that even if you can't say it back."

His star-speckled, navy eyes flick over mine. Considering. Processing. We've come a long way, but I know he's still learning to let people in. I don't expect him to return the sentiment.

"My chest feels strange when I'm with you," he rumbles. "It has for a while. Is that what this feeling is, Rip? Love?"

"Is that what you think it is?"

Xander peers away, his bottom lip clamped between his teeth. "I'm not sure. I haven't felt it before."

I look briefly at the other two. "Does your chest feel like that when you think about Lennox or Raine?"

"Yes." He clears his throat. "But in a different way. They're my brothers."

"Because you care about them."

"Yes."

As much as I want to drag the words out of him, I leave Xander with that realisation. His mind takes time to pick the world apart and translate it into terms he can understand. I trust that he'll get there.

Pushing open the apartment door, my nose wrinkles at the stench of thick dust and disuse. A massive pile of unanswered mail has been neatly stacked on the console next to the front door by whoever checked the place over.

The guys tentatively follow me into the vast, open plan space. Vaulted ceilings stretch all the way to the rafters, lined with huge steel beams. Light spills in through floor-length windows built into the brick.

I divided the space into two—living on the right side with the two bedrooms, a shared bathroom, glistening steel kitchen and restored, antique dining table. It's all still the same beneath inches of dust.

On the left, my studio space is separated by rows of drying racks and a bookshelf full of art books. Years worth of old canvases are stacked in piles, exactly how I left them.

"Bedrooms are over there." I gesture to the right. "I've no idea how clean any of the linens or towels will be."

"How did you pay the bills?" Lennox queries.

"I'd accumulated enough from selling art over the years." Dust particles tickle my nostrils. "Everything gets paid automatically each month so I knew the place would be okay while I was gone."

Leaving them to explore, I walk into the living area. Behind the table, I have a smattering of different coloured armchairs, all thrifted from my local antique dealer. I've always loved objects with history.

At the console table next to one of the windows, I flick on the Tiffany lamp, illuminating a collection of framed photographs I kept on display. My parents' wedding photo. A shot of me, all red and scrunched up, swaddled in my dad's arms.

The final frame holds one of me and Uncle Jonathan— my graduation from art school. I wore my robe with my hard-earned diploma clasped in my hands. But I can see the strain behind my practised smile.

It fucking hurts to look at him now. Younger but still immaculate in his charcoal suit and blue tie. Those same clear eyes, filled with schemes and secrets. I was still trying to please him back then.

Lifting the frame, I throw it at the brick wall and watch in satisfaction as it shatters. The smashed glass hits the floor, shredding the photo imprisoned inside.

"Ripley?"

"I'm fine!" I call back.

Someone stops behind me, breathing hard. I feel arms wrap around me, a firm chest pressing into my back. Spearmint washes over me, a refreshing comfort in all the stale air.

"Didn't like that one?" Xander whispers.

"No. Not anymore."

His lips press into the side of my head, cool and dry. Every clenched muscle relaxes at the feel of Xander holding me. Pulling me back to the present, where that man can no longer dictate my life.

"My chest hurts again," he murmurs. "I think I love you."

Laughter spills out of me.

"Fuck. Hell of a way to declare it, Xan."

"Want me to take it back?"

Pulling his wrists, I turn in his arms so I can see him. My swollen eye is still a badly bruised mess, but I don't need twenty-twenty vision to recognise the jagged angles and alabaster skin I've memorised.

"No," I whisper.

His mouth is drawn to mine, landing softer than I expected. The kiss is everything Xander isn't. Gentle. Tentative. Exploratory. All the traits I couldn't possibly ascribe to the man who thinks it's perfectly acceptable to gift me a tracking device.

I don't give a fuck, though.

Xander is perfect the way he is.

I'm so wrapped up in his lips, it takes Lennox shouting our names several times for us to separate. There's an odd ringing emanating throughout the apartment. Taking Xander's hand, I walk over to the front door.

The security system that Theo had his men install is demanding my attention. Next to the door, a small screen has been installed, offering me a view of the outside pavement and our floor.

"Someone pressed the buzzer." I study the image. "Do you think it was a mistake?"

Xander leans closer to study the four men standing outside the apartment building, all carrying shopping bags. His finger hovers over one—tall, raven-haired and radiating danger.

"That's Hudson Knight. He was in HQ when we first went. I saw him in the corridor afterwards."

"The Blackwood inmate?" Raine asks behind us.

"Wait, I recognise him too." My attention narrows on the guy wearing a pressed shirt and glasses, his pearly-blonde hair slicked back. "He was on those tapes that got leaked."

"Kade Knight," Lennox supplies. "Brothers, I believe."

"What are they doing here? Who are the other two?"

Jabbing his finger on the intercom, Xander offers a friendly greeting. "This isn't Blackwood. Fuck off."

"Smooth," Raine mutters.

The preppy-looking one, Kade, steps up to answer. "Uh, hello. This is a bit weird, but I kinda swiped this address from Theo's computer while he was busy."

My eyebrows feel like they've met my damn hairline.

"We just want to chat," he rushes to add. "Nothing sinister. This is my brother, Hudson, and our friends, Eli and Phoenix. We're unarmed and come in peace."

"What the fuck?" Lennox whispers. "Is this a joke?"

"He seems genuine."

"I don't trust genuine," Xander replies, hitting the speak button again. "Why are you here?"

"We have a peace offering." Kade lifts the white, plastic bag in his hands. "Thai takeout."

Looking at each other and silently deliberating, we leave them hanging. Hudson seems to say something to his brother, a stormy scowl carving his features as they both turn to face the others. Collectively, the group starts to leave.

I push past Xander to jab the button. "Wait! Come up."

"Ripley," Lennox hisses.

Ignoring his protest, I press to give them access to the building.

"Okay, then." Raine jostles on his feet.

The guys disappear from the camera as they walk inside. Lennox and Xander are both bitching while I wait for them to reappear on the second camera outside. They appear before a knock echoes on the door.

"Ripley," Xander warns.

Ignoring him, I pull the door open. Two friendly hazel orbs meet mine. Kade can't be much younger than us, though the dark circles beneath his black-framed glasses seem to age him.

"Hi."

"Hello," I reply timidly.

"Kade." He gives an awkward wave. "From the intercom."

Xander's shoulder pushes into mine, forcing his way in front of me. "Can we help you?"

A pierced, black brow cocked, Hudson gestures to the takeout his brother is holding. "We brought dinner."

"Why?" Lennox barks.

There's a snort from the blue-haired guy behind them, holding the hand of the fourth member, who avoids looking at us altogether.

"This is going about as well as expected."

"Phoenix," Kade scolds before turning his attention back to us. "You don't know us, but we've heard about your stories. You've probably heard some of ours. I figured we should all meet."

Looking between them, I'm filled with confusion. "What about... uh, Brooklyn? Brooklyn West?"

The silent, curly-haired one at the back flinches. That must be Eli. He's staring down at his shoes, a pair of ancient-looking Chucks, and seems deliberately secluded from the world around him.

When he finally looks up and I get a full view of his startling, rich-green eyes, I know he's hurting. Whatever they've been through to get here, it's left them battered and scarred. Just like us.

I offer him a tentative smile.

After a beat, Eli smiles back.

Phoenix is holding his hand in a white-knuckled grip. The pair seem glued at the hip. By comparison, Hudson and Kade feel like the team leaders, both standing shoulder-to-shoulder.

"She isn't with us." Hudson's stubbled throat bobs. "It's kind of a long story."

Nodding, I hold the door open for them.

"We've got nothing but time."

EPILOGUE

WHEN WILL WE BE FREE? – YOUNG LIONS

XANDER

Present Day

With Ripley's parting words describing that first encounter over Thai food, the documentary credits roll. I close my laptop, leaning back on the bed to blow out the breath it feels like I've held for an eternity.

The full, unfiltered truth is out there now.

Being seen is an odd thing.

Perhaps one of the most divisive opinions among humans. Some will sacrifice everything for the chance to be heard. For the world to know their name. No price is too high for fame.

Then there are those who stick to the shadows. Who thrive on invisibility. Striving to be forgotten by the sands of time. History erases us all in the end, but some make it their mission to expedite that process.

I never cared strongly enough about either before. Other people's opinions weren't exactly my concern—not when I lacked the emotions to care about their scorn or praise. I simply lived for the next thrill, the endless chase for the most exquisite pain.

Life looks a little different now.

I can't say I regret the road that led me here.

Stashing the laptop in the cluttered desk drawer, I catch sight of the faded military dog tags stuffed at the very back. Lennox never did quite summon the strength to toss them, but he hasn't searched for them in years.

He doesn't need that reminder anymore.

His family is right here in front of him.

Walking into our spacious living area, the three mismatched sofas we soon replaced Ripley's sparse armchairs with are fully occupied. Phoenix and Eli dominate one, trading whispers with their fingers intwined on their crossed legs.

Everyone arrived while I poured over my laptop, unable to stand another second without answers. None of the others wanted to watch with me. Not even Ripley.

"You know, Kade's winning the best husband contest," Eli grouses, his gaze fixed on the TV. "We need to outsmart him."

"How?" Phoenix moans.

"We get the others to have Logan and take Brooklyn out for sushi. You know it's her weakness."

"You hate sushi, Eli."

The green-eyed recluse shrugs. "I'll grin and bear it for her."

"We should rope in Jude when he finishes work. He can help us conspire."

"Late shift tonight," Eli replies. "He'll be a while yet."

Casting my gaze around, I spot Raine plucking the violin in his lap while sitting with Hunter, his younger brother, Leighton, and Theo. The men have a warm, healthy glow from their time in the Australian sunshine. It's rare that we see them.

They're back visiting England with Enzo and their newly

minted fiancée, Harlow. The past decade since Sabre's business exploded after Incendia was a bit complicated. They went through hell, but that's a whole other tale.

"Come visit us after your concert in Melbourne?" Hunter suggests, a tumbler full of whiskey in hand. "We'll put the four of you up for a couple weeks."

"Oh, awesome." Raine adjusts his rounded, black lenses. "I've got another show in Sydney the week after. I can get you all backstage passes if you want?"

Theo fiddles with his phone, engrossed in something. "Anywhere away from the crowds would be great."

"Consider it done."

"Xan?" Raine's head cocks, his nostrils flaring. "I know you're standing there. Can you get time off from work?"

"Haven't exactly got a boss to answer to while I'm freelancing," I reply easily. "As long as no major projects come in, it should be fine."

"You can code software on an aeroplane, Xan. Just say yes."

Sighing, I decide to humour him. "Yes, Raine."

"Perfect!" He grins broadly.

Turning away from them, I head for the kitchen where Lennox is arm-wrestling Hudson and failing miserably. Who the hell would challenge that massive oaf? It's giving Enzo and Kade some decent entertainment, though.

"Prepare to pay up," Kade boasts.

Glowering, Enzo watches them intently. "Never gonna happen."

"Double or nothing?"

Clasping his hand, Enzo shakes firmly. "You're on. Hudson's got this."

I halt while passing. "Did you bet against your own brother?"

Kade shrugs, unrepentant. "Hudson needs his ego checked every once in a while."

"Heard that!" the man in question grunts. "Fuck, dude. How are you so strong?"

"It helps to own a gym." Lennox strains to hold his position. "I have to look the part."

"I've got twenty on Lennox," I declare.

He flashes me a smirk. "Is that a vote of confidence? I'm flattered, Xan."

"Don't get cocky."

It's only another thirty seconds before I lose the bet. Hudson slams Lennox's arm down into the kitchen counter, much to his chagrin. With a series of imaginative curses, Lennox concedes defeat.

"How?"

Hudson grins smugly. "Wait until you're chasing around after a kid all day long. It does wonders for your stamina."

"Not sure that it's on the cards for us." Lennox chuckles, taking his hand to shake. "So I'll take your word for it. Good match."

"Come on then, Hud." Enzo takes a seat at the counter. "Let's see how you fare against a pro."

Hudson rolls his eyes. "Whatever, old man."

"Less of that. I'm in my prime."

Lingering against the stove, I watch the next few rounds. Hudson loses his winning streak. A short-lived challenge by Kade only intensifies Enzo's bragging. I decline a match, already certain of the outcome.

"That man's biceps should be fucking illegal." Lennox stops next to me, slurping a beer. "Like, shit. Reckon that's what Australia does to you?"

"Enzo's always been huge."

"Not that huge."

"You should take him down to the gym tomorrow. I'm sure he'd like to see the place."

"You think?" Lennox arches a dark brow.

"Yeah. Last time he was in the country, you were still extending the new weightlifting section."

"That's true." He nods to himself. "Alright, I'll take him."

"Good. Have you seen Ripley and the others?"

Lennox gestures towards the art studio. "Looking at some paintings, I think."

Slapping his shoulder, I head for Ripley's attached studio. These days, it's more like organised chaos. The space gets messy when she's having a bad week and can't stop. That and the times she doesn't have the energy to even move.

When those episodes hit, I come in and reset her workspace for her. We both work from home while Lennox is often at the gym he part-owns, and Raine makes use of a rented studio a few streets over to rehearse in peace for his upcoming tour dates.

Through the drying racks, I can see Ripley standing with Brooklyn and Harlow. Logan, Brooklyn's chubby toddler, bounces on her hip. Both women are a few years younger than Ripley, but they became fast friends.

She learned to love Brooklyn through the friendship we formed with her guys while she was gone. What began with an awkward drop-in and Thai food slowly blossomed through bonding over our similar experiences.

As for Harlow and how she ended up in our extended family, that's a whole other story. But having survived her own ordeal, she slotted into the close dynamic we've all formed over the last decade.

"How do you feel about the documentary airing?" Brooklyn asks.

A finished canvas clutched in her hands, Ripley stares down at the swirls of paint. "I'm glad the footage was salvaged from the memory cards."

"That's not what I asked."

Harlow runs a hand over her shoulder-length ringlets. "It's okay to have mixed feelings. This is a huge step."

"No… I'm relieved." Ripley chooses her words carefully. "I knew I'd never feel at peace until I told our version of events. We never had that closure."

Brooklyn coos over her little boy. "We just want you to be happy, Rip. Even if I didn't do an interview myself, I respect your decision to sit down with the journalist."

"You do?" Ripley glances at her.

"Of course."

"I was a bit worried about your reaction."

"No need to be." Brooklyn flashes her an easy smile. "You have to do what's right for you. We all heal in our own ways. I know I did. You've waited a long time to find your peace."

"I don't know if I've found it yet." Ripley hikes up a curved shoulder. "But this feels pretty damn close. I needed to purge myself of all the things I did back then."

"Are you worried about backlash?" Harlow asks fretfully. "I know firsthand how cruel the media can be."

"You know what? I'm not. What can they possibly do to me that's worse than what we went through?"

After Ripley puts the canvas back in its place, the three women embrace, all squishing Logan between them. He squeals loudly at all the attention. Brooklyn swipes under her silver-grey eyes when she steps back.

"I'm proud of you, Rip."

"Thank you."

Harlow rubs Ripley's arm, a warm smile making the burn scars that cover her neck wrinkle. "The world needs your voice. I'm proud of you for using it."

Letting them all hug again, I wait a second before interrupting.

"For the record, I'm proud too."

Her head lifting, Brooklyn points an angry finger at me. "You! Who the hell sets fire to a damn recording studio?"

Harlow bites her lip while Ripley just smiles exasperatedly. I keep my distance so Brooklyn can't slam her fist into my face. It's happened once or twice. She has the firepower of a fucking nuclear arsenal.

"Erm, me?"

"What were you thinking?" she demands.

"I was… feeling some stuff." I shrug it off. "Lots of stuff."

"Lots of stuff," Brooklyn repeats. "God help you, Ripley. You must have the patience of a saint to deal with this one's emotional vocabulary."

"Says the woman married to five men." Ripley giggles.

"Point taken. Speaking of…"

Winking at me, Brooklyn hoists Logan on her hip then tows Harlow from the studio, giving us some privacy. I linger by the door, feeling uncertain.

I haven't found the words to say since the documentary aired a few days ago. Hell, it took me this long to watch it myself. The backlash has been pretty fucking horrific. We've all had to turn off our phones to stop getting calls and emails.

But did the planet implode when the truth was laid bare for public scrutiny? No. Did armed assailants break our door down to throw us in some off-grid prison for escaped delinquents? Also no. The world did not end.

I can handle some assholes on the internet spouting half-baked opinions about things they'll never understand. They're irrelevant. Frankly, I don't need them to like what we did or even understand it.

All I need is for Ripley to be okay. We coasted for a long time, struggling to find our feet in the aftermath of what we survived. It took a long time to establish a semblance of normality before starting to rebuild our lives.

But she never quite got there. Her artwork has always given her some solace, and for years, I feared it became a cocoon. One she could hide in when the memories and guilt became too much to bear.

She's finally torn down all her barriers.

Ripley has told her truth.

Why did I ever doubt her motivations?

"Xan," she coaxes, a finger crooked. "You can come here."

"Wasn't sure if I'm forgiven or not yet."

"For running away from us to break into an abandoned building? Stalking a journalist? Or attempting to sabotage my interview?"

"All of it?" The words come out as a question.

Ripley rolls her green-brown eyes. "You're forgiven. We all make stupid choices when we're scared, right?"

"Apparently."

I step into her arms, letting my face hide in the crook of her shoulder. Ripley cups my neck, holding me close. She smells the same as always. A fresh, tropical thunderstorm. All things sweet and fruity.

"Thank you for organising this. It feels good to get everyone in the same room."

Abruptly straightening, I check my watch. It's past eight o'clock.

"We're short by a couple, but I've seen to that."

"Huh?" Ripley frowns at me.

"Come and see."

Taking her hand, I pull her from the art studio.

"Xan—"

"Just wait."

Logan is now snuggled up in Eli's lap, eating something he definitely shouldn't be while Brooklyn bemoans her husbands. Enzo has dragged the others in from the kitchen to gather the whole group.

Tucking Ripley into Lennox's side so he can hold onto her, I head for the front door. A flashy company SUV has pulled up outside the building. They're already headed up to us.

I open the door before Warner and Jude can knock. Both look at me in surprise.

"You're late by three minutes."

"Hello to you too," Jude remarks. "Where are my wife and son?"

Gesturing over my shoulder, I wave him in. He slaps me on the back as he passes, pulling off his medical lanyard to tuck it away. Warner follows him in, walking with a new, slight limp.

"You alright?"

He shrugs. "New prosthetic. Had a mishap with the last one."

"Do I even want to know what happened to it?"

"Probably not."

Smiling, I tug him into a hug. "You need to be careful."

"Bullets just seem to like me, Xan."

"Ripley won't buy that bullshit."

Admittedly, it took about six years for us to reach the touching stage. His steadfast presence in Ripley's life cemented my trust for him, though thick-skulled, younger Xander should've appreciated his actions long ago.

"What's kept you so busy?"

Warner releases me. "New client. Bit hard to explain. We're wrapped up in some messy shit."

"Sounds about right."

"We'll handle it." He flicks his hand dismissively. "How did the doc airing go?"

"As expected. We need to give you our new numbers."

He bites back a laugh. "That bad, huh?"

"It'll die down."

Guiding him into the bursting apartment, I watch for Ripley's reaction. Warner is her confidante. They talk regularly, but his work at Sabre pulls him in all directions.

Their most recent case—some complex, human trafficking situation—has led him to be absent since her interview. He had to undertake a long-haul trip to Mexico as part of the ongoing investigation.

"Did I miss the party?" Warner calls out.

Her head snapping up, Ripley turns to gape at us. "You're back!"

"I couldn't miss seeing this lot altogether in one room."

Ripley rushes to pull him into a hug. "I'm so glad you made it."

"Nothing could've stopped me, Rip."

I catch Lennox's gaze across the room. He's smiling at the sight of our girl, happily surrounded by everyone we care about. People we didn't know existed when we first set upon the road to this moment.

"Did I miss the live show?" Warner jokes, his eyes on Raine still plucking the violin in his lap.

"No." He shakes his head. "No live show."

"Oh, come on," Enzo cajoles. "Give us a preview. Then we'll all have bragging rights that we heard the great Raine Starling's latest hit first."

There's a chorus of agreements. Silencing them with a raised hand, Raine grins ear to ear as he stands up in front of the room. Sobriety agrees with him. His career has hit the damn stratosphere in the last few years.

"I have something, but it's rough," he explains, placing the violin under his chin. "I'm not sure if it counts, but I wrote this for the anniversary of our first date, Rip."

Sliding her arm around Lennox's waist and kissing his cheek, Ripley perks up at her name. She immediately looks down to the black chain bracelet she still wears, even though the tracker broke about five years ago.

"You remember the date?" She chuckles.

"Well, it's a rough estimate."

Raine lifts the bow, coaxing it over the violin strings with precision that will never fail to astound me for a man without sight. He plays like the instrument is an extension of himself—a living, breathing body part.

It's a complex song, layered with low, mournful notes that sound like deep sorrow. Then he flicks the bow with masterful expertise and adds lighter segments, blending the two contrasts into a seamless melody.

Light. Dark.

Hopeful. Devastating.

All of life's vast complexities.

Perhaps this is actually the most divisive opinion. Whether we can contain these multitudes at once. Hold evil and redemption inside us simultaneously. Strike with love and hatred in the same blow.

Raine's music is honest. Raw. Painfully realistic. A jagged blend of the two extremes. Just like Ripley's artwork. Both of them have immortalised our stories in their purest forms. Our voices will live on.

For many, we were the villains.

But we fucking deserve this happy ending.

The End

WANT MORE FROM THIS SHARED UNIVERSE?

The timeline of Harrowdean Manor runs parallel to Blackwood Institute. Learn more about Brooklyn, Hudson, Kade, Eli and Phoenix by diving into the dark and twisted world of another experimental psychiatric institute.

https://mybook.to/TwistedHeathens
https://mybook.to/SacrificialSinners
https://mybook.to/DesecratedSaints
https://bit.ly/BIBoxSet

Dive into Sabre next. Set in the same shared universe, the Sabre Security series follows Harlow and the hunt for a violent, bloodthirsty serial killer. Featuring cameos from all your favourite Blackwood Institute characters.

https://bit.ly/CorpseRoads
https://bit.ly/SkeletalHearts
https://bit.ly/HollowVeins
https://mybook.to/SSBoxSet

Finally, follow Willow's story next as she flees an abusive

marriage and takes refuge in the small mountain town of Briar Valley, assisted in her hunt for justice by Sabre Security.

https://mybook.to/WBWF
https://mybook.to/WWTG
https://mybook.to/BVBoxSet

Pre-order Warner and the Anaconda Team's story in an upcoming, dark why choose trilogy featuring a desperate heroine fleeing untold horrors and the complicated, morally grey security team who rescue her.

https://mybook.to/FracturedFuture

PLAYLIST

LISTEN HERE:
BIT.LY/BURNLIKEANANGEL

Twin Size Mattress – The Front Bottoms
Help. – Young Lions
Monsters – Foreign Air
Up In Flames – Ruelle
You've Created A Monster – Bohnes
Sincerely, Fuck You – Pardyalone
Freedom – Young Lions
Fixed Blade – Trade Wind
Said & Done – Bad Omens
God Needs The Devil – Jonah Kagen
Out Of Style – KID BRUNSWICK & Beauty School
Dropout
In Your Arms – Croixx
Roses – The Comfort
Sailor Song – Gigi Perez
Hate Me Now – Ryan Caraveo
Bleed – Connor Kauffman
SEE YOU IN HELL – Beauty School Dropout
Jerk – Oliver Tree
STRAY – jxdn
Pull the Plug - VOILÀ

Another One – Toby Mai
SPIT IN MY FACE! – ThxSoMch
Again – Noah Cyrus (Feat. XXXTENTACION)
Video Games – Good Neighbours
Higher – Croixx
Brain Stew – Green Day
End of a Good Thing – Cory Wells
Burn It to the Ground – Nickelback
S P E Y S I D E – Bon Iver
Violet Hill – Coldplay
When Will We Be Free? – Young Lions

ACKNOWLEDGEMENTS

The end of Harrowdean Manor is here! I feel so emotional writing these words. This duet has been a whirlwind in the last few months.

Ripley's story is one that many of us can relate to. I remember writing a blog post for a mental health magazine not long after receiving my diagnosis in 2019, admitting that I wished I could tell my loved ones it was something simpler and less enduring.

The stigma surrounding bipolar disorder is still prevalent, and helping to shed some light on how it impacts so many lives is something I feel deeply passionate about.

For anyone out there who feels alone, misunderstood, or abandoned — You are seen. You are heard. You have a voice. Please use it.

I want to thank the most important people in my life who have supported me to get this far: Eddie, Lilith, Kristen, Lola, Melinda, Zoe, Kaya. You all mean so much to me. I'm grateful to have such beautiful souls in my life, loving and supporting me along the way.

Thank you to my fabulous editor, Kim, for working her magic on this book baby. As always, you are my absolute rock. And I need to say a huge thank you to my publicist, Valentine, and the whole team at Valentine PR for supporting me with this release.

Finally, I'd like to thank you. The reader. I would be nothing without my loyal fans, showing up for every book I write, shouting about the shared universe, and recommending my stories to anyone who will listen. Thank you for inspiring me every day to continue showing up and telling these dark tales.

See you next time.

Stay wild,

J Rose xxx

ABOUT THE AUTHOR

J Rose is an independent dark romance author from the United Kingdom. She writes challenging, plot-driven stories packed full of angst, heartbreak and broken characters fighting for their happily ever afters.

She's an introverted bookworm at heart with a caffeine addiction, penchant for cursing and an unhealthy attachment to fictional characters.

Feel free to reach out on social media. J Rose loves talking to her readers!

For exclusive insights, updates and general mayhem, join J Rose's Bleeding Thorns on Facebook.

Business enquiries: j_roseauthor@yahoo.com

Come join the chaos. Stalk J Rose here…
www.jroseauthor.com/socials

NEWSLETTER

Want more madness? Sign up to J Rose's newsletter for monthly announcements, exclusive content, sneak peeks, giveaways and more!

Sign up here:

www.jroseauthor.com/newsletter

ALSO BY J ROSE

Read Here:

www.jroseauthor.com/books

Recommended Reading Order:

www.jroseauthor.com/readingorder

Blackwood Institute

Twisted Heathens

Sacrificial Sinners

Desecrated Saints

Sabre Security

Corpse Roads

Skeletal Hearts

Hollow Veins

Briar Valley

Where Broken Wings Fly

Where Wild Things Grow

Harrowdean Manor

Sin Like The Devil

Burn Like An Angel

Anaconda Tales

Fractured Future

Standalones

Forever Ago

Drown in You

A Crimson Carol

Writing as Jessalyn Thorn

Departed Whispers

If You Break

Made in United States
Troutdale, OR
12/01/2024

25574458R00268